Alberix the Celt

Book 1

Weep the Long Sorrow

The wind has broken us, the sea has drowned us, the eagles have torn us,
Oh, Lugos of the Long Hand. The flames have consumed us
as twigs are consumed in the crimson fire.

Bardic epigram

Albert Noyer

Books by Albert Noyer

The Saint's Day Deaths (2000)
The Secundus Papyrus (2003)
The Cybelene Conspiracy (2005)
The Ghosts of Glorieta / A Fr. Jake Mystery (2011)
One for the Money, Two for the Sluice / A Fr. Jake Mystery (2013)
Death at Pergamum (2013) Kindle
Unholy Sepulcher (2014) Kindle

Alberix the Celt

Book 1: *Weep the Long Sorrow*

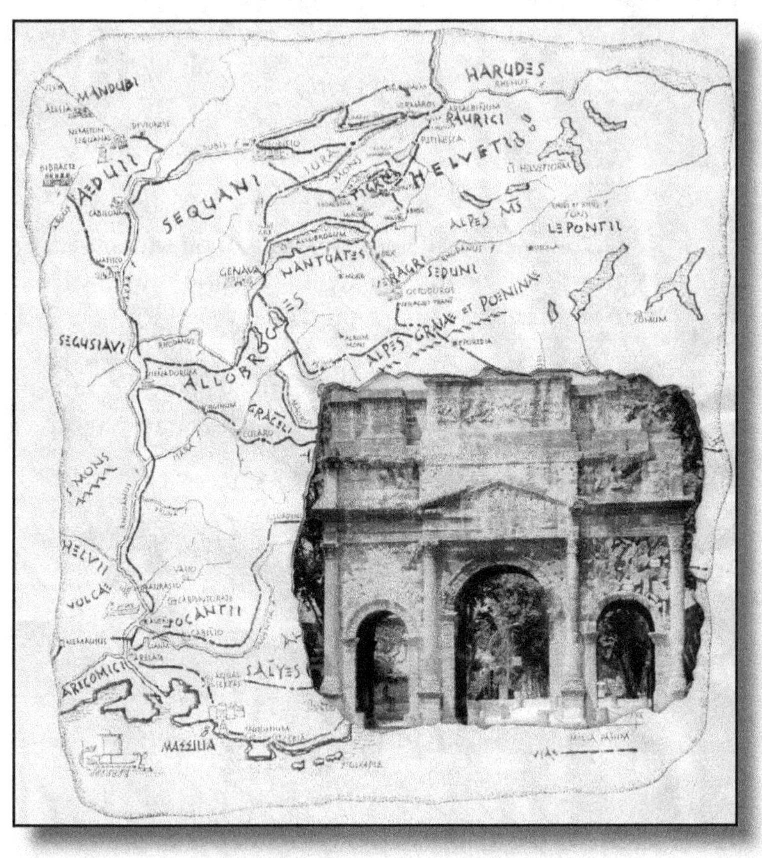

Albert Noyer

Plain View Press
1011 West 34th Street, Suite 260

http://plainviewpress.net
Austin, TX 78705

ISBN: 978-1-63210-000-9
Library of Congress Control Number: 2014903211

Cover art: Photograph of a Roman arch at Orange, France, commemorating victories over the Celts; map of Southern Gaul, and druidic calendar medallion by Albert Noyer

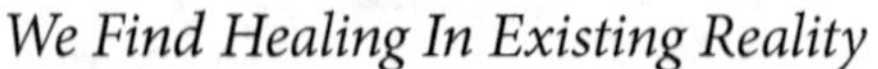

We Find Healing In Existing Reality

Plain View Press is a 36-year-old issue-based literary publishing house. Our books result from artistic collaboration between writers, artists, and editors. Over the years we have become a far-flung community of activists whose energies bring humanitarian enlightenment and hope to individuals and communities grappling with the major issues of our time—peace, justice, the environment, education and gender. This is a humane and highly creative group of people committed to art and social change. The poems, stories, essays, non-fiction explorations of major issues are significant evidence that despite the relentless violence of our time, there is hope and there is art to show the human face of it.

With gratitude to our critique group:
Jennifer, Carolyn, Roy, Sonni, Bob,
and the close collaboration of
John Zarro

BRITAÑIA IÆ
TRINOVANTES
CANTIACI
BIBROCI
DUROVERNUM
FRETUM GALICUM
GESORIACUM ITIUS PORTUS
NEMETOCENNA
SCALDIS
SAMAROBRIVA
ISARA F
ROTOMAGUS
MATRONA
DUROCORTORUM
GAL
OCEANUS BRITAÑICUS
SEQUANA F
LUTETIA PARISIORUM
METIOSEDUM
ISARA F
CASTRA ROXI
CARNUTUM
AGEDINCUM
CENABUM
AVTRICUM
LIGER F
NOVIODUNUM
ALESIA
NEMETO SEQUI
SALIMIS
CARIS F
AVARICUM
NOVIODUNUM
CONDEVINCUM
VIGERIUS F
BIBRACTE
DECETIA
VENETICÆ IÆ
OCEANUS
ATLANTICUS
CARANTONIUS F
GERGOVIA
VITERIUS F
UXELLODUNUM
ELAVER F
DURANIUS F
CESENA
MON
GARUMNA F
OLTIS
PROVINCIA
NEMAU
TOLOSA
CARCASO
NARBO
PYRENÆI MONTES
SI GA
HISPANIÆ
PARS
BARCINO

Author Reconstruction

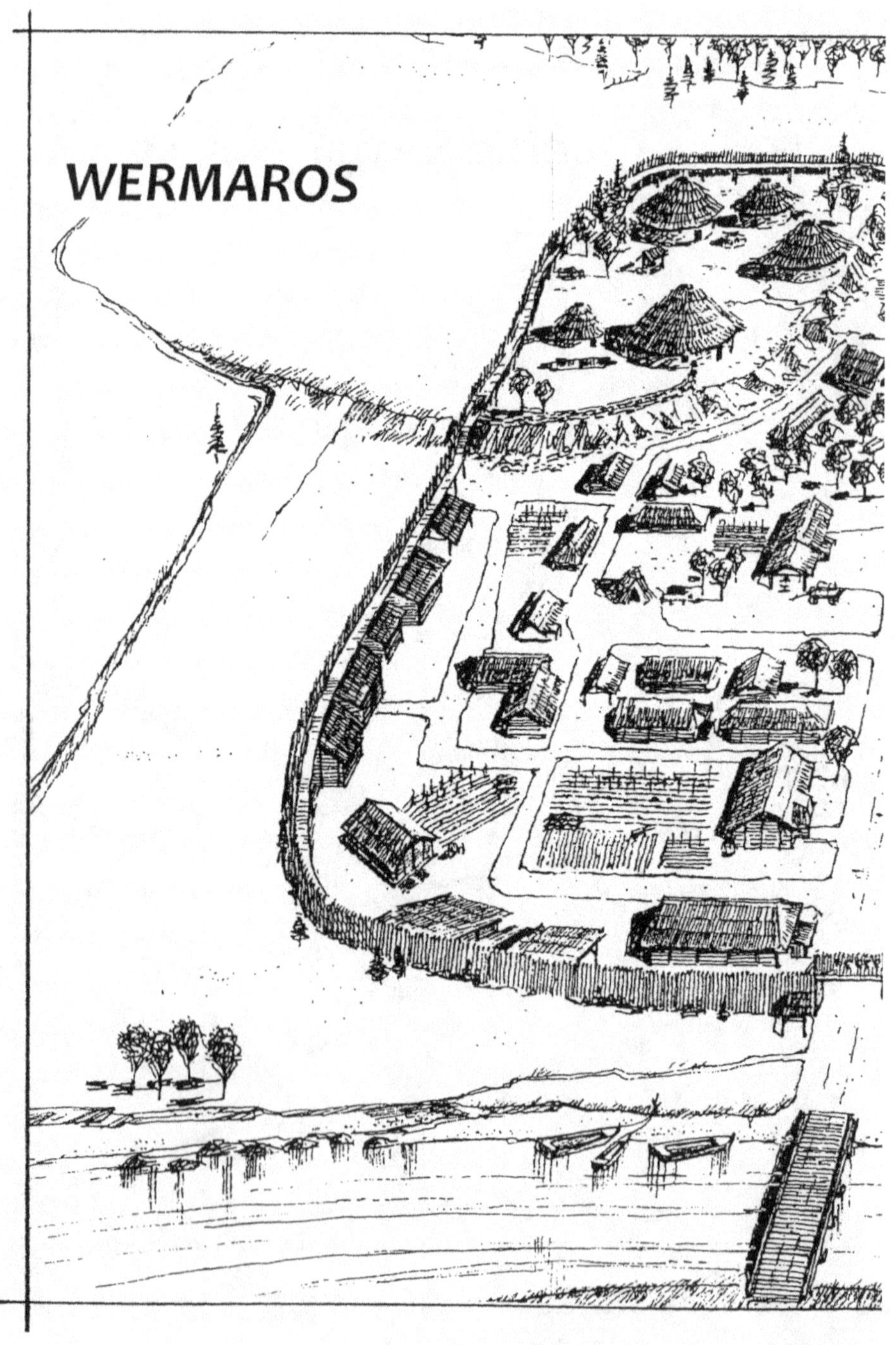
WERMAROS

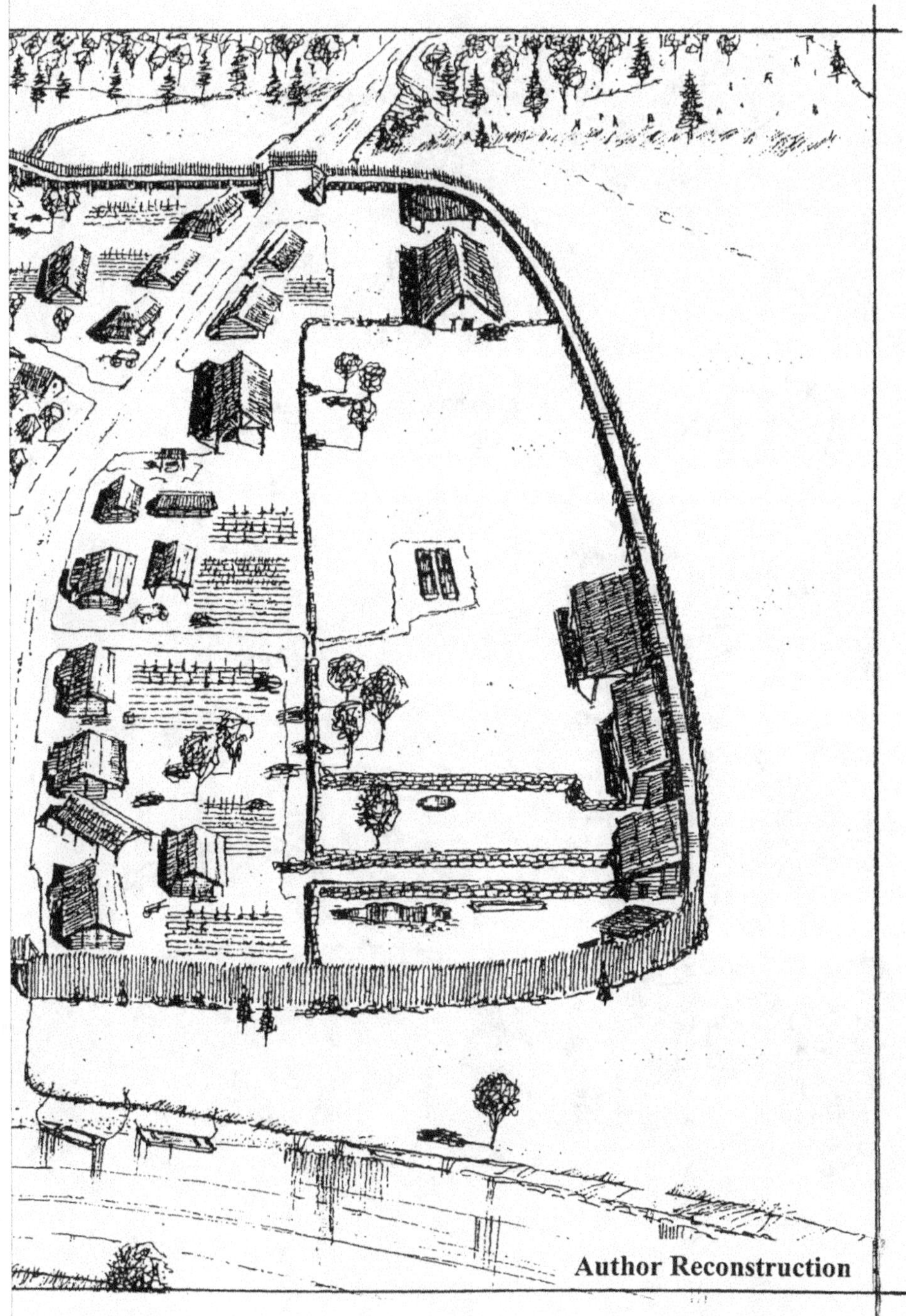

Author Reconstruction

Southeastern Gaul

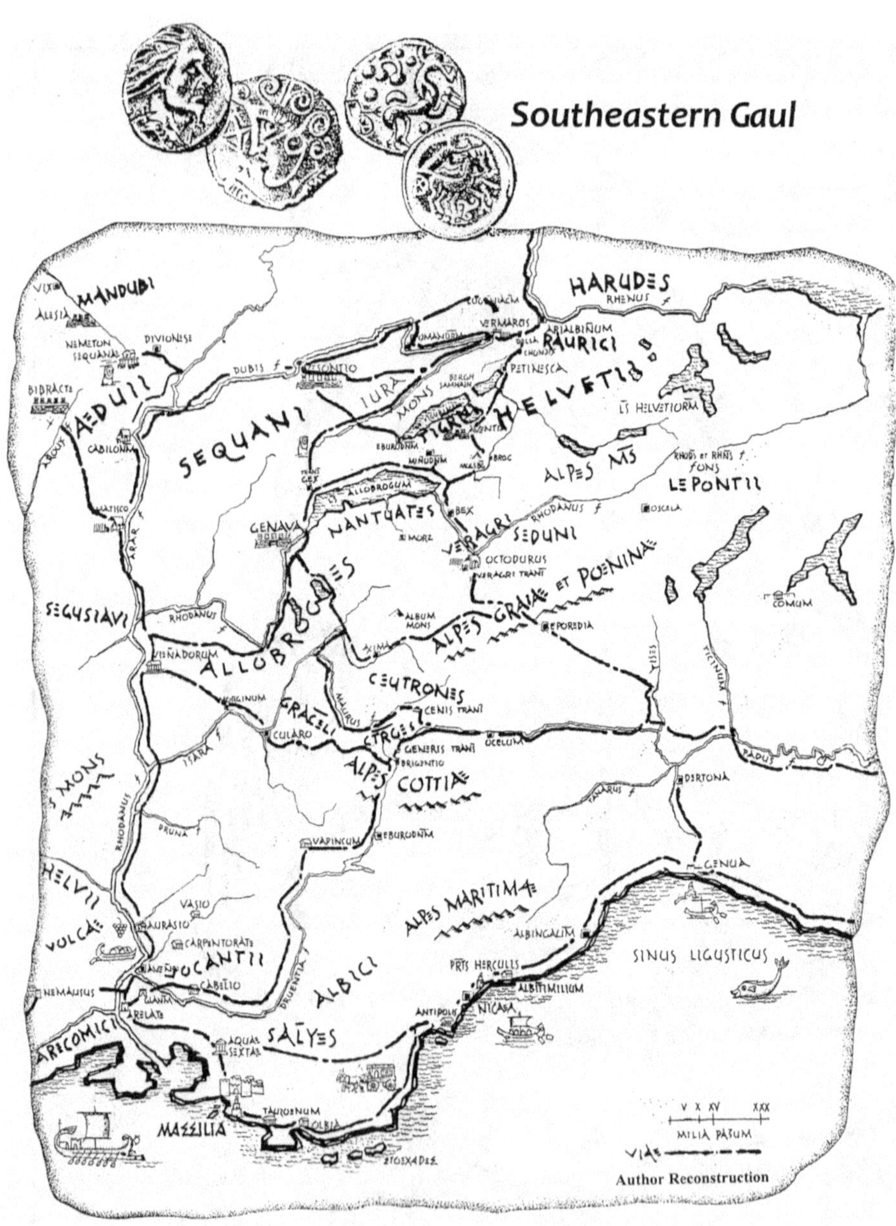

Author Reconstruction

PROLOGUE

In the spring of 58 BCE, the Celtic tribe of Helvetii, then settled in present-day west-central Switzerland and pressured by Germanic tribes from across the Rhine River, voted to migrate to lands in Gaul near the Atlantic Ocean. Gaius Julius Caesar opposed their passage through a Roman province, subsequently defeating an army eleven times larger than his available legions.

In eight campaign seasons, Caesar made Gaul part of Rome's growing empire: Roman institutions of government, law, and customs were veneered onto those of the Celts. A Gallo-Roman culture that prospered formed the matrix for much of modern European civilization.

That long ago Helvetian decision was the determining factor in ending a millennium of Celtic dominance in Europe, yet the Roman conquest assured that when devastating barbarian invasions erupted in the third to sixth centuries, those Germanic and Gothic tribes eventually would become Latinized.

This novel personalizes the Celtic struggle against Caesar by those tribesmen that opposed him, or those that supported Rome, and of the legion commanders who believed that bringing *Romanitas*—their civilization—to the known world was the sacred destiny of Rome.

Historical Persons

CELTS

Ambiorix — Chieftain of the Belgic Senone tribe

Brennos — Celtic leader whose warriors occupied Rome in 390 BCE

Casticos — Overchief of the Sequani tribe

Cingetorix — Treveri leader loyal to Rome

Diviciacos — Pro-Roman Aeduan, brother of Dumnorix

Divico — Leader of Tigurini who defeated a Roman army in 105BCE

Dumnorix — Anti-Roman Aeduan, co-conspirator with Casticos and
            Dumnorix

Nammeios — Helvetian noble

Orgetorix — Helvetian noble, co-conspirator with Casticos and Dumnorix

Vercingetorix — Arvernian noble, leader of the revolt of 52BCE

GERMAN

Ariovistos — king who crossed the Rhine River to settle his tribe in Sequani
            territory

Main Characters in Order of Appearance

Alberix   16, Son of Alrix, who is chief of the Raurici Alarian clan
Cluvios   36, A forge craftsman, brother of Alrix
Dividiac   68, Uncle of Briga, a druid priest
Arvos   30, A teamster
Briga   31, Mother of Alberix, wife of Alrix
Dirona   31, Twin sister of Briga
Liscos   55, Husband of Dirona, Sequani tribal chieftain at Wermaros
Ollam-Fodla   40, Druid from Inisfail (Ireland), former pupil of Dividiac
Pixtila   16, Girl from the Acantos enclave at Wermaros
S. Tullius Tilius   35, Quaestor attached to Legion X Gemina
Lucius Velcanius   38, Centurion in Legion X Gemina
Marcus Marius   25, Engineer of Optio rank
Gnaeus Cornelius   28, Engineer of Optio rank
Gaius Julius Caesar   42, Roman commander in the Gallic wars
Simonides   25, Gallo-Greek historian from Massilia
Psen-Ammon   40, Egyptian physician in Legion X Gemina
Apsa   18, Raurici slave girl at Octodurus
Frieda   20, Suebi woman in Germania

Glossary of Places

Present-day Switzerland
Arialbinnum — Basel   Brigantium — Bregenz
Noviodubno — "Newworld." Fictional village on the site of present-day Augst
Wermaros — fictionalized St. Ursanne in the western Jura Mountains on the
Doubs River
Genava — Geneva

France
Vesontio — Besançon   Bibracte — Mt. Beuvray near Autun
Arelate — Arles   Alesia — Alise Ste. Reine
Viennadunum — Vienne   Massilia —Marseilles
Avenno — Avignon
Germany
Bonaz — Bonn

Italy
Ravenna — Ravenna   Abellinum—Avellino
Roma — Rome

England was called Albion, Celtic "white," from the white cliffs of Dover that
are visible when crossing the English Channel, then named *Fretum Gallicum*
by the Romans.

Rivers
Renos/Rhenus — Rhine   Liger — Loire
Rodanos/Rhodanus — Rhone   Lagona — Lahn
Sequana - Seine
Moenus — Main

I. February — June / 59 BCE

Look before you to the southeast: the foxes run after the hare,
and eagles begin to shadow the green valleys.

Chapter I

The abrupt jolt shook me from an uneasy sleep.

My mind cleared a little as I heard the hollow sound of our wagon's iron-rimmed wheels crossing the planks of a bridge. *How long have I been asleep?* I shivered from the night cold and the recollection of a suffocating terror I felt during the surprise night attack on my father's village of Noviodubno.

After wild shouts outside my parents' lodge awakened us, I stumbled out with them into icy winter air. An acrid smell of grassy smoke stung my nostrils. Gray ash from burning thatch on lodge roofs drifted down on us like dirty snow. On the ground, orange flames cast dark silhouettes of enemy warriors fighting our men. They resembled shadowy spirits of the dead, who can cross over from the Other-world at our New Year's feast of Samain. Despite the present terror, I recalled that day, the beginning of the dark half of our year. Dividiac, my druid great-uncle, performs rituals during the long night to prevent the spirits from crossing over and harming the living.

Alrix—my father—ran back into our lodge for his sword, then ordered everyone except warriors to escape west along the Renos River road. Father led his men toward the river as my uncle, Cluvios, pushed me into his wagon. While teamsters struggled to harness their panicked draft ponies to carts and wagons by the glare of burning homes, I worried about my mother, Briga. *Had she been able to get to a wagon?* Most of the fighting was near the river, so I knew that the raiders were Germani. None of their tribes usually fought in winter, yet warriors must have crossed over the Renos on ice floes and surprised our night guards.

Taranis, I'm cold! I wish I had on more than my sleep tunic and the bear pelt uncle threw over me. With that thought I knelt to peer over the wagon bed's top board to find out where we were.

"Alberix, stay down!" Cluvios shouted. "We're not out of danger yet."

I fell back and felt a sharp pain in my shoulder. I had hit one of uncle's forge tools lying on the floor, but didn't cry out. *We're off the bridge...the wheels slid back into ruts on the roadway. Other wagons followed us.... Now we've stopped.*

I watched Cluvios crouch on one knee to glance over the wagon's side. A reddish glow reflected off his face as he shook his head in disbelief. "Arialbinnum is burning! We'll not find refuge there."

The village of Arialbinnum, where we lived before. That means we're at the great bend where the Renos turns sharply to the north. If the Germani are able to raid this far west in Raurici lands and get into the village—.

"Arvos!" Uncle interrupted my thought by shouting to the teamster who drove our shaggy draft ponies. "Arvos, our only hope is to reach Delsa. The

Germani will take time to loot Arialbinnum, so we cannot stay nearby. Their warriors would find us in the morning. Drive straight on."

Arvos protested, "We're running into a hailstorm and the road through the gorge is risky at night. There's only a quarter-moon for light and it'll set during this watch."

I looked to the southwest, where he pointed. Storm clouds scudded over the moon's pale crescent. A few grains of hail stung my face and the wind that brought them felt even colder than before.

When a voice near me mumbled a few words, I realized that another person was in the wagon bed with us. "Who is it?" I called out. "What did you say?"

"It is the tenth day of the new moon phase after the festival of Imbolc."

"Dividiac?" I recognized my great-uncle's voice. He's a druid priest and knows that this new moon for the month of Anagantios sets the date for our lambing festival of Imbolc. "Uncle, are...are you all right?"

Dividiac pushed aside a woolen blanket that covered him and impatiently gestured for my hand. "Boy, I want to sit up." After I helped him lean against his side of the wagon, he rasped, "We should have been prepared. Germani always start their bloody raids at the new moon. During the dark phase, the churls are too superstitious to do anything except sit and suck bones, and all because a seeress tells them it brings misfortune to fight at that time." Dividiac coughed a dry laugh at the notion that women could predict events—despite the fact that we Celts held the same belief. "Cluvios," he chided, "we should have been prepared."

Uncle ignored him to confront Arvos again. "I know this road well, and the sky god is helping us by bringing sleet. It may make controlling the wagon more difficult, yet this storm will keep the Germani from following us."

Dividiac glanced up at the sky, then predicted, "The frozen tears of Taranis have come to protect us, but they quickly will pass."

Cluvios pushed the driver, who had hunched down in his hooded cloak against the stinging pellets. "Arvos, did you hear? We don't know how many Harudes...if that's the tribe...crossed the river. Warriors may be following us "

"Where is Alrix?" Carried on the wind, a man's voice called out from the nearest wagon. "Has anyone seen him since the raid?"

A new spasm of anxiety wracked my stomach. Someone asked about my father, Cluvios's' brother and chieftain of our Alarian clan.

Another voice answered, "I saw him fighting without a shield alongside our men who were able to get weapons."

"He may not have been killed," the first man shouted back. "Those Germani were after slaves as well as loot."

Then Father may become a prisoner in some miserable wattle-and-mud hovel in Germania? At the thought, I slid back down onto icy granules coating the floor and pulled my bear pelt tighter around my body. *All because he decided to leave Arialbinnum and start his own village. I know the council disagreed with Father when he wanted the market truces to last more than a month...even to make Arialbinnum an open town and help mediate tribal infighting. Some of his vassos were of the same mind and went with him to build the new settlement upstream. Father even wanted Germani included in the treaty. And now—*Sleet granules showered me as Cluvios grabbed Arvos by the hood of his cloak and shouted at him.

"My brother and other warriors may have been killed to give us this chance to escape. If you won't drive, give me the reins..." Cluvios paused and tilted his head. "Wait! Listen!"

I also heard distant shouting. A smell of smoke from burning wood and straw blew in with them. I half-stood again and looked in the direction of Arialbinnum. "Uncle, the land gate is closed. Wouldn't fire show through the opening if the Germani got past the palisade that way?"

Cluvios shrugged. "If they were Harudes, they came from the river side, threw torches over the walls onto roof thatch, then set up ladders to climb the palisade. There aren't many guards posted in winter. Who expects a raid then?"

"The Germani caught us like forest animals out of hibernation," Arvos growled, then lashed the ponies into motion.

As the wagon lurched forward, I grabbed one side with my numb fingers to keep from falling.

Cluvios said, "*Dago*...good...we'll soon reach the Birsa River. Our draft ponies have traveled this road many times, and can sense its course."

Arvos grunted agreement. With the moon now hidden by storm clouds, the night was darker, yet patches of white sleet collecting in the road's wheel ruts marked out a dim, eerie trail. I heard the clatter of other wagons following us and glanced back. The ruddy glow at Arialbinnum had been absorbed into an opaque shroud of whiteness. Dividiac was asleep again, so I huddled against him for warmth, trying to understand how the Harudes could surprise our village. *The Renos River isn't frozen solid, but it is filled with ice floes. Their warriors must have taken advantage of an ice jam and risked a night crossing over the blocks to catch us with our shields down.*

I soon drifted into a restless sleep again, anxious about my father and mother.

❧

The road led south to follow the course of the Birsa, a rushing stream that cut through the eastern flank of the Jurassos Mountains and emptied into the Renos at Arialbinnum.

Cluvios squinted into the semi-darkness: the first forested height in Raurici tribal land would be *Benn Blevos*, "Blue Mountain." A stone shrine to Taranis was on its summit, with a statue of the sky god he had cast in bronze. "The figure should have been of our war god, Caturix," he muttered. "The Germani across the Renos would have seen him and been warned away." *Although Dividiac and I don't always agree about the power of the gods, he may be right after all. So far one of The Three...Taranis, Esus, and Teutates...seems to be guiding our escape. The old druid believes we can strike bargains with our gods. If that's the case, I certainly cast enough votive figures of them to have bartered for our safety many times over* Cluvios coughed and spat leeward of the wagon, spittle tinged with blood that tasted metallic. *My headaches are getting more frequent. Have I somehow offended Gobann, the forge god?*

Thinking back to Arialbinnum, the crafter recalled that the town had stone ramparts and a surrounding ditch filled from the river. *How did the Harudes get in so quickly? Had they recruited informers who told them the moat froze over, and about our new village upstream? Alrix thought it would be safe to continue work during the cold season, when Germani normally don't mount raids.*

Noticing Arvos's head nod forward, Cluvios nudged the driver. "The wind is at our back now. After the bend in the river, we'll come to a village where I know the clan leader. Givico will help us with shelter and food in the morning."

Arvos muttered another complaint, but straightened up. Cluvios slid back onto the wagon floor and fingered his neck torc. The silver circlet felt warm and reassuring. *Alrix was right to order those who were not his warriors away from the fighting, yet will I see my brother again? There is only a slim chance for his ransom. The Harudes only want loot they can carry back across the river.* He glanced at the dark form of his nephew, a shapeless lump huddled under the bear pelt. *Alberix is almost seventeen. At Beltaine he'll be two years past the time when he should have begun warrior training. Alrix let him stay with me to learn a crafter's trade, but insisted that he will teach Alberix how to fight and lead men in the spring. I know Briga doesn't want her son to follow a warrior's path, yet our traditions are hard to overturn. As the son of a clan chieftain, Alberix is destined to exchange his forge tools for a sword and shield.*

❧

Guided by the gurgling sound of the river, the draft ponies rounded the final bend of road before reaching the village. Cluvios half-dozed, but started awake when he caught the scent of wood smoke coiling back on the changing wind patterns of the ravine. He struggled up on cramped legs and leaned close to Arvos. "Stop up ahead...we're at Bireg. We can't form our wagons into a protective circle, so you and I will go back and tell drivers to move close to the wagon in front of them."

I awoke in the sudden quiet. I badly needed to urinate, but the warmth trapped in my fur pelt felt so comfortable that I again dropped off into a bloated sleep.

⋘⋙

It was light outside when the distant barking of dogs roused me. I shook hail grains off my bearskin, stood up on stiffened legs, and glanced around. A clear sky was tinted the warm blue of alpine penstemon blossoms, a color that mocked the coldness of the air. Yet Dividiac had been correct. The late winter storm was a short one.

I shielded my eyes against the whiter glare that shone everywhere. Sleet-crusted boughs on firs bent low in sparkling sweeps. A glaze of opaque crystals coated the framework of branches on bare trees. White birches were invisible among their darker neighbors, now covered with a pale shell of rime ice. Across the road, where the course of the Birsa was marked by a steaming vapor that hung over its surface, snow-draped forest trees still brooded in gloomy shadows, but behind me the distant whitened height of *Benn Blevos* shimmered in a rose-yellow haze.

Squinting at the dazzling beauty, I stood to relieve myself over the side of the wagon, sure that my father had escaped and caught up with us.

I recognized the wooden lodges of Bireg in the distance, because I had come here with Cluvios to repair farm tools. I heard barking again: about a spear's throw away hounds bounded in front of a group of armed men. Dividiac awoke, muttered complaints, and slipped as he tried to stand. I steadied him and told him where we were. "Uncle, this is Bireg and villagers are coming this way. I hope they don't think we're Germani."

The mens' breathing mimicked vapors over the river. Some brandished hunting spears. A few had ovoid shields and swords clutched in their hands, but most made threatening gestures at us with woodcutting axes. *Where are Cluvios and Arvos?* After my numb fingers fumbled to bare my right shoulder, in our Celtic sign of peace, the men lowered their weapons. Some grinned and pointed at our wagon.

"Dividiac?" Their leader, Givico, had recognized uncle's reddened face in his ice-crusted fur hood. A swing of his spear quieted the dogs' yelping. "Druid," he asked, "by the winter gods, what are you doing here? Who are in the wagons? We thought you might be Harudes."

Dividiac invoked a god. "Let Taranis strike the Germani with his sky fire! Their warriors crossed the Renos and raided Alrix's new village. Arialbinnum is burned."

Givico spat aside and cursed their common enemy, "'May clouds of blood descend upon them.' Even now, Harudes winter near our warm springs, bold as foxes." He looked back along the wagons. "Where is Alrix?"

"My father is missing," I blurted out, "and I haven't seen Mother since last night."

After he nodded without commenting, I understood. A late winter raid meant the Germani were desperate for food and would not waste rations on captives, nor risk the threat of a counter-raid to rescue them. Had my mother also been killed? Thank Lugos, I heard Cluvios call out behind me.

"Alberix, I found Briga! She was in a wagon with the family of Tutios."

I jumped down and ran over to her. Mother looked tired and the borrowed cloak she wore was too large, but I mumbled thanks to the god that she was safe. Lugos was the first deity I thought of, because Dividiac said that he protected travelers.

"Have you heard anything about Father?" I hoped Briga knew what had happened to him.

As she shook her head, copper-colored hair strands straggled out of the cloak's hood. Givico doffed his fur hat. Briga was the *bena*, the wife of a clan chieftain and due the same respect as her husband. "Mistress, wh...what happened?"

"You are?"

"Givico, chieftain of this village."

Mother nodded and brushed a lock of hair back from her face. "I...I awoke with Alrix," she explained in a quiet voice, but her blue eyes had hardened into a frown. "We heard shouting and went outside. Warriors carrying torches and weapons came from the direction of the river. Alrix ordered me to go with our son and Dividiac to the south gate, where he kept the wagons. We were to escape with those who were not fighters. He...he ran back into our lodge for his sword, then went out to rally his few warriors. I last saw my husband fighting close to the river, near burning lodges. Everything happened so quickly...." Briga passed a hand over her eyes as if to wipe away the scene of horror, then pointed to the line of wagons. "Givico, those are *vassos* of my husband. They must be fed and sheltered."

"We will help, Mistress." He turned back to Cluvios. "Crafter, have you counted how many of your people escaped?"

Uncle pulled at his blond mustache in the nervous mannerism he affected when upset. "Forty-three villagers survived, in nine wagons."

"Nine?" Dividiac echoed. "Nine is a sacred number, a good omen."

"Good?" Cluvios scoffed. "You can find *good* in this disaster, old man?"

"Crafter, every sign that the gods give us can be interpreted." Dividiac gestured toward me with an impatient hand wave. "Boy! Get me out of this wagon!"

After I helped uncle down, Cluvios motioned for me to go with him to the lead wagon. Perhaps he wanted the villagers to know that the son of their chieftain was safe.

Briga came over to knead the old druid's stiffened shoulders. "Uncle, even after so many years of serving the gods your memory is still keen as a new blade."

Dividiac's breath came in steaming gasps as he narrowed his eyes against the glare. "Yes, and before I join Cernunnos in the Other-world, I plan to teach Alberix the secrets of druids, the Men of the Oak."

"Men of the Oak?" Briga protested. "It takes twenty years to learn all that druids teach. Alrix wants our son to follow him as clan leader...perhaps some day be elected over-chief of the Raurici tribe—"

"Niece," Dividiac interrupted, "is that what *you* want?"

"No, and we quarreled about that," she admitted. "I don't want Alberix to continue the cycle of clan brawling. I hoped to convince Alrix that it would be better for our son to stay at the forge and make useful implements our people need. Cluvios has felt more and more ill lately. He needs Alberix's help."

Dividiac snorted, "A druid priest is closer to the gods than any of our people."

"I know that.... Oh, I see Cluvios returning with Alberix. I want my son to go back with me and thank Tutios."

After the two left, Cluvios took Dividiac aside. "Druid, the survivors want you to ask the gods what we are to do next. A few wish to return and rebuild the village, yet most fear new raids and want to settle elsewhere." He lowered his voice. "If....if Alrix is dead, Briga wants to take her son to Wermaros, where her sister's husband is chieftain. She would start a new life among the Sequani tribe."

Dividiac countered, "Crafter, the Earth Mother will decide where we go. She will tell us where our future will be."

Cluvios frowned at a possible delay. "Then do so quickly. Givico offered us food at his lodge, yet we cannot stay beyond mid-sun. His winter storage pits are nearly empty."

Dividiac pointed back to the wagons. "I took my amulet case and a bundle of tunics along with me. Ask Alberix to bring them to the lodge. A bird augury will point out the direction we are to travel."

The old druid limped away toward Givico's home to begin arbitrating the group's destiny through omens pointed out by the gods.

❧❧

By the time all the survivors had crowded into the lodge's common room, the women of Bireg had cooked pots of barley porridge and sweetened them with crusts of maple sap. After I received my bowl, welcome warmth flowed into my stiff fingers and empty stomach as well. I watched Mother arrange for the distribution of clothing and footwear collected by the village women for those who had not had time to dress warmly. Briga's father, my grandfather Cavaros, had been of a nobleman's rank in our clan, warrior-head of the council at Arialbinnum.

Of the forty-three survivors, only a few older men, artisans, and teamsters had escaped, but many of the women married to warriors brought children with them. Mother spoke quietly with each one, realizing that they might be widows now and their children fatherless.

I put down my empty bowl when a woman gave me a pair of checkered woolen trousers that were too large, a worn fur jacket, and mismatched boots. After dressing, I helped Dividiac put on a long white ceremonial robe, decorated in a pattern of green interlacing swirls at the sleeves, neck, and hem. He asked me to bring the oak statue of our clan god, Alar, wrapped in a shiny cloth that came from a land far to the east of Germania, where our sun god, Belenos, rises. Alar is a human image, not an animal god like many others. Father once explained that Alar holds peaceful tools, a pincer and sickle, yet his hand rests on a sword hilt to show that our clan warriors are ready to fight if they must.

Before we went outside again, Uncle led a petition to Lugos, asking the patron god of new ventures for protection, and then listened to the individual wishes of those assembled in the lodge. Those who did not want to return to the village site outnumbered those who did.

After the count, Dividiac announced, "Now is the time for augury. Through the spirit of one of her creatures, the Earth Mother will point to our destiny. Givico, the occasion is critical. Bring me a caged bird, even someone's pet if need be. People of Dagda, follow me into the woods."

In stories about our people, Dividiac told us that Dagda, "The Good God," was an ancient patron of druidism and magic, so I was anxious to see how he would help us. Uncle led the way to the river, carrying Alar and the amulet case. I brought a nervous finch in a reed cage, but felt sorry for the sniffling girl walking beside me. It was her pet.

While waiting for villagers to chip rime ice off flat stones that bridged the stream, I looked for Cluvios, who lagged behind. Despite the cold, his skin was a sallow color, and he frequently cleared his throat to spit. He had lost weight. I remembered that Klega, my small cousin at Wermaros, also looked ill, except that her face was flushed. What evil spirits could have entered their bodies?

After we crossed to the stream's far side, Dividiac pointed toward a young oak and told the fugitives to hold hands in a circle around the sacred tree. As they did so, he chose a silver medallion from his case and held it up.

While slipping the chain over his head, Uncle explained, "On this talisman, the crystal eyes of Taranis, Esus, and Teutates look out on the past, present, and future of our people. The three gods will counsel the finch to choose wisely."

I had seen the disk before, which also depicted waxing and waning moon cycles, each phase divided into the twelve-month segments of our year. In a thirteenth section, Greek letters spelled out the names of our four main Celtic festivals: Samain, the eve of our new year. Imbolc, the lambing festival that Dividiac had mentioned in the wagon. Beltaine was the sun god's spring festival, and Lugnasad a harvest celebration in late summer. The medallion was a small calendar of our months and festivals.

Dividiac told me to give the cage to Cluvios, so he could hang it on a branch of the oak and let the finch absorb the strength of the tree. Then he placed the figure of Alar at the base of the trunk, facing the direction from which we had come. After that, Uncle turned to the east and held the round talisman high enough to block out the bright newborn sun from his eyes. As he stared at the medallion, he fell into a trance and began to chant in a voice that was loud enough for everyone to hear.

"The strength of the oak touches the past,

as the fire of Belenos awakens new life.

Alar, clan god who is our protector,

finch, spirit of the Earth Mother's power,

show us a new spoke on the Wheel of Life.

Point out our path to a rich destiny."

In the silence that followed, I trembled with an expectation I imagined each person felt. Even the awakening sun and a morning breeze seemed to pause as echoes of Dividiac's exhortation were absorbed into the forest. Finally, Uncle roused himself and unlatched the door of the cage. The finch crouched down, hesitated a moment, then flew out of the opening. I was a bit worried about consigning our future to the whim of a bird, yet, with the others, watched it flit in a southwesterly direction until it was only a black speck absorbed into the bright glare.

At the instant that the finch was lost to view, I heard harsh croaking come from across the stream, and turned to see a trio of ravens preening themselves in the bare trees. Fearful murmurs of "*Badb-catha*" and "*brandubh*" rippled through the survivors. Our people consider the char-black birds to be symbols of death. When I looked back at the oak tree, I shivered; the figure of Alar now faced in the same direction that the finch had flown! Had Dividiac moved it while the ravens distracted us? I glanced back at Uncle. Dressed in his white robe, he blended in with the snowy background and resembled some spectral being from the Other-world more than a living person in our Now-world!

Dividiac spoke again. "People of Dagda. The augury and our clan god point to a road leading west. Both the Earth Mother, through the finch, and Alar declare it. Look to the north. Only the dark birds of death wait to greet us there."

The ravens seemed to agree with the druid's prediction. As if satisfied with their part in the ritual, the ebony birds gave a final series of hoarse cries and flapped off in the direction of the Renos River.

A moment later, I heard the rumble of a carriage that I guessed had alerted the birds. The teamster struggled to halt his team at the end of our wagons. Cluvios hurried back across the stream on the flat stones to question the man. I ran after him, sure it was Father.

"Adiantos...it's you!" After uncle called the name, I recognized one of our carpenters. Cluvios told him, "The Germani raided our village. Are you coming from there?"

"No, we visited my brother's farmstead upstream and went back this morning."

Anxious, I asked, "What did you find? Was anyone there?"

His reply was bitter. "Lodges...the unfinished palisade...all burned! What livestock the Germani did not take across the river were slaughtered in their pens."

"But...people?" I persisted, as mother came alongside me. "Did you see any survivors?"

"I went down as far as the river. Saw stripped corpses among the ice floes."

Briga asked him, "What of Alrix? Did you see my husband? Your clan chief?"

Adiantos shook his head and glanced away.

Mother seemed about to embrace me in a gesture of sympathy, but looked toward where the ravens had flown. She was reluctant to show any emotion that might embarrass me in front of a tribesman of inferior rank. If my father *were* dead, I, as his son, had become a person for whom clan members might one day vote as their chieftain. It was a disturbing, yet at the same time, somewhat boastful thought.

"Dividiac has divined our clan's destiny by augury," Briga told Adiantos, looking him directly in the eyes. "As soon as they can, our people will leave here to build new homes in the west. Your skills, your wife's, and even your children's will be needed."

"Mistress"—Adiantos glanced at me and then touched his lips—"Mistress, I swear by the god by whom my father swore that I will serve you."

I flushed and turned away, ashamed at my arrogance in thinking I would ever be capable of leading free men, and much less warriors, the way my father did—or even as my mother had done in evoking an oath of obedience from a carpenter and his family.

Chapter II

As I watched Belenos arc up to his late winter height, the sun god's brilliant rays warmed the morning air and melted grainy layers of rime from tree branches. Amid the brittle echoes of ice dropping in the mountain forests, Mother told Cluvios to order that the wagons move on to Delsa. My uncle, as Father's only brother, now shared responsibility with my mother for the well-being of our surviving villagers. Under Celtic laws, Briga was the equal of her husband in matters of inheritance, but if Alrix were dead, Cluvios would be obligated to marry her. I didn't want to think about that. I lay back in the wagon on furs and turned my face to the sun. After a bitter night, the warmth re-assured me, and I again felt hopeful that Father was safe.

❧

Briga sat on the wagon seat next to Arvos, thinking about her son. *He has the blue eyes of the Alrixian men, but he's slimmer than his father was when I first met him. Alberix never really has known his father well, because Cluvios raised the boy. Sometimes I don't understand our custom of fostering out a son until he's old enough to begin warrior training. Is it that by then it's like teaching a stranger to kill?*

When Mother half-turned to glance back at me, she looked worried. It was natural in view of her uncertainty about Alrix. To reassure her, I said with as much confidence as I could, "Father will find us at Delsa."

She nodded slightly. "We're going on to stay with your aunt, Dirona, at Wermaros."

"Then Father will find us there." I waited a moment before asking, "Are we ever going back to Arialbinnum?"

She shook her head. "Dividiac wouldn't allow it. That finch flew toward the west, and our clan god agreed with the augury."

I understood and fell silent, thinking of my early life at Arialbinnum. Because Father was the leader of a prominent clan, we had lived in the village's only stone house, one with a slate roof. The other lodges were timber with steep roofs covered in grass thatch. From the age of seven on, one of Dividiac's pupils had taught me about our people's customs, and the responsibility that was mine as the son of a chieftain. I was around adults most of the time and learned some Germanic words from our slaves, even a fair amount of Latin from a Roman sausage merchant who lived in the village. When I reached the age of twelve, I went to live with Cluvios at his forge near the river gate.

I was working with Cluvios when Father had a disagreement with the town councilors about market truces called among local tribes, to trade for goods that each needed. Alrix wanted the fairs to last longer than a few days and include Germanic tribes from across the Renos. He felt this might result in more understanding and less infighting. The council disagreed, yet some townspeople, about twenty families, were of the same mind as Father and went with him to build a new settlement upstream. He called it Noviodubno, "New World," and thought it might become a center for peaceful negotiations between Celts and Germani.

I glanced up at Mother. She still looked anxious, so I thought I would try to distract her with more pleasant memories. "Mother, I'll miss the spring and autumn trade fairs."

"They were exciting..." Briga turned and smiled a little in remembrance. "Tribes brought in trade goods from different places in Gallia. Your aunt Dirona loves that flaxen cloth the Cadurci make."

I pointed at Cluvios, lying in the wagon bed next to Dividiac, both men asleep. "Uncle admired the silver work of the Gabaldi. He said they live near a western sea that has no end."

"Alberix"—Briga's quiet laughter mimicked the ripple of the river—"I think you may mean the Aquitani. The Gabaldi are a mountain tribe."

"You're right." I fell silent, recalling my own memories of a time that might never return. "Mother, remember that some people made fun of the Tigurini warriors? Why were they carrying weapons that weren't like those of our Celts?"

"Didn't Cluvios tell you?"

"Something about...Romani? I forget. Who are they?"

Mother turned in her seat to face me. "Alrix explained it to me. Romani live to the south around a Middle Sea and they aren't a Celtic people. In a battle years ago, they tried to stop the Tigurini from migrating through their province in southern Gallia, but the tribe defeated them."

"I remember now. They killed the Romani over-chief and humiliated his warriors by forcing them to pass under an arch of crossed spears."

"Yes. Some of the older Tigurini men still wear the short swords and helmets taken as loot, but those younger ones were not even there. The whole event is becoming one of our myths, like Dividiac's poems about Brenn's voyage in a crystal boat, or about Lugos, the god who taught our ancestors farming and metalworking." Mother reached down to toy with the sleeve of my jacket a moment, then looked into my eyes. "Alberix, I must tell you this. Dividiac has taught many young men to be druid priests. Now he wants you to be his final pupil."

The offer took me by surprise. "Why, Mother?".

"It's a great honor, Alberix. A Man of the Oak has the highest rank that our people can offer...even above that of *cunovalos*...over-chief."

"But it takes twenty years," I objected. "Not that I don't want to learn new things. That's why I liked the trade booths." I wasn't sure that I wanted to be a druid and changed the subject back to the fairs. "I think the Kephestos brothers had the most interesting trade goods. You, know, the two Greek traders."

"Those drunken importers of wine?" she scoffed.

I said, "Our men like wine better than the wheat *cervisa* that Celts brew."

"Don't *I* know that!" Briga agreed. "You're correct, they were Greek, but wasn't Fulvius, that sausage seller, a Roman who once served in their legions?"

"Yes, I liked him and went over to his shop whenever I could. He taught me some Latin and used that language when he told me stories about the places he'd seen."

"You did spend a lot of time with him."

"Fulvius wrote Latin words on a wax tablet and made me memorize them. I was getting quite good..." I fell silent at the thought that all this was lost. At the fairs I'd also seen dark-skinned merchants with hair like black lamb's wool, and short, swarthy people who were unlike our tall blond Celts. I was curious about the world beyond mine, yet it seemed so unreachable. It was time for me to take my place in the tribal position my father had chosen for me, and he expected me to become a warrior. I might have inherited Cluvios's forge shop, but now Dividiac wanted to train me as a druid. In either of those three ways, I felt trapped in a direction not of my choosing.

I heard Mother ask, "What are you thinking about, Alberix?"

"Thinking?" I looked up into her blue eyes—still reddened from weeping she had not wanted me to see. "That...that I sometimes think life is like one of the wheels I help Cluvios make."

"Oh? How is that?"

"Well, the spokes that support the felly are like the different members in our tribe. Warriors, crafters...herders. Shopkeepers. The rim of tradition holds them all in place."

"And?"

"What if...if your spoke isn't the one you want, or that the rim is too confining? Dividiac is always talking about a Wheel of Life that extends even to the Other-world of the dead." I thought uncle was dozing, but he heard me and called over.

"Yes, my boy, and the gods have put our lives onto a new spoke."

Briga asked in a tone colder than the air, "What of Alrix's spoke?"

Dividiac caught her sarcasm and hedged. "Only the gods know its direction. Don't forget, Niece, Death is merely the center of a long life that connects us with the Other-world."

"So, druid, I'm to travel a new spoke with my husband absent among the dead? I'm going into another tribe's land where I have no standing. Dirona may be my sister, but her life in a remote Sequani village is not one I would have chosen for myself."

Uncle mumbled something about the unreasonableness of women, then turned over and pretended to sleep again.

I reassured Mother that Alrix would find us. Bireg villagers would tell him where we went, then I looked away at the gorge's snow-covered crags hemming us in on either side. Now, instead of bracketing our route to a new freedom, they seemed like ominous barriers to my future. Dividiac and Mother had just talked as if my father *were* dead. If that was true, my life had become disconnected from a predictable future, one now as void of direction as Mother's.

⸾⸾⸾

By late afternoon, our wagons had moved from the blue shadows of the gorge into pinkish light that flooded a long, narrow valley below Delsa. A bluish haze of wood smoke hung over the height where the village stood. I stood up in the wagon bed and saw a group of horsemen riding out of the gate. Mother craned her neck for a better view. I joined her on the seat, thinking that both of us imagined that Father was among them.

When the horsemen reached us, we saw that he was not. Givico had sent word ahead of the Harude raid, so the villagers knew that we were arriving. They sent out villagers to escort us into Delsa.

⸾⸾⸾

In the house of the main clan leader, my mother suggested that Dividiac grant an unconditional annulment of debts owed her by Father's *vassos*, the clients who rented his land and herds. The way Mother put it was that she wanted the refugees to weave a new cloth of their lives with unborrowed yarn. Yet, she herself had lost every possession— her clothing, household utensils, and the jewelry she inherited or bought over the thirty-three years of her life. Again I realized how proud I was of her, and how beautiful she looked. Even in the dim light of the common room, her hair shone like a new-spun copper dish, and the rosy cast to her skin set off the blue of her eyes. They were frowned in seriousness now as she listened to the wishes of the survivors of her husband's doomed settlement.

Some of the women who came with us elected to stay in Delsa, with kinfolk. Others said they would leave with us the next day to find homesteads of relatives or friends who lived in the valley. Afterward, Dividiac was too tired to repeat a ritual to Lugos for a safe journey on the next day; he went straight to a sleeping compartment vacated for him.

Before we left in the morning, I helped Cluvios and Arvos inspect the wagon Uncle had built, and the small, shaggy work ponies he had traded from, ironically, Harude tribesmen. He preferred the stocky Germani breed to the larger war mounts of our Celts because they endured northern winters better and were ideal for his hauling needs. Fortunately, most of Cluvio's forge tools were with us. He kept a set in the wagon, ready to go out and repair work implements and house wares when villagers or farmers summoned him.

The horses showed no signs of strain and their bronze bridle fittings had no blood on them. The wagon, too, was sound.

After provisioning us with a day's supply of bread, smoked pork, and a skin of *cervisa*, the villagers gave Dividiac a feather-stuffed bolster and two bearskin pelts to spread on the wagon floor. He did mutter a short invocation to Lugos before we left, then lay down on the bolster.

We moved out of the palisade gates around high sun. I decided to walk alongside the wagon for a while, rather than sit or lie down again for an entire day.

Cluvios ordered Arvos to follow a dirt road that paralleled the Sorna River. We passed through snow-covered cropland that was sheltered on both sides by low northern mountains of the Jurassos range. Stone walls dividing farmstead fields were mostly buried by the winter's snowfall, but the many storehouses, cattle herds, and blue smoke, drifting from openings in lodge roofs and smokehouses, told of how well our Raurici tribe had settled and cultivated the area.

Melting winter snows softened the frozen road and left it a rutted trail. Now, as Belenos continued to warm the surface, a reddish, sticky mud gripped at the wheels, slowing down the ponies, and miring my mismatched boots. I recalled that after leaving Delsa in the spring and fall, it took us about three sun hours to arrive at Wermaros. This time we would not reach the village before dusk.

I jumped aboard the wagon again and tried to get comfortable on the floorboards and lean against the side. I passed time by looking at the details of Cluvios's wagon. Uncle had designed it to be a work of beauty as well as useful transportation. The bed's tapered sides were carved in symmetrical, swirling patterns that I painted in bright colors. He shaped the ends of the oak frame supports into human heads, a common figure that reflected our Celtic belief that the soul resides in the head and contains the basic essence of a person. Possessing the head controls an individual's spirit. *Had Cluvios been serious when he said that in an earlier time the actual rotting heads of enemies might have decorated our wagon?* Iron fittings allowed a leather canopy to be pulled over curved ashwood staves and keep wet weather off the inside. In our haste, we had left the covering behind. Bronze bindings held the spokes of wheels that were fitted with heated outer iron rims, which cooled into a tight fit on the circular edge. I was proud to have helped Cluvios make them.

The air grew colder as the sun slanted down toward the Jurassos crests. My body ached from the jolting ride, and no amount of shifting position could make me feel much better. Mother had become silent, surely dreading what lay ahead.

By the time we rested our team at a crossing, where a road to the right led toward Wermaros, we were alone—all the other wagons had turned off onto farm sidetracks. Here, the muddy way began a steady rise to a mountain pass above my aunt Dirona's village. At its highest point the road forked off toward Vesontio, capital of the Sequani tribe. Still hopeful that Father had survived, I became more and more excited about arriving at Wermaros. I looked below at the patches of white cropland that checkered off into the darker forests around them. This high winter view was an orderly panorama that resembled the square patterns on woven cloth made into tunics, trousers, or cloaks. Before today, we only had gone to the village at the spring and autumn festivals of Beltaine and Lugnasa, to attend trade fairs organized by my aunt's husband, Liscos, chieftain of the village.

It was late afternoon, with a low sun dissolving the land into a white, blinding glare, when I felt a penetrating chill. The road had entered a dense forest above Wermaros. This final stretch was gloomy and frightening. Even at midsummer the sun barely shown through a heavy overhang of fir, oak, and pine branches. Travelers always hurried through the shadowy arches of the trees, especially near evening. At dusk, when the balance between light and dark became equalized, Dividiac said that the spirits of the dead in the Other-world might try to cross over into our land of the living. Animal gods could shape-shift and take human form. I had never seen either, but then, I had been fearful of looking directly into the dark recesses of the woods. Arvos loosened the reins to let the ponies pull us up the long grade without straining them. Both of my uncles were under the bear pelts, still asleep. When Cluvios awoke from time to time, coughed, and spit blood over the wagon's side, Mother would glance back at him, worried about his health.

The day seemed endless to me. We Celts mark time by the monthly phases of the moon, reckoning on the nights instead of days. Now, the remaining daylight was quickly fading and last night's waxing moon would be only slightly more full. The evening air felt uncomfortably raw, when I finally caught sight of Wermaros, in a valley at the bottom of the road's down-slope. The village's scattering of lodges was encircled by a log palisade that was built on the near bank of the Dubis. The river's swift, dark surface reflected the last of the sky's brightness.

As we approached the village in the half-light, abruptly, as if experiencing a vision, I imagined that the circular palisade was the rim of a huge wheel. The village streets and paths were its spokes!

"Mother!" I cried, standing up and clutching the wagon's side. "It's the Wheel of Life I was talking about! The wheel that Dividiac says holds our destiny. Is Wermaros where ours...mine...is going to be?"

Briga did not reply to my question, but reached back to squeeze my hand and stare at a dark village sprinkled with yellow-orange dots of street-corner bonfires. If she also envisioned a wheel of the future, I realized that it must be with little pleasure. She could not control events that had moved her into the territory of a foreign tribe, to a remote Sequani village where she had no husband, no status, no possessions. A place she would not voluntarily have chosen herself.

I felt Mother's apprehension too, yet, strangely, it made me think of the Romani we had talked about on the way, the people that the Tigurini had humbled. I knew that no Celtic tribe would let such a defeat go unchallenged. This outside threat of danger was an additional spoke of the wheel that I had not considered.

Fulvius the sausage maker once told me that each year his people commemorated their defeats in war, as well as their victories. What Celtic tribe ever celebrated battles they had lost? *Taranis! I'll wager a new dagger that these Romani will come back some day, on one excuse or another, to avenge that long-ago insult.*

With that disturbing thought, my vision faded. Wermaros returned to what it actually was—an isolated mountain community of thatched wooden lodges and storehouses, whose only connection with our family was that my aunt had married the village chieftain.

Is this where my future is to be forged?

Chapter III

After the last flush of pink in the sky had etched distant trees on the Jurassos crests into a black filigree of lines, only the brilliant dusk star kept a silent vigil over the darkening valley. As we approached the mountain gate to the village, the warning yelps of dogs sent guards scrambling from their bonfire to challenge us.

Arvos asked in a nervous whisper, "Th...they'll know who we are?"

Cluvios told him, "Briga's sister is the clan chieftain's wife. One of his wives, I should say. Liscos has three."

I pictured my aunt's husband, a stocky, red-faced man who had only one arm, yet many of our warriors are scarred or mutilated in some way. When I was younger, the stump of Liscos's shield arm always held a morbid fascination for me and the other boys with whom I played in the village.

Four guards formed a line on the road, holding their spears horizontally as a signal to halt. When the wagon clanked to a stop, Cluvios identified us.

"The family of Alrix, a Raurici clan chieftain, who is kin to Liscos."

One of the sentries recognized him. "Cluvios? What forge work brings you here before Beltaine?"

"Not work, Germani! They raided Alrix's new settlement. He...he's missing."

"May clouds of blood fall on their heads!" The man spat in the snow after pronouncing the curse, then said, "We...we also have poor news. Little Klega has died."

Briga heard him and stood up. "My niece is dead? When? Why wasn't I told?"

The guard doffed his hat to mumble, "Lady, we sent to Arialbinnum for Dividiac. Didn't Docis bring him the message?"

"We were at Noviodubno, my husband's village. What happened?"

"Lady, an evil spirit in the child's body took her to the Other-world."

"And where is she...her body...now?"

"Inside her father's lodge."

Briga ordered, "Arvos, take me there. My sister is Klega's mother, wife to Liscos. Their lodge is at the far end of this road, near the river gate."

The driver glanced over at Cluvios. He nodded agreement.

After the guards moved aside, Arvos maneuvered the team onto a central dirt track running through Wermaros. Except for the muffled barking of dogs inside lodges, the village was quiet at the time of an evening meal. Warm light shown from triangular openings at the top of the lodges' steeply pitched, thatched roofs, where wisps of blue cook-fire smoke vented.

I felt sad about Klega, even though she usually stayed inside when we came to visit. Thin and pale, she had coughed up bloody spittle much of the time. Other village children kept away, repeating to each other their parents' warning that an evil spirit had taken over their playmate's body.

As we neared her sister's lodge, Mother told me to awaken Dividiac. When he stirred, she told him, "Klega has died. Have you a rite to comfort my sister?"

"Eh? The girl is dead?" Dividiac extended a hand to me for help in sitting up. "Then Cernunnos has a new daughter."

Dividiac meant his remark about Klega being with the god of the Otherworld to be comforting, not callous, but Mother did not reply.

When we arrived at the lodge, Arvos stayed outside to stable the ponies. Cluvios led the way through a low door that went into a small anteroom, then down an earthen ramp to the common living area, six hand spans below ground. Rough timber walls rose equally high above the top of the lowered area. The dimly lighted space smelled of wood smoke that hazed the air and came from a cooking fire enclosed by a flat stone wall set near the ramp. I smelled a meaty odor of simmering pork rising from a cauldron suspended over the flames, but news of my cousin's death tempered my hunger.

The room was as I remembered it in late summer, at the Lugnasad festival. The underside of the straw thatch overhead extended down to log sidewalls. Dusty bear and elk skins draped along its length closed out drafts. A sickle, scythe, shovel, and wood-cutting axe hung on the end nearest the ramp. Below the tools, ranged alongside each other, pottery jars held grain, oil, and herbs. In a far corner, the stone querns for hand-milling grain were still, but I saw a lamp nearby and noticed a slow movement at the household loom. Trauna, the chieftain's oldest wife, treaded the shuttle; even in death, routines to sustain family life continued.

Illuminated by the flickering light of a double-spouted oil lamp and cradling a drinking horn in one beefy hand, Liscos slumped in the shadows next to the wicker partition of one of the sleeping rooms. His battered shield, spear, and sword hung on the wall behind him, next to a banner with a white image of his clan's boar-totem embroidered on a green cloth.

After he noticed us enter, Liscos slurred his words in chiding Dividiac, "Druid, y' came too late. My little daughter is dead."

Cluvios explained, "Chieftain, we never received your message. Harudes attacked our settlement. Only some forty of us escaped and Alrix is missing."

Liscos grunted, but did not ask for details.

Dirona heard us and came from her vigil at the small bed, where her daughter's emaciated body lay. My aunt and Mother embraced in silence, then we went to see the dead girl.

My cousin lay on her own oak bed, covered with a calf skin that would be her burial shroud. Klega's small face was pale as the moon that had risen and begun to move toward the dusk star. Dirona had placed a golden diadem in the shape of a crescent over her red hair. Boughs from spruce trees surrounded the thin body.

A shrine to the goddess Sequana was set on a ledge behind Klega. Liscos built it for his daughter after the evil began to ravage her body. He hollowed out a limestone slab to hold water in imitation of Sequana's sacred spring, the source of a river that Father said eventually emptied into a narrow sea channel that separated Gallia from the island of Albion. Clusters of white mistletoe and fresh holly twigs draped the goddess's oaken image. Sequana's features were serene, with her hands spread out in a gesture that might either radiate an internal power or signal helplessness in the face of a more powerful god's action.

On a table nearby, Klega's favorite jewelry and playthings would be buried with her—silver bracelets, golden rings, wood and cloth dolls, and her favorite toy, a small, wheeled, bronze horse that Cluvios had fashioned for her last birthday.

Liscos stared at the twin sisters a moment with bleary eyes, drained his horn, and stood unsteadily to confront Dividiac again. "Man o' th' Oak. A warrior is th' vassal of Death, but explain t' me why my little girl had t' die."

Without hesitating, Dividiac replied, "I will speak to you of this death as the center of her *life*."

On hearing the druid, a white-haired man, lounging on the furs of an earthen sleeping ledge, sat upright and began to strum a harp. I had seen Celtillos before, but the line of scar that slashed across his forehead, and the milky sphere of his mutilated eye, looked even more hideous by the flickering light of the cook-fire flames.

Dividiac went to sit cross-legged near the bard. He closed his eyes and inhaled the short breaths I had seen him use to induce a trance state. The firelight set his face's wrinkled flesh in motion and threw a fluttering shadow on the log wall behind. When he finally spoke, Dividiac's voice was a low sing-song, intoning verses I had heard before. They expressed belief of a reincarnation in the Other-world.

"The grave squared in Mother Earth is not the end of human-life,

just as burial in a furrow is not the death of seed-life.

The seed is covered over, but soon new life arises from its grave."

Celtillos caught the word rhythm of the verses and strummed a soft accompaniment. Dividiac did not need a notched memory staff to help him recall words that he had sung countless times at the death of everyone from stillborn infants to warrior kings slaughtered in battle.

"The spokes of the Wheel of Life hold together
the rim of our oneness with the Earth Mother.
Each happening has a time, each event its season,
before it returns to the clasp of the Mother.
Look into the Mother and you will know
that all life returns upon itself.
As the spoke of a wheel returns to the position
it once had, and yet the rim moves to a new place,
so the small spoke of Klega's life
has turned to a new place, a new life.
Our own existence is like a wheel:
the spokes turn and re-turn,
to move past the place that was,
and stop again at another place.
So it is with Life and Death.
Death is only a pause in Life,
a waiting to move on again,
perhaps in a new form."

Dividiac was in a full trance now, swaying slowly from side to side with the cadence of his words. I tried again to understand what they implied. A wheel was the image used to express a life cycle that Celts believed rolled on into the Other-world of the dead. Yet the cycle did not end there, it continued back to this world with the dead person reborn in a new form. Uncle continued his explanation of Klega's death.

"The laws of our gods are just laws.
They demand appeasement, asking like for like.
So what god would ask for Klega's life,
except to sweeten it?
Justice demands that Cernunnos, king of the Other-world,
release the girl.
Release her from the prison of sickness,
to live awhile in the Land of the Young,
where a hundred years are as a single day.

Afterward, he will give Klega the spirit-form of a bird,

the most free of the Mother's creatures.

We shall soon hear her singing in a new sun,

see Klega flying to the pillars that hold up the sky.

Then, the Wheel will turn again.

This time the bird-girl might come as a woman.

A druidess who knows the secrets of Cernunnos,

come to prophecy to us."

Dividiac's head dropped forward. Celtillos put down his harp.

I was stunned at way the death of my little cousin had been made bearable. In my mind and those listening Klega might eventually return to the Now-world as a priestess second only to a Man of the Oak.

Dividiac slowly roused himself, looked around, then ordered in a hoarse whisper, "Light three bonfires of oak and yew wood at the burial site. Carry the girl there." He motioned to me, "Alberix, bring the image of Sequana."

Liscos carried the front of his daughter's bed, with Cluvios holding the back as they went up the ramp and outside into chill night air. Dividiac and I walked behind them. My aunt and mother were further back. The image of the goddess felt warm in my hands, as if the latent power of Sequana, now trapped in her wooden form, would be released in Klega's grave.

The guards had alerted the village men and women of Dividiac's arrival. All were *vassos* of the chieftain, who came from lodges to join the procession. The men carried pine-pitch torches to light the way.

We passed back through the mountain gate and turned left onto a communal pasture. At its north edge, where dark forest trees began to climb a rocky slope, I could see the bright blaze of bonfires reflecting a pale orange on the surrounding snow. Anticipating little Klega's death, the villagers had dug a grave and stacked yew and oak wood for the girl's burial.

At the site, the old druid invoked three gods to whom the fires had been dedicated, then directed that the bed be passed through the purifying smoke. By the light of the fires and torches, two women covered Klega's body with the calfskin. Then her bed was lowered into the grave's black emptiness. Cluvios reached down to lay a pine box containing the girl's treasures next to her body, and motioned for me to place Sequana's statue on the other side. The patron goddess of the Sequani tribe would protect the little girl during her travels in the Other-world.

After we stepped back, the village women arranged fir boughs over the leather shroud, and threw apples and nuts around the bed as symbols of immortality. Afterward, several vassal men spaded earth into the grave and heaped it into a small mound.

There was little weeping at the funeral. Death was common and Dividiac's promise of a new life for Klega had tempered grief with hope. Yet, when we returned to the lodge, Mother went with Dirona into her sleeping compartment. Liscos motioned Dividiac, Cluvios, and me to a table, then slumped down and stared into his drinking horn. After an interval of silence, broken only by the snap of pinewood in the fire, he roused himself from his thoughts.

"Food," he demanded thickly. "Arduinna, bring us food."

From her loom, Trauna motioned to her husband's newest wife, who watched from the door of her room. Arduinna went to the cauldron, ladled out three bowls of pork stew, and brought them to us. I thought the woman looked young, perhaps barely older than I was, but she did not glance at my uncles or me. She refilled her husband's horn with *cervisa*, and then brought pottery cups of the frothy, sweetened beer for us.

I was hungry. Dividiac ate well, but Cluvios picked at his food. Liscos devoured his in silence, his head bent low over the bowl. I knew he was grieving, yet I felt he was also ill at ease with Dividiac, knowing that his own rough mountain speech was no match for a druid's eloquence.

Liscos gulped down his beer, motioned for the horn to be refilled, then looked up at Dividiac and stammered his understanding of what the verses had meant.

"Druid, is…is my daughter gone t' Cernunnos, then?"

When Dividiac sucked froth from his cup without replying, I answered, "Uncle says she's healthy again. Klega will only pause in the Land of the Young before returning to the Now-world."

Liscos glared at me, took another gulp, wiped his mouth on his right sleeve and stared down at the table again.

After his interval of silence, Dividiac muttered, "The moon is rising in the sign of the Fish. It is good, a feminine sign whose element is Water."

From his memorized knowledge, the old druid had culled astronomical signs concerning Klega's death. Liscos scowled at him, but said nothing.

Curious to know more, I asked, "Uncle, what does that mean?"

He reached across the table to pat my cheek. "My boy, the stars have wisdom in them for us to read." He pushed his bowl and cup away, eager to interpret signs that would tell more about his niece. "Klega died two nights ago as the moon ascended into the Water Carrier. The element was Air, a masculine sign—"

Dividiac paused. With him, I realized there were two Water signs and only one of Air, a contradiction of his prediction of a bird reincarnation for the girl. In moments, his face relaxed and he chuckled as the puzzle resolved itself in his mind.

"*Cranes!* The water birds of the god Esus! I have seen their images in the sanctuary of the Parisii. The girl is truly favored and will be his attendant."

Liscos looked up, flushed with anger. His daughter was dead and all the cranes of Esus could not take her place. When he stood up, muttering "Falern'an," then went to a wine amphora set on a wall rack and poured out a pitcherful, I guessed that he needed to counter Uncle's babble about stars and water birds with something he knew about.

"Falern'an, a wine of th' Romani," Liscos boasted, sloshing some into the dregs of Cluvios's and my beer. "An' I have information no one knows." He leaned forward unsteadily and affected a confidential tone, "Romani are coming *here* t' Wermaros. My village. Import'nt chiefs of theirs t' parley with *me*."

Cluvios looked at him, trying to grasp the significance of what he had said. What Uncle had drunk didn't help, so his response was slurred. "Romani? Their province is t' th' south. Why come to your Sequani lands?"

Liscos wagged an unsteady finger, pleased to be the center of attention again. "Ah...I can't tell y' *everythin'*, but they're coming after th' festival of Beltaine."

"Beltaine? In th' spring?"

I imagined that Cluvios's numbed mind could think of no reason why Romani would come to Gallic territory, unless they planned to annex Sequani lands. Father told me they had done so with Allobroges to the south. *Then Germani warriors are not the only threat to us.* I remembered, as we came down the road above Wermaros, wondering when the Romani would come back to avenge their defeat by the Tigurini. That could be the reason, yet would they warn an enemy first?

Dividiac interrupted my thoughts. "Liscos, your talk of Beltaine reminds that it soon will be spring. Have you an equinox *menhir* in your village?"

Liscos shook his head; there was no such stone marker.

Dividiac continued, "Then, at sunrise, Alberix and I will find a location for one." I was surprised, but before I could question Uncle, he clutched my shoulder for support and stood up. "To sleep, my boy! We must be out before daylight every morning for the next year to observe and record where Belenos rises."

I agreed, yet had no choice. Dividiac had begun his promise to teach me the secrets of the druids.

After I helped him lie down on a sleeping ledge and covered him with furs, Uncle motioned me to a place further along the shelf. I pulled a covering around myself, but leaned against the clay wall instead of lying down.

I heard drunken snoring. Liscos's head rested on his one arm as he slept.

Cluvios's chair squeaked as he turned it to stare at the glowing coals of the fire. I wondered if he was trying to read his own future at Wermaros in the dying embers.

I glanced up at stars glimmering in the blackness outside the smoke vent at the top of the roof gable. Dividiac had tried to point out the names of constellation patterns to me, but I hadn't been that interested. I had learned the most obvious one, Arctos, the seven stars that formed a bear's outline. I only saw a ladle, like the one Mother used in cooking. Now, after hearing uncle's prediction for Klega, I wanted to learn more about the star patterns he had called *Zoidiakos*.

I recalled my brief vision of Wermaros as the Wheel of Life. The spoke my father had chosen for me was that of a warrior, one on which I might take his place as *vlatos* of our clan. Liscos's talk about Romani coming would add a new spoke to the wheel. I felt very tired and crawled under the fur coverings, aware of the rustle of mice in the roof-thatching overhead. The ledge and my fur covering would be speckled with their droppings in the morning.

❧❧

Briga watched her brother-in-kin's heavy sleep from the curtained edge of her sister's room, then glanced over at Arduinna, who washed the stew bowls and cups.

"I see Liscos has a new doe," she commented in a sarcastic tone.

Dirona shrugged acceptance. "Arduinna is more like an un-weaned calf, but I like her. Our gods can be merciful. She will help him forget his pain over Klega."

"Sending a child to replace a child?" Briga scoffed. "But, then, you were always the gentler of the two of us. What does Trauna think?"

"She has little to say. You remember that Trauna was a free servant when Liscos contracted to marry her. She is content to weave and know that she has two fine sons in Vesontio."

"*You* weren't a servant, Dirona. Father gave Liscos a herd of cattle as your marriage price. He leased them out and made enough money to become a trader. That's what eventually made him respectable...for a Sequani."

Dirona pushed her sister in mock reproach. "What a thing to say!" At Arial binnum they had shared jokes about Sequani men being without polish, like one of Cluvios's rough forge castings. "You must admit that Liscos was handsome," she retorted. "I may have felt sorry for him because of the arm, but he has been good to me...and his only daughter."

Briga began to undo her sister's hair braids and smooth down the reddish tresses with a silver comb. "I'm sorry about Klega. We all knew some evil had entered her body. Her death was a matter of time."

Dirona sniffled and wiped her eyes on a sleeve. "I heard Dividiac's prediction. It's of some comfort, I suppose. What...what of Alrix?"

"Only the gods know his fate."

"The gods..." Dirona turned to look at her twin and take her hands in hers. "Briga, there's something supernatural about how all of you came here tonight."

"Supernatural? Why? Our Raurici people have always lived in the shadow of Germani raids."

Dirona explained, "I think that it's Alberix with whom the gods are concerned. *They* brought him here."

Briga began combing again, puzzled by her twin's remark. She had conceded that Dirona often possessed perceptive insights. Had she not married, she might have become a druidess. "Sister, I'm not sure what you mean."

"Wasn't Alberix about to begin warrior training?"

"In about two months, at Beltaine."

"What does Cluvios say about having to return the boy?"

"He wants him to continue at the forge. To complicate things, Dividiac told me he wants to train Alberix to be a Man of the Oak."

"It would be a great honor for your son to be a druid."

"And twenty long years of study." Briga worked her sister's hair into a single braid, thinking that Alberix would be more content making swords than killing with them. Yet, it was impossible to alter custom. Alrix had tried. He had left Arialbinnum to create a neutral place, where treaties, rather than bloodshed would settle disputes between clans.

Dirona's intuition surfaced again, seeming to have read her sister's thoughts. "Briga, they say that Alrix wanted to include Germani in his treaties. Would their chiefs have agreed?"

"Can a wolf be taught to guard sheep? Alrix did think that it was time to sheath swords, that a common law would benefit both banks of the Renos."

"Like laws the Romani are said to have in their provinces?"

"Romani are not Celts..." Briga tied a linen strip to hold the bottom of the braid in place. "Sister, I heard Liscos boasting about some of their chiefs coming to see him. What is that about?"

"He doesn't discuss such affairs with me."

"I suppose not." Briga gave the knot a final tug. "Sleep now, we'll talk more tomorrow. I'm going to look in on the men." She turned to embrace her sister. "I...I'll miss Klega. She was small, yet so brave in accepting her illness."

When Dirona pulled away, tears dampened her eyes. "Sister, may the night bring you bright dreams."

"And you, my Sister."

Briga went to throw a plaid blanket over Cluvios's shoulders and let him doze in the chair. She tucked in the loose fur covering at Dividiac's neck, and saw that Alberix was asleep. With a final scowl at Liscos, she went to a sleeping compartment next to her sister's.

Despite the tiring day, Briga knew that sleep would not come easily. Alrix and the prospect of an uncertain future without him were foremost in her mind. She also felt numb from the shock of Klega's death. At the end of Dividiac's prophetic verses, no one had spoken much of the little girl. It was as if her dead niece briefly had gone away and would soon return.

Cluvios worried her. In the past few months, he had become increasingly irritable over small incidents. He complained of frequent headaches and a constant metallic taste in his mouth. He tired easily. Now he spat up blood. What manner of evil forge-spirit had attempted to enter his body?

Dirona's comment about Alberix being the concern of the gods was still unclear. *I suppose that every aunt thinks her nephew is special, yet what is Dirona getting at? Alberix is about to enter a traditional path for Celtic youths, except that he is the son of a clan chief. And the Romani, those conquering strangers from the south, can be deadly as Germani. Dividiac says that they persecute druids who live in their Gallic province, and destroy their sacred shrines.*

What could be their business with Liscos? Whatever it is that the Romani want is sure to affect his tribe's way of life, and now ours. Dividiac, Cluvios, my son and I, all of us may be snared like hapless trout in a Dubis River weir.

Chapter IV

It was still dark when Dividiac shook me awake. I hadn't slept that well —gnawing worry about what might have happened to my father, the long, tiring wagon journey, and the still face of my dead cousin—these images had clogged my mind.

I raised myself on one elbow and looked over the edge of the fur coverings. The room was cold, smelling of wood smoke and boiled pork, along with spilled wine and *cervisa*. Cluvios, still in his chair, snored lightly. Liscos was gone, probably bedded down with his new wife.

"Trauna brought you clothing." Uncle handed me woolen trousers, a tunic-shirt and belt with a short dagger attached to it, elk-hide vest, and boots. "We will return to Givico what he lent us."

Glad to have clothes that fit, I stuffed them into the warmth of my bedding, then noticed that pre-dawn stars glimmered in the open triangle near the roof.

After a few moments, I took a deep breath, shook mouse droppings from my covers, and stood on the cold dirt floor. Since light barely shone from the remnant of cook-fire coals, I threw on a handful of dried moss. The kindling flared up long enough for me to pull on trousers and slip the shirt over my head. As I belted the tunic, Dividiac rummaged through his amulet chest, which Arvos evidently had brought in during the night. He pulled out a round leather case that held cakes of black ink, reed pens, and sheets of papyrus.

Uncle slung the case over his shoulder and handed me a deerskin pouch to carry. "Bread, dried meat, and a skin of *cervisa*. We shall be out all morning."

I looped its strap through my belt, put on the vest, and followed Dividiac through the inner vestibule and out into icy dawn air. During the night, a fresh fall of light snow had whitened the streets and thatched roofs of lodges. Overhead, the sky was clear, speckled with stars that resembled a white splash of salt flung across a black cloth. I saw that Arctos the Bear had turned his nose down to the northwest horizon, searching for honey.

The crunching sound of our footsteps in the snow alerted dogs inside several lodges. They barked viscously, but none charged out to threaten us. At the river gate, I tucked cold hands into my armpits and waited while the guards spoke to Dividiac. Word of the druid's arrival had gone around the village and they recognized him. The men even nodded to me in respect as the son of a chieftain.

I followed Uncle onto the planks of the wooden bridge that crossed the Dubis River, hearing the loud rush of water and feeling the span tremble as the dark current forced itself against the piers. Even in daylight, the somber reflections of forest trees made the water appear black—*dubi*. Our Celtic word had given the river its name.

On the far side of the stream a dirt track led upward through cleared land, where timber for the lodges and palisade of the village was cut. I knew the area; on earlier visits I had played among the stumps with village boys.

After the roadway leveled off, Dividiac turned into a field that would give us a good view of distant crests on mountains east of the village. After he chose a fallen log on which to sit and wait for sunrise, I brushed snow off and sat next to him. Uncle motioned toward the pouch. I opened the drawstring, broke off pieces of bread, and cut the tough, smoked elk meat with my new knife. We shared the food and gulps of *cervisa* in silence.

As the crowing of roosters announcing dawn drifted up from the village, Artos and his starry neighbors melted away into an overhead pool of milky sky. A mountainous horizon materialized across the Dubis valley—dark, jagged lines set against the rose-tinted background. Dividiac uncurled a sheet of papyrus from his case, took out a reed pen, and moistened a cake of ink with snow. I watched him sketch the outline of trees on the opposite mountain, exaggerating the size of a skeletal fir where the light was brightest.

"Our point of reference," he explained. "I'll put a circle here, where Belenos rises today. You will see the god continue north until mid-summer, then again turn and begin his slow retreat toward southern regions."

I watched the first bright shafts of sunlight gleam through the gaunt framework of trees. Dividiac circled Belenos's position on his sketch, then wrote something above it.

I asked, "Uncle, how is it that you know what those marks mean?"

"Our people have no alphabet of their own...no letters...but druids use Greek characters to make words in our language. See..." Dividiac held the papyrus toward the light to show me the marks, XXIV ΑΝΑΓΑΝΤΙΩΣ. "This is the twenty-fourth day in our month of Anagantios. You will learn how to read all this, Alberix," he said as he replaced his materials back into their case.

We stayed on to watch the sun disc move upward and change the sky from a tint of watered milk to the color of glowing coals in our forge at Arialbinnum.

"Uncle," I admitted, "I haven't paid much attention to where Belenos rises, or that dawn could be so beautiful."

Dividiac chuckled and patted my cheek, then stood to test the air with a wet finger. "Despite the winter storm, Belenos gives us the sign of a warmer rain. The wind of *Toshaight Aree*...'Beginning of Spring'...will soon blow in from the Western Ocean."

"How do you know that?"

"Signs! That is why we came here, Alberix. I will teach you to interpret the Earth Mother's signs."

As the sky turned to pale lavender, I wondered about how long that might take.

After Belenos cleared the tops of forest trees, Dividiac turned and put a hand on my shoulder. "Alberix, it is time you learned the lessons of the Mother. Your father became a great warrior, yet I think the ways of Men of the Oak are more to your nature." He pulled his hand away and indicated the far-off crest, now clearly showing the shapes of firs and skeletal oaks. "Today you have seen the first secret of the silver disc I brought out at Bireg."

"Secret, Uncle? Wasn't it a small calendar of months?"

"Our people see Belenos each day, but are ignorant of his lessons," Dividiac continued, as if he had not heard me, and pointed at an area to the right of where the sun had risen. "In seven days the god will come about there, by that white birch. On the sixth morning after the new moon of Ogron, we will mark the place where he is on the equinox, when day and night are of equal length. On that day, the dark half of the year gives way to the bright. That spot is where the *menhir* will be built." Dividiac abruptly grasped my hands and stared into my eyes with an intensity that almost was frightening. "Each day, Alberix, you shall learn the secrets of our Earth Mother! In time you will hold the highest position of any man beneath that of the gods." He tightened his hold on me and decided that if Cernunnos permitted he would offer the total of his knowledge to me as his final pupil.

After Uncle released my hands, tears glistened at the corner of his eyes. Then he picked up his case and turned to walk back down the road. I hopped behind him, my step falling into my previous snowy footprints. The druid's words had reminded me of last evening's funeral rite for Klega, but also of Liscos's drunken boast.

I caught up with him. "Uncle, what do you know of the Romani?"

"Romani?" He turned to me, frowning. "Why do you ask about the 'Shorthairs'?"

"Shorthairs?"

"Our name for *them*. They mock us because our Celtic men wear their hair long and call us 'Long-haired Galli'."

"Last night Liscos boasted that their chiefs were coming to meet with him. I wondered if—"

"Dirona's husband is a fool!" Dividiac interrupted in an angry tone I rarely heard him use. "Romani kill Men of the Oak and destroy our sanctuaries and *nemtons*."

"Why do they do that?"

"Some druids perform sacrificial rites that displease the Shorthairs, and... and even me. Alberix, speak no more of these outsiders."

We had reached the point where the road dropped down toward the village. The snow-shrouded lodges were washed in a rosy light and beginning to absorb the warmth of Belenos's rays. Where patches of white glided off the steep-pitched roofs in silent waves, children screamed in delight and ran to let the cold, feathery mass drop on them.

As Dividiac started down the slope, I called after him, "Uncle, I want to stay up here awhile longer."

He nodded absently without looking back. I still wasn't sure why my questions about Romani had upset him. *What sacrificial rites did he mean druids performed?*

While I thought about Dividiac's hatred of the Shorthairs, a finch flew from a fir stump in the field alongside me. I didn't consider it a sign, but tramped over to brush softening snow off the flat surface and sit down. Below me, in the village, the spokes of the Wheel I had imagined last evening were in motion. Blue cook-fire smoke curled from lodge vent holes. A sharp sound of axes chopping ice from water troughs echoed up to me. Pigs squealed and cattle lowed in contentment as they ate food. I located the lodge where we had spent the night and thought that Cluvios might be talking to Liscos about setting up a new forge for him. A crafter would bring honor to Wermaros as well as more coins to the chieftain's purse.

My ultimate place on the Wheel was to be ready if the council of elders voted some day for me as chieftain of our clan. *Chieftain, but where? The people of our Alarian clan are scattered among the farmsteads of the valley where we passed. Dividiac is offering me a new spoke, one I had never considered. Here is a chance to touch the gods through ritual, and to control unseen forces that are beyond the sweep of a warrior's sword blade. Working among the Sequani, despite being the son of a chieftain and nephew of the village leader, I'll have no privileges that I haven't earned.*

Dividiac has traveled all over Gallia. I remember stories he told around our evening fires of new tribes and strange places. Yesterday, I talked with Mother about the different people at our trade fairs. Men with dark skins. Swarthy ones like the Kephestos brothers, and both blond and dark-haired Celts from other tribes. All these lives are tightly connected to the Wheel by the rim of tradition.

I recalled what I had learned this morning and then about Klega's death, which Dividiac in a sense had made understandable, even relevant. Yet I realized that even though Uncle could observe the seasonal journeys of Belenos, he could not explain what the brilliant disk actually was. Even a ritual like the bird augury that brought us here was a way of fitting mysteries onto the Wheel and keeping our people together. I had watched enough of

Dividiac's rituals to know that law and tradition held tribal life in place, and yet I was questioning whether I could submit to a life that was so confining.

The thought of tampering with tradition—and the will of the gods—disturbed me so much that I bolted from the stump and half-ran, half-slid down to the river gate.

❧❧

The weather stayed unusually cold, but, as the winds turned southerly, clouds saturated with warm rain came in with them. I watched much of the snow melting on the mountains around the village. Ogron, the month we call Middle Spring, blossomed forth so quickly with fields of sunblossoms and moondaisies that the flowers might have been mistaken for banks of colored snow set among white drifts that lingered in north-facing forest hollows. The Dubis ran full, sweeping in a broad, sparkling arc as it rounded the Great Bend that gave Wer-Maros its name, then surged westward toward Vesontio, to what Dividiac said was a far-off joining with an Arar River.

Over Klega's grave, the small mound of eroding dirt sprouted weeds and grasses. By the next moon, that of our month of Cutios, the pitiful earthen hillock would be completely hidden by a lush growth of green vegetation.

❧❧

We stayed in the guest lodge until Cluvios could set up a forge and have his own house. He began to train some village men in making charcoal for his smelting pit, and appointed Arvos as their supervisor. Before month's end, thick smoke from the smoldering piles hung in a blue, translucent layer over the greening valley. At night, a ruddy glow from the oven mouths shown through a latticework of tree trunks.

Each morning that was not cloudy I went with Dividiac to record the location of the sun's rising on his drawing. Afterward, I helped Cluvios build a forge like the one we had at Arialbinnum. Under the roof of an open shed, we dug a square pit two paces long on each side, with a shallow ditch in front that channeled wind into the pit and fanned the smelting fire. To increase the draft of air we made a bellows of calfskin sewn into a bag and fronted with a copper funnel. Through a pulley and counterweight device, one person could operate a treadle that pumped the bellows.

Men indebted to Liscos repaired a smaller lodge next to our forge, which was near the center of the village. The chieftain sent others to make tree trunk anvils and haul an immense flat granite stone to the forge on log runners. Its hard, smooth surface was ideal for pincering and hammering the iron rim of a wheel into position around its wooden felly.

It pleased Cluvios that we finished just before the new moon of Cutios. That was a lucky month—*Mat*—on our calendar, and Dividiac told him it was a good omen to begin a business with the waxing moon.

Over two months had passed and yet there was no word about my father. Mother refused to accept his death by removing her jewelry and loosening her hair as a sign of mourning, yet neither did she continue to speak of him. Fostered out to Cluvios for four years, as I had been, seeing Father primarily on our festivals, I nevertheless missed him.

I worried about Cluvios, and so did Mother. Neither of us could think of a reason for his sickness. He was more irritable with everyone and complained of dull headaches. That metallic taste still fouled his mouth, and blood flecked his spittle. Mother reported that gossip around the bake ovens suggested that Cluvios had offended the forge god, Goban, and was punished with an evil spirit. Is that what our gods did? Perhaps, yet, if so, what had little Kelga done to deserve her illness?

❧

On the day that we finished building the forge, Cluvios and I relaxed outside in a soft, spring twilight. Uncle seemed to feel better during the last weeks of being away from the acrid smoke of his metal pourings.

Mother brought two horns of sweetened beer to us from our new lodge. "You've both earned these," she said, smiling again for the first time in a long while.

Cluvios took a sip of the frothy brew. "The work went faster than I thought it would."

"Liscos gave us as many men as we needed," I added, then noticed Uncle studying my face. I had grown in the last few months, and even blond beard stubble roughed my cheeks. "What, Uncle?" I asked, flushing at his scrutiny.

Cluvios grinned and wiped a smudge of charcoal off my forehead. "Alberix, we'll take a wagon to Chondix tomorrow for a load of iron loaves and copper ingots, then try out the forge."

I was surprised. "Chondix? That's to the south. Aren't we going to the old pits near Arialbinnum?"

He shook his head. "Too close to Germania. Rumors are that raids have gotten more frequent. In the past our Helvetii have always beaten Germani warriors back, but now it seems the tribe is preparing to migrate west and escape them."

"The Helevetii are migrating?" Briga asked from the doorway. "Where did you hear that?"

"Merchants told me."

"*Merchants?*" Mother scoffed. "Come to the bake oven if you want the latest rumors. The women are afraid that what occurred at Arialbinnum will happen here. If our Raurici migrate with the Helvetii, there will be no one left to stop the Germani."

To divert Mother's anxiety, I said, "With Arialbinnum lost, Liscos now may want to hold bigger trade fairs here at Wermaros."

"That's true," Cluvios agreed. "Mountain tribesmen have no village that's any closer." He drained his horn and wiped the back of a hand across his tawny mustache. "Liscos is crude, yet I admire the way he recast his life after he lost the arm."

"And having you in his village and hosting Dividiac won't hurt his fortunes," Briga commented dryly. "Any chieftain would trade his clan standard to count a druid in his household..." She paused while Cluvios suffered a bout of coughing that left him gasping for breath. "I'll make a hot tussilago and honey drink to soothe your throat, then you'll go inside and rest."

Uncle made an impatient gesture with his hands and stood up. "Alberix and I need to get our wagon ready and be back here in time for the festival of Beltaine."

Mother shrugged in the helpless way I had seen her use with Father. As she went to prepare the remedy, she muttered about the stubbornness of all men.

While I helped inspect the heavier wagon that Liscos had lent us to haul ore, I thought of Beltaine. The festival dedicated to the sun god's return was on the first day of the month of Giamon, one of the times we had come to Wermaros. On the way, Dividiac always spoke of our Celtic deities. There were about four hundred of them, but he said that only a fourth of that number was well known. I didn't remember all their names, but some are visible, like Belenos, Selena the moon, and Taranis the sky god. There are also rain gods and others who animate rocks, trees, water, and forest animals. A few are invisible, lurking inside the dark body of the earth. It was these latter, Dividiac warned, who were always ready to tamper with the cycle of seasons, or health and prosperity. He said that the function of druids was to neutralize these powers, or better, to control and direct them to beneficial ends through rituals and sacrifices.

Dividiac implied that some of the older rituals included human sacrifice, when men and women shut up in wicker cages were burned alive. He said this no longer happened, except in some remote backcountry areas. A runaway slave might be drowned to appease Teutates, or hanged to Esus, perhaps burned in an oak grove to appease Taranis, but the omens would have to be unusually disastrous, and the druid who performed the ritual particularly fanatical. *Those must be the sacrifices he meant.*

One of the disturbing, yet fascinating, aspects of the gods was that some could shift into other shapes and come from the Other-world in forms that deceived humans. When these gods gained your trust, they might suddenly revert to their true shape and destroy you. The most common one to warriors was *Babd-Catha*, whom they called "The Raven of Battle." When the ravens appeared at Bireg, some of the raid survivors had muttered her name. Bards recited songs about a beautiful woman who appeared on battlegrounds. She would encourage warriors and help the wounded, only to abruptly shape-shift into a red-eyed hag, riding in a chariot pulled by a terrifying horse form. The effect could paralyze the warriors of her enemies. After their defeat, she would change again into the raven-form and strut among the bloody dead.

Druids could master the secret of shape shifting. At Beltaine, during the Burning of the Fires of Belenos, the priests could become a beast that might harm cattle. By entering the predator's spirit, they gained control over its will and lessened the danger that it would ravage herds. I had never seen this happen, yet Dividiac swore it was true.

∾

Cluvios and I left Wermaros five days before Beltaine. When we reached the open pit mines at Chondix, I spent the first afternoon watching ironsmiths operate the stone smelting furnaces built many generations before. Iron-rich red earth was pick-axed out of surface deposits or shallow mines, then washed in a sluice to remove rock impurities. After the ore dried, workers pushed the lumps through openings at the top of pine cone-shaped furnaces, onto a bed of red-hot charcoal. After a time, along with a sponge-like loaf of incompletely melted ore and slag, a flow of relatively pure iron was collected at the kiln's base and in a hollow on one side.

During that first evening's long twilight, I drank with my uncle and the village men. The locals told of a road that led farther south toward the Tigurini, and described three lakes near that tribe's land. Aventia, the fortress capital of the Helvetii, was close to the shore of the middle lake. These veteran ironworkers mocked Tigurini toll road guards, who wore helmets that their grandfathers and fathers had taken from defeated legions in a battle decades ago, which most oldsters could not recall. The strutting Tigurini at Arialbinnum that I asked mother about also had flaunted their Roman loot.

Cluvios bought the more costly pure iron pourings, rather than spongy, yellowish loaves. Heating and hammering out the latter's impurities was hard, time-consuming work. He also bargained for tin and ingots of shiny copper that reminded me of the color of Mother's hair.

To not strain Liscos's draft horses with the heavy load, we returned home at a slow pace. In greening fields, myriads of colorful spring blossoms replaced the white shroud of winter that had covered the land during our escape from the Harudes. Farmers cut furrows in the dark valley soil with iron share heads on their wheeled plows. Others waved to us as they sharpened scythes for the first of three hay cuttings. I saw the products of the forge everywhere: kettles outside the farmstead homes, rakes, hoes, and saws. Shoes for horses were strapped onto their hooves. Liscos realized the demand for such items, and had not asked Cluvios for an indenture contract to repay the money he had lent him to build the forge and buy supplies. Profits from the iron and bronze implements we made would quickly repay the chieftain.

As Cluvios braked the wagon down the heights east of Wermaros, cattle had been brought out from their winter stabling and into fields around the village. After their recent confinement, newborn calves gamboled in the freedom of unfamiliar open spaces. I remembered that on the day of Beltaine the cattle would be purified with smoke, then led into mountain grazing meadows for the summer months.

As soon as our wagon rumbled through the mountain gate, Dividiac hurried toward us on the road. He had been awaiting our arrival and looked upset.

"Too long!" he chided, waving his arms. "You have been gone too long! It is two days to the festival and the bonfire stacks are not yet built—"

"Calm yourself," Cluvios reassured the old man. "I'll tell Arvos to have his charcoal makers put them up."

"The games! The games of Beltaine begin tomorrow!"

"Liscos will referee the contests." Cluvios jumped from the wagon and held Dividiac by the shoulders. "Druid, your only duties are to bless the clan god images and attend when cattle pass through the smoke, before herdsmen take them to the highlands."

"A heifer must be sacrificed," he babbled, "and an altar built."

I worried about his confusion, and called out to him, "Uncle, I'm your pupil. Let me help you with Beltaine preparations this year."

"Eh? My pupil?" The offer seemed to soothe him. "Then, Alberix, be in the meadow at high sun. We shall set up an altar for the sacrifice."

"I will, Uncle."

Cluvios took the ponies' bits and led them on foot toward the forge. "I'm glad you offered to help him. Dividiac has been getting forgetful since the raid."

"I'll help him, but I want to work with you, too."

"We'll see."

At the forge a group of village men waited to borrow our iron hammers and bronze ingots, wanting to throw them in one of the game contests. After I passed them out, Cluvios told me not to start a fire in the pit; he would close the forge for two days and enjoy the displays of skill. When he fell into another fit of coughing, I was glad he would be absent from the acrid fumes.

❧❧

Shortly after high sun, I was helping Dividiac drape robur oak branches around the bench we had set up as an altar for the herders' clan gods, when six strangers came out of the forest and walked across the meadow toward us. I didn't recognize the foremost man, but took him to be a druid. He was dark-haired, with a sallow-complexioned, angular face, and a thin body clothed in a black tunic. Following him were two young women, druidesses identified by blue face and arm markings and decorated tunics. Of the two Celtic-looking men, one toyed with the strings of a harp. The sixth person lagged behind the others, a muscular black man, wearing only a loincloth and leather vest.

I alerted Dividiac to the group. "Uncle, do you know those people?"

He squinted at the person in front, then scowled and turned away. "It is one of my former pupils."

When the dark druid was about ten paces off, he called out, "Master. I thought I recognized you."

Dividiac replied without enthusiasm, "You've changed since you left me, Danach."

"Danach?" He corrected him, "I am called Ollam-Fodla now, which is 'Doctor of Wisdom' in the language of my island."

"Inisfail, wasn't it? I wondered what had become of you." Dividiac had a clear recollection of the youth who had appeared in Arialbinnum, some fifteen years earlier. After he had befriended the lonely boy and accepted him as a pupil, Danach had gorged on learning the way a starving dog devours meat. Yet the boy had been attracted to the more occult druidic rituals, and after a decade of training, abruptly disappeared. The memories were not pleasant ones. "Danach, you left like a thief in the night. Why do you return now?"

Fodla ignored the question to introduce his companions. "These are my disciples. The two women are druid priestesses. Those men, Finan and Fithil, are a harper and juggler. That sooty fellow is Bocchus, from Mauretania on the Africa coast."

When Dividiac ignored the group, Fodla waved them back to the forest. The women strolled off in silence, arm in arm, but Finan gave an impudent flourish on his harp strings before following them. Fithil snatched up and juggled three of the four apples on the altar that we brought to eat, then tossed two of them to Boccus and crunched into the third as he walked off with the Mauretanian.

I was sure Fodla was aware of me, yet he continued to ignore my presence. "Master, you look well," he said to Dividiac. "This village is fortunate to have you."

"I am no longer your master." Uncle handed me a white leather thong. "Alberix, secure the oak branches to the altar with this binding."

Fodla watched me a moment, then turned back to Dividiac. "I must talk to you about Beltaine."

The old druid looked hard at his pupil. "You came from your island to talk of the sun festival?"

"What animal have you chosen for the sacrifice?"

"A white heifer calved between last Beltaine and the Lugnasad. Have you forgotten what I taught you?"

"Of course, a heifer..." Fodla brushed the grass with the toe of a shoe. "Let me come to the point. On Inisfail our people are more devoted to...to older ways. It seems that your Gallic tribes have become less faithful. Was not the hay season late last year? Even now snow still lies on the high meadows. Grass is thin—"

"Danach, why do you speak of this?" Uncle interrupted in anger. "What has it to do with the festival?"

"The sacrifice."

"What of it? Speak up, man!"

"The gods"—Fodla lowered his voice even though no one else was nearby—"the gods obviously require a sacrifice that will please them again. A human victim."

"*Human* victim?" Dividiac exclaimed in disbelief. "Are you mad, Danach? There have been few human sacrifices since the Romani came to the Rodanos valley. Certainly, I have no love for the Shorthairs, but I think it one of their wiser prohibitions."

As if he had not heard, Fodla continued, "Choose someone of no importance. A criminal perhaps, or one from whom the gods are owed retribution."

Dividiac trembled in responding, "I recall...Danach...that you did not stay for all of my instruction. Whoever finished it starved both your mind and your heart. Go back to your Inisfail!"

Fodla bowed in mock humility. "As you wish, old one, but we have a warning on my island. 'Those who displease the gods are cast up to melt like sea foam on the sand'." With a smirk at me, he turned and strolled back up to the forest edge.

Uncle did not look after his former pupil, but I watched until the druid in the black tunic disappeared—absorbed, it seemed—into the gloomy darkness of the woods.

I wanted to ask Uncle more about Danach...Ollam Fodla...but the man had upset him, so I finished decorating the altar while speculating to myself. *Where is this island of Inisfail, where druids still practice human sacrifice? That must have been the 'custom' that Uncle said Romani were suppressing in Gallia.* As I stepped back to see if I had properly drapes the oak branches, then again looked up at the silent forest, I wondered why Uncle's old pupil had turned up so unexpectedly. *The druid wouldn't have traveled from his distant island just to find his old master and talk about Beltaine. Fodla must have more important reasons for bringing his five disciples to Wermaros, and I'm sure it's not to submit to Dividiac's authority once again.*

Chapter V

Before setting out for Chondix, Cluvios had wanted an estimate of the tools we might have to make. That would be based on the number of village households, so I went with him to speak to Liscos's clan advisors. They said that the twenty-three lodges in Wermaros housed about two hundred freemen and thirty slaves—sixty-nine men and fifty-six women, with seventy-seven children under the age of fourteen, some fostered to relatives.

Father once explained about our tribes and clans. Family gelfines and derbfines, who are blood relatives up to the second generation, make up our clans. Celts are not a unified peoples, in fact, there are several different names for us. Those Kephestos brothers at Arialbinnum called us *Keltoi* in their language, yet also referred to our people as *Galatae*. The Romans named us *Galli*, as well as *Celtae*—what we call ourselves. Dividiac said the word meant "hidden," or "secret," because druids do not write down knowledge. The priests rely on a memorized tradition to hand down information. Dividiac points out that Romans make fun of us because we wear trousers and have long hair. *Gallia Comata*—"Long-haired Gaul"—is what they call our lands. We're mocked as *"Brachatae,"* from our word for trousers. Well, let them spend a long winter along the Renos River, and then decide if woolen leg coverings make sense or not!

☙ ❧

From my previous visits to Wermaros, I knew that the sporting contests on Beltaine's festival were less extensive than those of the late summer Lugnasad. Local tribesmen are mostly farmers or herders and warriors only if the call comes from clan chieftains against some sudden threat—they would not risk injuries at the start of a work season. Later, after harvests were in and cattle brought down from mountain meadows, men could afford to spend idle winter days healing broken bones.

By the morning before the festival day, I had forgotten about Dividiac's pupil, "The-druid-of-the-night-eyes," as I called him. Belenos rose brightly, arcing across a sky that was as blue as a mountain lake. White swells of cloud foretold good weather. For his trade fair, Liscos set up merchandise stalls on the meadow outside the palisade's eastern wall. Leather or linen awnings covered pine tables displaying trade goods that his wagons had brought from Vesontio. His two sons there acted as agents in purchasing, primarily from the Lingones and Aeduii Celtic tribes to the north and west.

Booths spaced at intervals along the merchandise tables sold local beer and honey-sweetened Greek and Roman wines that had been barged up the

Rodanos from Roman Gallia. Festival goers bought these along with millet bread and bowls of pork stew, or smoked pork meat that was a Sequani specialty.

A mild westerly breeze drifted a combined smell of food and animal manure toward the tents of visiting tribesmen that were pitched farther east of the trade stalls.

The mountaineers stripped off winter furs and heavy cloaks to stroll the line of booths in short-sleeved, homespun tunics. Ruddy arms and faces soaked up the welcome heat of Belenos's rays.

Shouted greetings over filled drinking horns and cups of wine hailed friends unseen for months. Women shared gossip collected during a winter of isolation on snow-bound farms. Comparing colorful woven tunics, capes, and trousers, and fondling brooches, rings, and bracelets displayed in the stalls, the women weighed the intensity of their desire for the ones they wanted against a willingness to part with the few bronze and silver coins they were able to hoard.

Liscos was everywhere, his single arm gesturing commands, shaking hands, collecting traded goods or money after haggled agreements, and supervising the *vassos* who managed his booths. The chieftain's beefy voice boomed above the crowd's babble and the metallic clink of hammer throwing contests. In the common meadow, players' shouts sounded in hurley games, where men kicked a leather ball towards a post.

❧❧

I was helping Arvos sort out hammers for the throwing contest when Cluvios came and pulled me away.

"Alberix," he said, "it's time you took part in the contests. You know more about the weight and balance of those hammers than any man here."

"I'm not sure, Uncle. I– "

"Nephew"–he interrupted me with the word he used instead of my name whenever he was irritated–"in six months you will be seventeen. I blame myself for persuading Alrix to let you stay at the forge this long and isolating you, but it's time you moved into the world of men."

"And make a fool of myself?"

"It's said that folly and learning often live together!" Cluvios called over to Arvos, "My nephew will be in the next contest. Save him a hammer."

The teamster-turned-charcoal maker, unshaven, in a grimy tunic smudged with charcoal dust, grunted acknowledgement, yet avoided looking at me.

I had watched the games before and knew there were two hammer competitions. One was for distance and the other for accuracy in throwing close to a stake set at the center of a circle, about fifteen paces away. I realized there were men stronger than I, who could toss greater distances, so I decided to try for accuracy.

The hammer throwing area was set up outside the river gate, on a narrow strip of land between the palisade and water. I had stopped to talk to Mother, who had asked me how Cluvios was feeling, so I missed seeing the distance throws. When I hurried out through the gate, teams were forming for the centering contests.

Arvos, still wearing his grimy tunic, had gone there ahead of me to compete in the first contest. Living near the charring kilns had made him take on the careless look of the few vagrants I had noticed at Arialbinnum. I saw him when he brought charcoal to the forge, but hadn't thought much about the teamster who had escaped the raid with us. Since he did not seem particularly friendly, I wondered if he was resentful at having been assigned difficult and dirty forest work that isolated him from the village.

Arvos motioned me over to him and picked up the heaviest hammer off the ground. "This is yours, *boy*," he said, extending it with a sarcastic sneer that I didn't expect. "You're competing against me."

I took the tool, wondering what I had done to anger him. The hammer Arvos chose for himself was our lightest one. *He figures I won't be able to control mine, giving him the advantage.*

"Let a *man* throw first," Arvos boasted as he stepped up to a gypsum line on the ground. He sighted along the hammer handle, pulled a brawny arm back, and sent the iron tool arcing through the air. It hit grass, bounced twice, and, incredibly, came to rest with its handle leaning against the stake. "Match *that* throw," Arvos dared me, but he was not smiling.

I found the balance point of my hammer and decided on an underhand thrust that would slide it into the circle. The tool skidded through the grass and raised a puff of white dust when it slid through the chalk ring. With a loud clunk, it struck Arvos's hammer broadside and pushed it outside the boundary. The other contestants gave whoops of praise for my feat. I considered it more good fortune than skill.

"Charrer, try for the best of three," a man shouted to him. "Maybe the *boy* was just lucky!"

Arvos glared at him, then turned and stalked away around the corner of the palisade. The man who had taunted him came over and extended a hand.

"I'm Docis. When Klega died, I tried to bring Dividiac here from Arialbinnum. I couldn't find him."

"He was at my father's new village—"

"Yes." Docis gave me a friendly slap on the back. "Pay no attention to Arvos. An envious man reveals his inferiority."

"Why be jealous of me?"

"I heard that the man lost everything in the Harude raid, but doesn't appreciate that he kept his life. Stay and throw with my team. We'll use hammers that are equally matched."

I agreed, despite an uneasy feeling that I had unwittingly made Arvos an enemy. I won a few close contests, yet never repeated my previous skillful throw.

❧

The booths' and people's shadows were lengthening into afternoon when a *carynx*, our war trumpet, announced the call for the chariot racers to assemble.

Docis had invited me to drink a cup of Greek wine with him. At the booth, he grinned, drained his cup, and boasted, "That's for me. Come and watch a real competition!"

Although Father told me that Celts had abandoned war chariots generations ago, men still built lightweight frame-and-wheel carts with wicker sides and floors, to race on festival days. A course ten paces wide, marked off with clan flags, circled the palisade. On the eastern side, it passed between merchandise stalls clustered near the wall and tent area of tribal members.

The river gate was the starting point. Liscos stood on the back of a wagon to preside over the race with a two-headed referee staff he had carved with a boar's figure, his clan totem. He wore his old bronze war helmet, and a long sword dangled at his side. His face florid with heat, wine, and frustration, he bawled out instructions to warriors trying to harness shaggy work mounts into unfamiliar chariot yokes. "Taranis's Thunder, Epanactos, get that animal into line! Docis, go over there. *Over there!* Are you drunk? You're driving on the outside."

I joined a crowd that lined the bank of the Dubis and spilled out onto the wooden bridge. Other spectators had positioned themselves along the length of the course. Food and drink spattered on bettors as coins flashed in drunken wagers on the contestants. Even before the races began, several fights had splashed off the riverbank and into the dark, swift water. I thought that Sequani certainly lived up to our Celtic people's reputation for fighting each other.

Liscos waited until three chariots were reasonably in alignment and then waved down his staff. The trio lurched off in a shower of gravel and dust. Even before the chariots rounded the palisade once, onlookers yelled for contestants to show off their riding skills. The drivers climbed over their chariot's wicker front, to run back and forth along the spruce-wood poles that yoked the horses to the pitching platform, and lash their teams into wild-eyed frenzy. As the chariots jolted along the rough course, I moved around the palisade corner to get a better view of the straight section, where they went the fastest. Amid the crowd's shouts and taunts, it was evident that Docis—the most reckless —was their favorite. In passing me, he grinned, stood on one leg for an instant, then effected a half-turn on the pole without losing his balance. However, on his final rounding of the northeast corner of wall, my new friend turned his team in too short an arc and plunged them into a beer stand. The owner dived out of harm's way, but the booth, kegs, and most of his pottery mugs were shattered.

Docis still was unconscious when teammates carried him to his lodge.

Liscos's good arm flailed the air with his baton, signaling races and winners for a watch period. At another trumpet signal, charioteers took overheated horses from their harnesses and walked them in the long shadow of the palisade. Bets were paid and drinking seriously resumed, but I heard muttering that the action had been disappointing rather than exciting: aside from the accident involving Docis and his shattered left leg, only one chariot wheel had snapped its linchpin and fallen off. The charioteer limped away from that tangle of wood and wicker.

Evening twilight brought a cool wind down from the darkening forest heights above the village. Fires were kindled to drive off the chill and roast suckling pig carcasses over the crackling, smoky coals.

Old Celtillos, the bard with the slash scar and milky eye, strolled among the supping groups, stooping occasionally to strum his harp in accompaniment to a song about their Celtic ancestors. Twice he began a poem of praise to Brennos, the chieftain who had once driven the Romani from northern Italy and ransacked Roma itself. Twice an angry Liscos stopped him. The visit by Romani officials was to be in the next month. Casticos, the Sequani over-chief at Vesontio, had insisted that the visitors be treated with cooperation in whatever they wanted, and he probably had agents with sober ears listening among the campfires.

I stood on the walkway of the palisade rampart watching darkness creep in like a dank autumn fog that obscured Wermaros and the mass of tents alongside.

Fires re-stoked against the night chill sent swirling columns of sparks into the blackness overhead. The smell of pine smoke gradually overlaid food smells from evening meals. Looking down at the yellow-orange circlets, I remembered that the moon would not rise until near the end of the first night watch. Selene—Dividiac's Greek name for the goddess—neared her last quarter, a time when unsuspecting persons were vulnerable to the forces of evil that lay dormant in the Earth Mother. I felt uneasy about Arvos's hostility, yet, in the dusky light I also thought back to the dark druid who had upset Dividiac. What had happened to him and his companions, or his talk about a human sacrifice at Beltaine?

An orange flare-up in the distance attracted my attention. Some of the tent people moved toward a large bonfire near the edge of the forest. I went down to find the reason.

"What's happening over there?" I asked a bearded mountaineer, whose face looked as weathered as the limestone cliffs above the village.

"That druid who came a few days ago is putting on some kind of ritual."

A druidic ritual? Then Danach still is here. He called himself Ollam Fodla, Doctor of Wisdom, so is he trying to compete with Dividiac? Curious, I joined the crowd gathering at the forest's edge.

A circle of white powder had been drawn on a flat outcropping of limestone, where grass was sparse. Finan, the harper I had seen, had seated himself just outside the ring, strumming a lively accompaniment to the juggling antics of Fithil.

Finan's harp fascinated me, an instrument that put to shame the ancient worn harp of Celtillos. It was larger, about four hand spans in height. The sounding box, neck, and curved willow wood fore-pillar displayed sculpted plant tendrils that curled along the surfaces. Silver-inlaid animals gamboled through the foliage. At the joining of the neck and fore-pillar, a wide-eyed face of our god Lug Lamfota, "Lugos of the Longhand," stared out at listeners. Even the harp's storage bag was elegant otter fur ornamented with seashells and lined with white deerhide.

I watched Fithil juggle knives and pottery cups in a graceful arc to the rhythm of the harp's melody. The first three fingers on Finan's hands move deftly over the strings, coaxing out a sprightly tune. He tinkled high-pitched short strings above the roll of low tones, whenever Fithil performed a particularly dexterous throw, or used the music to soothe the ruffled pride of a spectator if the juggler snatched up his drinking cup to add to the circling objects.

Fithil caught the knives and cups in succession and bowed. As the crowd called out approval, he turned and seemed to dissolve into the shadows beyond the fire.

Finan teased his strings into an opening cadence, then began to sing of adventures on terrifying seas that no inland Celt could imagine. The harper played with such intensity that his verses became pictures in each listener's mind: Salty waves washed over imaginations. A cold sea foamed off the prow of a boat in "The Voyage of Bran," as the adventurer searched for the Happy Isles of the Land of the Eternally Young. Then, it was as if each man stood with the warrior Cuchullian, spear in hand, as he shouted that he did not care if he died the next day or the next year, as long as his valiant deeds lived after him in their retelling. I knew some of the stories, because I had heard bards sing them at Arialbinnum.

Finan was praising a Celtic hero of ancient times, Conal the son of Conn, who had been spirited away to the Other-world by beautiful girls in a crystal boat, when the crowd suddenly gave a collective gasp. Even I was startled: the two druidesses I had seen with Ollam Fodla materialized out of the gloom. The women were naked, undulating their bodies to Finan's rhythms and to music unheard except in their sinuous limbs. They had dyed their skin blue with juice extracted from leaves of the isatis plant, a color Dividiac said was sacred to the Earth Mother. Whirling circle designs and the tendrils of young vines were painted on their arms and legs in charcoal mixed with animal fat.

Teasing the spectators, the priestesses moved in and out of the gloom beyond the circle of firelight. They passed into the darkness behind the flames, them emerged again wearing animal masks and dancing the mannerisms of forest creatures. Fithil imitated the animals' cries from the gloom.

Gradually the fire burned lower. Watchers forgot the chill air, entranced by the blue dancers. When they glided away, darkness clothed the twin druidesses in obscurity. Then, advancing, the feeble light once more molded their limbs into indigo flesh, until the reeling minds of those watching could no longer distinguish solid from shadow, flesh from spirit.

I heard the sound of new drumming that came from darkness beyond the fading ring of light, and caught a glimpse of Boccus the Mauritanian, whom we called *Dubver*, "Black Man." The African beat out rhythms that were as alien to northerners as what I could only imagine were the endless suns and sandy wastes of his homeland. The steps of the dancers quickened at the sound. Their swaying became more frantic.

Caught up in Boccus's drumming, Finan played more softly to allow the drum beat be absorbed into the dancers. Highlights of sweat glistened on the women, blurring charcoal lines that had dissolved into a salty bluish wetness. Only their dark pubic triangles remained a shape, along with the flashing of their eyes and white teeth barred in hallucinated ecstasy.

Boccus's drumming reached a climax, then dropped. Barely audible at first, Finan began to recite verses that told of rebirth. As the crowd swayed in unconscious accompaniment, one of the priestesses threw a handful of powder into the dying fire. It flared up in a small explosion of blue and green flames. Blackish smoke drifted into the crowd. Even from where I stood, I heard murmuring begin in the front row, then grow louder. Hands jerked up to point toward the forest. A child awakened, looked up, and screamed. I saw it too.

A tall figure slowly emerged from the shadow of a hollow space formed by oak trees behind the dancers. It stood upright in the form of a stag, reaching almost to the lower branches of the oaks. Its antlered head raked the base of the leaves, a tall, bizarre apparition swaying back and forth to the low beat of the drum.

"Cernunnos, th...the Horned One!" a man cried out, terror turning his voice to a higher pitch. "It...it is the Lord of the Other-world!"

The animal body merged into the darkness, then reappeared behind the smoke of the fire. I thought, *Shape-shifter. The druid-of-the-night-eyes transformed himself into the antlered god, Cernunnos.* Standing further back and not being drunk, I could sense, if not share, the panic gripping the throats of those watching.

Boccus stopped drumming. Finan began a song-poem whose verses edged the onlookers along an abyss where their present world merged with the supernatural realm of Cernunnos. Even the bravest of Liscos's warriors sat rigid, helpless with fear and cowering in the presence of supernatural powers so strong that they could turn the steel of their swords into clay. Yet before the terror could damage, the second druidess agitated the fire with a stick. When the surge of colored flames and smoke subsided, the antlered god was gone.

Now the verses of Finan's song brought spectators back to the Now-world with visions of another realm in which the nude, blue-skinned dancers became,

> *"'Full cream-white girls in brilliance dressed,*
>
> *And thick as blossoms from springtime trees.*
>
> *When the smell of the air is sweet and blessed,*
>
> *And the men walk young in the warming breeze'."*

The vision was as yet a phantom of a better future.

> *"'But the Land of the Young is beyond a sea,*
>
> *Where the mists of Now drift over the shore.*
>
> *Bran's boat will come, we will all be free.*
>
> *And sail with him to that golden shore'."*

The harp strings fell silent, their dying chords wafting up into the smoke of the embers. After a time, a few villagers cautiously stood up, staring at the forest. Others sat stunned, as the last shower of sparks danced up to merge with the white speckle of stars overhead. They had glimpsed the Other-world and sleep would come only after many restless turnings. I remembered that little Klega was in that Land of the Young.

Is this is what Dividiac wanted to train me for? I had never seen shape-shifting happen, but I wondered if this appearance of Cernunnos was a trick, an illusion. Fodla could have dressed in a deerskin and put on stilts to give his body more height. I was at the back of the crowd, but after the druidess made the colored flames appear, I had detected an acrid smell in the smoke. Had it been some kind of mind-dulling herb, like the mandragora that I had seen Dividiac use to ease pain? Many mountain people who watched Cluvios break apart the clay mold of a casting, and saw a bronze god appear, considered that a manifestation of magic.

Whatever the cause of the apparition, I liked Finan's stories. Whenever traveling bards came to Arialbinnum, they stopped at our lodge and I listened to their tales of adventure. I'd never seen any body of water larger than a lake, but I believed that an endless western sea, with islands in it, existed. Crystal boats might be another matter—ours were made of wood—or a land where people remained eternally young, such as the one where Klega now lived.

The dark druid's performers had been absorbed into the forest murk. Only the embers of their fire, which cast a feeble light on the stone slab, were evidence that they had appeared. Men, and women carrying small children, walked back to their tents or lodges in silence, shaken by that fleeting glimpse of supernatural beings. As I went back with them, I again wondered whether I had actually witnessed the Other-world. Had we been tricked by the harp music, the startling appearance of Cernunnos, and the mind-pictures in Finan's vivid imagery? If so, it was entertainment, not a spiritual vision of the world beyond this one. Twice now, in recent months, I had questioned the existence of our gods and this made me more uneasy than seeing the unearthly apparition among the trees. How could I reveal these feelings to Dividiac?

Arvos's unprovoked hostility also disturbed me. Cluvios hadn't watched the hammer throws, so I decided not to tell him about what had happened. Not too confidently, I hoped that the charcoal maker's unexplained anger would melt away like the last of the winter snows that still blanketed deep hollows in the forests.

Chapter VI

I slept fitfully that night, my mind choked with the terrorizing images I had seen by firelight in the forest clearing. Still awake when morning stars moved into the open triangle at the roof, this time I shook Dividiac and told him it was time to go up the mountain for Belenos's rising. It was the first day of Giamon, the sun god's festival.

By the familiar misty light of dawn, the forest no longer seemed terrifying. I didn't tell Uncle what I had seen. Now Fodla's shape-shifting, even the blue-painted druidesses, seemed like frightening night dreams of a child.

∾

As Dividiac and I recorded the sunrise from a shelter we built in the field, we heard the bellowing of *carnices* from the palisade ramparts—war trumpets announcing dawn on the festival of Beltaine. The harsh sound echoed from high limestone crags above Wermaros and sent roosting birds circling the village in chattering protest.

These curved instruments, whose bell openings mimicked animal mouths, fascinated me as a child. Father spoke about constant Celtic inter-tribal wars and incursions by Germani from across the Renos, yet the war trumpets had been silent for two years. Then, Ariovistos, over-chief of the Suebi tribe, led his people to the western side of the river. They defeated the Aeduii, then the Sequani, and settled in the northern part of their tribal lands. Mother said that bake-oven gossipers worried about Suebi moving south into the Dubis valley.

I was looking over Dividiac's shoulder, when he turned, handed me the scroll, and mumbled, "Here, boy, draw the location of the god's rising. I'm getting too feeble to climb the road up here every morning."

"Uncle, I think I could do this for you now."

He nodded in replying, "Alberix, the gods have blessed you with a keen mind."

"A keen *mind?*" I mocked. "I could have used other skills in the games yesterday."

"A sharp mind is worth the honed swords of ten warriors, who only can boast of their strength." Dividiac stood and looked at my sketch. "Good, put away the scroll. We must go down to perform the sacrifice and purification ritual for the herds.

∾

After we reached the village, I walked among the tents, reminding herdsmen to bring statues of their clan gods to the meadow where cattle grazed on the dew-soaked grass. Dew was another of those mysterious in-between states that druids considered magical. The droplets were neither rain nor spring water, and some villagers rolled in the grass to absorb whatever supernatural power might be present.

A day before, each cattle had been painted with the clan symbol of its owner's family: a boar, crane, bull, or other animal form. Now, women and girls finished garlanding the cattles' horns with sprigs of ground ivy and Moondaisies. Uncle said the flowers were sacred to Selena—white blossoms with yellow centers that protected our beasts against lightning strikes through the intercession of the moon goddess with Taranis, who controlled sky-fire.

Young fir trees, trimmed of branches except for a triangle of green boughs at the top, were set around the edge of the meadow. Village clan standards and lengths of colored cloth fluttered from each pole, a rallying point for bringing the decorated cattle.

I helped Dividiac unwrap the clan gods from cloth or fur casings, then set the images on the ground facing east, toward the rising of Belenos. As the brilliant orb cleared the mountain summit and warmed the small statues' ancient wood, the gods cast long shadows on the grass, toward a white, ceremonial heifer tethered near our altar. I noticed Ollam-Fodla with his druidesses, standing at a distance up the forest slope to watch the ritual. The women still bore smudges of blue dye on faces and arms. Near them, the African hunkered down on his heels, scanning the scene with impassive sepia eyes. Finan and Fithil were not there. I imagined the two entertainers were still snoring on their sleeping furs, wherever it was the group stayed.

After the previous day's confrontation, Dividiac would not include his former pupil in the Beltaine ritual. I noticed that most herdsmen avoided looking up at the dark druid, as if the night apparition at the mystical circle had been only an icy dream that would melt away in the day's warmth.

Charcoal workers had set three stacks of oak wood in such a way that cattle were driven to one side and through the sacred fires' purifying smoke. The beasts then would be led around the palisade, across the Dubis bridge and onto ancient trails that wound up into mountain pastures of fresh spring grass.

Once the clan gods were in an orderly row, Dividiac motioned me to the altar that I had decorated with oak garlands. He wore his white ceremonial robe with an embroidered gold thread pattern he told me was Greek, not Celtic. The two ends of his golden neck torc terminated in wide-eyed heads of Belenos, the patron of the festival. I wore my silver torc and a shorter linen tunic Mother had made. With a green inter-twining decoration at the sleeves and hem, I thought I looked the part of Uncle's pupil.

Dividiac had placed a bowl of fresh spring water holding sprigs of mistletoe on an altar, next to his amulet box and a golden knife. Liscos, Cluvios, Arvos, and three older men I didn't recognize, stood waiting behind the altar.

Uncle ordered me to open the amulet box. After I did so, he selected three shards of crystal and held them up to recite an incantation. "Spirit of the crystal, gather the fire of Belenos into yourself and join it to the oak. Cause its smoke to drive away the evil spirits of winter and purify these cattle.

"Sacred oak, preserve the beasts from the evil spirits of summer, seen and unseen. May Taranis, who holds up the sky, be our witness to this rite, along with Belenos, to whom we offer the sacrifice." He turned and handed me the crystals. "Give these to Arvos that he may light the fires."

As I handed him the shards, Arvos avoided my eyes. He gave them to the men who would focus the sun's rays onto the wood stacks until the kindling smoked, then ignited into flame.

"Bring the water," Dividiac ordered. I held the clay bowl while he took the mistletoe sprigs and walked along the row of clan images, sprinkling each of them. At the end, he offered a blessing to the four directions, then speckled a grazing sacrificial heifer on the head and flanks with water. "The knife, Alberix."

After I handed him the golden blade, Dividiac's slashing of the heifer's throat was so rapid that I hardly saw it severed. Without even a muted protest, the beast dropped to its knees, then fell sideways onto a quivering flank. Uncle's second thrust to open its belly was equally swift. The heifer kicked feebly at the air as its entrails slid out in a glistening mass that steamed on damp meadow grass the victim had been nibbling moments before.

When it lay still, Dividiac knelt, trying to discern omens from the animal's death throes and contours of its viscera. He had told me what to look for. The killing was clean, favorable, the sacrificed beast had not struggled, but there seemed to be an abnormality in its spleen: the organ was enlarged and gorged with blood. I recalled that this was a sign of war. Uncle hesitated, seeming confused. *Surely, he understood the omen.* I helped him stand, then Dividiac raised his hands and cried out to the elders.

"The omens are favorable! Bring the cattle through the purifying smoke"

I was stunned...that was a lie! Did Uncle misinterpret the sign or had some evil spirit seized the old druid and spoken for him?

"Uncle, why..." I started to object, but it was too late. The herders cheered and brought tethers to sort out their cattle and lead them through smoke swirling out of the stacks. Left alone with me, Dividiac stood rubbing his forehead, eyes closed, as if unsure of what to do next. "Uncle," I suggested, "let's go back to the lodge. You've finished the sacrifice."

He looked at me as if not quite understanding, yet did not resist when I took his arm and led him through the mountain gate and into the village.

At our lodge, Mother spooned out a barley-milk porridge for the druid to eat, then took me aside. "Alberix, your uncle seems confused. Did the ritual go well?"

"The herders were pleased." I did not want to upset her by mentioning his deception. "I...I think he's just very tired."

"My great-uncle has spent over two-twenties of years performing rituals to appease the gods. Traveling to distant nemetons to teach others—"

"And now," I broke in, "he wants me to do the same thing. Last night..." *Should I tell mother what I saw at the edge of the forest?*

"Last night, Alberix?"

"What do you know about uncle's former pupil?"

"Danach? He's still here, isn't he?" After I nodded, Briga went on, "It's been at least eight years since I last saw him. I admit I didn't like the boy. He reminded me of one of those rock lizards that change color. Danach would ingratiate himself to Dividiac, but was curt to anyone he felt could be of no use to him. He sucked knowledge out of your uncle without replacing it with anything substantial, any affection or even gratitude. He tried to win my approval with flattering remarks and gifts, but that ended after I caught him throwing live frogs into Cluvios's fire pit."

"That's cruel. Did he say why he did that?"

"Danach stammered something about sacrifices to the forge god, Goban, but never came near me again. Soon after, he was gone." Mother looked toward Dividiac. He had pushed his food away without tasting it. She went to sit opposite him and slide the bowl back. "You must eat or your strength will slip away like morning river fog."

Dividiac grunted refusal and massaged his brows with a blue-veined hand. "I...I have a malignant spirit troubling my head."

"I'll get you a cup of thyme brew." Briga clasped the druid's hand, which felt cold. "Danach is back. What does he want?"

"He spoke of reviving the old sacrifices to the gods."

"Burning human victims to appease Taranis, like he did those helpless frogs, or strangling a victim to Esus?" she scoffed. "What did you tell him?"

"I sent him back to the forest with his followers."

Briga recalled, "I heard about them at the bake oven. The druidesses are twins named Moira and Sabia."

"The harper is a talented bard," Dividiac admitted, "but that juggler and the *Dubver* could be sentries in the Other-world." The old man stood up, clutching the table edge for support with one hand and massaging his eyes with the other. "The thyme drink, niece. Then I wish to rest."

Late that afternoon I still worried. After I returned the herders' clan gods, rather than watch the boat and log games at the river, I wondered about Dividiac's confused mind and decided to walk up to the flat stone, where the strange apparitions had taken place the night before. The spring sun had heated meadow grass until ground plants exuded a soft fragrance that filled air alive with the buzz of insects. After a long winter of breathing wood smoke in the lodge, I deeply inhaled the clean outside scents.

"I don't understand why the month of Giamon is considered *Anmat…* unlucky… in our calendar," I mused half aloud. "It begins with the festival to Belenos, when the renewed earth is so beautifully green after the long snows." I turned and looked back down to where the heifer was sacrificed. *I suppose Dividiac lied about the omens to not worry herdsmen, yet how can animal entrails really predict future events? At Bireg, the finch flew to the west, the ravens north, but the cage was facing in that direction and a wagon's arrival alerted the birds. They would tend to fly away from it.*

When I reached the white circle, the shouts of teams competing in the river games below me sounded far off and faint. The women dancers' feet had blurred the white–powdered edge and trampled flat small plants and lichen growing in the limestone's crevices.

With a sense of unease, I walked to the back area where the stag-god, Cernunnos, seemingly had materialized. I wanted to search among shrubs growing between the oak trees, yet wasn't sure of what I was looking for. Grasses and weeds were flattened by the human footsteps, yet I found none of the cloven depressions that a deer's hooves might have made. Would a spirit even leave such impressions?

Where the woods began, I found a clay bowl thrown beneath budding sumac bushes. After I ran a finger around the inside, it came away blue. *The coloring those druidesses painted on their bodies.*

Farther in, late sunlight filtered through tree branch openings in almost horizontal rays. As I moved aside the sun-speckled greenery, my eye caught an alien shape and color in the near distance. Pushing saplings away to get closer, I stopped, shaken at what I saw in a clearing ahead.

A human form of an old man hung against the forked crotch of a robur oak. I was sure the body was in line with the white circle's center.

"Taranis," I blurted aloud, "that oldster is the sacrifice Fodla wanted!"

It was obvious that the man was dead, strangled with a golden cord that circled his neck. The rest of the binding's length trussed his body against the tree in a grotesque pose, several hand-spans above the ground. His arms and legs had hardened in the stance of their final flailing. His weathered face now a lifeless blue-gray, the man's bulging eyes stared out far beyond the Now-world. I imagined that the dead victim's swollen tongue was on the point of asking why the god Esus, he of the Bull and Cranes, required the hanging death of a human as a sacrifice? If it was the African who tightened the golden garrote, perhaps Fodla had whispered the words that Dividiac used whenever he could not think of an answer to one of my questions: "Thus, old man, it has always been since the moon was made to please the gods."

I felt weak, sickened, but held down a retch. Dividiac's rituals were benign, yet he implied that those of some other druids were not. Uncle believed that the Now-world was controlled by male and female gods, who were responsible for what happened. They were to be contacted, honored, and ritually appeased in order that crops should grow strong, that animals would give normal births, and human affairs remain orderly. Yet, I wondered how the death of this helpless oldster could have any effect on such things. Or why my little cousin Klega had to die and serve in the sanctuary of Esus.

Goban, the forge god, seemed unable to protect Cluvios from a sickness steadily invading his body, yet Uncle had cast images of him and other gods all of his life. If we *could* bargain with the gods, Cluvios should be healthy, and why had Dividiac not told the truth about the sacrificial omen?

Confused by these questions, I ran back down to the village and reported the ritual murder.

⁊⁊

I found out that the victim had been "someone of no importance," yet far from the criminal whom Fodla had suggested for sacrifice. The old man's name was Acos. He lived by himself in a hut on a mountain slope overlooking Wermaros. I had never seen him, but the eccentric loner was reported to have gestured wildly and jabbered to himself, whenever he came into the village to trade small animal pelts for supplies. Children taunted him until he disappeared up into the forest again with a sack of millet flour, smoked pork, and skins of cervisa carried in his arms.

His spoke on the Wheel of Life had been that of a hunter. I realized that Acos had experienced the terror of the hunted in the moments before his capture and execution. What had been his last thought? Was it that the whispered response of the dark-eyed druid, "Thus it has always been," was no explanation at all for being sacrificed to an unseen crane bird "god?"

Again, I seriously questioned the nature and purpose of our Celtic gods, and yet there was no one in the village to whom I could safely confide my doubts.

Chapter VII

Liscos kept the ritual murder of Acos secret. Ollam Fodla disappeared from the village. Because of the expected visit from Romani chiefs, I guessed that Dirona's husband felt there was no point in beginning an investigation that might embarrass him in front of Casticos, the Sequani over-chief at Vesontio. Besides, Liscos realized that no one would bother to ask for the whereabouts of a peculiar old recluse who rarely came down out of the forest.

In the warming days after Beltaine, Mother and I were pleased that Dividiac seemed to recover his health and good spirits. Cluvios agreed to let him teach me his druid's knowledge on the condition that during the moon's waning phase I still help at the forge each month. This actually fit in with my druid uncle's plans. As Dividiac became familiar with farmsteads around Wermaros, he went out to bless livestock, mediate quarrels, and search for sacred mistletoe in remote oak groves. A druid, he became excited at the reports of underground grottos inside cliffs that were located west of the village. Uncle wanted to explore these openings, which he believed reached deep into the sacred interior of the Earth Mother and could reveal many of her secrets.

At the beginning of the dark moon of Giamon, Dividiac told me to keep the daily record of Belenos's rising alone, and then rode along the river road on a borrowed horse. He took only a water skin, millet bread, hard cheese, and a new leather pouch to protect his magic talismans. I only had been in Wermaros a few months, but already felt more of a man. Now Uncle was entrusting me with a task that only druids performed, and perhaps his lessons about the gods would counter the skepticism I felt after discovering the murdered body of Acos.

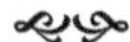

Our presence in the village still caused resentment because we were not Sequani. Yet Liscos boasted to everyone that his patronage of a druid and craftsman, and hosting the wife and son of a clan chieftain, meant that the misfortunes of a Raurici tribe could only bring good fortune to his own people. Just as merchants, the gods always kept their affairs in balance.

For both Mother and me the expectation that Alrix would appear at the mountain gate became as fragile as dawn mists hovering over the black surface of the Dubis. With each passing day that hope evaporated as rapidly as the river's haze, yet always renewed itself in the evening. Were we deluding ourselves? The only certainty was that the lengthening warm days followed each other without word of my father.

Nine days after Beltaine, on a luminous morning of the day called Mergher, Dirona asked mother and me to stroll through the village with her. She wanted us to know the lodges and their people. We had seen Wermaros many times, even joked about its rusticity compared to Arialbinnum. Not to offend her sister, Briga agreed. Cluvios allowed me to go, since he prepared small moulds of votive images to Sequana while the forge fire heated up. I'd help him later with pouring molten bronze. Liscos would send the statues to Vesontio, where they would be sold at the sacred spring where her river had its source.

I put on light woolen trousers and a short-sleeved, linen tunic. Mother wore a belted green gown and the gold enameled earrings her twin had given her at Beltaine. She had skin that was still clear and taut, yet tiny lines around her mouth and eyes had become more noticeable since the Harude raid. Ersa, Dirona's Germani slave girl, arranged Mother's mass of reddish hair into plaited braids that passed over her head and were held in place by a silver comb. She hadn't darkened her eyebrows with blackberry juice or heightened her cheek color with ruam, although I noticed my aunt had done so.

After Dirona saw her sister, she laughed. "Briga, you'll have to put on more jewelry than that! Liscos wants his wife *and* his kin to show signs of wealth. My husband pretends that it pleases the gods, but I think he just wants to boast about how well off he is."

"Then, Sister," Briga replied, without sharing Dirona's amusement, "I will need to borrow some of yours."

Mother's forced request was another painful reminder of what she had lost. I knew that she preferred to wear only a few ornaments, despite the fact that our people—both men and women—decorated themselves with many products of the goldsmith's art. Brooches and pins held our cloaks in place and circular neck torcs warded off evil powers, yet Celts wore rings and bracelets for the sheer love of personal adornment.

Dirona chided, "Even if my tunics fit you, you'll need new clothes of your own when..." She abruptly caught her twin in a tight hug. "Briga, even if Arialbinnum is rebuilt, you *can't* go back!"

"No, not even if...if Alrix were here. He would return to Noviodubno."

"No matter." Dirona released her hold and forced a smile. "Liscos ordered new clothing from Vesontio to sell and it should arrive soon. Really, Sister, Vesontio is larger than Arialbinnum. My husband keeps promising to take me there, but all he does is describe the trading stalls..." She beckoned to her slave. "Ersa, bring my jewel case."

After Dirona slipped three bracelets over Briga's wrist, she shook her arm and remarked, "I feel decorated enough for the feast of Lugos, and that's three months away."

Dirona teased, "Remember, we're only doing this for Liscos." My aunt realized, as I did, that if Liscos took anyone to Vesontio, it would be Arduinna, his new "doe."

When we stepped out of the lodge's vestibule, the smell of manure on the morning air mingled with a sweet scent of hay plants and bread baking in the common oven. We started along the pathway on the inner side of the west palisade. The first building we passed was the lodge where we had been housed after we arrived. It was a shelter for visitors and village elders supervised elections there. Beyond the lodge, built against the stockade posts, the slanted roofs of Liscos's storehouses angled toward the path. Farmer and herder homes made of wattle-and-daub construction ranged in front of the flimsier huts of their slaves.

I kicked back a leather ball to children in a fallow garden, playing with sticks and the ball in imitation of their adults' hurley game. Women, with girl slaves carrying wicker baskets of clothes to wash in the river, bowed and stepped aside to let us pass. As the path moved upward toward the northwest part of the village and its more substantial upper class lodges, we passed granary sheds set on flat stones and raised on stilts to keep out rodents.

"The oldest families live in these homes," Dirona explained, indicating well-built wooden lodges. "They're *vassos* of my husband, but have their own clients, like Alrix has...had..." She stopped, touched Briga's arm and glanced at me. "I'm so sorry."

"It's all right, Sister. Sometimes it's hard for me to realize that my husband isn't away just visiting his own *vassos*."

We circled around toward the bake oven. Several women holding infants watched slaves rake out coals through the oven mouth before putting in a row of raw loaves. The flattish dough was set to one side, attracting flies and yellow jackets. When we approached, the women stopped talking and acknowledged Dirona and Mother with a slight bow. A few smiled at me, yet, even before we were out of earshot, they huddled together to talk in hushed tones. I guessed the three of us would be a topic of new gossip.

Garden plots were next to all the homes. Stooped-over men and women worked black earth newly planted with onion, leek, bean, and cabbage seedlings, but stood up to touch their shoulders in greeting as we passed. Some had paused to drink from water or *cervisa* skins, but none offered us a sip, knowing we would not accept. With the exception of our great festival days, even Father rarely drank with his clients on a semblance of equality. *The rim of the wheel is tight,* I recalled.

As we walked, I absorbed the various sounds and smells of the village: a hammer's distant thump echoing back from cliffs along the river; dogs barking somewhere; the soft cluck of poultry; those laughing and shouting children at their hurley game. Even a pungent odor from fly-infested dung heaps at the side of lodges was the smell of abundance. Father had come to value these indicators of peace above a warrior's furious yells, the metallic clang of weapons in battle, and the inevitable smoking ruins of gutted homesteads. *If only he had warnings about the Harudes or enough men to defend his village .*

Dirona's voice brought me back to the present. "That is the oldest part of the village," she said, pointing to buildings set on a high stone escarpment at the northwest palisade corner. A rock wall enclosed them, and a stench of pigsties came from the area. "You can tell what they raise up there," Dirona said, puckering her nose. "Their homes are round and made of stone. Dividiac said the same type is only found in far western Gallia. We don't intermix and Liscos doesn't bother them. I think he feels they settled in this valley first."

I asked, "Aunt, if they aren't Sequani, who are they?"

"They call themselves *Acantos*. 'People of the Rim'."

Some of the residents came to peer at us over the wall. One of them waved. I recognized a black-haired girl, who twice had spoken to me at the marketplace. I signaled back. *What is her name...Pixtella...something like that? It seems that her people are strangers just as we are, trapped here on an alien spoke of the Wheel.*

We turned away from the unpleasant smell, back onto the village's main road, walking past granaries and livestock barns in the common enclosure. Now that the cattle were grazing in highland pastures most pens stood empty, except those of draft horses and mules.

Our newly built lodge and forge shop were beyond the bake ovens, set in front of a grove of oak trees. As we approached, Dirona noted, "Cluvios is not at his forge."

"Uncle probably went inside to rest," I told her. "His headaches are getting worse."

"Sister, he has no woman yet?"

Briga shrugged helplessness. "The forge is his wife. All husbands should be as faithful as Cluvios is to his craft, yet I'm worried about him. He's losing weight and still coughing up black, bloody spittle. He gets irritated easily, even at unimportant matters."

Dirona remarked, "Cadurcos the potter told me that evil in Cluvios's metals, which his forging drives out, can enter the crafter himself."

Briga shook her head in frustration. "And I cannot get him to stop or take a woman who might be able to make him do so."

Cluvios had talked with me about not being married, jesting about women disliking the smell of forge smoke and claiming that he liked it as well as the fragrance of perfumed oils. I don't think he was attracted to other men, as were some of the young warriors at Arialbinnum. These men often had relationships together as naturally as if they had chosen women.

Briga stopped. "We'll stay here, Sister, and visit the rest of the village another time. I must see if Cluvios needs anything."

After we both embraced Dirona, Mother watched her walk toward her lodge, then turned to me. "Alberix, I hope Liscos's new importance won't make him neglect my sister. He's already taken a new wife and... Never mind. Let's find Cluvios."

❧

Dividiac returned the next morning in the middle of the first day watch. His face looked ruddy, less haggard, as if his sojourn in the forest had rejuvenated him.

"Cluvios, the boy is mine today," he announced with an exaggerated cough at fumes coming from the smelting pit. "We'll go out to fields and breathe air that is with-out the sting of your metal-smoke, to look for plants the Earth Mother gives us for health."

Cluvios objected, "Druid, this day is within *my* moon."

"Get some idler to work the bellows and file burrs off your kettles," Dividiac retorted. "The boy is mine."

I sensed Cluvios's disappointment, knowing that he was resentful of Dividiac for the time he spent teaching me. "Take him, then," he snapped, turning back to the figures of Sequana we had been casting.

I didn't want to be the cause of bad feelings between them. I should have told Dividiac that I needed to stay at the forge, yet also was pleased at the prospect of being away from it for a day. Despite being outdoors, metalworking is hard and the shed's air heated by the forge coals. Distant Belenos was less torrid than our smelting fire, and it would be cool in the forest. Still, I was about to tell Dividiac that I should stay with Cluvios, when I saw Mother coming out of our lodge, carrying a basket and woven net bags.

"Alberix," she called out, "I convinced Dividiac to take me along. I know as much about the uses of plants as any druid. Who do you suppose prepares remedies when any of you is sick?"

"Fine, Mother." I was pleased, but heard Uncle mutter something under his breath. He had wanted to be alone with me.

At a vendor's stall just inside the river gate, Briga stopped to buy bread, hard cheese, and a skin of sweetened wine. The merchant recognized Dividiac and refused payment, but asked him to intercede for him with Rosmerta, the goddess of plenty.

79

Uncle mumbled a greeting to the gate sentries, and then stalked across the bridge ahead of us, to climb a road that now was familiar. A short distance away, on the right, was the covered shelter we built, where I recorded the sun's rising each morning, earlier and earlier now that the equinox had passed. I expected Dividiac to ask me if I had remembered to come each of the days he had been gone, but he was already searching for plants among fungus-covered tree stumps.

"Over here!" he called out. "The Mother-plant that Greeks call *cadiaca*." We went to where he knelt, fingering greenery with square-stemmed, branching fronds that resembled those on a maple tree. "It is too young, we will return at the next moon to pick the leaves." When Uncle did not explain further, I asked him what the plant was used for. "Eh? Oh, for women who have pain at the time of their moon-bleeding. Syrup made from it eases pain in the chest and heart."

Briga added, "It's called the Mother-plant, because it's also useful to women at birthing."

Dividiac stood again and walked on, stooping to push aside field grasses. Today, he seemed a man half his age, transported in spirit by his nearness to the gifts of the Earth Mother.

"Look here!" he cried out in excitement. Uncle had found a clump of plants whose dark-green leaves had a silvery undersurface. After he crushed one and thrust it under my nose, I winced at its pungency. "Artemesia." He chuckled at my reaction. "This is also for women's bleeding, yet its power goes beyond helping rid a body of evil. Alberix, you must carry these leaves when you travel. If you do so, you will never tire on a journey." Dividiac sniffed the fronds and handed me one. "This is the oldest of plants born of the Mother at the beginning of things, in the time the moon was made. Because the plant saw the separation of good and evil, the gods gave it the power to prevail over evil."

I smelled the crushed leaves again, not sure of their magical properties because I hadn't experienced them. The spicy smell reminded me of Fulvius's sausages at Arialbinnum.

We moved higher into the mountain meadows, picking plants that Uncle indicated or that Briga found herself. At the sun's highest point, we had filled the net bags with several remedies for various ailments.

As Dividiac's early enthusiasm gave way to fatigue, he became short of breath and stopped to rest under a fir tree. Its lowering branches cast speckled shadows on field grasses beneath. He opened a sack to spread his withering plants on the smooth curve of a fallen tree trunk, sending carpenter ants scurrying off in a senseless panic. He leaned back against the log, massaging his legs and muttering, "Belenos is fierce today."

I moved with Mother into the shade of a nearby oak. The fragrant smell of the hot fields was exhilarating. Soon, crickets disturbed by our presence chirped again. Far beneath us, I could trace the silvery line of the Dubis, etched into the valley as the river meandered off in the direction of the sun's westward path. A haze of bluish smoke marked the charring ovens where Arvos and his sooty workers kept the villagers supplied with the black fuel. A hawk, hunting prey, circled dark against the valley mist. Wermaros was out of sight, its lodges, storehouses, our forge—all that was good—left behind, as well as the evil of the deadly Harude raid on Father's village. It was easy to close my eyes and imagine that none of them had existed, that the world was as innocent as it had been when Dividiac said the moon was new and gods separated good from evil.

All might seem good now, yet I realized that evil was present, most recently in the person of the druid-of-the-night-eyes from Inisfail. Abruptly, I felt Mother rummaging in the food bag that hung from my shoulder.

"We should eat," she said. "Even a sip of warm wine would go well now."

Briga brought the skin container to Dividiac, along with chunks of the bread and cheese. After he drank, she passed the container and food to me. The sweetness was warm in my mouth, the cheese I bit into, salty and rich.

After eating, I lay back and closed my eyes, then heard Dividiac call to me. I went to where he knelt next to his plant collection, which he arranged in a row on the log. He had used his knife to lever up a small plant with broad green leaves and the beginning of seed stalks.

"My boy," he asked, "what do these leaf shapes remind you of?"

Lately, uncle had become impatient with wrong answers, so I took a moment to study the plant. To me the oval leaves looked like iron or bronze blade points on warrior lances, so I ventured, "Spearheads?"

"The point of a spear?" Dividiac frowned, then thought a moment. "Yes... it could be. Yes, *good,* but what part of a body does plantago resemble?"

I braced myself for a flash of temper. "The tongue?"

"Excellent, my boy! Indeed, the tongue." Uncle swept a hand over all the plants on the log. "The Mother shows us the remedies in her plants by signs... their shapes... colors, even taste. Plantago is one of her most plentiful and useful. Spread over a wound...yes, even one that a spear would make...the crushed seeds will stop bleeding."

"But how does it help the tongue, Uncle?"

"The plant's boiled juice is helpful for treating redness of the mouth and throat during the cold season." Dividiac plucked one of the immature seed stalks. "These will form into a rod, like a serpent, and protect against poison if worn around the neck. Boiled in animal fat and rubbed on the body, the leaves ward off evil spirits that bring the pock disease."

"How can something outside the body protect from an evil that's inside?" I immediately regretted a question that Dividiac might take it as criticism.

Briga looked over; she heard me and felt the same. "Dividiac," she called to him, "let's go up higher. I want to find bitter gentian to go with our supper."

The old druid grunted and gathered his plants back into net bags. We had walked in silence for a while, when he called me to an area that shimmered with what I already knew were blue-flowered cichorium plants. The thin, bristly leaves resembled a serrated blade, like a fish-scaling knife. The blue heads were turned to face Belenos. Although it was just past high sun, the blossoms had already closed in on themselves.

Uncle plucked one and handed it to me, "Germani have a legend about what they call Waywatcher, yet our people also tell the story. The flower is blue, like your eyes, and the legend says that the Waywatcher was a maiden. Belenos fell in love with the girl and wished to marry her, but she was proud, thinking herself too good for even a god. Belenos became angry, so he shape-shifted her into a plant whose flowers were as blue as the maiden's eyes. Then he forced her to look at him from sunup to sundown."

"But the blossoms are closed."

"There's more to the story, Alberix. The maiden-flower called out to her mother, a powerful sorceress. Her magic was not able to return her daughter to a human form, but she did weaken that of Belenos enough to close the girl's eyes at high sun."

Briga added, "Germani believe that this flower was created by the sky-fire of Taranis, and that with its blossoms one can open mountains, just as his blinding fire breaks rocks during a storm. Inside the mountain, the flower will lead one to treasures of gold and gems."

"Bah!" Dividiac snorted. "Germani know nothing of mystical things, only stories to amuse. It's all women's talk...tales by crones and idle wives at the bake oven."

I recalled uncle's reluctance to credit our enemies with anything of value, but the mention of caverns had evidently reminded him of the underground caves he had gone to find. He motioned me to the slope of the mountain and pointed to the Dubis Valley.

"The clans speak of enchanted grottos, there, across the river toward Vesontio, and yet not far off."

"How are they enchanted, Uncle?"

"My boy, great forests were frozen into stone by sorcerers. Bodies of giants are imprisoned in the Earth Mother because they tried to rob her of secrets." Dividiac took my shoulders and turned me to face him, his eyes gleaming with an intensity I had seen only once before, the time he had accepted me as his last pupil. "We will find them, Alberix, you and I. And mistletoe, the most sacred of the Mother's gifts—"

He abruptly turned away, leaving me feeling even more confused about the doubts I had experienced after finding the body of Acos.

❧❦

I spent the rest of the afternoon searching for plants and listening to Dividiac and Mother tell me about them. I realized I would have to memorize all this information, just as bards who sang their stories from memory.

We found the yet-blossomless stalks of a plant commonly called Westflower. The plant's narrow, blue-green leaves twisted around to face west, with serrated edges pointing north and south. With their help, a traveler could always be sure of directions during an overcast sky or even at night, if Artos hid behind clouds.

I learned about the plentiful sorell, whose tart taste mother used to add flavor to boiled meat and vegetables. Uncle said it was useful for treating rashes or the swelling that entered a cut or deeper wound. Handling sow prickle took practice, but the plant's milky, bitter juice assured lactation in nursing mothers and relieved skin diseases or eye ailments. Dividiac warned that the spines were considered to be harbingers of evil, yet he would teach me incantations to render them harmless. The Earth Mother was a woman, he warned, and, like all females, often fickle. Just when men presumed to know her ways, she might suddenly release the spirits that shared her rule over the world of shape-things. Druids knew the charms that soothed her, just as a husband might soothe a disgruntled wife with soft words and gifts of jewelry.

Mother was amused by her uncle's words—I caught her smiling—but she did not contradict him.

Another common plant was the fast-growing melilot, whose clover-like leaves were boiled with goat fat to make a poultice for wounds and skin sores. It was said to preserve eyesight. During the waning phase of the moon, Dividiac always wore a circlet of its roots over his neck torc to help his vision.

❧❦

As Belenos moved further down toward the western horizon and a mound of gray clouds gathering there, it was obvious that Dividiac had gotten exhausted. Mother suggested that we go back. He agreed, but first separated the leaves we had found into three groups, depending on their usage. Uncle repeated the properties of each and the legends associated with them, then told me to shut my eyes and picture in my mind the shape and name of each—whether they were to heal wounds, or for women's moon-bleeding, or to assure milk after childbearing. I was to say nothing on the way back down to the village, only continue to picture them so that, as he put it, they were impressed into my memory like designs in the soft clay of a potter's bowl.

While I studied the plants, Uncle lay down in the lengthening shade of an oak. In moments soft snoring told Mother and me that he was asleep. She came to sit beside me.

"Dividiac's mind is as restless as the design on the back of Dirona's mirror. He's served our people a long time, but lately seems overly concerned with the Other-world. He's upset about Danach's return and I'm concerned about why his former pupil actually came here."

I didn't know and asked, "Where is he living?"

"Gossip is that he's in the old hut of Acos with his priestesses and the others."

"Living in the forest is harmless enough."

Mother brushed a lock of hair away from my eye. "Alberix, it's more serious than that. They say Danach is bewitching Liscos and that the chieftain will invite him into the village to take Dividiac's place."

I shook my head. "Cluvios would never allow it."

"Sometimes your uncle only has eyes for his smelting crucibles. He is not Sequani, and Liscos and his advisors make the decisions here. Alberix"—she reached for my hand, then pulled away, as if I were no longer to be caressed like a child—"Alberix, be watchful of Dividiac. You're his last pupil, one he much loves, even if he is slow in showing it."

"I will, Mother…" I paused, hearing the sound of thunder rumbling in the distance. The massive cloudbank had gotten closer, black and angry now. "A storm is coming. I'll awaken Uncle."

While Briga returned the plants to their sacks, I helped Dividiac stand up on his stiffened legs. He listened a moment, then tested the feel and smell of the wind. "Taranis calls out to tell us that his wetness will flood into the Earth Mother and make her fertile, like the laying of a man with woman that gives birth to children."

There was no embarrassment in the old man's comparison. Some of our tribe's unmarried girls lay with any warrior of her choice. Offspring resulting from this union were raised as foster children by the clan. So it was with Taranis—The god's fruitful waters fell everywhere and continued life for men, animals, and plants.

Dividiac said, "Let us offer soothing words to Taranis that his passion may be controlled and he not harm the homes of our people, or their cattle, nor that his sky-fire destroy forests. Like a careless boy collecting bird eggs and crushing them, the power of the god is often greater than he intends." He took a small bronze statue of Taranis from his talisman bag. The god was shown holding a wheel and thunderbolt. Uncle held it up toward the west, mumbled an incantation, and then touched the figure to the earth and an oak tree. "Away now! Let us go back to the village ahead of Taranis's fury."

We had almost reached the shelter where we recorded our sunrise locations, when the first drops of cold rain spattered on our backs. After we hurried inside, its leather walls flapped in the wind. A sound of raindrops drummed on the swaying leather roof. Yet, this time as a lover, Taranis was gentle, sending down sheets of rain in soft gusts as he emptied himself into a receptive Earth.

I watched rivulets of water form in the road and wash down toward the village, now hidden in a veil of translucent mist. Colors darkened. The smell in the air changed from the fragrance of hot fields to that of a faint fish odor like that of the river. Above our tent, fir branches swished down low, scattering raindrops on the leather in random patterns. Birds gripped the swaying limbs, their feathers ruffled by the wind. I imagined that ground animals inside burrows dug deeper into their tunnels to escape water from above that seeped in.

I thought of what I had learned that day, what I would have to memorize. *Do I really want to begin twenty years of such lessons? Dividiac won't live that long, so with whom would I finish training? Certainly not the dark-eyed druid, if he stays at Wermaros. I could work at the forge, but Cluvios seems to have gotten his sickness there .*

Dividiac's voice broke into my thoughts. "We must prepare for the arrival of the Romani. The Shorthairs."

Uncle's unexpected comment startled me. I glanced at Mother, who also looked surprised. "Have you heard any more about when they'll arrive?"

"I don't trust them," he grumbled without answering my question. "That churl, Liscos, refuses to tell *me*, a druid priest and his own kin, about the nature of their business. Yet it can only bring us evil. If I were not new to this place, I would exclude him from my rituals...drive him from his own village!"

I knew Dividiac could do that. As Mother had pointed out, a druid's power was even greater than that of an over-chief.

"Uncle, calm yourself," Briga admonished, rubbing his back. "You're tired...upset over Danach—"

He retorted, "Cluvios and I are making Liscos too rich and proud. One day he will be crushed by the Wheel."

I wasn't sure what Dividiac's predicted threat meant, but I didn't share his opposition to the visit by the strangers from beyond the White Mountains of the Helvetii. It might be a chance to talk about Romani lands, about new things beyond the reach of our traditions.

I felt the wind sweep over our shelter in a final gusting that set the forest sighing. Mother glanced at the sky outside our shelter. "The rain is over. Alberix, help your uncle stand up. We must get back to the village."

As we followed our long shadows on the muddy track, the sun emerged from an edge of ragged cloud and warmed our backs. Rainwater sparkled in side gullies or rushed with soft gurgles in miniature waterfalls down the road, toward the muddied Dubis. By the time we greeted the gate sentries in their wet cloaks, my mind was no longer as much on the day's plant gathering, as it was on wondering about the reasons why Dividiac so hated—or feared—the "Shorthairs" who soon would come to the village.

Chapter VIII

Two days earlier, when the youth accompanying the two women had looked up at her *Acantos* quarter, Pixtila waved to him from the wall that surrounded her family's pig wallow. Twice, when she brought her father's smoked pork to sell at the marketplace, she had seen the son of the copper-haired woman and even been bold enough to talk to him about his arrival at Wermaros. He said that his name was Alberix.

Sixteen years old, the black-haired *Acantos* girl was born with the stink of pig dung in her tiny nostrils. When she was eight, her father had told her that his ancestors belonged to the ancient Eberari people, but stronger tribes long since had taken over their lands. Survivors migrated to the east and went into craftwork or trade. The women tended goats and pigs, all occupations that needed little land.

Even though Pixtila's father forced her to care for his porkers, then smoke and sell their meat, she did not intend to remain a pig-keeper all her life. Yet, lying awake on a sweet-smelling hay mattress at night, the girl despaired of ever breaking out of the tight hold of tradition—Sequani men stayed clear of *Acantos* women. Alberix appeared unexpectedly, as if in answer to her devotions to Arduinna. The goddess lived in dim forest haunts that were Pixtila's favorite places to visit, whenever she could escape the drudgery of pig-tending for half a day.

She had initiated her conversation with Alberix by jesting, yet immediately perceived a lack of prejudice against the *Acantos* in this blond youth, who was about her age. He might respond to more serious flirting. When necessary, Eberari women had survived by utilizing their bodies. After she learned that Alberix worked with his uncle, a crafter named Cluvios, in a forge shop beyond the oak grove, Pixtila decided that he would not turn down an invitation to explore the forest above Wermaros.

Pixtila's chance came on a spring morning so brilliant that it seemed as if even the Earth Mother had lent her charms to make Alberix's refusal impossible. The girl was sure that in the cool dimness of a forest glen Arduinna would grant an answer to a devoted girl's many tear-stained pleadings.

After bathing in the downstream section of the river allotted to the *Acantos*, Pixtila put on her favorite blue linen tunic, one short enough to reveal a length of graceful leg. Having massaged her breasts with ewe's milk every evening, she hoped their nipples were firm enough to dimple the material. She put fresh convellaria lilies at a shrine by her bed that honored Arduinna, and one sprig in her hair. After packing a flat loaf of oat bread, slices of smoked pork, two apples, and a skin of her father's honey-sweetened wine into a wicker basket, she made her way down to the forge.

❧

I barely noticed the black-haired girl with a basket coming up the road to the forge, and thought little of it until she called out my name and greeted me in accented Celtic.

"*Slano*, Alberix. Health to you."

"P...Pix?" Surprised, I used the shorter form of a name I couldn't completely recall. "What are you doing here?"

Instead of answering, she asked, "Is that your uncle Cluvios?" When I nodded, she went to him. "My name is Pixtila. What are you crafting?"

His reply was amiable, "Preparing moulds to cast axe heads, young woman."

"I see." She turned back to me. "Alberix, the day is so beautiful that I brought food. We could go up to the forest and breathe air that doesn't smell like my father's porkers, or forge smoke." After I glanced over at Cluvios, she added, "Your uncle *could* come with us."

"No, no," he declined, flushing to the tint that probably colored my own face. "Go with the young woman, Alberix. My eyes ache. I'll rest inside."

Pixtila smiled. "Do you like my blue tunic?" she asked, watching me take off my gloves and apron. "It's my best one and my favorite color."

"It...it's nice." I ducked my face into our water bucket and washed off charcoal grime, unused to giving compliments to a girl. After I dried, Pixtila handed me the basket, then held onto my bare arm with hers. Her touch felt good, exciting in a way I hadn't expected.

From the door of his lodge, Cluvios watched the couple walk toward the mountain gate. *Alberix has little experience with girls. Alrix always insisted that only the daughter of a chieftain or highborn noble would be a suitable wife for his son, but with Dividiac teaching Alberix the secrets of the Men of the Oak, he'll have no time for a pregnant doe of any status.*

Pixtila ignored the crude jests of two gate sentries, who eyed her, and pulled me across the communal meadow toward the forest, while chatting about the solitude and beauty of the forest. Beyond, a high ridge of limestone towered above Wermaros and the Dubis.

Her laugh sounded like a harp-string trill, then she said, "Let's climb to the top of 'Giant's Pillar'. The view of the river is breathtaking. Have you been up there?"

"No, only as far as the charring ovens."

"Ugh"—Pixtila made a face—"Those charcoal makers destroy Arduinna's forest."

"Arduinna? That's the name of Liscos's new wife."

"Then she was named after Arduinna, the goddess of these forests. My... my friend. I want you to see the village from up there, where buildings look like the small houses that children make in river sand. You can see your forge, too." She squeezed my arm. "I watch you a lot, Alberix."

"I...I didn't...didn't know that, Pix," I stammered.

"Yes, I look for you whenever I'm on the Pillar. Come."

Pix held my hand until we had climbed beyond the furthest common pasture shed, then led the way into the forest along a trail that was a little wider than an animal track. As she went ahead of me, I had never before realized that a girl's walk, her bare legs, ankles—even the sandals she wore—could look so graceful. I felt a new stirring in my groin. At the end of the climb, we emerged, breathless, on the flat crest of the limestone ridge. I saw the remains of old bonfires scattered about, their ashes leached gray by rain and winter snow.

"Samain fires," Pix explained. "Villagers come up for the New Year rites. Even we *Acantos* are allowed to do that."

"Why don't the villagers like you...that is, your people?"

She shrugged her shoulders and bent to pick a blade of grass. "We're different. We settled here from another part of Gallia. No one has much, but it's always been that way." Pix tickled my chin with the grass, then reached for my hand again and pulled me toward the edge. "Come see my secret view."

After I reached the brink of the dizzying height, I laid aside the basket. Looking down, I was fascinated by the miniature scene of the village that spread out far below. I easily located our forge, where Pix said she watched me at work. Our lodge and the other village buildings did look as small as child's toys. Faint sounds of playful screaming came up to me from children splashing in the shallows of the river. A few women sat on the bank watching them, while female slaves further downstream rinsed out laundry.

On the communal meadow, two boys on horseback galloped their mounts around its edge. Undisturbed by the movement, a flock of sheep quietly grazed in the center of the field. A short distance up the river, a trio of white-haired oldsters had thrown fishing lines from a skiff anchored in the river's center—and far enough from wives who might object to the full wineskins they brought with them.

Pix grasped my hand and pointed to the west. "Look down the valley. When I'm up here, I like to pretend that I'm a bird flying over the river. Sometimes I'm a lark, at others a hawk, like...like *that* one circling the hay field over there."

When she leaned against my shoulder and held up my hand to point out the predator, I was conscious of her body pressure and scent, an herb fragrance that was stronger than the moldering leaf smells on the rocky ground. She abruptly kissed my cheek, then broke away and half-slid into a deep hollow space a few paces from the side of the ledge. Well screened by a tangle of shrubs, I never would have noticed the hidden recess by myself.

"Bring the basket," she called up to me. "We'll eat down here in my secret hiding place."

I scrambled down and sat beside her on the leaf-covered bower, aware of the stirring in my groin. Pix broke off a piece of bread and chunk of pork, then placed them on a small rock altar she had put inside a niche on one side.

"For Arduinna," she explained, then, giggling, teased pieces of pork into my mouth. "A drink of wine?"

I nodded, my face hot. She sipped from the skin first and then leaned toward me to pass the cool sweetness into my mouth from hers. We drank again, savoring the exciting flow on our tongues. After a third exchange, I suddenly bent to kiss Pix's neck and nuzzle her black hair, conscious of her breasts and the uncomfortable pressure of my erection. She lay back and brought my hand under her tunic, slowly guiding my fingers over her soft roundness, helping me stroke the nipples erect.

"Take off my tunic," she whispered, yet it was more a command than suggestion. I hesitated, never having been this close to a girl. "Take it off," she repeated, her voice husky this time.

When I knelt to help her slip the dress over her head, I felt terribly awkward. Pix eased herself down, nude, her tanned skin glowing against a thick mat of withering field grasses and leaves that cushioned her body. I realized that she had come up the day before to gather the plants and spread out this bedding for us.

She pulled me down to her. "Kiss me again."

I bent to find her mouth, then slid my head down to tongue her nipples. After a few moments, she pushed me back, sat up, and began to pick at the leather laces of my now-taut trouser front, all the while looking directly into my eyes and smiling in a sensual way I had never seen a girl do before.

The lacings were almost free when, abruptly, Pix stopped. Her motion froze. As she slowly brought a cautionary finger up to block my lips, the inviting look in her eyes changed to one of terror. Moments later, through the lattice of shrubbery, I saw a figure appear above us, about six paces away. A man stood at the edge of the cliff, looking down at the village. Pix had caught his smell before she saw him silhouetted against the sky. Now I did...a mixture of horse sweat and human urine.

As we watched, terrified, two other bearded warriors joined their companion. Bare-chested, the men wore only dirty leather trousers laced around their boots at the ankle. Leather straps that passed over their left shoulders held sheathed long-swords at their sides. Each had gathered his reddish or blond hair into a side knot above the right ear. Once the trio exchanged a few guttural comments, I realized they were Germani. Their leader seemed to be called Bodos.

Grunting in evident satisfaction with what he saw below, Bodos barked a command to his two companions. They raised cattle horns to their lips and blared out a signal. With the echo of the twin sounds still reverberating off nearby crests, the three men turned and ran back down the trail we had taken. Pix and I remained quiet until we no longer heard the sound of their footsteps on dry leaves and twigs.

As I held onto the girl, I tried to control my own shaking. We lay still for a time, her bronzed body trembling against mine. My erection had long since gone limp, and all thought of my first lovemaking attempt had vanished with that last trumpet echo.

When I felt it was safe to move, I helped Pix into her tunic, whispering, "What were those Germani doing this far west? Has there been a new breakthrough of tribes across the Renos?"

Still frightened, Pix shook her head as an answer that neither of us could know. After I scrambled out of the hollow and crept to the edge of the overlook, the scene below answered my question. A troop of some twenty or so mounted horsemen had streamed out of the woods and fanned out onto the pasture in front of the village's west palisade. Two of the mounted warriors had slashed down the boys on horseback and led their captured mounts back to the forest's edge.

"They're Germani heading for the mountain gate!" I blurted. "I must get down there!"

Pix grasped my arm to hold me back. "To do what, Alberix, throw forge tools at them? You have no weapon and are not trained as a warrior."

I knew she was right. Watching the enemy attack, we saw our sentries struggling to close the massive gate doors. Then the harsh blare of our Celtic war trumpets was heard above the distant yelling. Liscos had raised the alarm, calling herders in from the fields to help defend his village.

After shouting their individual war cries, and breaking into a sonorous chant, the raiders galloped their horses across the pasture, panicking sheep up into the woods. At the forefront of the warriors, four bodyguards formed a protective pocket around a man who evidently was their leader. Each of his other men seemed intent on being first to reach the palisade gate, before it could be pulled shut.

The river entrance to the village was further away from the attackers. Already alerted by the trumpets that had sounded from atop Giant's Pillar, mothers frantically herded their children out of the water and ran toward the half-closed portal. Slaves left clothes floating downstream and ran to catch up with the women, barely entering to safety before sentries could barr the gate.

The old men beached their skiff on the far side of the Dubis and hurried to the concealment of shrubbery along the bank.

As Ogerth rode in the lead, flanked by his guards, the Suebi sub-chief cursed his short-legged horse for not running more swiftly. He turned his head to glare at the pillar of stone above the village, and spat abuse at the three warriors who had sounded the signal to attack. Bodos had wanted to scan the palisade from above, then, if all was quiet, sound the battle horns. Ogerth had agreed, yet forgot that because of distance the signal would reach the villagers before his own hidden warriors heard it, at the far edge of the forest. A crucial time interval of moments dulled the surprise of his attack.

"Spawn of chicken droppings, you ride like blind serving girls!" he screamed, seeing two of his horsemen catapult to the ground in a blurred arc of animals, men, smashed shields, and spears.

Yet this was the part of a raid he liked best—moving with his horse as one organism; feeling a stream of cool wind fanning his face; hearing and seeing the panic of victims up ahead as they scattered to escape his deadly attack.

Gripping his sword hilt with a sweaty hand, Ogerth held the long blade low under a round shield and used leg signals to angle his mount toward the still partially closed palisade gate. Abruptly, he heard the blare of enemy war trumpets above the thumping hoof falls and waning war chant of his men as they rode closer to the crucial opening.

"Ride into that dung heap of a village!" Ogerth yelled back to his warriors. "Smash the Kelten like clay pots. Stop them from closing that gate!"

Sequani warriors outside the portal strained to shut the two gates by pushing them together, while others pulled from the inner side. Looking back and seeing the horsemen closing in, the men frantically tried to squeeze inside through the tightening space. Ogerth was upon them, slashing at the Kelten in a spray of blood and bits of tunic cloth. With his bodyguards, he tried to force an entry, yet the small space still open was too narrow, even for the Suebi's smaller horses.

"Dismount," Ogerth bellowed. "Fight on the ground, you sons of swine dung! Push into that opening!"

Despite their leader's angry orders, most of his men reined away, feeling more secure on horseback than as ground fighters. Ogerth's face flushed to a reddish-purple as he rode among them, slapping at their shields with his sword, cursing for them to attack on foot. Some slid off their mounts and lunged for the narrowing open space, but, now, spears angled down from the top of the palisade.

Wermaros's defenders had climbed to the rampart walkway. At the gate, a Suebi went down in a scream of pain, clutching at a spear in his side. His companions ignored him to hack at the few Kelten still outside, or slash at long spears thrust through the gap.

The Suebi warriors who had not dismounted rode their horses in helplessness around the palisade stakes, able only to throw spears up at the defenders, and dodge those arcing down at them. With surprise evaporated, the thrust of the Germani attack faltered as quickly as it had begun.

Epanactos, leader of Liscos's bodyguards, rallied the men who had run up to defend the gate. "Outside," he shouted. "'Hedgehog' under your shields!"

Ogerth saw a file of defending warriors squeeze through the portal and crouch behind long ovoid shields. They protected each other in this tight mass, and jabbed out at his men with long spears. As mounted warriors were unseated in a tangle of screams, weapons, and flailing hooves, the attacking foot warriors fell back. Hearing the defenders' own furious battle shouts, Ogerth realized that his attempt to force the gate had stalled. He backed his horse away, while his gray eyes studied the line of painted shields. Only ten Kelten were holding off his faltering companions.

Cursing them again, Ogerth jerked his mount toward the row of shields. Deftly avoiding enemy lances, he swung his steel sword down in savage strokes, cleaving through the bronze rim of shields and helmets in a clang of blood-reddened wood and metal shards. He struck repeatedly, gripped by his own rage, slowly forcing the defenders back before his deadly strokes. Four men fell in his savage attack until, his sword hilt slippery with blood and perspiration, Ogerth felt his hand losing its grip.

Reining back, expecting to have given his horsemen the advantage, the chieftain was infuriated to see his remaining mounted warriors still circling the palisade. A few of them carried lighted torches and threw them over the surrounding wall, but most looked for an opportunity to exploit their own particular moment of glory.

At the sound of the horns that signaled the attack, Liscos had climbed onto a wagon behind the gate to direct its defense. Now he yelled for slaves and women to pull down burning thatch on the lodges and storehouses with rakes and pruning knife staffs.

Hearing the shouts, Cluvios awakened, came out of his lodge and realized the village was under attack. He stumbled to the common lodge, whose thatched roof was on fire. Briga was there with her sister, helping beat out pulled-down heaps of burning straw.

Anxious for his nephew, he asked Briga, "Has Alberix come back with the girl?"

"What girl?"

"One of the *Acantos* came to take him to the forest for the afternoon."

Briga's eyes widened in alarm. "No, but perhaps they...they went back to her house. Go and find out."

Although ill, Cluvios hurried to the cluster of round stone dwellings on the limestone shelf. The *Acantos* men and women had ranged themselves along their section of the palisade, using slings to pelt the attackers with stones. None had seen the pair. Coughing from the exertion, Cluvios returned to help fight the fires.

A spear thrown from the wall slid along the neck of Ogerth's horse, panicking the animal in a sear of pain and spurting blood. With effort, he brought his mount under control, then shouted again for his warriors to resume the attack. It was too late. Kelten, who could be counted on two hands, lay dead or wounded outside the gate, tangled among his own warriors. Ogerth's men had captured a few defenders, but did not breach the entry. The gate now was closed and barred.

Breathing in gasps, Ogerth tore at his sweat-stained tunic to bare his right shoulder, as his enemy did. Seeing a truce sign, the village men paused on the ramparts. At Ogerth's command, Suebi warriors dragged their dead away and laid them in rows on the meadow. The injured defenders sat a circle a short distance away, heads bowed.

Calmer now, Ogerth called up to his enemies in guttural Celtic, "Bring the *vlatos* of this swine's dung heap to the wall. I have words to barter with him."

In a moment, Liscos came and taunted him. "'Knot-hair,' have you come to add your head to my trophies?"

Ogerth glanced at the skulls nailed above the gate, but ignored the insult and lied, "I have many other warriors nearby, yet I am a Suebi of honor. Swear by your clan god that I can bury my dead in peace, and your own warriors will live."

Liscos hesitated. He was sure the man had no other companions, yet his own herdsmen had not heard the trumpet signals. Would it be worth continuing the fight, losing the captured men, and more village buildings by fire?

Briga climbed the ladder to the rampart walkway. "Liscos, what do they want?"

He resented her interference, but answered, "To bury their dead in return for the lives of our captured men."

"Allow them to do it," she ordered firmly.

"No!" Epanactos's shout of rejection startled everyone. "Let our warriors enter the Other-world as shining ones!"

Liscos hesitated, scratching his beard stubble. The words of Epanactos, one of his advisors, held authority. "Th...the Suebi say they have other warriors nearby."

"They lie," Epanactos screamed. "All Suebi lie!"

Briga touched Liscos's sleeve. "Even so, you know that there are many more warriors to the north led by Ariovistos. Will your dead Sequani come back from the land of Cernunnos to defend us from them?"

Liscos knew her logic was sound, but resented a woman advising him, a Raurici at that. "I will decide if he speaks falsely," he muttered, but raised his voice to Ogerth. "'Knot-hair!' Take your dead beyond the river. Bury them deep to not foul our air with the stink of your kind. You have until the shadow of my palisade wall stretches out four paces to leave here." Ignoring Epanactos's glowering stare, Liscos ordered, "Have the *carnyx* signal a truce. We fight no more today."

෪ඥ

I had put an arm around Pix as we sat at the edge of Giant's Pillar to watch the action unfolding around the village below us. The fighting seemed to have ceased, but thick yellowish smoke still rose from thatched buildings around the inside perimeter of the stockade. I recognized our latest war trumpet signal.

"They've called a truce," I said, helping Pix stand up. "We should go down and see what damage has been done."

She nodded, still frightened by the closeness of our escape. "I...I hope my parents are not hurt, or your mother and uncle."

I tried to reassure her. "I doubt anyone inside the village was injured, although men were killed defending the gate. Even the fires look like burning storehouses, not family lodges."

While Pix went to bring back her basket, I thought of how the secluded hollow had probably saved our lives, but also of the sight of the girl's supple body, when she had slipped off her tunic. In light of the devastation below, I felt guilty that I harbored such distracting thoughts.

Hurrying back down the pathway, we had almost reached the bottom of the forest trail when Bodos, on horseback with his two companions, spotted us. The three had watched the unsuccessful assault from the edge of the woods, now aware that they had compromised the timing of the raid. None wanted to face Ogerth's wrath.

The *Acantos* girl had caught their horses' smell, but too late. The warriors clucked their mounts into motion. Pixtila turned and ran back into the forest, hoping the trees and tangled undergrowths would slow her pursuers. I followed her as she ran ahead of me, swiftly and gracefully as a fawn, dodging in and out between tree trunks.

I had lost sight of her when I heard the thump of a horse's hooves close behind me, then felt a sharp pain across my upper back. I pitched forward into a clump of weeds and fallenleaves, stunned by the force of a blow one of the Germani had given me on my shoulders with the flat of his sword blade.

I lay still until the bright light behind my eyes became less intense and the pain in my shoulders was only a dull throbbing—yet expecting at any moment for the returning warriors to drag me to my feet. Glancing around, I cautiously stood up. No one was among the trees, so I hobbled back to the trail we had taken to reach the Pillar.

Desperate to find out what had happened, I walked in among the pines that bordered the path, searching for Pix. A short distance away, I found her basket with the wineskin and food scattered about. Beyond, was her rumpled blue tunic, but no sign of the girl herself.

Pix's probable capture stunned me as much as the sword's blow. In a daze, my back stinging, I stumbled down across the meadow, past dead warrior mounts and the bodies of the two horseback-riding boys. I recognized one; he had helped us set up the forge. At the mountain gate, our men placed the bodies of guards who were killed onto carts, while wives and relatives wailed at their loss. Further off, Germani hoisted their dead warriors across the backs of mounts. They would take them over the Dubis bridge, to where companions dug graves in the sandy soil.

I felt a glimmer of hope because our enemy hadn't left yet. *If one of the men in the forest brought Pix back, he might still be here. I could try to ransom her from him!* I thought a moment, then recalled the name Bodos, and even the Germani word for girl.

Approaching the nearest knot-haired warrior, I asked, "Bodos? *Magadina?*"

The man squinted at me. "Bodos?" He spat on the ground, then spewed an outburst of guttural abuse directed against the three warriors who had not dared return.

My slim hope for Pix's safety vanished. Arduinna had failed to protect the *Acantos* girl who was so devoted her.

Inside the village, the fires at storehouses no longer burned, but log walls and center posts still smoldered. I saw Mother outside our lodge at the same moment she saw me. I ran awkwardly toward her because of my injured back. I felt that she wanted to embrace me, but held back in public.

"Alberix, your uncle and I were worried. You...you went up into the forest with a girl?"

"From the *Acantos*, Mother."

"Cluvios told me."

"She.... Germani warriors captured her," I mumbled.

"Ten men here were killed in the Suebi attack, with as many wounded." Briga paused to look at me. "You're standing strangely. Are you hurt?"

"I was hit in the shoulders by the flat of a sword blade."

"Taranis be thanked it was not the blade! Come inside and I'll put a poultice on your bruises." After we went in, Mother hugged me in the privacy of the lodge. "I...I'm glad you're safe, Alberix, but what happened to the girl?"

"Near where we had hidden on the Pillar, three Germani gave that trumpet signal for the attack. After I thought they left, we started back to the village, but one on horseback caught me with his sword. The other two captured Pixtila."

"I see." Briga turned toward a shelf that held her medications. "I'll apply your poultice, then I must help the survivors. We'll talk more about this girl later."

❧❧

That evening, despite her concern for our wounded and dead warriors and damage to the village, Mother tried to comfort me about my new friend's disappearance.

"The girl. Pixtila, is that her name?" At my silent nod, she continued, "Perhaps she'll be traded for money or supplies. It is possible that you'll see her once more."

"Just as I'll see Father again?" I snapped, then quickly apologized. "Mother, I'm sorry, but I'm no longer a child. If Pix is alive, I realize she'll live out her life as a slave in some Germani village on the far side of the Renos."

Cluvios broke in, "I thought those might be renegade Harudes from the group that attacked Noviodubno, but they were Suebi allies of Ariovistos. One of the tribe's ambitious sub-chiefs probably recruited followers and decided to mount a raid. The fool hadn't gotten enough men for that."

Briga remarked, "Dividiac is still away, searching for his enchanted grottos. May Lugos grant that those Germani don't find him."

"Uncle can take care of himself," I said, mainly to ease Mother's fear.

"I still worry, Alberix. I wish he would return from looking for those cave entrances."

Cluvios asked, "For that matter, why is Danach still here? I hear he's living with his followers in the old hut that belonged to Acos."

"They say the druid bewitches Liscos so he can take Dividiac's place."

"I'll never allow it!" Uncle exclaimed. "And what *do* these Romani want? Every day I hear Liscos boasting that they'll soon be here."

I stood up. "None too early, Uncle, if other Germani decide to raid Helvetii lands this far west of the Renos." Both my shoulders still ached despite the pine oil-and-lard salve that Mother had smeared on the bruises, and I was tired. "I'm going to sleep now. In the morning I'll go visit Pix's family and explain to them what happened."

"Alberix, it wasn't your fault."

"Mother, I know..." I gave her a light embrace. "May the night bring you pleasant dreams."

"And you, Alberix."

Mother turned away, but I was sure no one in the village would rest easily that night. Another raid might occur at first light.

❧

Sleep came fitfully to me. Along with the throbbing ache in my shoulders, thoughts filled my mind about what more I might have done to avoid the three warriors. I wrongly surmised that they would rejoin their companions and help in the attack on the village. What would Pix's family say after I told them she might be a captive—or worse, raped and murdered?

Cluvios had wondered about the Romani, and that also was on my mind. Whatever their business, I hoped that once they were here, Dividiac would moderate his antagonism towards them.

As it turned out, I didn't have a long wait to find out. Seven days before the new moon of Simvisson, a villager, who had joined the cavalry auxiliary unit of a Romani legion in their Gallic province, rode into Wermaros with written notice of the imminent visit. I couldn't understand every word in the Latin message, but read the name of the signing Romani chief on the papyrus scroll as Tribune Sextus Tullius Tilius.

Chapter IX

Sextus Tullius Tilius felt hot and uncomfortable. An early June sun heated the iron rings of his *lorica* until the chain mail shirt burned his upper arms whenever they touched them. Underneath the links, a woolen tunic irritated his skin; his silk neckerchief was soaked with perspiration; and he long since had become insensible to the smell of his own sweat and his horse's. A dull soreness in his lower ribs was a daemonic companion, a painful reminder of sunup-to-sundown days in a hard leather saddle, and nights lying on the least rocky ground he could find. There were no public baths or hot water tubs in which to ease the ache. At night he could only wrap himself in his cloak and try to sleep.

A few weeks ago, Tilius was at Aquileia, on the upper Adriatic Sea, attached as Quaestor in the winter quarters of Legion X Gemina. He thought back on how difficult it had been to gain his appointment as financial officer to the new governor of Illyria and Cisalpine Gaul, a rising politician by the name of Gaius Julius Caesar.

It cost you a pouch of sestercii on each influential senator's seat to get the post before you were of legal age. Couldn't wait another two years until you were thirty, and you wanted to impress this Caesar now that he's a consul. Some impression! Because your mother's family is from the Po River region, and you know a smattering of the Celtic language, he sent you into eastern Gallia, to a barbarian tribe you've never heard about, to negotiate the building of signal towers on their land. It wasn't the gods-forgotten assignment you expected when you left Rome for your two years of tribune service.

Despite his discomfort, Tilius half-smiled when he recalled that to cover his ignorance of military procedures he decided to affect a haughty manner in dealing with the three thousand or so legionaries whose salary accounts he supervised. *After all, I had no experience in deducting from the men's pay the cost of their food, bedding, clothing replacements, or stipends for the retirement banquets given those who had served twenty years and were eligible for discharge. Even worse was trying to convince scheming veterans that they could not borrow from the legion's funeral fund, or attempt to extort the extra sums they innocently termed "boot money."*

Humility had soon replaced Tilius's initial haughtiness. These veterans of Julius Caesar's Iberian campaigns had seen many fresh-faced Patrician tribunes come and go. They reincarnated their stock of affable excuses—and a few "jested" threats—to successfully cajole money out of their inexperienced *quaestor*.

Squinting in the bright June sunlight, wondering why he had felt it necessary to order that his companions wear protective mail shirts, yet grateful that he had not insisted on heavy shoulder doubling, Tilius noted that the narrow trail along the Dubis River had moved out of the forest shadows and onto a grassy plateau. He glanced back at the men with him, Centurion Lucius Velcanius and two engineers of optio rank, Gnaeus Cornelius and Marcus Marius. They looked as uncomfortable as he felt, yet he was pleased that after thoroughly interviewing a number of men in the legion, a bit of Etruscan luck had prompted him to choose these three legionaries to accompany him to Gallia.

At age 38, Velcanius was ten years older than Tilius, and born in the Campanian *Ager Falernus*, southeast of Rome. The public farmlands were in sight of a dramatic, cone-shaped mountain named Vesuvius. His family name did not rank among the noble ones at Rome, yet it assuredly was more honest than many of those. The centurion had said that his father believed that the blood of long-dead Etrurian kings flowed in their descendant's veins—Velcanius being a Latinized derivation of the Etruscan "Velchanas."

At age 17, Velcanius decided that field sweat, no matter how honest, was not to his liking, and enlisted with Roman legion recruiters raising a military levy in the Campania region. By exchanging the pruning blade for the short sword, the youth had found far more travel and adventure than his recruiters had promised.

Following four years of peaceful service in Sicilia, Velcanius was assigned to then-praetor M. Lucinius Crassus, whose legions were desperately trying to crush a massive slave revolt led by a Thracian gladiator called "Spartacus." After that campaign ended successfully at Bruttium, he joined Legion XII Fulminata in the Asian Province. During an ambush by forces of Parthian king, Mithradates VI, Velcanius had taken command of his cohort and rescued the legion's standard, after the *aquilifer* who carried the banner and four of the legion's six centurions were killed. Although wounded, Velcanius and the two surviving centurions rallied the panicked men and saved them from annihilation. After recovering on the family farm at Abellinum, his reward was promotion to centurion rank.

With the Servile and Asian wars ended, Velcanius found military life tolerable, if not exactly enjoyable. His pay as a centurion was much higher than it had been as a legionary, and he found that his new rank had a certain prestige among the Patrician class at Rome—as well as with the newly moneyed Equestrian order. Each group sent their sons to serve an obligatory two-or-three-year service in the legions as Tribunes. Since Velcanius had helped several men return unharmed for the civil service jobs that awaited them, not a few influential Roman families were in his unofficial debt.

Amid training there also was leisure time, especially when his legion was in winter quarters. Velcanius hired a tutor and learned to read, discovered the Greek geographers, and began a hesitant correspondence with an historian,

Sallustius Crispus, about the new places and customs he had encountered. Crispus, in turn, was pleased to have a reasonably literate officer whom he could question about campaign outcomes, without having them distorted by self-serving tribunes or legates.

Tilius knew less about the army service of Cornelius and Marius, but the fact that they were literate and familiar with the work of a young architect-engineer, Marcus Vitruvius Pollio, was reason enough to choose them. Vitruvius's language might be inelegant and utilitarian, but his notes on scorpione or onager catapults, siege tactics, and defenses against them, were of practical value to engineers. The men also understood some Celtic, learned at Rome from the hostage sons of Allobroge chieftains raised in the capital. That had been fortunate, because a Senone tribesman, from Gallia Cisalpina, hired to interpret for the Sequani, deserted at Genava. Without an experienced interpreter, Tilius correctly worried that none of the Gallic tribesmen with whom he would negotiate understood Latin.

The journey was the longest and with the most spectacular scenery that Tilius and the others had yet taken. Allobroge guides met the men at Augusta Taurinorum, then led them over the partly snowbound Mons Cenis Pass to Genava, their tribal capital at the south end of Lake Lemannus. "The Lake of the Allobroges," the Celtic tribe called the crescent-shaped body of water, but it had been renamed Lemannus on Roman strip maps. The route was well to the north of the more familiar Genevris Pass that led to Cularo, a safer road, but much longer. It would soon be the midsummer solstice and Julius Caesar had made clear the urgency of his mission to build watchtowers.

From the summit of the Cenis pass the men experienced awesome views of the southern Cottian and Maritime Alps, of Mons Album, a massive white mountain to the north, and a glimpse into the valley of the Rhodanus River, far to the west. Late spring snow squalls had cut the viewing short, but they completed the descent along the Maurus River to Genava without mishap.

Perhaps rightly, Tilius mused, *not all the deities had forgotten him.* He dedicated the four men to the watchful eye of the goddess Fortuna, and invoked her each morning with a generous libation of their wine ration.

"What the...?" Tilius was shaken from his reverie—and almost from the saddle, when his horse shied at a boar abruptly scurrying out of the shadow of an oak tree.

As he reined his mount under control, he heard Velcanius shout, "*Quaestor!* Looks like we may get in some hunting!"

Tilius grinned at him. "At least we won't starve among the barbarians."

He refrained from voicing what other problems they might encounter. Tilius, whose father's ancestors hailed from a noble Alban clan, had come to respect his men. The forced companionship shattered some of the prejudices about the Plebian class instilled in him by parents and tutors. *After my quaestorship is over, I might be wise to throw my support behind the Populares party, rather than with Optimates and all those conservative senators. This Gaius Caesar seems to know how to deal with them in getting what he wants. His success in Iberia... election to consul...shows that he knows whom to impress. Or perhaps bribe? Either way, the man's star is definitely rising.*

Tilius called back, "Centurion, ride up here with me. There are things I should tell you about my mission for Gaius Caesar."

Velcanius cantered his horse alongside the officer. "You mean beyond getting permission to build signal towers?"

Tilius nodded, took a swig from a leather water bottle, poured some over his matted hair, and squeezed dripping water from a week's growth of beard. "Felt good. Yes, a few tribes from Germania are trying to cross a river called the Renos. In fact, a Germani over-chief named Ariovistos did cross and defeated our Aeduii allies. The barbarians also took land belonging to Sequani clans who supported him."

"But," Velcanius pointed out, "that's far north of both the *Mare Internum* and our Gallic province."

"That's partly true," Tilius agreed, "but now this Ariovistos is asking for more Sequani land. Seems several thousand Harudes have gone over to him, and they demand settlement space. Rumors are that the Celtic Helvetii are getting nervous enough to try and migrate out of their territory into western Gallia."

Velcanius whistled his surprise. "That would leave completely empty land for other Germani to fill up."

"Exactly, *Centurio*, and an area from which to launch further attacks. The tribes would be on the border of Roman territory and our transalpine province, including the southern end of Lake Lemannus. That's a direct route for the Helvetii to take into Gallia. They could leave through there, or cross around the northern end of the Jurassos Mountains, into Sequani territory. That's where we're going."

"So watchtowers would give the Sequani a few days advance notice."

"And us. We signed a treaty with their old over-chief...some unpronounceable name I forget...but his son, Casticos, recently took over tribal leadership. Gaius Caesar needs to find out where *his* loyalties lie, and if he's a threat to the security of Gallia Transalpina."

"So the towers are also a good excuse to burrow into Sequani territory and learn if this Casticos is up to anything treasonable."

"Indeed." Tilius rode on in silence for a moment, then glanced over at Velcanius. "You have a good grasp of diplomacy, *Centurio*. It's a shame you weren't born into a class above that of...ah...that of Pleb."

Velcanius replied with a straight face, "Yes *Quaestor*, too, too bad."

Ahead, a Sequani guide who had met Tulius at Genava, signaled and spurred his horse forward toward two of his fellow tribesmen coming from Wermaros to meet him. The Allobroge escort halted, their work done, and turned back without a parting word.

Tilius muttered, "So much for our so-called allies, and any of them who might have understood some Latin." He eased a bronze helmet he had tied to a saddlebag strap over his damp hair. It was important to make as impressive an approach to the barbarian village as possible.

The tribune was pleased that they had made good time, estimating the group had ridden fifteen miles since dawn. They had left Genava five days earlier and followed narrow forest trails. Yesterday morning, they forded the Dubis River over to its left bank, well before encountering a steep gorge further on that their guide said would make a crossing impossible. Tilius had ordered a halt at the gorge in order to arrive at Wermaros around midday.

After the riders entered a level meadow area above the village, the trail widened at a field of tree stumps, and then led downward to a plank bridge crossing the Dubis. Beyond, they saw a rough palisade enclosed a scattering of thatched-roof homes and storehouses. A gate facing the river was open in a gesture of trust. Brightly painted square and oval shields hung at intervals from the top of the weathered pine stakes. Above them, on poles, banners fluttered of each family's animal totem figure. Images of boars predominated.

Tilius looked back at Velcanius to mock, "Imagine, they've brought out their barbarian finery to impress us."

"*Quaestor*," he chided, "Gallic men in our auxiliary cavalry fight from horseback better than any Roman. Now, *that* impresses me."

Tilius cleared his throat at the implied reprimand and tugged at his helmet strap. "Wonder who's in charge down there?"

A stocky, one-armed man stood a few paces in front of the open portal. He was flanked by several tribesmen who were both older and younger than him. Other villagers clustered a few paces back. All the men wore plaid trousers and short-sleeved tunics. A few had blue arm and facial tatoos. None of them were armed.

Up ahead, the Sequani guides turned and gestured for the Romani to approach the bridge.

"*Centurio*, ride up here with me," Tilius ordered, suppressing nervousness. "It looks like everyone in the village came out to gawk at the 'Shorthairs.'"

"'Shorthairs."—Velcanius chuckled—"I've been called worse to my face, but I guess we're even. We refer to their lands as *Gallia Comata*, 'Long-haired Gaul.'"

"Halt here. That one-armed man in front must be the village chief with his bodyguards and advisors."

Velcanius noted, "His red hair and drooping mustache is almost a caricature of the Celtic race. A handsome people, though, and like Po Valley Galli, they're taller than Romans by at least half a head."

Tilius frowned. "I'd like to take this infernal hotbox of a helmet off, except the furcing thing makes me look bigger."

"Sir," Velacanius warned, "the men aren't armed, but there could be warriors we can't see crouched on the palisade rampart."

"Good point, *Centurio*. What was the name of that village chieftain again?" Tilius retrieved a square of stained parchment from his writing kit to read. "Liscos, that's it. I think I know how a gladiator might feel if he came into the arena and saw that he'd been pitted against half a barbarian tribe!"

"*Quaestor*, there are four of us," Velcanius quipped. "Three may only be Plebs, but don't you think those are good odds for Romans against barbarians who wear their hair long like women?"

Tilius glanced at him sharply. *Is Velcanius being sarcastic and mocking me? Well, whatever his true feelings, the die is cast.* "Let's go down and see if we can make ourselves understood. I hope I won't have to report to Gaius Julius Caesar that his whole venture has been a colossal waste of time and effort!"

Chapter X

Cluvios, Mother, and I stood directly behind Liscos as the four mounted Romani approached across the bridge, their horses' hooves making hollow clunks on the weathered boards.

I turned to Cluvios and whispered, "They're dressed like they expect war."

"Trying to impress or intimidate us, Alberix." Uncle put his arm around me. "You may get to use whatever Latin sausage-maker Fulvius taught you."

I watched Liscos bare his right shoulder in our sign of peace. The lead Romani in the helmet, whom I guessed was a chief or sub-chief, dismounted and came forward to grasp Liscos's forearm. Fulvius had told me his people did this in greeting each other.

When the man spoke, I understood him to say, "I come in the name of the Senatus and Romani people, sent in peace by the consul Gaius Julius Caesar."

There were many strange words. I didn't know who or what a senatus and consul were, but guessed that the last three words were a name. Liscos looked puzzled. He grunted something to Epanactos, next to him, who shrugged and shook his head. Neither had understood the response. We were off to poor start. I was about to say something, but another of the Romani dismounted. I took him to be a bodyguard, even though he looked older than his chieftain did. He translated the words into halting Celtic.

Liscos responded with a mocking grin and his own welcome.

After hearing the reply, I understood the guard to say to his chief, "Tribune, Liscos of the Sequani says that he welcomes you to his village in the name of his *cunovalos*...his over-chief, Casticos, whom the Senatus has declared 'Friend of the Roman People.'"

I blurted out, "Liscos also said, 'May the gods grant us both peaceful bargaining'."

The man called Tribune looked at me and grinned. "Good, young man, you speak some Latin. I am Tribune Sextus Tullius Tilius. How are you called?"

"Alberix, son of Alrix."

"I'm pleased that your Latin is at least understandable, yet it might be better if I let you translate with *Centurio* Velcanius present. He'll help your vocabulary."

"I would like that, Tribune-Sextus-Tilius-Tilius. How many names *do* you have? I thought it was Tribune."

"It's a little complicated, so 'Tribune' will do." Tilius motioned Velcanius away to murmur, "I caught most of what the chieftain said, but it might be wise to let him think I don't understand Celtic. Remember, the Casticos he mentioned is the Sequani who deposed his father. I need to find out if the tribal leadership is still friendly to Rome. Introduce yourself to the young man."

Tribune's bodyguard came forward and reached for my forearm. "I'm Centurio Lucius Velcanius, but just 'Lucius' will be fine. Your accent isn't Sequani, is it?"

I tried to return a grip as firm as his while saying, "If I have one, it would be Raurici."

Liscos looked irritated at being left out of a conversation he could not understand, and shook my sleeve. "Tell the Romani that I have prepared a meal in their honor. We will parley afterward."

I did as he asked, but Tribune only gave a slight nod in reply, as if he had other plans. When Liscos turned to lead the way through the river gate into the village, I saw the Romani pause to look up at the trio of hollow-eyed, slack-jawed skulls nailed above the open portal.

"The heads of clan chief men who try take village one time," I explained to Lucius, but my Latin wasn't as smooth as I intended.

Tribune heard me, grunted acknowledgement, and said, "About that meal. Tell your chieftain that we'll be pleased to eat with him, but only after we conduct the business for which I came." He evidently wanted to impress Liscos about Romani firmness in dealing with friends, and by implication, with enemies. "First," Tribune added, "my men and I would appreciate a quick cool-off in that river."

After I told Liscos of the request, he barked orders to some of his *vassos*.

The Romans dismounted, laid aside their metal shirts and wool tunics. Stripped to loincloths, they were in the river, when four village girls, carrying towels, ran down to the water. They giggled and pushed at each other, showing off for the dark-haired strangers. Bronze bracelets and bells sewn to the hem of their tunics added a musical tinkling to their laughter. They took off loose summer shirts, baring firm white breasts, tied their tunic hems above muscular thighs, and waded in, bringing a suet-like lump in their hands. After Lucius noticed that it foamed on his body and washed away sweaty grime in a way traditional scraping with a strygil did not, he examined a piece.

We call it 'sapo'," I called out to him from shore. "It's made by boiling animal fat with wood ash in a kettle, then letting it cool. It gets hard."

"That's not *all* that's hardening," Marius boasted, eyeing the bosom of a red-haired girl scrubbing his chest.

"Enough of that talk," Tilius warned. "I took a chance on getting us in the river unarmed, without you also propositioning women. Their men are watching us from shore. Everyone out, *now!*"

On the grassy bank, one of the girls dried Lucius's back. He motioned me over. "Alberix, where are we billeted tonight?"

"Bill-et-ed?"

"Where will we stay while here?"

I understood that. "You've been given the common lodge. We just finished repairing the old roof that burned. Lucius, could you use simple Latin words? I'm not that good at your language."

"Fine, Alberix." The centurion smiled at the girl drying him, but motioned her away and finished toweling himself. "Was that lodge fire an accident?"

"No, from a Suebi raid at the last new moon. In our month of Anagantios, Harudes destroyed my father's village near Arialbinnum. He...he is still missing."

"Is that why you came here?"

"Yes, my mother's sister is married to Liscos."

"Your mother is safe, then?"

I nodded. "Briga was standing next to me, watching you arrive."

"I recall her. Stunning. A...beautiful...woman—"

"My father will return!" I snapped at him. *This Romani has no right to be interested in my mother.* "Put on your...your clothing," I half-ordered. "We should go to Liscos's tent."

For the banquet and talks the chieftain erected a colorful pavilion of dyed calfskins, set beneath a grove of trees outside the east palisade. In the center a table and benches were scrubbed with sand until their ashwood surfaces shown with a metal-like patina. Clay amphorae of *cervisa* and wine cooled in a wooden tub filled with river water, next to the small table that once held Klega's playthings. On its top was a silver ceremonial goblet decorated with the design of an interlaced gold band and enamel work.

Farther away, under a linen awning near the river, village women prepared food to be served after bargaining negotiations were completed. A pleasing fragrance of wood smoke, baking bread, and roasting meats already overlaid the forest's pine scent.

The leather pavilion undulated in the valley's afternoon breeze as our Celts approached the parley site and seated themselves on wooden benches around the table. Epanactos and a limping Docis, along with three older men I didn't know, already sat there. Dividiac was with them to ratify any agreements made and perform the sacrifice that indicated whether bargaining results would be favorable or not.

I walked with Lucius, just behind Liscos and Tribune. Liscos carried his oak clan staff of the carved image of a boar set above an array of fluttering wolf tails. The two Romani who had not said much walked behind, carrying bundles taken from their packhorse. I assumed they contained treaty gifts like the ones I had seen Father give out at Arialbinnum.

Liscos's *vassos* stood back from the table, dressed in checkered trousers, short-sleeved linen tunics, and light woolen cloaks thrown over their shoulders. Even the mild air of Simvisson could turn cool in the shadows. Each man's silver or gold neck torc gleamed softly in the shaded light. I knew the Romani were less comfortable, having again put the on iron-ring shirts over their woolen tunics. They wore leather kilt strips that reached just above the knee—which made the village girls renew their giggling—gray cloaks, and bronze helmets. I surmised that the red horsehair crests on the headgear were intended to make the Romani look as tall as our bareheaded warriors.

After Liscos indicated where everyone should sit, an awkward silence followed. I wondered if there would be a standoff in pride over who would be first to speak.

Liscos finally motioned to me. "Tell them I have an excellent Romani wine, Falernian."

After I translated, Tribune declined. "Tell him I never drink before negotiations."

Trying to soften his curt, even insulting, reply, I added a vague reference to the man's digestion and noticed Lucius hide a smile behind the back of his hand. Liscos shrugged off the refusal.

Tribune, nervous at perhaps offending Liscos so early in the talks, ordered, "*Centurio*, sh...show him the gifts. What did we bring for...for the chieftain?"

"A ceremonial sword."

"A *sword?*" Tilius muttered. "The man has only one arm and may think I'm mocking him."

"We didn't know that, but it's too late." Lucius ordered Marius and Cornelius to unwrap the bundles, then cleared his throat. "Alberix, tell Liscos that this beautiful damask steel sword is a gift to him from our commander, Gaius Julius Caesar."

I couldn't understand why Liscos should be given a sword of damaged steel, but perhaps I misunderstood the word. It didn't matter. Before I could translate, Liscos took the weapon with unconcealed pleasure, held the scabbard between his knees to remove the sword, and swept the air above his head with the blade. Epanactos, Docis and the other advisors showed approval by calling out praise and banging their fists on the table.

Cluvios remarked, "Superb craftsmanship! Later, I'd like to look over the blade more closely."

"Well, that wasn't bad," I heard Lucius remark to Tilius with a sigh of relief. He unwrapped the second bundle. "This is a gift for his wife, a silver mirror tooled on the backside with a scene of Venus and Eros."

"For your wife..." Tilius smiled as he pushed the mirror across the table to Liscos and whispered to Lucius, "The barbarians should be impressed with the workmanship on *that* gift."

After Liscos frowned and muttered something, Lucius turned to me, puzzled. "Alberix, what's wrong? He is married, isn't he?"

"To three wives. He wants to know which wife the mirror is for."

Tilius said, "I caught that. Zeus! What else do we have for a woman?"

"A bronze lekythos of perfumed oil," Lucius recalled.

"Worth four hundred sestercii at Aquileia. Anything more?"

Marius held up jewelry. "This ivory bracelet with gold ram-horn terminals."

"Those should do." Tilius pushed them over to Liscos. "For your wife...*and* your wife." He leaned towards Lucius to whisper, "It would be less complicated if the Celt was involved with a mistress, rather than a trio of wives."

Lucius replied, "Sir, Caesar was told that in Gallic society priests and craftsmen rank next to a chieftain. He has gifts for them, too."

"Ask the boy if there are any of those men here."

I heard Tribune. "Cluvios, my uncle, is a crafter. Dividiac, my other uncle, has been a druid for over two-twenties of years."

Two-twenties?" Tilius asked, puzzled. "What ?"

"Celts reckon on multiples of twenty," Lucius said before I could explain, and then asked me, "That oldster over there is Dividiac?"

"Yes. Cluvios is the one who admired the sword."

Dividiac grudgingly accepted a gilded bronze statuette of a sacred bull. Lucius told him it came from a far-off land called Aegyptus and was one of their gods. He presented Cluvios with a silver serving dish, decorated with a scene that he explained as the Roman forge god Vulcan and his wife Venus. She ran off with the war god, Mars.

I thought that was the end of the gifts, but Lucius brought out a narrow bundle wrapped in red-dyed calfskin, and handed it to me. "For you, Alberix. It was made at Roma."

"Me?" I flushed as I unwrapped a waist-bladed belt dagger, its sheath decorated in gold and red enamel inlay. I lapsed into Celtic, "A *bid*. It...it's beautiful."

Lucius reached across to touch my hand. "May it never be used against your Roman friends."

I hadn't failed to notice that the presents were carefully chosen with the interests of the recipients in mind. Even the dagger might have been intended for a chieftain's son. Whatever these Romani wanted from Liscos was very important to them. He realized it, too, and now it was his turn to impress them.

"Tell them," Liscos ordered me, "that Casticos, our Sequani *cunovalos*, gives this to the over-chief of the Romani as a token of friendship."

As I translated, Docis slid an exquisite necklace of gold links that terminated in a lump of amber set in a golden bezel. It had been traded from Germani who, Cluvios had told me, lived near a cold sea far to the north. They found the rare material on the beaches, a gift of their sea god. Visible, encased in the golden translucence, was a winged insect, trapped there, Docis swore, since the world was made.

"*Glaesum* is all the rage at Roma," a delighted Tilius murmured to Velcanius, fingering the necklace. "This piece alone is worth all our gifts combined. Have the boy thank Liscos, but don't start explaining how Romans don't have a single over-chief. The last consul who came close to being one was Sulla, who declared himself dictator."

With the admiration of the gifts complete, Tribune came directly to his purpose. I translated his remarks, as I understood them, to say that advisors to Senatus—undoubtedly their over-chief—were worried about rumors that the Helvetii were planning to move from their lands to western Gallia.

Liscos betrayed no surprise that the Romani knew this. Even I realized that with our Celtic auxiliaries in their service, a few coins could buy any tribal information.

Liscos had me respond, "The Germani press on them, and the Helvetii are a proud tribe who will do as they wish."

"They will have to pass through our Gallic province." Tilius worked a touch of his old haughtiness into his response, "The Roman Senatus finds this unacceptable. Of great concern is that Germani will flood into empty Helvetii lands and threaten Roman borders as well as Sequani ones. This Ariovistos has already done so in the north."

After the translation, Epanactos and the other advisors murmured among themselves. Undoubtedly, the Harude and Suebi raids, and those of Ariovistos, were the first of more to come. Tribune's imagery was correct: it would be as if the dam on a river had broken and water flooded their lands.

"What do you want of me here at Wermaros," Liscos asked, although I recalled his boasting and guessed he already knew.

Tilius said, "To lease land for the building of two signal towers. From them we can relay information to Vesontio about the direction Helvetii might take, and about any other threats. We already have the consent of Casticos..." Tilius motioned to Velcanius, who handed him a papyrus scroll. "This has your over-chief's name and clan symbol with the terms of the agreement."

When Lucius showed me the scroll, I had trouble with the size of a unit of land measurement, the *jugera*. I suggested that Tribune decide where he wanted the towers, then mark off the area with stakes. A yearly fee for five years, employment of our stonemasons for the work, and the clearing of a road between the towers were agreed upon—although I learned something about bargaining. Liscos objected to each term in the original proposal, the Romani countered, then everything was compromised to what each had already decided they wanted.

A section called for the eventual quartering of forty-eight Roman warriors, whom Lucius called "legionaries," with half in each watchtower. He explained that the men trained together in units of eight. When Liscos objected to the number, Tribune settled for thirty-two men in all.

After the amendments had been inked in, Liscos stood and touched his clan staff to the document, then repeated the oath that Father had told me was the most sacred one that could be sworn.

"'I swear by the goddess Sequana, by whom my tribe swears, that I have not harnessed my tongue to falsehood or deceit in this agreement.'"

As the ratifying marks and seals were about to be applied, Dividiac interrupted, "Before the sacrifice, there is one other condition."

Frowning, Tilius put his reed pen down.

"What is it, old man?" Liscos demanded, impatiently slapping his clan staff against his thigh. "We're finished here."

Dividiac pointed to the eastern crest, where we took our daily readings of the sun's rising. "I wish a stone menhir of twenty Romani feet in height erected on that crest, where I marked the spring equinox. This is to be completed within a year."

Velcanius whispered the request to Tilius, who glanced up at the place, nodded agreement, then looked at me. "Now, young man, what is this sacrifice that the druid mentioned?"

"To make sure the omens are favorable for this treaty."

"Of course, our own priests sacrifice before important decisions are made. Where will this take place?"

"Follow my uncle."

The men rose. With the villagers following, we went to where Dividiac and I had raised a low cairn of fieldstones and topped it with an oak board. I had checked the plank's levelness with a bowl of water marked by a ring. When tipped out, the water had spilled evenly down the altar board's four sides.

I went to fetch a white calf tethered nearby and brought it to the altar. As I held its head over the board, Uncle mumbled an incantation, then deftly slashed the animal's throat with a golden sickle.

The omens were not good. The startled beast reared out of my grasp and thrashed on the ground, flicking jugular blood on Dividiac, Liscos, and Tribune. Its great eyes were wild with pain and incomprehension at its betrayed trust in humans. What blood got on the board seeped to the west and dribbled off that edge. As at Bireg, several ravens gave harsh cries from a grove of oak trees at the near edge of the forest.

Tilius had seen enough Roman priests bungle a sacrifice: he drew his belt dagger and gave the bellowing animal a slash to the back of its neck. The blade bent and blood ran over his hand.

Uncle raised his arms, evidently seeing no point in examining the calf's entrails. His body shook and his voice trembled as he predicted, "The legions of Roma will be bent and bloodied, but not broken. To the west, the future of our people is with the birds of death."

Stunned at the prediction, no one spoke until the sacrificed calf ended its death struggle and lay still. Then Dividiac asked Tilius, "How many legions does your Caesar have?"

The *quaestor* hedged at revealing the information. "I...uh...I'm not exactly sure."

"Count the ravens," Dividiac ordered, and stalked away.

Tilius eyed the four black birds preening themselves in the oak trees. "Great Jupiter!" I heard him exclaim to Lucius. "At this moment Julius Caesar commands that exact number of legions."

Liscos sounded nervous when he ordered me to tell the Romani that the meal was ready. "We...we should go back to the tent for food now," I said, also shaken by the ominous results of the sacrifice and Uncle's prediction. This time he had not lied.

"Fine, fine," Tilius agreed. "And I'm ready for a full cup of that Falernian your chieftain mentioned. Have it served *unwatered!*"

Chapter X

Since Celts prefer to eat sitting or squatting on the ground, the parley table had been moved outside. High-ranking clan families brought in low eating boards and placed them in the shade of the tent. Surrounded by hides and furs on which the guests would sit, the boards were in a U-shape, so that diners could observe the four strangers from beyond the White Mountains of the Helvetii. As the heads of each family seated themselves in order of rank, I noticed Arvos sitting at the furthest end of the boards nearest the river, with the children and women. The charrer avoided looking at me, but Cluvios had invited him to the dinner out of pity for his self-imposed isolation.

Liscos sat at the center of the arrangement, facing the long row of boards on either side. His new sword hung from a tent pole behind him. Tribune was to his right, with a place for me between the two, so I could help translate. Lucius sat on the chieftain's armless side, next to Cluvios. The two Romans who had not said much—their names were Cornelius and Marius—were at the longer side with their backs to the river. If they were also Tribune's bodyguards, they did not seem much like warriors to me. Dividiac, next to them, ignored both men.

Liscos gestured for me to bring him the silver cup from Klega's table. "Tell the Romani that we will seal our agreement by drinking as *carantos*... as friends."

After I explained to Tribune, Liscos drank first then gave him the cup. The Roman spilled a small amount on the ground before taking a sip and passing the cup to Dividiac. As the silver goblet made the round of the villagers, I wondered if any *Acantos* from Pix's area were there. I had not gone to see her parents.

Celt slaves captured in tribal raids brought wooden trenchers and pottery platters of roast and boiled pork, haunches of grilled ox, broiled Dubis trout, and loaves of millet bread. Bowls of goat and ewe cheese with their milk, and quantities of porridge were set out to be eaten after the meats were gone. It was too early for pears or apples, but there were reed baskets with wild raspberries that children had picked.

As the guests ate, beer from pitchers foamed into drinking horns and splashed onto the boards and food. Tribune swallowed a sip of the Falernian wine.

"Strong," he muttered to me. "We usually add water to our wine."

"Celts like it full strength," I said, pleased that he was commenting to me.

Mother was seated with her sister and Liscos's two other wives at the far end of the men. Several times I was annoyed to catch Lucius intently looking her way. Briga seemed not to notice him.

By what I guessed was either cunning or too much wine, Liscos decided to ask Tribune about the man who had sent the Romani to Wermaros.

"The Romani over-chief," he said to me, "is called Julianos, a name like that. Ask him to tell us about him."

After he heard my question, Tribune told Liscos, "Our commander's name is Gaius Julius Caesar."

The name meant nothing to Liscos. "What kind of warrior is he? How many enemy skulls has he taken?"

"Skulls? I...ah...really don't know," Tilius stammered. "I was assigned to his legion only a year ago and he wasn't there much. Velcanius was with the commander in Hispania." He looked past me. "*Centurio*, tell us something about Caesar."

"The commander is very energetic, you must be 'on your shield' with him every moment. In Hispania he raised ten new cohorts in just a few days. That's over three thousand legionaries." Velcanius watched a red-haired child refill his drinking horn, then continued, "We only had a short period of training, but I never saw men toughen up so fast. Caesar seemed touched by a god, yet instead of dining with officers, he shared legionary rations with his men. They pretty much worshiped him!"

The man named Marius called to him, "What of fighting? When did you move out against the barbarians?"

When Lucius glanced at me, I imagined it was because these 'barbarians' were Celtic tribes, like ours. "Ah... we took on the Calaici and Lusitani, who had never seen Romans before. By the end of the campaign season we bathed in the Western Ocean."

After my halting translation, Liscos asked thickly, "Ocean? What is that?"

"A sea that marks the limit of the world" I told him. "Celtillos sings about its magical islands."

"The boy is right," Lucius said. "Except for Atlantica, a few islands beyond Hispania, there is no more land."

I was translating as best I could, using a mixture of Celtic and Latin, but words like "energetic," "cohort," "rations," and "campaign" were beyond me. I reminded Lucius that he had promised to use simpler terms.

Liscos, in no mood for geography lessons, interrupted. "Tell me more of this Julian."

Lucius diluted his wine with a splash of sweet beer. "The favorite camp story is about a time when the young Caesar was captured by *piratae... pirates.*"

"Pirates?" I asked.

"Bandits, Alberix, thieves. Perhaps *ladronos* in your language."

I understood, but after talk turned to Caesar, I saw Cornelius ignoring the village girls who had pampered him with food and drink. "Indeed a good story," he called out. "Again, *Centurio*, how much ransom did they ask for?"

"Twenty talents of silver, a weight that adds up to almost two thousand sesterces, and yet young Caesar had enough nerve to tell them he was worth at least fifty talents. He acted insulted and even offered to raise the money for them."

"What happened then?"

"They agreed to let Caesar's aides go out and get the ransom and that's exactly what he had counted on, to gain time. While they were gone...it took over a month... Caesar made himself at home. He played their games, ordered them to be quiet while he wrote poetry, and even forced them to listen to it. If they complained, he called them barbarians and illiterate oafs. That amused the Cilicians..." Lucius paused. "Are you getting all this, Alberix?"

"Enough of it." Lucius wasn't speaking too fast and I was cutting the story short for Liscos.

"Good. Well, Caesar became on such friendly terms with the *piratae* that he joked about hanging the lot of them for having dared to capture him. They got a laugh out of *that* threat. After the ransom was paid and Caesar released, he sailed to Miletus and persuaded authorities there to let him have a galley and a few soldiers "

"The overconfident fools were still on the island," Cornelius interrupted with a drunken chuckle.

"Yes, Caesar surprised them. He took back ransom money and everything else they had, including their boats, and brought them back to the governor. He would decide on their punishment."

When Lucius paused to sip wine, Liscos wiped foam from his mustache and glanced around, bored from the tedium of the translating. Even I didn't think it much of a story compared to the ones our bards told. And it was straight narration, rather than verses that were sung and accompanied by harp music.

Liscos yawned and told me to ask if the thieves were sold as slaves.

"No," Tilius broke in, "and that's the best part. Caesar crucified the lot of them at Pergamus, *just* as he had vowed to do when he was their prisoner!"

Hearing the Romani laugh at the ending, Liscos looked perplexed. I understood that his merchant's mind could not see the logic of killing men, who could be sold as slaves. Yet the concept of vengeance was as strong among our people. In such a case they would not have waited until later to seal the bandits' fate; all of them would have died on the island.

Those warriors who had been close enough to hear the story had not understood, and called for more food. Slaves brought pitchers filled with unwatered Falernian or our sweetened beer. Liscos staggered to his feet to examine his new sword again.

Lucius leaned toward me to comment, "Your Gallic people are a handsome race. I like the bright clothing, so unlike those monotonous white togas seen at Rome. The neck rings—"

"Torcs."

"Yes. Those torcs could become all the fashion in the capital. I'd heard criticism that your women put on too much face coloring, yet they don't need anything at all. Nature already made them quite beautiful."

I didn't reply, but the recollection of Pix's swelling breasts, bronzed body and impish smile came to me. I shook the image and guessed that wine loosened his tongue, and Lucius would ask about Mother next.

"Take your mother down there," he said, just as I predicted. "You said her name was Briga?"

"Yes."

"Well, the Gauless next to her isn't an identical Gemini, a twin, but close."

"Dirona *is* my mother's twin sister. I told you she was married to Liscos." Annoyed at his interest and not wanting to talk about Mother, I looked away at the river.

Lucius realized Briga was holding his gaze and hid his embarrassment with another drink. *What are you thinking? The woman is Alberix's mother, not a camp follower. She has the bearing of a Patrician...a woman of good family. If her husband is dead, every warrior in the village will want her as wife.*

In glancing around, I noticed Arvos stand up unsteadily from his place at the far end of the guests. Some of the men had gone to urinate in the river so I thought he would do that. A newcomer not living in the village, Arvos had not attracted any girls as a potential husband. In fact, Dirona told me that they made fun of the charcoal maker's squat body and soot-stained clothing by nicknaming him *Dubadzo*, "Black-stick."

Instead of going to the river, Arvos clutched his drinking horn and lurched toward the end of the table where Tribune's two bodyguards sat. He stopped behind the one named Marius, gave him a mock salute, and spilled beer on both of them in the process. The girls giggled at the man's awkwardness and tittered the name *Dubadzo* among themselves. Arvos's face turn florid in a jealous rage as he looked toward the women, then glared at Marius.

"Shorthair, I heard warriors talk about your swords," he goaded in the poor Latin he had picked up at Arialbinnum. "They joke that you prick with *short* ones."

After Arvos repeated the taunt in Celtic to the girls, they laughed at the sexual reference. Encouraged, he continued, "Shorthair, I seen your weapons. Celtic swords are long and sharp, more than a match for yours. Ours *fill* the sheath!" Cluvios heard the taunt and called for him to sit down. Arvos ignored his warning and leaned over until he faced Marius a hand span away. "Not a man here got a blade short as yours."

Liscos, sensing a brawl, turned and took down his sword.

Lucius stood and touched the chieftain's arm. "Let me fight the drunken fool with words, defeat him that way." He called to Arvos, "I've seen your long swords, but it's not so much length as endurance that counts. Yours bend after only a few thrusts."

Arvos reached for his missing belt knife: Liscos had ordered men to leave weapons at their lodges and bring only eating knives to the meal.

Marius stood up to intervene. "This is my quarrel, *Centurio*. I don't think I'm as drunk as he is, so with Bacchus's help I'll succeed in using some of my wrestling tricks on the sooty boor."

Lucius looked toward Liscos. He shrugged, then grinned at his warriors, who had become frenzied at the expected confrontation. They hooted approval by banging the handles of knives and their cups against the board tops.

When Arvos threw down his drinking horn and lurched forward to grapple with Marius, the Roman spun away from the tent and onto the sandy bank of the river. *The gritty footing is reassuring, with the familiar feel of a palaestra training arena, so why does the thought of Arrachion flash into my mind? The wrestler was killed defending his title.*

Arvos stumbled forward, reaching out to clamp a stranglehold on his adversary. Marius knew it was the obvious move to expect from an untrained opponent; the counter-move was the first one taught by wrestling instructors. He ducked under Arvos's beefy left arm to lift it up. At the same instant, he dropped to his knee and reached behind the man's right leg. Grasping the limb, Marius pivoted on his knee and sent his adversary spinning around to land flat on his back on the sand.

Arvos rose up slowly, red-faced, breathing hard from effort and humiliation. He dived for Marius's waist, confident that he could reach around the man, encircle him with both arms, then could crush his ribs like sticks of charcoal.

Marius leaped back, out of the charrer's reach, but the sandy bank crumbled and sent him falling backwards into shallow water at the river's edge. Arvos lunged in after him, grasping one of Marius's sandals in a tight grip. He tried to reach for the other foot and flip his antagonist over on his face. In the wetness, his grasp slipped. Kneeling in thigh-deep water, Arvos coughed out inhaled water.

Marius regained his balance and saw his opportunity. Before Arvos could stand again, he caught the man's head in a full arm lock, forced it into the water, while his legs scissored his opponent's body and held it helpless. *Keep the brute under long enough to drown the fight out of him!*

When Marius released his vise-like hold, Arvos staggered from the river, gagging.

"Charrer, go back to your hut!" Cluvios ordered. "To help the fool would be a further humiliation, yet he can't insult guests and endanger treaties."

As I watched Arvos skulk off towards the forest, I knew that a Celt's pride was wounded more easily than his body—an internal hurt that did not heal as rapidly or permanently. I looked around at the men: rather than the charrer's loss angering them, the brief action brought out stories of other feasts and boasts of other fights.

The eating and drinking went on unabated as Belenos dropped below the western Jurassos crests and ushered in a long twilight. The girls who teased Marius and Cornelius during the feast had overcome their initial shyness. Now, they urged their fathers to approach the newcomers with offers of sharing sleeping quarters for the night. When asked, Tilius politely declined and had me explain that it was not the Roman way.

Lucius Velcanius also refused, but smiled to himself after hearing the *quaestor*. An offer from the Gaulesses was straightforward admiration for the manliness of their guests, a high compliment. In contrast, the "Roman way" was, often enough, for the bored wives of magistrates to secretly sleep with any man willing to do so—that is, the most immoral of citizens.

By twilight, drunken brawls broke out among the men who had not fallen into a stupor next to the eating boards. When their women quietly removed the small knives, the besotted antagonists attacked each other with half-eaten haunch bones and bowls of rancid curds. After globs of food spattered his guests, an equally drunk Liscos roared for the warriors to stop, waving his new sword in arcs of frustrated helplessness No one paid attention to him.

Finally, with an oath to Taranis, Liscos pushed the Romani out of the way and hacked the main support pole of the tent in half with his sword. The calfskin covering settled down over the startled brawlers, who feebly struggled under the food-stained leather, then fell asleep face down in the dinner dregs.

Even Sextus Tullius Tilius, who had attended banquets of unusual depravity at Rome, was hard put to suppress amusement. He staggered off with Liscos to his quarters in the guest lodge. Cluvios and I followed them, half-supporting Lucius.

As he looked up at the evening star, I heard him mutter something.

I asked, "What did you say? Do you want something?"

Lucius shook his head. "Th' evenin' star. We call it Venus...goddess of love."

Appropriate, I thought. The last time I saw Marius and Cornelius they were surrounded by a group of amorous, red or blond-haired, very determined village girls.

❦

As he lay on the furs of his sleeping ledge inside the lodge, Lucius's reeling brain could not shake the image of the copper-haired woman with the lake-blue eyes. Briga had briefly returned his gaze before the quarrel with Arvos and distracted him, but she had left during the brawl.

❦

Briga did not enjoy the day. The feasting was an unhappy reminder of her own husband's banquets after signing a mutual treaty, or ending a successful campaign against enemies of the Raurici tribe. She rejoiced then because he was safe, yet at the same time dreaded the interval until he took up his sword again. If the face of one of the dark-haired Romani lingered in her mind as she prepared for bed, Briga did not assign it much importance. He was a warrior from an alien race. She, the law-wife of a clan chieftain who would soon return.

❦

I couldn't fall asleep, too excited at the long day's events. I had done a passable job of translating until no one paid much attention to what was being said. This made me think of Fulvius. I felt grateful that he had befriended me and taught me rough Latin. But now he, Arialbinnum...even Father...were pictures in my mind as indistinct as the flickering shadows cast by the dying embers of the cook-fires outside.

Fulvius had told me stories about his travels, how he had marched great distances with what he called the Eagle Standards. Might the wheel of my life turn with that of the strangers, whom some of our people derisively called, "The enemy from beyond the White Mountains."

❦

Ollam Fodla had watched the Romans from a vantage point at the edge of the forest, above the clearing where the parley tent had been set up. The talks, sacrifice, feasting, and brawling over now, he stood up under the darkening sky to go back to his hut. Fithil approached.

"Did you see that today?" Fodla asked him. "The Shorthairs are here to obtain something that is in the interest of their nation, or of their provincial over-chief."

"I'm not interested in politics," Fithil replied, without breaking the juggling rhythm of the three sticks and a smooth stone that he picked up from the ground.

Fodla ordered, "Nevertheless, find out why the Shorthairs are here. It may be an excuse to bring in their legions, as they did in the south."

"Romani, Graeci, Galli," Fithil scoffed, "What does it matter? Three designs on one dish."

"You reckon without the Germani."

"*Four* designs, then." He caught the juggled items in unison and threw them aside.

"Fithil, a dish may hold porridge or manure. Which would you prefer for breakfast?"

"Druid, manure was porridge first."

Fodla gave a dry laugh. "Your philosophical mind astounds me. Our 'porridge,' if you will, is that manure-filled village below. I need to convince its one-armed chief that the Shorthairs are more of a threat to his Sequani than even Germani to the north. These Gallic Celts must be forced to stop intertribal wars or they'll be partitioned by the Shorthairs, like the body of a dead elk is torn apart by wolves."

"How will *you* do this? The old druid you called 'Master' is kin to Liscos, *and* his advisor."

"Dividiac is away in the forest much of the time gathering mistletoe... seeking entrances into the Earth Mother. Perhaps you should let Boccus know that."

Fithil shrugged at the deadly suggestion. "The smell of that roasted meat has aroused my stomach. I'm going down to charm those village girls, who also arouse something else on me. I'll get pork and beer, and something infinitely more honeyed between their thighs."

Ollam Fodla watched the juggler saunter down towards women tending the last fires that burned near the river, then glanced at the moon rising in an early night sky. He murmured to the orb, "I shall convince Liscos that these Romani are his enemies, as sure as you are to change your crystal face each month."

Chapter XI

Blinding rays of a June morning sun, slanting through the lodge venthole and across the room's bluish air, brightened a triangular patch of earthen floor. Cornelius and Marius awoke on their wolf-fur pelts with aching heads that felt stuffed with the same fuzzy hair. An aftertaste of Falernian soured their belches. The two Romans vaguely recalled being taken to their sleeping quarters by incredibly strong, beautifully long-haired, and unbelievably insatiable village girls.

A sense of the present returned to Cornelius. He sat up on the ledge, picked a wolf hair off his tongue, glanced down at his now-flaccid "gladius," and then over at his prone companion.

"Marius," he called out, "no pun meant, but I hope my gladius *upheld* the honor of Roma last night."

"Ugghhhh...." The engineer moaned and rolled over on his back, licking at dry lips with a tongue that felt as if it rotted overnight. "Wh...at? Oh. I do seem to recall that before I wrestled with Arvos, he bragged about Gallic versus Roman sword lengths. I think I told him I preferred a javelin."

"Friend, every soldier compares his little cockerel to a weapon, either a javelin or a short sword." Cornelius lay back again, unwilling to risk his throbbing eyes to more daylight. While waiting for the room to stop revolving, he continued to jest, "Ah, yes, to 'He-who-relies-on Dionysius' for his sexual prowess, a javelin *is* a formidable weapon, yet once it is hurled, it usually bends and becomes useless. Give *me* the shorter gladius, which can be thrust again and again, and yet again before it..." He moaned. "What in Hades's name am I babbling about?"

Before Marius could respond, a window shutter pushed open and let in the sounds of girlish laughter. He abruptly sat up. "What is Tilius's reaction going to be to our little overnight escapade?"

"I'll wager the tribune hasn't awakened yet."

"It must be halfway through the third hour! Ahhhh"—Marius touched his forehead—"I'm going to soak this swollen head of mine in that cold river."

"The river will have to do, but I'd give a day's rations for a morning at the Stabian Baths in Pompeii."

"No argument there!"

Wearing only cloaks, the two men staggered to the riverbank. The water felt like an analgesic to their throbbing skulls. Kneeling in the shallows, they ducked underwater as long as possible to drown out the loud giggles and undoubtedly lewd comments of red and blond-haired vixens upstream.

The women washed clothes or cleaned up the banquet tent on shore. A few warriors still lay in the sodden mess, snoring loudly.

Cornelius remarked, "I imagine even a kinperson would not lightly awaken, even an unarmed Celt sleeping off the effects of Dionysius."

"No.... Uh, uh, look," Marius warned. "Here come the tribune and *centurio*. Let's avoid them, ease ourselves into the water and drift downstream."

Tilius and Velcanius strode toward the river with exaggerated dignity. Once in the river they lathered themselves with the sapo lumps. Liscos appeared with two village girls holding towels. "Fine linen from the looms of Vesontio," he boasted. "After you're dry, stretch out on the ground and let the girls massage you in the Romani manner."

After Lucius translated, Tilius muttered aside, "No need. I don't want to come into this barbarian's debt. We should start talking with him about the next step in building the signal towers."

"My feast pleased you?" Liscos probed. "A great expense to buy the wine—"

"Fine, an enormous honor," Tilius told him. "Velcanius, tell him that I want my two engineers to find locations for the towers and draw up a lease and construction contract. If the Helvetii do carry out their threat to migrate west, time is short. Get that young man who was translating to come to our quarters."

After hearing the request, Liscos growled something to the girls, then stalked off, peeved at a lost opportunity to boast further about the quantity and cost of his banquet.

"We'll get started..." Tilius looked toward the village. "Now, what in Jupiter's name happened to those engineers?"

Lucius indicated them with a nod of his head. "Cornelius and Marius are floating over there, trying to hide from us."

"Order them out of the water, and send those girls away. We'll towel ourselves dry."

⊷⊶

A slave of Liscos summoned me to his lodge. When I entered, Tribune, Lucius, the Romani who fought Arvos, and his companion stood around a table with Liscos.

"Alberix," Lucius called to me, "we need your help here. Ah, how...how is your mother? Briga? When I answered by a quick shrug, he indicated a square of animal skin on the table. "This diagram Liscos gave us shows the land around Wermaros with site names written in Greek. Where did it come from?"

I looked at a chart I had not seen before. "Dividiac or another druid could have drawn it up."

"I know enough Greek to identify the Dubis River and Vesontio over here. Liscos says the road to the Sequani capital follows the waterway. Are there villages east of Wermaros called Boia and Delsa?"

"Yes, we came through them on our way here."

Cornelius nodded. "However crude, this map will be of enormous help. After we scout out the best tower locations, we'll mark them in red ink." He unrolled a papyrus scroll. "I've made a drawing of what the towers will be like, and we'll build a model."

"Model?" The drawing interested me, but I didn't know the word.

Marius held a hand above the table. "A small construction this high to help us plan what they'll be like."

Tilius said, "Young man, I'll summarize our business here, and if you don't understand everything Lucius will explain. My commander has decided that two towers are needed. One should be on the highest crest above this village that overlooks the road running from Delsa. The Helvetii will take that, if they choose a northern route to the plains beyond the Jurassos. That way the tribe will bypass our Gallic province, yet must travel through Sequani and Aedui lands."

"The other tower," Lucius elaborated, "should be built along the Dubis road to relay a signal on to Vesontio. If hired scouts at Delsa are trustworthy, we'll have at least four or five days warning of any migration. That should give the affected tribes...and us...enough time to oppose the Helvetii."

"Sir," Cornelius suggested to Tilius, "I'll look for locations with you and Velcanius. "To save time, Marius can remain here to build the tower model and hire stoneworkers."

The *quaestor* nodded approval. "Young man, tell Liscos we'll need a guide, preferably one who speaks Latin."

"I'll do my best."

"Good. We'll leave at sun up with horses and enough rations to scout the area for three days."

After I told Liscos the request, he said that Epanactos would accompany the Romani.

Cluvios felt worse the next morning: he was irritable, complained of a violent headache, and seemed too exhausted to work. I banked the forge coals and went to see what Marius was doing. It would be a chance to speak more Latin and find out what his country was like.

I found him whittling down a length of pinewood into a square strip of finger- width. "*Slanos*, health," I said, greeting him. "Do you mind if I watch you?"

"Watch?" Marius grinned. "How about helping? I understand you work at a forge."

"With my uncle Cluvios."

"Then finish squaring this wood. It's another floor beam for the tower model. Look over here."

On a table Marius had built up a three-sided square of pebbles that was ten fingers high and cemented together with pinesap. Five of the small beams were in place, with thinner strips laid over them, two hand spans high. "This represents the floor of the first level," he explained. "There will be four levels, including the top for the signal fire   I'm leaving one side open so I can work out the interior plan."

I looked around the sides. "There's no door to get in. Is it on the open side?"

"No, the entrance will be at the first level, about fifteen feet off the ground."

"Fifteen *feet?*" I didn't understand.

"A Roman measurement. Twenty of them are about from here to that far wall."

I was puzzled. "Why so high? Our doors are at ground level."

"Don't you have a great deal of snow in winter?"

I laughed at his words. "Not *that* much." When Marius turned away and began whittling down another beam, I realized his answer was an excuse. It was a clever precaution and convinced me that the Romani didn't entirely trust us. "Why did your friend go to look for tower locations instead of you? Is he your over-chief?"

"Cornelius is senior to me, but we both have the rank of *Optio*. We construct things for the legions."

"What things?"

Marius hesitated a moment before asking, "Didn't you say there was a recent Germani raid on your village."

"Yes, by renegade Suebi."

"What happened?"

"About a twenty of them tried to get inside an open gate before we could close it."

"Some raiders were killed and several of your warriors, too?" After I nodded, Marius said, "I've inspected your palisade. The wood stakes are old, rotted. Your gates don't have an offset entrance to trap attackers. A protective ditch should have been dug around the outside, with that river diverted into it. There are no towers spaced along the wall. We would have gotten inside in half a watch period, without losing a man."

Angry at his criticism, I demanded, "So, Marius, how would you do that?"

"First, by using an onager to batter down the palisade."

"Onager?"

"It's an African wild ass, but also the name for a machine that 'kicks' heavy stones from a distance."

Marius went back to working on the small beam. He was not going to tell me any more about Romani battle tactics. I hadn't understood everything, so I asked where he came from.

"Arpinium, a town over fifty miles east of Rome."

"Is your family *uxello*...a noble one?"

"Noble?" Marius chuckled as he sighted along the wood to check straightness. "We're Equestrian Class, not Patrician. That's in the middle between Pats and Plebs, but I am a distant relative of Gaius Marius. He was Julius Caesar's late uncle by marriage. Gaius reformed the army, lowered property qualifications for recruits, and enlisted landless volunteers. Is this too much Latin for you to follow, Alberix?"

It was, yet I didn't want to admit that. "I did ask the question."

"Even so, enough for now. Let's get this model finished. Caesar gave us until the ides of September to build both towers. That's a little over three months from now."

Our month of Edrin. The weather will be colder. Leaves start to turn color and snow could fall. Should I tell him that the leaders of the Helvetii won't wait for it to be that close to winter to move from their lands? I didn't.

During the three days that I helped Marius, I learned a lot about building towers. The height of these was eighty of his feet, built in the unmortared stonework that is familiar to our masons. The first level, which Marius called a 'barracks,' was the sleeping and cooking area for the agreed upon sixteen men in each tower. Space under the floor would store supplies. Above were two half floors reached by ladders. The second held kindling and wood for signal fires at the topmost level. They burned in a clay firepot set on slate and filled with sand. Marius said the garrison would bring barrels of a thick, oily liquid that would create black smoke for daytime signals.

Liscos was as good as his word. Over the next few days, stone workers and carpenters arrived in Wermaros. Some brought their families. They set up leather tents in the field where herder clans camped during Beltaine.

I helped Tribune draw up a contract that said workers would be paid in coin for working each of the three months of our lunar calendar—a few days less time than the Romani sun calendar. Liscos would receive the sum and make payments, but Tribune would record the amount each man received. Since resolving disputes would be the chieftain's responsibility, I hoped he would be more competent in controlling the tower workers than he had been his banquet guests!

Tribune kept an account of the construction supplies he wanted to buy, and the lease payments for the land. I was a little baffled by his insistence with written records. Our merchants kept track of trade transactions in their heads, and Dividiac said that debts were payable in the Other-world.

Lucius was in charge of making sure the towers were completed on time. He suggested a bonus of a gold coin for each man in the crew, who finished his part of the work ahead of the estimate time. Liscos said they would have preferred receiving a slave instead, but found the money acceptable. At Vesontio, Casticos made silver and gold coins copied from Greek ones he received, but I found Romani coin designs more varied.

Even though I resented Lucius's interest in my mother, I still couldn't help coming to like him.

The cavalry legion auxiliary from the village that brought the message about the arrival of the Romani was sent back to report that the tower agreement was concluded.

Legionary garrisons could be sent. He had not been gone long enough to reach Genava when the first men arrived. This Julius evidently anticipated the success of his mission or sent the men here early to make sure it would be in his favor.

Lucius assigned men to each tower site, ordered them to dig a ditch around their camp, and surround it with sharpened stakes they brought with them in their baggage train. Leather tents sheltering eight men were set up in the center. After I commented to Lucius on his men's efficiency, he told me that a legion of several thousand soldiers did this each time they halted for the night. Tribune was with him and boasted, "The race that wears the toga shall rule the world.' I wasn't sure what he was talking about.

Tribune labeled his accounts *Turris I* and *Turris II*, but Marius called them Castor and Pollux. He told me these were the names of the twin sons of Jupiter, the over-chief of Romani gods. They had sailed to the ends of the world in search of a golden sheep-skin. At the time, Belenos was passing through the constellation of Gemini, a sign of Twins in Dividiac's zodiac. To Romani its two brightest stars bore the names of Jupiter's sons. To Liscos's ear "Castor" and "Casticos" were similar enough for him to make a connection with his over-chief at Vesontio. Work on *Turris I* went more rapidly than on the other, but then Pollux was further away on *Benn Terix*, the area's highest mountain.

❧❧

As the nights lengthened toward the summer solstice, Belenos arced out of the sign of the Twins and into the stars that formed the Great Crab. The winds blew warmer. By the time that the Month of Hay merged with Harvest Month, Sextus Tilius and Lucius Velcanius were familiar figures in the village.

Tilius became reclusive at the tower site. The *quaestor* kept to his account books, or rode along the river to throw pebbles in its backwater pools and estimate in the circling ripples the number of months before he could end his tour of duty and return to Rome. He looked around at the mountains, wondering if he would be assigned to winter quarters at Aquileia, or be stranded in the deep snow of forested slopes that cut off too much of the brilliant sky he loved seeing on his father's villa in Latium.

Cluvios fashioned iron door hinges and retaining rings for the towers, so Velcanius often stopped by the forge. The centurion's star had led him along a soldier's path, yet he appreciated adeptness in any calling. Amid the hot, sooty bustle of the forge, he watched smoking metal spill into clay molds. The energy was creative, the smells clean and acrid, unlike the death-stink of the battlefield. Foundry casts birthed shining metal children that were different from bloated corpses that spawned maggots and carrion flies.

Lucius Velcanius enjoyed talking to Alberix. The young Celt had an inquiring mind and seemed interested in the exchange of ideas, yet he realized that a chance to see the boy's mother was also a reason for his visits. An initial awkwardness in the presence of the Celtic woman who had intrigued him at the banquet disappeared. The image of her comely face and gentle manner dominated his thoughts. He found new excuses to visit Briga in the late afternoons: Cluvios and his nephew took respite from the forge to eat a little food before a late evening meal served during cooler twilight hours. Briga would be with them.

❧❧

Cluvios and I were outside with Mother, sharing the cheese, bread, and horns of frothy *cervisa* she had brought us, when Lucius came toward us from the direction of the river gate. A short sword hung at his belt, but then some of our warriors always walked around armed. He greeted us, then held out a silver medallion dangling on a leather thong to Mother and explained, "Briga, this...this is to recall that the towers have made us friends. It shows Castor and Pollux on one side and commemorates one of our victories. We celebrate with games called *Ludi Apollinares*."

Mother blushed as she thanked him. To save her from embarrassment, and actually not that pleased that Lucius had brought her a gift, I changed subjects. "How *is* work on the towers coming along?"

"Very well, Alberix. You'll have to come see Castor. We're up to the second level. Your stone setters are skilled men."

Briga hung the medallion around her neck and looked at one side. "What are these games you mentioned?"

"Citizens at Rome are entertained with horse races...plays in the theater... fights between wild animals. This morning my men pitted a weasel against a young boar they trapped." Lucius paused after seeing a frown on Briga's face, then mumbled a weak excuse, "They're good men. There...there is not much here to entertain them."

I broke a strained silence. "Lucius, are you from Roma?"

Relieved, he replied, "No, from east of Latium, where Liscos's wine is made."

Briga asked, "Do you have family there? Perhaps, a...a wife?"

Lucius shook his head and laughed. "A legionary makes a poor husband."

When he did not go on, I guessed he remembered that Mother needed no reminder of that fact. "Why *did* you join the legions?"

"Adventure, I suppose, Alberix, but mostly to get away from the farm."

"You stayed."

"Thank Fortuna, I *survived*." Lucius thought for a moment then continued, "Some of our writers say that Roma considers it her destiny to bring a *Pax Romana* to the world. Others...Stoics...teach that a brotherhood can exist among different nations. Peace could happen. Look at us here...potential enemies now as friends."

Briga agreed, "My husband felt the same way."

"Yet could a fox bring harmony to the chicken yard?" The question came from Epanactos, who stood next to wicker windscreens that shielded the forge's pit fire.

Lucius reddened, but Liscos's bodyguard came forward to smile and extend a hand. "That was a country saying, nothing more. I've wanted to talk with you." Retaining the grin, he turned to Briga. "Woman, a horn of beer would go well on this hot day."

Mother glared at his impudent request, but went inside for the *cervisa*.

Epananctos had the rough manners of a warrior. I recalled that he was an Arvernian brought here as a child, when his highborn parents were exchanged as hostages in a war against Aeduii.

"I overheard something about games," The grin vanished as Epanactos sounded less amiable. "Do you Shorthairs not have professional warriors who fight as entertainers?"

"Gladiators," Lucius confirmed, "but they're not part of the *Apollinares*."

"You've seen these men kill each other?"

"I've gone to arena bouts."

Epanactos's new disarming smile revealed a stretch of eneven teeth. "And have you not learned a few fighting strategies from watching them?"

"I suppose."

"Then, Cluvios, you..." Epanactos paused to sip from a drinking horn Briga held out to him, then handed it back without thanks, and wiped foam from his mustache. "Cluvios, you have long banner poles. Bring two of them. I wish this Shorthair to show me his skills. Let him play with me a bit."

Cluvios protested, "The man is a guest in our village. He should not be—"

"It's all right, "Lucius interrupted. "Alberix, bring us the poles."

At uncle's nod, I came back with two ash-wood rods the thickness of a man's wrist, and an arm-span in length.

Lucius hacked one down to the shorter length of his sword, explaining that he did not want an advantage over his opponent. Epanactos's mirthless grin congealed in place as he tested the balance of his longer weapon.

The two men moved out of the shadow of the lodge and onto a grassy area near Cluvios's wagon. Once there, Epanactos warbled a lark's call. At his signal, several fellow warriors came out of the oak grove and stood around the edge, to form a makeshift arena. They were unarmed, yet Lucius felt that he had been tricked into an ambush.

"Shorthair," Epanactos smirked, "I see that you carry a sword although you are a 'guest.' Do you not trust Long-haired Galli?"

Lucius did not respond, but unbuckled his sword and laid it aside.

Epanactos ran a hand through thinning hair and tousled it into a semblance of the stiff strands Celts affected in battle. His smile now a scowl of hate, the Arvernian grasped his wooden pole in both hands, moved forward, and swung it in deadly swishing arcs, forcing Lucius back against the wagon. "No...countermoves?" he gasped in the sultry heat, and savagely swung down at his opponent's head.

As the centurion sidestepped, he felt the wagon side vibrate from the force of the blow. Knowing that Epanactos's hands were stinging, he stepped forward to thrust upward with his short sword-length of wood, then moved back—a standard legionary tactic. The jagged end had caught the Arvernian below the rib cage. He staggered back with a grunt of surprise. An oval stain of blood seeped out to color his tunic.

After his comrades shouted taunts of shame at him, Epanactos lunged forward, jabbing rapidly with the length of wood as he would a spear. Lucius swung down at it with his shortened pole, then twisted aside and slid the wood upward until it smashed into the fingers of his opponent's left hand. Epanactos clenched his teeth in pain, but said nothing. Pivoting his pole upward, he caught his opponent on the side of the face. With an ooze of blood from an earlobe reddening his cheek, Lucius swung to his left, again, catching Epanactos in the side and knocking out his breath.

As the Arvernian fell back, clutching his stomach, Lucius paused to dab at the blood on his face with a neckerchief. He had no wish to humiliate a Gallic noble and one of Liscos's advisors. There was an instant of awarness that Briga held her head in a gesture of horror. Then one of Epanactos's comrades tossed the Celt a round cavalry shield. Feeling confident again, the warrior leveled his pole and threw it like a spear. All in the same quick movement, Lucius sprang away from the arcing shaft, threw down his pole, and ran forward. He reached Epanactos, grasped the lower edge of his shield in both hands, and forced the metal rim up into the warrior's throat.

The Arvernian's head snapped back. He slid to his knees, gagging in short, rasping gurgles. Lucius wheeled around, expecting to be attacked by the warrior's friends, but the men were silent, or grunted reluctant approval for an action well fought. Two of them came to lift their comrade by the arms and help him back to his lodge.

Velcanius's ear burned and his head throbbed. Briga had hurried inside to bring out a bowl of water and linen cloth.

"Lucius, you will have a painful bruise." Her hand trembled as she dabbed cool water on his ear. "Hold this cloth in place, while I go back for mint-mullein ointment."

Cluvios promised, "I'll speak to Liscos about Epanactos. There is no excuse for his attack."

"No, sheath your anger," Lucius advised as he held the cloth. "Besides, it's not often that I fight against only wooden weapons."

Despite the light humor, Cluvios insisted, "The fool upset Briga by provoking a fight that reminded her of Alrix."

"I'm sorry for that. How long has her husband been missing?"

"Over five moon periods."

Lucius asked softly, "Do...do you believe he's dead?"

Cluvios shrugged uncertainty. "Germani have been known to ask for ransom."

"But almost six months and still no word of him?"

"Why all this interest in Alrix?" Cluvios snapped. "My family may think of you as a friend, yet we are barbarians in the eyes of your people."

"Of some perhaps, but not—"

"Roman, let me finish! We have our laws, our customs. My brother had a sharp vision, the eye of a falcon that saw the possibility of a peaceful future. I try to look beyond my forge fire, but the light from the coals shines only so far..." Cluvios paused, racked by a bout of coughing.

After he recovered, Lucius came to sit beside him. "Friend, we want the same outcome, peace. Together we can check Germani raids and secure the Renos frontier."

Briga came out to apply the ointment. As she smoothed the balm on with her fingers, Lucius held back, desperately wanting to reach up and press her hand against his cheek.

"Soak this cloth, Lucius, and keep it on for tonight. It will help the swelling."

" I...thanks, Briga. I...I should get back to the tower."

As the centurion walked back to the camp, swelling on the side of his face reminded him to not be tricked into an ambush again. Now, a humiliated Epanactos might urge his hot-headed warriors to attack his legionaries in revenge.

That night, only the coolness of Briga's touch mattered. And, for the first time, she had called him by his name.

❦

No warrior assault came on the legionary tents. Peace among the valley tribes continued as hay season merged with the hot days of Elembiv, the harvest month.

I continued to take the record of Belenos's rising on most mornings, watching the bright disc move further and further north. From the shelter, I could see activity at the tower named Castor, but Lucius never again invited me to the site—the Romani kept whatever they were doing away from curious eyes. I hoped he had not lost trust in me.

At mid-month, a detachment of Gallic auxiliaries brought the worker and legionary salaries, along with a message for Sextus Tilius.

After reading the first paragraph, the *quaestor* exclaimed, "*Centurio*, our Caesar has indeed seduced the goddess Fortuna! The Senate appointed him governor of the Narbonensis Province."

"Old Metellus has died?" Lucius asked.

"Presumably. Our commander has the entire coast now, from Hispania to the Maritime Alps."

"An unprecedented command!"

"Exactly." Tilius lowered his voice, "Between us, Gnaeus Pompeius and Marcus Crassus have amply repaid his legislation on their behalf. Of course, Caesar does deserve the province."

"What of Caesar's co-consul, Bibulus?"

"No mention, but he can't be too pleased." Tilius read on, then chuckled. "Why that fox! Caesar married off his daughter, Julia, to Pompeius."

"Wasn't she engaged to Servilius Caepo?"

Tilius glanced up sharply. *Velcanius knows as much as I do about the commander, perhaps too much for a rural centurion.* "This marriage will strengthen two important families."

"Is there mention of Helvetii intentions?"

"Yes, here. A leader called Orgetorix is recruiting supporters. His daughter married an Aeduan over-chief named Dumnorix. Caesar wants us to find out if there's any sort of conspiracy being hatched." Tilius read on, then commented, "This is of interest. The Helvetii have sent envoys to the Allobroges at Genava. Our agents report that their clan leaders are buying up wagons and draft oxen. For the second year the tribe planted an enormous quantity of grain."

"Collecting transports and provisions for a move," Lucius surmised.

"Indeed, *Centurio*. Caesar goes on to say that he wants the towers completed post haste, and any reports of Helvetii movements sent to Titus Labienus, commander of the Tenth Legion. The legate is on our Allobroge frontier, near Genava."

Lucius recalled, "It's not like Caesar to wait. I learned in Hispania that he makes totally unexpected moves against an enemy."

Tilius rolled up the papyrus. "And this isn't some remote land at the end of the world. The Narbonensis and Allobroge lands both touch Italia itself. Any rash action by the Celts could repeat that long ago barbarian invasion by Brennos." He slapped the scroll against one hand in frustration. "If only I had accurate information."

Lucius thought a moment before saying, "*Quaestor*, I have an idea."

"Go on, *Centurio*."

"We could tell Cluvios and Alberix to go to the Helvetii capital at Aventia, on the pretext of asking if they needed forge items. The site is to the south, on the road they take to the ore pits."

Tilius thought differently. "Cluvios could go, but his nephew is too young."

"About the age Caesar was when he hunted down and hung those pirates," Lucius countered. "And I'm sure the commander would be most appreciative of anything *you* could find out...and did so...before anyone else told him."

"Before anyone else told Caesar," Tilius repeated softly, seeing the advantage of informing his commander about a budding conspiracy that could be dealt with before it leafed out of control. "Fine, it might be worth a try. I'm positive that Casticos knows more than he's told us."

"Nor would Liscos forego an opportunity to make a profit. It should be easy to convince him that the whole idea of selling pots was his."

"Start with Liscos, then talk to the boy's uncle,"

"Kinship or not, Cluvios is in indebted to Liscos. He'll order the crafter to go."

Tilius held up the scroll. "Now I'll burn this. I'm positive that old druid can read some Latin."

As the men watched the manuscript curl into dark ashes on the coals of a brazier, Alberix ran into the tent, out of breath.

"Tribune, a...messenger just arrived...at the mountain gate...from Aventia. He's telling everyone...that Orgetorix of the Helvetii has been...arrested for treason!"

"Treason?" Tilius glanced at Velcanius. "Then, there might be something to rumors of a plot between the Aeduii and a Helvetii faction, after all."

"What plot?"

Lucius grasped his arm. "Alberix, we were just talking about that. We need you to go on a mission that could save many of your people's lives, as well as protect their security *and* that of Roma."

Chapter XII

Aching in every muscle, I slid down from the back of Derka onto the rippling grass of a meadow on the slope of a mountain named *Benn Samain.* After I removed my wide-brimmed leather hat, cool wind blowing through damp matted hair felt good. Tethered together nearby, the packhorse and that of my guide, Cimbris, nibbled at sweet-clover plants that crowded aside orange-red poppy blossoms and waving stalks of field grasses. Cimbris moved off to sit in the shade of an Arolle pine and was asleep in the time it took an orange butterfly to investigate the bursting white pods of a milkweed stalk. I thought we had stopped to eat and rest the horses, not catch up on sleep.

I recalled how I had gotten here, a day-and-a-half's journey from Wermaros. When Cluvios felt too sick to travel to Aventia with me, as Tribune wanted, I persuaded Mother to let me make the journey in the company of an experienced guide who knew the Helvetii. It hadn't been easy, but we both were becoming reconciled to Father's probable death. I told her I was only going with articles from our forge, pans especially, since the clan tribesmen were collecting metal cauldrons, instead of breakable clay ones. I argued that no one would suspect a lone boy selling pans, especially once they found that I had a druid uncle, another training me as a metal crafter, and that my father was killed fighting the hated Germani. Liscos saw profits in the journey and finally convinced her that I would be safe with Cimbris, a distant relative of his.

Dividiac still was away, so we left at the new moon of Elembiv. My guide is from Sego, a hamlet more than halfway up *Benn Samain,* which is on the southeastern edge of Sequani lands. Like Liscos, the mountaineer has only one arm. He isn't very talkative and didn't mention his loss, but white scars on his face and remaining arm indicate that a farm accident had not caused his mutilation. A warrior's assault in a tribal quarrel undoubtedly had cost him the limb.

Our first day's travel had been easy. We followed a forest trail along the slope of the Jurassos that paralleled the bed of the Dubis River. The path snaked over a pass and by afternoon wound down through flatlands to pick up another trail inside a gorge. That followed a twisting stream that Cimbris did not name. The roadway passed under a natural arch formation before joining another stream. By sunset we had arrived at Sego, whose stone houses dotted a steep trail that led to the summit of *Benn Samain.* Since the height's name was that of our New Year festival, druids surely celebrated rites on the mountain.

We were not at the summit, yet high enough for a fantastic panorama to unroll before us toward the south. Never had I experienced anything as breathtaking, not even the view from the road above Wermaros. Directly below, the flat surfaces of three lakes reflected the sky and mountains. To my right, a morning sun glinted off the south end of the largest lake. Surface wavelets made it resemble a bar of hammered silver that melded into darker blue or green reflections. At this distance, the furthest and smallest lake was only a flash of brightness that I barely glimpsed between low hills. Down the slope in front of me lay a medium-sized expanse of water. A finger of white sand pointed from the shore to its center, and a stream connected it to the largest lake.

Beyond the three lakes stretched broad patches of dark-green forest and ochre fields, until landscape colors blurred in the hazy foothills of immense white peaks that loomed in the distance. I wondered about a few columns of black smoke, dotting the plain, but the autumnal mists of Fogmair had not yet obscured the outline of the distant range. Its peaks spread a jagged barrier across the horizon. Snowy summits stood out so delicately against the blue sky that it seemed that I could reach out and rub them away with a finger. I couldn't estimate their distance, but they seemed more like a sorcerer's apparition than actual mountains.

"*Benn Vindos*...The White Mountains," Cimbris said behind me.

He had hardly spoken during our night stopover and had crept up on me in total silence. I would have to be more alert. "How far off are they?"

"Three day's journey. They guard us from the Romani on the other side."

I wanted to keep Cimbris talking. "What are those lakes below us?"

"Largest is Lake of the Helvetii..." He pointed to its near end. "There, where the river flows into it from the lake below us, are ancient signs of our people."

"How ancient?"

The guide shrugged uncertainty. "Before the time of my grandfather's father, the village was destroyed by the sorcery of Tergwath. We will avoid the place and not touch on its *geis*...its curse."

Cimbris volunteered no more information about this sorcerer, but since he seemed talkative, I asked about what I had come to find out. "Is there truth to reports that the Helvetii plan to migrate to new lands?"

"Sego is far from what happens outside our valley," he hedged, handing me a thick slice of cheese on a chunk of bread. "Eat. We must be on our way."

I chewed and swallowed a first bite, then decided to be persistent. "Have you heard of Orgetorix?"

"Orgetorix?"

"An over-chief at Aventia."

"Aventia." Cimbris pointed toward the smallest lake. I squinted along his arm and noticed a cluster of shapes that were alien to the forested landscape. "There is the *dunum* of the Helvetii."

"*Dunum?*" He used a Celtic word I didn't know.

"Fortress. Their capital is built on a flat hill protected by walls."

"How long will it take to get there?"

"Sunset."

Cimbris moved off toward our mounts. I stuffed the rest of the bread into my mouth and followed him. The man had never looked directly into my eyes, even when handing me the food. Mountain people did not share many secrets with strangers, even those who paid them. I had perhaps given away my real reason for going to Aventia, but if Cimbris had guessed it—or already knew—he said nothing after mounting his horse.

I climbed onto Derka, and reined the packhorse away from its nibbling. We started down on the rock-strewn trail, passing areas of scorched grass and fire-blackened earth that lay between upright stones. I surmised that this slope was where druids lighted Samain bonfires that could be seen at Aventia and farmsteads scattered around the lakes.

After the trail circled the ruined remains of Tergwath's sorcery, at the north shore of the smallest lake, it joined a wider roadway coming from the east. Many tribesmen and their families were traveling the road with supply carts or wagons of household furnishings. Most herded cattle, sheep, and pigs, heading toward Aventia. The columns of dark smoke in the distance still puzzled me. Cimbris said nothing, but I was sure he came to the same conclusion that I did: the Helvetii *were* on the move and burning their abandoned farmsteads behind them.

Toward evening, with Aventia in sight, some of the wagons turned off the road into newly harvested fields alongside. As we neared the capital, campsites grew crowded, as more and more families pitched tents for the night and built fires to cook food and temper the chill air.

Aventia was built atop a rise of ground and surrounded by a stone wall topped with a log barricade. I could see high towers at the corners, where the walls turned to encircle the hill. The ramparts reminded me of Arialbinnum's defenses, except that these were more massive and solid.

Cimbris explained our business to the gate sentries with words in the Helvetii dialect. We left the riding horses outside town in the care of some boys, but paid a "trading fee," a bribe that allowed me to bring in the packhorse. Since there was only about a watch period of daylight left, I did not have much time in which to find a location and sell the forge items I had brought.

Inside Aventia, people, mostly men, clogged the main street. The lodges resembled those at Arialbinnum—log constructions with steeply pitched, thatched roofs. Other shed-like warehouses or shops abutted the stone ramparts. Some dwellings were of squared timbers neatly dovetailed at the corners, but most had rough-hewn logs with shreds of bark still clinging on their weathered sides. Wagons, many newly carpentered, stood alongside houses. Large numbers of barrels, jars, and lumpy bales of supplies were stored against the lodges.

With Cimbris walking ahead, I maneuvered the packhorse through the crowded street. Armed men clustered on corners, speaking in serious tones while eating food and drinking. Other warriors came from side streets, headed in the direction we went.

Cimbris fell back alongside me. "You can show your craftwork at an open space in Aventia's center."

I nodded, but felt uneasy in this atmosphere of unrest among the men. I heard the name of Orgetorix repeated in angry conversations—In this tense situation would anyone bother with my metal-wares?

The main square of the town was about a hundred paces on a side. A stone building dominated one section; the broad porch over the doorway suggested a communal lodge. Houses of high-quality construction, with iron fittings and painted decorations on front, were on the other three sides. I guessed these were the lodges of Helvetii noblemen or sub-chiefs. Most of the crowd was at the stone lodge, listening to a white-haired man speak.

As we were jostled into the square, Cimbris muttered, "Orgetorix has called his *vassos* together and they summoned their clients. I have not seen this many warriors since a tribal assembly was called to oppose Ariovistos, the Suebi king."

I had little time to reflect on the fact that Cimbris *did* know about Orgetorix—and probably a lot more than he let on—before he ordered, "Get your pack horse off to one side. This crowd is in no mood to buy."

As I led the animal to the edge of the lodge, I heard the oldster on the porch respond in an angry voice to hecklers in the crowd. "The charge is treason. Regardless of his rank, Orgetorix will be tried tomorrow under our laws."

Cimbris identified the old man. "Marcios is *vergobret*, chief judge of the Helvetii."

"Orgetorix thinks only of our nation," the heckler shouted. "His alliance with the Aedui and Sequani will make us masters of Gallia. It is the right of the powerful...of the sons of Lugos of the Long Hand!"

The man tried to lead the crowd in a chant of Orgetorix's name, but another oldster came out the door. He stood alongside Marcios, calling for silence.

"It is Nammeios," someone called out. "Listen to Nammeios!"

The feeble chanting died away.

"It is a traitor's 'long hand' that is in this, not that of a god," Nammeios began, tempering the crowd's hostility with sarcasm. "And the dagger hand of Orgetorix will eventually reach Dumnorix and Casticos, just as it tried to reach your *vergobret*."

"His trial will be at dawn," Marcios added. "Now, just as the fire becomes ashes, our words are ended."

Both men turned to enter the lodge. After the door closed, Orgetorix's followers continued to shout protests at his arrest. Shoving matches broke out among opposing factions.

Cimbris pulled me away. "We will sleep outside the gate. Guest lodges are full and there will be drinking...."

He did not need to finish the thought. At Arialbinnum I had seen an argument over a portion of banquet meat end in the death of one of the brawlers.

As we pushed through the crowd, pulling the packhorse along toward the gate where our mounts were tethered, bright red poppy flowers began to appear, pinned on tunics, belts, or sword sheaths. A young, beardless warrior tried to force a blossom into Cimbris's cloak brooch, but the guide shoved his hand away with his good arm. When we found our horses, Cimbris clinked coins into the boys' palms, then led the way to the edge of the camp area. While looking for a suitable place to place our fur bedding, he hailed a man he recognized, sitting at a fire with others. Most of them wore a poppy.

"Trevos. I didn't know you were in Orgetorix's debt. How did you come under obligation?"

"Not I." Trevos pointed to another man sucking marrow from a split beef bone.

"My sister's husband rents cattle from a client of Orgetorix. He was told that if he didn't show support, the *fehu*, the rent, would be doubled."

Marrow sucker, probably hoping for additional backing, motioned for us to sit with him as friends of Trevos. Cimbris introduced me around a circle of suspicious faces, but the group relaxed after they found out I was a crafter and chieftain's son.

The talk turned to Casticos, the Sequani over-chief. A freckled herdsman, with hair as fire-bright as the coals he poked, spoke up.

"His father was friendly with the Shorthairs, but Casticos won't sleep with them once the alliance between Orgetorix and Dumnorix is sealed. They may have to defend Roma again, just as in the time of Brennos."

After the laughter and grunts of approval ended, a toothless farmer thin as a wheel spoke spat into the fire. "As a Sequani, I fought against Dumnorix's Aedui a half-twenty of years ago. A skunk keeps his smell. He will try to control us again."

A blond Sequani warrior disagreed. "The Shorthairs had a treaty with the Aedui, yet they didn't help them when they attacked us. It's Ariovistos and his Germani we shouldn't trust."

"You speak truth," a bushy-bearded giant, wearing two poppies, agreed. "Orgetorix only wants to strengthen our tribes against this common enemy."

"Marcios is the lawful *vergobret* of the Helvetii," the toothless farmer objected. "I wear a poppy because I rent Dumnorix's land, but he tried to take power through a conspiracy. This is a matter for druids to decide."

"Men of the Oak travel through the land as they wish," a man without a poppy scoffed. "If they were as restricted as we Helvetii are, druids would quickly find the omens favorable for our move."

The blond Sequani took up the cue. "Helvete, I saw the smoke from your burning farms and villages. Will you also destroy Aventia along with them?"

The man's blue eyes, brownish in the firelight, glinted defiance. "After we migrate, we'll have no need of what is here. Should we leave our villages for Germani to occupy?"

I realized he had confirmed rumors about a Helvetii move. After red-hair tossed his stick in the fire, it blazed up along its length. The men became silent, trying to read their future in the gyrating flames. Some spread furs and wool cloaks on the damp ground and lay down to sleep.

Belenos had long disappeared on the other side of a mountain that backed the lake. Behind the tent encampment a sliver of new moon stood above the darkened eastern crests. The crescent was outshone by the brightness of the dusk star and its near twin, which Lucius said was named Jupiter. Cimbris told the men who were awake that I had bronze and iron pans to sell. I let him bargain for me and he soon handed me a pouch of coins. I offered him part of them, but he said he already had been paid. Too tired to argue, I lay down wrapped in our furs,with the pouch clutched to my chest.

When a guard opened the door to a room in the common lodge and admitted a man, Orgetorix looked up from the corner where he sat, brooding. Hearth-fire flames gave enough light to see that the visitor wore the long tunic of a druid. Without standing, the nobleman asked, "Who are you, Man of the Oak?"

"I am called Ollam-Fodla."

Orgetorix shrugged ignorance of him. "Your purpose here?"

Fodla came closer and held up a clay tile inscribed with the name Verucloetios. "It is because of this man that I speak with you, but I come from Casticos of the Sequani."

Orgetorix squinted more closely at the gaunt druid dressed in spectral black. He seemed to have come from the Other-world, yet perhaps Casticos had sent more substantial warriors with him. "Affairs have not gone as I hoped," he admitted. "My *vassos* are here in support of me, but Marcios was not intimidated and convened my trial. What has Casticos to say?"

Fodla moved into the circle of firelight. "He has men here among your followers. They will help you escape to avoid the trial and your possible execution."

"Go on, druid."

"There would be one condition "

"Condition!" Orgetorix stood so quickly that he overturned his stool. "Casticos dares bargain with me, as he would with a horse trader?"

"Would it not be wise for a snared wolf to bargain with its captor?" Orgetorix did not reply, so Fodla explained, "He asks only that your Helvetii be diverted to attack Ariovistos."

"Ariovistos? Impossible! His warriors are well to the north of our route."

Orgetorix set the stool up with a foot. "Druid, Casticos need not concern himself about Germani. They soon enough will find their way into vacant Helvetii lands."

"Or they will send more of their kind flooding across the Renos. Even now Harudes and other tribes prepare to cross while the river is low."

"Bake-oven rumors, druid."

"I have spoken with Dumnorix of the Aedui. With Ariovistos destroyed, you and your tribe might remain in the lands he had captured. The road through Gallia to the Western Sea is long and dangerous."

Orgetorix showed interest in the proposal. "We would remain on Sequani lands?"

"Is not a herder in debt to those who save his sheep from the wolf?" Fodla's mouth creased into a smirk. "More to the point, are not rescuers of greater strength than the rescued?"

A knowing smile tugged at Orgetorix's lips. *This dark-eyed druid is clever if he is behind this. With the Germani beaten, Casticos can have only feeble objections* to another Celtic tribe occupying land that he had already lost. *Perhaps we need not travel far to the west. A coalition of Helvetii, Aeduii, and Sequanii could more firmly move against a tribe like the Arverni, who might challenge our scheme for ruling Gallia.* "Fodla, what is your plan?"

"At the dawn change of guards a straw roof above this room will be torn away. Casticos's men will stage a diversion. Wagons will be waiting to take you to safety on *Benn Giblix*."

Orgetorix nodded—any action was preferable to a humiliating trial. "Tell Verucloetios, thus it will be."

Bowing, Ollam-Fodla left the room and nodded to the door guard. Once outside, the druid siddled along the edge of the unruly crowd until he reached the lodge of Verucloetios. The waiting Helvete nobleman admitted him in.

"Orgetorix agrees!" Fodla's nasal voice sounded triumphant. "He will flee in the wagon."

"Suspecting nothing?"

"He went for the bait like a trout to water dragons. By mid-sun tomorrow, Orgetorix will lie dead in the caves of *Giblix*. There will be no trial, no dissenters to delay preparations for your migration. His own men will announce his 'suicide' as an honorable act."

Verucloetios poured out two cups of wine and handed one to Fodla. "Once we control the Arverni, we can deal with Ariovistos. You know your duty in this?"

"To recruit any clans of the Raurici that say they will not join Marcios in the migration."

The nobleman sipped wine while looking at Fodla over the rim of the cup. "Druid, this Alberix you mentioned?"

"Young, but the son of a Raurici clan chief. I will use his father's name as an incentive. More important, I control Liscos, the chieftain of a border Sequani village where your Helvetii can assemble."

"Wermaros?" At the druid's nod, Verucloetios said, "Romani are there."

Fodla scoffed, "An insignificant garrison easily dealt with if need be."

"Then we have only to await the rising of Belenos." Verucloetios took back Fodla's cup as an indication that the meeting ended. "Druid, once joined with Dumnorix's Aedui, we can drop the pretext of migration and force the Arverni into a treaty. By the end of next planting season, we will control half of Gallia!" He grasped Fodla's arm. "Your help will not be forgotten...'Arch-druid'!"

Shouts and the sound of approaching horses and rattling wagons abruptly awakened me. For a scalp-tightening instant the sounds reminded me of the raid on father's village. I pushed my fur covers aside and bolted up. A flush of pale light on the eastern horizon mophosed into a brightening band, transforming the landscape into a black silhouette. The hour was near dawn.

Shouted warnings became distinct. "Fire! A blaze takes hold in the town."

I looked toward Aventia. The side furthest from the gate displayed a pale orange glow where bits of flaming straw spiraled skyward in a slight pre-dawn breeze. Warriors stumbled out of their tents to gawk, or run toward the town's open gate. When Cimbris joined me in watching, I asked him how I could help. Before he could answer, three wagons, escorted by a cluster of horsemen clattered out through the gate. I distinctly saw a red poppy on each man's tunic.

As the group passed us heading south, Cimbris remarked, "I'd wager my best hunting bow that Orgetorix is in one of those wagons."

A short distance off, at a fork where the main road divided two smaller ones, each wagon took a different route. Caught by surprise, any Helvetii loyal to Marcios's faction, who pursued the wagons, would be unsure about which one harbored the fugitive.

I asked, "If that was Orgetorix escaping, what will happen now?"

"With their man in exile, his supporters will go home until he sends them new instructions. Before that, Marcios's advisors will ratify his migration plan." Cimbris looked at me. "Next Middle Spring would be a good time for the Helvetii to start."

I felt good when I returned to Wermaros. I had been successful in selling our craft-work and confirming Helvetii intentions. I decided to no longer shave off the fuzzy growth on my face and grow a man's beard. Well, at least to try.

When Liscos came to hear about my mission, his breath smelled of wine. His red eyes had a bleary look. He seemed puzzled at hearing of the conspiracy and escape of Orgetorix, repeating what I told him. "He wanted his Helvetii with th' Aeduii and Casticos, to be over-chiefs in Gallia? Fodla tells me that th' Romani want t' make Sequani lands another of their provinces. Th' towers are a ruse. A first sword thrust."

Surprised, Cluvios asked, "You spoke to the druid? Where is Fodla?" When Liscos looked away, he warned, "Ariovistos, not Romani, should concern your Sequani. The Suebi king has a stranglehold on your northern lands."

"Fodla knows that," Liscos muttered defensively. "He's going t' lead warriors against th' Germani."

"*Warriors*," I scoffed. "The druidesses and his three entertainers?"

Before Liscos could react to my rebuff, Cluvios added, "Indeed, it would be better to have the druid's recruits help strengthen your mountain gate against another attack."

Stung by this reminder of the Suebi raid, Liscos stalked off. I imagined he would drink more and continue brooding about who were his real enemies. Cluvios shook his head. "Both wine and the dark druid are corrupting his mind."

An unrelenting bout of coughing wracked Uncle's body. Concerned, I asked him if we couldn't shut down the forge for a while.

"I will, Alberix, when Dividiac comes to instruct you. He's late and never came during his moon phase."

In jest, I predicted, "Uncle has found the enchanted cave he's been searching for!"

Chapter XIII

My words about a magic cave were to come true, yet Dividiac had not returned for me by his moon phase. Although worried, I continued working with Cluvios.

Four days before the new moon of Edrin, the month Lucius called September, Dividiac came back to the village. Cluvios and I were outside at the forge, but the druid dismounted and hurried into our lodge, agitated, without a word to us. He came out almost at once and shouted to Cluvios.

"The boy is to come with me! The matter cannot wait!"

Uncle's face was gaunt, dirty, his drooping mustache blending into facial hair that he usually kept clean-shaven. The same woolen tunic and cloak he wore when he left were soiled and matted with leaves and twigs, as if he had been sleeping on the ground.

"Calm yourself," Cluvios soothed, no doubt alarmed as I was on seeing Dividiac so restless. "It is not yet your time of the moon and we have an agreement. I need Alberix here. The Romani have commissioned ironwork for their towers."

Wild-eyed, he predicted, "The Shorthairs will soon have more than towers in Gallia. I tell you, the boy must come with me now!"

Cluvios muttered to me, "Perhaps I should humor him. By morning he will calm down. As you wish, Dividiac," he called out, "but the last day watch is beginning. Leave after dawn."

"We go immediately!" the old druid insisted. "Alberix, I spoke to Briga. She prepares a food pouch. Bring your mare to the river gate with that oil lamp the Romani gave you. Bring extra oil."

Before I could question him, Uncle hurried back inside. I was in Derka's stall when Mother came in carrying a leather bag and pelts. She looked worried. "Dividiac told you where we're going?"

Briga shook her head. "Not even where he's been and his mind is elsewhere. I don't know what good or evil spirits he found in that forest, but he insists on returning with you." Mother handed me the pouch and two bear-fur coverings. "Here is food and warmth." When she brushed at smudges on my face, I saw tears welling in her eyes. "Alberix...see that no harm comes to your uncle."

"I will, Mother."

"Then take Derka out. I don't want Dividiac more upset than he is."

As I removed my leather apron, she kissed my cheek. At the forge, Cluvios grasped my hand, then turned away, caught up in a racking cough. Dividiac came out of the lodge, clutching a cloth-wrapped box that he put in his saddlebag. He mounted the animal and turned it toward the river gate without a word of farewell to Briga or Cluvios. I placed a bridle on Derka as quickly as I could, put Mother's food and the lamp in my saddlebag, and followed Dividiac. I caught up with Uncle beyond the bridge and rode behind him along a road that followed the meandering right bank of the Dubis—the route that Liscos's trade caravans took to reach Vesontio.

Belenos arced down in front of us in a bright glare of light. I still took a record of his risings and knew that the god had almost returned to his position at the spring equinox. It was several days before the autumnal balancing of night and day hours, and the late afternoon was cool. Brilliant red and yellow leaves already tinged some of the maple trees, wiping splashes of brightness across a blue-green forest, spreading up the slopes. These, and the rust-brown color of scrub oak, reflected in the river's black water.

Dividiac rode ahead without looking back at me, or halting until early evening. The sky reflected a red flush on the surface of a pond formed by a beaver dam in a backwater of the river. When he raised his hand in a signal to stop, I estimated that Wermaros was about two of Lucius's hours behind us.

After I came alongside, Dividiac said, "We stop by this water for the night. Let the horses drink."

He trotted his mount into trees at the roadside and dismounted. I led Derka and his horse to the water, but impatient, Uncle came to pull his animal away and up toward a limestone ridge a short distance off. After we reached a shallow cavern formed by the overhanging rock, I noticed the white ashes of a recent campfire. A small stack of dead wood was nearby. Looking back toward the pond, a rosy glimmer shone on its calm surface, where rings spread from the sweep of insects flitting into the ruddy mirror. The dull sound of a splash betrayed a trout breaking the surface to catch one.

"Tether the horses, boy," Uncle ordered, "then build a fire with that wood."

He sounded more tired, yet less upset. While I struck sparks into moss and pine-twig kindling, he rummaged through my saddlebag and brought out the smoked meat and bread Mother had packed.

Dividiac crouched by the nascent flames and ate in silence. In the cool forest dusk, emerging insects began shrill chirping harmonies. Some stung us after a determined flight to reach our skin. It was not until it was dark enough for Uncle's face to reflect the glow of firelight that he spoke again. His voice was hoarse.

"Alberix, I...I have found a way into the womb of the Earth Mother, the entrance of which hunters speak."

Hunters? Dividiac has been gone for over a month, searching out the caves he spoke of on the day we gathered plants. Now he's found a cavern?

"Their tales were true," Uncle said. "Only in the lands of the Cadurci have I heard of such grottos. They tell of caves-with-animal-pictures, where a sorcerer changed living creatures into images on stone walls."

Skeptical, I asked, "Uncle, how can that be?"

Not hearing me, Dividiac raved that it happened so long ago that the reason was forgotten, then stared at the flames as if he were inside this grotto and saw the animal pictures in the flickering shapes. His eyes reflected the dancing orange light and gleamed with a frightening vacancy. "Here," he rasped, "I believe, we are at one of the entrances to the Other-world, where beings are frozen in stone between birth and death. Alberix"—he grasped my arm in a tight grip—"the secrets of Cernunnos are close at hand!"

I shivered despite the fire's warmth, recalling the antlered apparition at Beltaine. The shadowy figure had seemed to move between the Two Worlds before the harper's music brought the terrorized villagers back to the Now-world. To temper Uncle's irrational fervor I quietly asked, "How did you find the cave?"

"I prayed to Arduinna, boy, and slept in her forest for many nights. The shape-shifters came, as in a dream."

"How do you know it *wasn't* a dream, Uncle?"

He ignored my question. "First I became hawk, soaring over the land to search for the cave, then deer, looking for the entrance on the ground. Arduinna led me here. I found the entrance and became fox...yes, one night I was fox and entered the opening. I smelled the cold vapors coming from the Mother's womb and crept in."

The intensity of his vision fed my curiosity. "When will we go inside the cavern?"

"In the morning..." Dividiac looked away from the fire and at me. "We will enter at dawn. I am too tired now. My...my head aches."

Uncle's fatigue had broken the spell of his shape-shifting. I helped him roll up in his cloak and one of the furs Mother had given me. He looked small and fragile when he poked a hand out of the covering and motioned me closer to whisper, "We are not far from the grotto. Perhaps Arduinna will favor my pupil. Shape-shift you into a fox to sniff out the entrance and...and...." He turned his back to the fire's warmth.

I stacked more wood on the blaze and lay under my fur. Uncle had begun to teach me how to concentrate on freeing the spirit from my body and merge into the shape of another creature, but I was exhausted and quickly fell into a sound asleep.

During the night, no animal came to give life to my imagining. I awoke shivering. The fire was out, its gray ashes blending with an eerie, vaporous mist that pervaded the woods. In a stillness broken only by the hesitant twitter of awakening birds, I clearly heard the gurgle of the Dubis flowing over the beaver dam and entering the pond. When something rustled the leaves beyond the huddled form of Dividiac, I looked up to see a reddish shape resolve itself into the body of a fox. The animal's wary eyes watched me a moment. Its graceful snout tested the air, then it trotted into the forest.

The instant the fox disappeared, Dividiac awoke. Had Uncle shape-shifted into the animal for the night and returned to the Now-world? His all-too-human groans answered my question. He had not.

"My body hardens like winter ice," Dividiac complained, struggling upright. "It will be up to you, Alberix, to carry my teachings out to the clans as a Man of the Oak—"

"Uncle," I broke in, "I'll get the fire started again." I avoided another argument about my future.

"No!" he screamed. "We must enter the Mother before wood gatherers come upon us and discover the cave. Bring your lamp."

We found the horses nibbling at dew-soaked forest growths. When I took out the lamp and oil jug, Dividiac removed the box he had brought from our lodge. I noticed that it had a strong cedar oil aroma and seemed heavier than its small size would warrant. He tied his talisman bag onto his tunic belt and cradled the box with one arm.

The grotto was further away than Uncle had implied, up a steep ridge and along a faint trail that was marked by newly trampled forest growths. A thick stand of beech and juniper trees screened the cave's entrance, as if the Mother had sought to hide her virginal opening with the most simple of means. It would take a small animal like a fox to penetrate the underbrush and discover the cave.

Dividiac pushed his way through the tangled growths. Even before I saw the opening, a flow of cool, dank-smelling air betrayed the entrance to me. Uncle squeezed through and I followed him in. A mound of mossy tinder and a few pine-pitch torches lay nearby. "Is your lamp ready?" he whispered in a husky voice that faintly echoed along in the passage.

"I need to put in oil."

I loosened the jug's beeswax seal and filled the lamp through its center hole. Uncle struck sparks into the moss. The dry plant smoked until a small flame sprang up. While I lighted the oil-soaked wick, Uncle pushed two of the torches into the blaze, watched them flare up, and handed me one. I stamped out the kindling. Dividiac held his torch low to light the uneven ground and led the way through a narrow passageway. Without looking back, he said, "Just ahead is a temple to the Mother the size of which even Romani cannot have built in their capital."

My lamp and torch illuminated a low ceiling and rough walls glistening with moisture. The cold air smelled of decay—as if animals had entered and died because they could not find the entrance again. After a twenty of paces, the narrow tunnel abruptly opened up into an immense domed chamber. The area was so high that our torch and lamplight could not fully reveal its ceiling, but their orange flames reflected off cascades of water and icicles on the sides that had frozen into stone. Ripples of wetness slid down other fantastic formations, which I could not have imagined before. I could only relate the shapes to ones that Renos River ice took on whenever cold froze the tumbled blocks together.

Dividiac marveled, "To the top of this room alone is as high as the Romani towers!" He took my torch and wedged it upright with his between two pillars. "Put your lamp on this ledge. We will offer a prayer to the Mother."

Stunned at the overwhelming sight, I barely heard Uncle's order. Sheets of the stone ice-forms hung from the gloom above my head, or rose up from the floor in twisted, misshapen towers. At one corner, the flickering torchlight revealed a massive shape encrusted in liquid stone that had congealed in such a way that it resembled the head and body of some gigantic creature imbedded in the earth.

"We are in the womb of the Mother, the source of all life and truth, the primal origin of the Now-world." Dividiac began an incantation whose distorted words slid around the walls and returned to him. He paused to whisper, " Alberix, there are passageways I have not entered. They may lead to the Land of the Eternally Young."

I could believe anything about this fanciful inner grotto. Uncle resumed his chant, coaxing words about eternal secrets that he accepted as real. A lifetime of memorized information raced in converging streamlets though his mind, like the passages that branched off from this chamber. In the dim light, his head seemed to glow and his white robe shimmered with a radiance that resembled the curtains of pulsing color I had seen in northern skies.

Caught up in the repetitious phrases, the normal time periods of day and night seemed suspended in a liquid gloom; only the flickering light served as a spiderweb-thin contact with the world outside. Beads of clammy sweat broke out on my face as a penetrating fear replaced my initial awe. If the flames went out, there would be only darkness, nothing to distinguish time and place, up or down, even less than in the black void of night, where at least familiar stars gave orientation to the black expanse.

Shivering from the chill air and my unsettling thoughts, I suddenly realized Dividiac was speaking to me. When I looked at him, his eyes hosted a vacant gleam and his face had contorted into a demonic mask. Was it the play of light on his features?

"Son of Alrix, there is a reason I have brought you here."

Son of Alrix? Uncle rarely called me that. What was his purpose? Before I could ask him, Dividiac's voice boomed out a name, and echoes flung it back to us from the sculpted walls until it was too faint to hear.

"D-A-N-A-C-H...D-a-n-a-c-h...danach...."

Silence. A spark glimmered in the darkness above us. Two lamps slowly flickered into a smooth flame in the windless air, to light up the features of the dark-eyed druid who had been Dividiac's pupil. My neck skin rippled in dread. I barely heard the babble of Uncle's explanation.

"Danach has returned with news that will affect the Sequani and all Gallia itself."

Danach? I didn't understand Dividiac's connection with the druid—I thought he detested the former pupil who deserted him. Fodla'a voice increased my puzzlement.

"Enough, Dividiac! Attend to your relic and I will speak to the boy." The dark druid's command to Uncle was chill as air in the cavern, yet his tone turned persuasive in speaking to me. "Boy, come nearer. Bring your lamp."

Ollam Fodla had seated himself cross-legged between two upright towers, as if on an unearthly throne. After I came closer, I saw that a row of niches beneath him held human skulls. In the feeble light, they seemed to grin in mute amusement at my fear.

"I call you 'boy'," Fodla continued, "but you are a young warrior. Your uncle and I have come to an agreement. Whatever our differences the danger to us as druid priests is of greater concern." Dressed in his black tunic, Fodla had seemingly dissolved. Not a glint of light reflected from his eyes. Only a disembodied voice spoke from the gloom. "The challenge by our common enemy must be met with force."

I asked, "What common enemy? Romani?"

"I am not yet concerned with them. I speak of Ariovistos and his Suebi."

I felt more confident in talking about something I knew. "Ariovistos is in Sequani lands—"

"True," Fodla agreed, "and he has allowed the Germanic Harude tribe to settle alongside his Suebi and the Sugumbri."

Dividiac screamed from behind me, "To invite Harudes is the final insult! They killed your father, Alberix. You must avenge his death!"

The outburst startled Fodla. "Enough, old man!"

Dividiac ignored him and grasped my tunic sleeve. "Alberix, you are the son of a warrior, a clan chief. I will train you in the wisdom of the Men of the Oak. You will be a warrior-druid, leading our people." Spittle flew against my face as Uncle ranted on, "Lead them against the Germani...the Harudes who killed your father. Through you, the gods will place them in our hands. Teutates...Caturix—"

"Uncle..." I touched his arm to calm his babbling.

Dividiac shook my hand off. "Vengeance, Alberix, vengeance! As the son of Alrix you must lead our clan... our tribe...to destroy Germani." Dividiac's voice lapsed into an exhausted whisper. "My magic will help you. My talismans...."

I was sure Uncle was beyond reasoning. "I'm not a warrior. Besides, Father wanted this cycle of hatred to end."

Ignoring my protests, Dividiac bent down and opened the box he had brought. The smell of cedar oil and decay were powerful, as he groped inside and pulled out an oval shape. When he held it up, drops of pungent oil stained both our tunics.

"Swear vengeance!" Dividiac shrieked, dangling the object in front of my face. "Swear, Alberix, by your father's head that you will destroy the Germani!"

I watched as the oval in Dividiac's hand became recognizable. Glistening with the aromatic oil, the sallow face of Alrix my father swung before me in a gruesome pendulum. The hyalescent eyes were turned upwards. His teeth gleamed in an unlikely grin beneath damp strands of blond mustache.

I almost dropped my lamp in backing away from the horrifying talismen. Dividiac stared at the head for a moment. Now that he revealed his awful secret, he dropped the relic and sagged to the floor. As my father's head rolled beyond the dim circle of light, anger replaced my revulsion.

"You're both insane," I shouted, "and shape-shifted into evil. Alrix put down his sword, knowing that in war only the *Babd* claims victory. He put our clan mark on treaties with the Germani...to end this cycle of blood...." I finally choked. Despite its vast size, the gloomy chamber now felt oppressive... the smell of cedar oil nauseating. I lost my sense of direction, then recalled the passageway through which we had entered.

"Uncle, I'm getting you away from here," I said, but he only looked at me with uncomprehending eyes. One side of his face and his mouth were stiff. He tried to speak, but I only heard chilling, guttural sounds. I took my lamp in one hand and started to pull Dividiac away with the other, when I heard the high-pitched voice of Fodla scream out.

"Boccus, stop him!"

The echo of the druid's command still resounded in my ears, when a shadowy stone formation moved on my right. The Mauritanian rose to block my escape and was in front of me. His huge hands lunged for my throat. Desperate, I dropped Dividiac's arm and flung my lamp at the bulky shadow. A rivulet of flame spattered on the African's face and trickled down his bare chest. Blinded, he bellowed in pain and wiped at his face with fingers that only spread the fiery coating.

Circling around him, I slipped on the wet limestone floor, recovered, and groped my way in the dark to where I thought the entrance might be. Scraping my knees and shoulders against the stone floor and walls of the narrow passage, I crawled in the dank blackness, sniffing fox-like, to pick up a scent of clean outside air.

The commotion had aroused a colony of bats clustered at the grotto entrance. Now, black night creatures fluttered in frantic dartings above my head. In abruptly standing to push away the frenzied horde, I grazed my head against the rough ceiling.

Rivulets of perspiration and blood half-blinded my vision. The bawls of the Mauritanian gradually faded into the distance. I worried about Dividiac, yet I would not have lived had I stayed with him. Although only evil in uncle's mind could have persuaded him to join his former pupil, I was sure that Fodla needed him. The druid would make sure that the old man safely left the cave.

I finally glimpsed a sliver of gray light that marked the cave's opening. I squeezed out to a drenching rain pouring down outside. With bats still circling the entrance in high-pitched chatterings, I slid down the ridge's indistinct trail. Blood trickled from my head wound into my mouth as I reached Derka. My fingers trembled when I struggled to loosen the animal's wet leather strap. Mounting, I galloped the mare past the pond as fast as I dared and back along the river road to Wermaros.

I was grateful that the first autumn rain misted the mountains in low clouds. The opaque veil curtained the terror I had left behind in the grotto, and the pungent pine smell of the wet forest eased me back to the familiar limits of the Now-world.

I knew I couldn't tell Cluvios or Mother about Dividiac's relic, but, strangely, I wanted to confide in Lucius about the horror I had seen.

Chapter XIV

As Derka's hooves splashed through puddles on the rutted roadway back to the village, I rose in the saddle with my face full to the wet wind, letting this clean force of the Mother drench away the dankness of the cave and the horror of seeing my father's severed head. I smelled the cedar oil that spotted my shirt, and felt the fear that had gripped me when the hulking form of Boccus arose from the cavern floor.

I desperately wanted to see Lucius, but had never gone to *Castor,* the tower closest to the village, from this direction. I knew it was located on the mountainside above this road. Watching for a way that might lead up to the structure, I eventually spotted a wide path leading into the forest. Turning Derka up the muddy trail at the same reckless pace, my mare's hooves scattered small frogs that ventured out from the rain-soaked woods. Here, among the wet trees, the air had a fishy scent that mingled with an acrid odor of rotting leaves and the sharp smell of wet pine needles.

After the trail leveled off, I reined Derka back, then impulsively pulled off my woolen shirt, threw it into dead weeds alongside the trail, and rode bare-chested in the forest's chill. I knew I was nearing the tower as soon as I caught a whiff of wood smoke in the layered strands of fog among the trees. Reining Derka a short distance into a clearing of charred stumps where Taranis's sky-fire had once touched the trees, I dismounted and stripped off my trousers. With only my silver neck torc gleaming above my chest, I stood naked to the rain, letting the cold drops wash down the cuts on my forehead and arms, and with them—I hoped—the memory of what I had seen in the grotto.

When my shaking became unbearable, I huddled against Derka's warm flanks. At Wermaros, the mare had been my gift from Liscos, when the chieftain tried to convince Cluvios to set up a forge. I had trained the mare. At my command she lay down, un-comprehending, yet obedient. After unstrapping my blanket from the saddle, I spread the covering over myself and clung to the animal's heaving sides to warm my body. Dividiac said that horses were the gift of the goddess Epona, who had brought them to Celtic tribes from unending grasslands far to the east, where Belenos rose. I had seen a statue of Epona at Arialbinnum, a short, wide-eyed, woman who held a bird and rode sidesaddle.

Gradually, my shivering under the shelter lessened: Derka's heat flowed into my body until it seemed that the animal's own energy merged with mine and restored my exhausted spirit. In the enveloping warmth, I closed my eyes.

The dream came a moment after I fell asleep.

A she-fox and her pups were by a stream, wanting to cross, yet the vixen only trotted nervously up and down the bank. The tree trunk used as a bridge had rotted and fallen into the water, but the she-fox easily could have swum the span, even with a pup held in her mouth by the scruff of its neck. The vixen's true anxiety was that a row of poisonous serpents, coiled and ready to strike, guarded the far bank.

The sound of yelping hounds came closer. Frantically, the she-fox nuzzled her pups away from the stream and towards the flimsy cover of nearby bushes. The hindmost pup was not quick enough and dogs tore it to bits. Despite the vixen's efforts to herd her pups into the scanty protection, all were destroyed. She herself was left torn and bleeding before the hounds were called back by the distant blare of a horn... .

A low grunting and the whinny of my mare awoke me from the disturbing dream. Derka bolted upright, throwing me roughly to one side. From the ground where I had rolled, I looked directly into the narrow, red eyes of a boar that stood five paces away. Attracted by the refuse of the tower garrison, the beast sniffed the air in search of food, even as it confronted the now-familiar scents of horse and man.

Derka pawed the ground, her head lowered. I lay still, naked and weaponless. Not even a fallen branch was nearby, but a bloody image of the fox pups was vivid in my mind. Boars are unpredictable; I spoke soft words of reassurance to Derka, hoping that her presence would discourage any attack by the beast. I was right. Not scenting food, the boar gave a final snort and trotted back into the wet underbrush, poking at my cast-off trousers as it went.

My body shook from relief as I prayed. *Thanks to Moccus the boar god, and Arduinna of the forest, that it was not an enemy in a shape-shift, trying to ambush me.* As I calmed Derka, I was annoyed with myself for thinking that the boar might have come from the Other-world. *Isn't anything ever as it seems, only an animal, a thunderstorm...the diseased liver of a sick calf? Must all things be as druids tell us, supernatural beings hidden in the many forms of the Now-world?*

I wrapped the blanket around myself, remounted Derka, and continued along the trail to the watchtower. When the gray, stone shape appeared above the treetops, I felt relieved. I could speak to Lucius without fear of antagonizing either one of my uncles.

On one side of the tower the garrison's tents were pitched in orderly rows behind a ditch-and-palisade defense. I had been in a tent once, but not the tower, and recalled from the model that its entrance would be set high on one wall. I rode around until I found a wooden door in the stonework. After I threw a few rocks at the portal, it was partly opened.

"I want to see Lucius," I called up to a ruddy, dark-bearded man who peered down at me.

"The *centurio*'s not here."

"I'm Alberix, his friend. I'll come in and wait for him."

The legionary grunted, turned away, and shouted for a companion to help lower a ladder down to me. I tied Derka to one of the iron wall rings we had forged in our shop, and climbed the rungs. As I stepped through the doorway, the men inside noticed my bare legs under the blanket.

"Who got your *brachae?*" one grinning legionary taunted.

I didn't think the comment about my missing trousers funny. "Where *is* Lucius?"

He winked at his companion. "Probably in the village visiting that copper-haired Gauless. What 'doe' you been chasing'?"

I ignored both comments and controlled my anger at the reference to Mother. "When is Lucius coming back?"

"Ask Marcellus"–the legionary jerked his thumb toward a man sitting by a fire pit in the room's center, whittling on a block of wood–"He's 'centurio-for-the-day.'"

Having overheard, Marcellus looked up. "Lucius is at *Pollux* tower...should be back in time for the third watch." With the block he indicated an iron cauldron hanging over the fire's coals. "You're his friend aren't you? Help yourself to venison stew."

I shook my head in refusal and went to sit away from the men and look around. A puppy ran over to play with me, but was whistled back by a man holding a pet ferret he had let out of its wicker cage. Marius had described this barracks room, quarters for the garrison. I counted sixteen rectangular shields hanging on the walls, each decorated with painted eagle wings and four of Taranis's sky-fire bolts. A wooden rack held long spears, half of whose length was a slim iron shaft tipped with a triangular point. Metal shirts like the ones the Romani had worn on arriving at Wermaros were draped over kegs. Helmets lay on top.

The odor of fresh wood was tempered by cook-fire smoke and a savory smell of onions and stewing meat coming from the cauldron's steam. By the dim light of the fire, and two windows set high on opposite walls, I saw some of the men building wooden bunks for their straw mattresses. Near the ferret owner, others played a game with small bones. Others waterproofed their boots with goose fat. The men were mostly dark-haired and shorter than Celts, but well muscled. I had no doubt that these "legionaries," as Lucius called Romani warriors, were effective fighters.

I dozed, when the sound of the ladder being dropped out the door startled me awake. Lucius stepped off the top rung with Marius, evidently discussing the equinox marker that Dividiac wanted built.

"...So we must at least get started before winter snows. A foundation, if nothing else. Get the druid's sketches for where he wants it..." Seeing me stand, clothed only in a blanket, Lucius exclaimed, "Alberix! What happened to you? Briga told me you left yesterday with Dividiac, and didn't know where you'd gone."

"Lucius, can I talk privately with you?"

"Of course, come to my quarters. *Optio*," he told Marius, "later on Alberix can give you his drawings for the exact marker location."

Marius nodded in recognition and went to the cauldron for a helping of stew.

Lucius slipped off his damp cloak and ordered Marcellus to bring me dry clothing, along with two bowls of the stew and bread, then led the way to a wicker-walled room furnished with a cot, table, clothes chest, and folding stool. Inside, he grasped my shoulder. "Sit down and tell me where you've been! You look as if you've come from the realm of Hades."

"If that's your Other-world, I may have."

"Make sense, son."

I told him about Dividiac's obsession with finding an opening into the Earth Mother, the fantastic cavern we had entered, then the confrontation with Ollam Fodla and his African disciple. The hardest part to relate was the moment Dividiac brought out what he had kept in the chest. An expression of shock and disgust shadowed Lucius's face. When Marcellus came in with the clothing and food, I paused to put on a loincloth under a pair of the plain woolen trousers the legionaries wore, and a heavy tunic shirt.

"Now eat something," Lucius said quietly. "What you told me is truly horrifying, but not that surprising."

"How so?" I asked.

"We've destroyed druid shrines in the Narbonensis that displayed skulls and human heads. Alberix, your people have a fascination with them. From what I saw in Hispania, Celts are about as civilized...if that's the correct word...as we Romans were before the Republic. Your people have only a druid's memory to tell them what are their traditions and laws. Very little is written down."

"We have...*vergobrets*...judges," I objected through a mouthful of stew.

"Your gods tell them what a ruling should be. Look at that botched sacrifice at the parley."

"Don't you Romans have priests?"

Before Lucius could respond, Marcellus looked into the room. "Permission, *Centurio*. Watch sentries are ready for inspection."

"Fine. Come and watch, Alberix."

Four men had lined up, wearing the clothing I had seen lying on the kegs. Each had a short sword at his belt and held one of the spears, but was without a shield. Marcellus called out a memorized checklist of equipment, while Lucius noted the condition of each.

"*Lorica* — shirt armor!"

"*Caligae* — boots!"

"*Cigulum* — belt!"

"*Gladius* — *pilum...gale!*"

The men's swords, spears, and helmets were in as good condition as their other equipment. With a warning jest about staying awake, Lucius dismissed them to their posts atop the tower. After I went back to his room, I said that I wanted to stay at the tower for awhile.

"What? What would you do?" he asked.

"I could repair equipment. Make myself useful."

"Did you tell Briga that?"

"No," I admitted. "Dividiac wants me to take his place as a druid, but I'm confused about some of his teachings, his superstitions "

"We Romans have plenty of those," he said with a wry chuckle.

"I'm even questioning our gods. I need some place to think things out."

Lucius looked at me for moments before saying, "Alberix, I'm not ready to sign you into an auxiliary cohort, but if you stay you'll be subject to military discipline. Some of your villagers work here, so I can't show favoritism."

"I understand."

Lucius indicated the stool. "Sit down again. You're questioning your gods?"

I sat and told him that I had found an old hunter sacrificed to one of them at Beltaine.

"So I heard. Liscos is suppressing the fact, yet the villagers gossip."

"What of the gods, Lucius? Do you think they exist?"

He sopped cold stew from the sides of his bowl with a last crust of bread, then looked up at me. "For some people they're necessary. I'm called a Stoic for what I believe. Our teacher, a Greek named Zeno, lived two hundred years ago and saw the world as a single great community, not lands with many differences, but a place where all the inhabitants are as...as kin. I saw a small example of that on the farm, where everyone and everything were dependent on one another...even our slaves."

I told Lucius he was speaking too rapidly, that I didn't understand all of what he said, then recalled that at the parley he had poured out wine as an offering to a god.

"Tribune's idea, for good fortune. Zeno taught that we're ruled by an all-knowing spirit he called 'Logos.' It's not really a person, more of a concept that is understood depending on your level of intelligence. Terms he used are 'Divine Reason,' 'Universal Spirit,' the cosmic purpose of nature. I don't know if Celtic has a word for it, but Briga told me she believes in an Other-world where everything is beautiful and perfect. We can come close to that in this world by bringing our lives into line with the Logos, and pretty much accepting and making the best of whatever life brings us."

"But you left the farm to become a warrior."

"True, I didn't like the farm and wasn't *always* a stoic."

I pushed my empty bowl away. "Lucius, I'd like to stay and learn to read Latin better, if you have time to teach me."

"Marius likes you, so he'd help. With cold weather coming on we'll be cooped up here like chickens, yet secure. The Helvetii won't move in winter. Informers told us that Orgetorix committed suicide, so that means that his conspiracy is dead too."

"Their over-chief, Marcios, seemed determined to migrate."

"We'll deal with him in the spring. If you stay here, we'll have to work something out with Cluvios and your mother. I'll not go against their wishes and risk more trouble in the village. Not after that incident with Epanactos."

"I only work with Cluvios for half of the month. Couldn't I come here for the other part?"

"We'll see."

I was sure Uncle might agree, but what would Dividiac's reaction be when I saw him again? I felt he was safe because Fodla needed him. The African was another matter, and yet I hoped his burns were not serious.

When I finally fell asleep on a straw mattress, the bloody dreams came back.

Dividiac had not returned when I went back to Wermaros the next day to tell Mother that I was safe. After I decided to tell Cluvios about the incident in the grotto, he was shocked, yet not surprised, and wondered how Dividiac had gotten the "relic," as he called it. All had been confusion the night of the raid, yet Uncle had been in the wagon with us, and Mother had seen Alrix alive before she left in the wagon of Tutios. The incident put aside any doubts about my father's fate. Cluvios insisted that he did not yet want to tell Briga about what I had seen.

That evening I wanted to ask Cluvios about our people's fascination with the human head as a cult object, and walked down to the bridge with him. We watched the leaf-speckled, black water of the Dubis flow underneath us before he explained.

"Druids teach that the spirit of a person can, in some magical way, go on living through their head. To possess such a relic is to control the life force of that person. One of our legends tells of an ancient king, Brenn, who went on directing a battle after his head was hacked off."

I recalled the story from Beltaine. Without asking Cluvios if he thought it was true, I pointed back to the blanched trophies above the gate. "Like those skulls over there?"

He nodded. "Liscos thinks he's been able to absorb his enemies' strength."

"What do you believe, Uncle?"

Cluvios coughed in a spasm that racked his body and spit blood into the black water. The evil had not left him in my absence. After the spell subsided, he replied, "It doesn't much matter what I believe. In the back country there are druids who still hoard skulls for their ceremonies."

"When will you...we...tell Mother about Alrix?"

"There's time for that."

I didn't agree, but Cluvios was head of our family now. His decisions were binding.

❧

Soon after the line of mountains beyond Aventia was chalked in white against gray clouds on the horizon, the snow came to Wermaros. It was only near the end of our autumn month of Fogmair, yet great wet flakes drove in on the winds that crossed Gallia from the western ocean. The snow filled in meadows where a moon earlier cattle had grazed on the toughened grasses. Forest creatures denned themselves underground as Belenos's dull disc appeared further and further south of the dead fir tree, where the Romani had cleared space for Dividiac's equinox marker.

On days when snow clouds scattered and the cold weather turned clear, rays of that distant sun sparkled off frozen facets of spray along the river's edge. Icicles touched the ground from the low eaves of the lodges' thatched roofs, crystal struts that were broken and melted to save women a difficult trip to the river for water. In the common pens, cattle were crowded into narrow stalls they had forgotten while in their highland meadows, yet the sweetness of hay plant fodder cut under the hot sun of Middle Summer succored the discomfort of the close space.

On some days, the wind blew snow on the mountainsides and misted the forests in a swiftly moving white fog. Soot from the charring ovens coated the white drifts with black granules that were layered dark and light, as snowfall followed snowfall. The air of the valley was tinted blue by the perpetual haze of wood smoke. I wondered about Arvos—I barely had seen the charrer in the village since the Beltaine games.

Dividiac's return coincided with the coming of the snow. Uncle had aged terribly, looking as white and fragile as the driving flakes. One side of his face and mouth were tautly stiff. In speaking, he slurred his words. He avoided me and refused to talk to Mother or Cluvios about where he had been. Over his feeble protests, Briga tucked the old man into the furs of his sleeping ledge near the cook fire. She fed him hot broth along with extractions of the herbs she had picked on the day we had gone to the high meadows to find them.

Ollam Fodla appeared at Wermaros a few days later, and went back to the abandoned hut of Acos, the old hunter strangled on the eve of Beltaine. Liscos soon offered the druid a lodge rented by one of his *vassos*, crippled in a fall from a hay wagon, and who owed the chieftain money. After he and his family were evicted into the snowy street, the tenant tried to obtain a judgment in his favor from Dividiac. Uncle refused to see the man.

Dividiac had not brought back the cedarwood box, but I was determined to eventually recover my father's head and give it...give *him*...a chieftain's burial.

Chapter XV

In the coming days Dividiac rallied under Briga's care, but a new obsession in his mind was about the approaching rites of Samain at the end of our month that Lucius called Octobris. On that last day, the eve of our new year, druids performed rituals that let the spirits of the old year pass across the abyss of that final night, and on the first day of Samon to merge a safely with those of this opening year.

In his continuing corcern with the Other-world, Dividiac mumbled to himself, as if speaking to spirits seen only in his fevered mind. I heard one frightening, slurred comment. "This Samain I will look across the abyss and into The Land of the Eternally Young, see the gods there, and return to tell of it. Like a woman playing a game, the Earth Mother tricked me in her cave, yet I will win this one."

One evening Dividiac reminded Cluvios that in the long winters at Arialbinnum he had begun a story each night about ancient Celtic heroes. They helped to pass time until deep snow melted and the outside world was once again accessible. Calling for his notched memory staff, the old druid said he would have Cluvios fill in details that might lie fallow in his imagination. Ill himself, Uncle still agreed to humor the old man.

Dividiac's contorted lips moved with the telling as his mind became one with the events and people in his legends: he was *there*, in the boat with Brenn and his companions, crossing an enchanted sea as they sailed to the Island of Beautiful Women. He *became* Conn of the Hundred Battles, setting out over the horizon in a crystal boat to search for the realm of Cernunnos. He believed himself to be the Archdruid of the Dagda, as his king fought against the encroachment of the Firblogs. In his favorite tale, Dividiac lived with the ancient Tuatha, tribesmen of the goddess Danu, who taught them the magic and sorcery she possessed. He fashioned the all-conquering spear of Lugos, charmed the sword of Nuada into invincibility, guarded the Cauldron of Abundance, and moved in the company of god-artisans—Goban the smith. Diance the healer. Credne the brass-worker. With them as companions, Dividiac convinced himself it would be easy to cross the abyss into a land without age or aging, envy or hatred, sorrow nor arrogance.

As the old druid's fantasies deepened, he insisted on being taken to the summit of *Benn Samain* for the New Year rites. He called it the "Mountain-of-the-Coming-Together," a sacred high place that was close to both earth and sky gods. I had gone there with the guide, Cimbris, yet apart from the difficulty of reaching the height with two sick uncles, I was concerned that Ollam Fodla would be left alone in the village to further influence Liscos into replacing Dividiac as his druid.

Cluvios gave in to the old man's agitated requests and agreed to go. I helped fit our wagon with curved ash-wood struts, and fastened leather coverings over them to keep out poor weather. Mother lined the wagon bed with straw and covered it with furs and feather-stuffed bolsters. Supplies of food and drink were stored in barrels.

I knew the wagon couldn't manage the narrow forest trail that Cimbris and I had taken to Aventia. One of the villagers told us to go up the road that led to the pass above Wermaros, then back down to Boia and south along a road that bordered the Sorna River until it joined with the wider roadway we had taken.

⚘

The weather was clear two mornings before Samain eve—the day of my seventeenth birthday—when I clucked the team of mares through the mountain gate and onto the road we had come down nine months after the Harude raid.

We stayed overnight at a farmstead with a family where Cluvios had done iron-work, then reached the village of Sego on the afternoon before Samain. Cimbris was not at his lodge. A number of pilgrims had arrived in the village and pointed out a road that twisted around several times before reaching the summit of the mountain. We joined an ascending caravan of wagons, carts, or horse riders and arrived at the wind-swept height late that day.

The ochre and green landscape I had seen in late summer now lay under a colorless shroud, a snow-covered monotony that stretched to the distant, equally pale barrier of the White Mountains that Cimbris had called *Benn Vindos*. Threads of blue smoke marked the location of farmsteads below us, but the far-off, a darker dash that was Aventia lay under a smear of black. Only the windblown, metallic surfaces of the three lakes below gave a contrast to the desolate scene.

Wagons from different clans had stopped on the crest, where druids and their followers set up leather tents as shelters. Nearby, sacrificial sheep and calves waited in crude pens built largely from the bones of previous years' victims. Cartloads of kindling and firewood had been brought up the steep road. Now the summit, almost swept clean of snow by the relentless wind, was dotted with cone-shaped wood stacks that would be set alight when darkness fell. Cluvios explained that except for a deep shaft, where worshipers threw offerings down to contact the gods of earth and sky, the mountaintop had no shrines or totems.

Cluvios told me to drive the wagon toward a firewood stack nearest the wooden roof that covered a ritual shaft. As I turned the mares, a hare, disturbed by the unexpected move, darted from under our wagon in erratic leaps, searching for its burrow. The creature scampered in the direction of the animal pens, where a herder—with the sure reflex of experience—smashed its head with his staff. As the hare's blood stained its white fur and a patch of snow underneath, the man received an angry reprimand from a druid: the first killing of Samain was non-ritual and therefore a poor omen.

Posts wreathed with mistletoe had been set up near some of the fuel stacks. While dusk came on, several druid priests fastened human skulls to the tops of the upright supports. In the gloomy light, their open mouths seemed to gape with broken-toothed amusement, as dark eye sockets watched with mute patience for the ceremonies to begin. I looked away to the distance. A flight of ravens flapped in a broken rhythm toward the shore of the lake below to feast on silvery carcasses of fish that waves cast up on the ice-rimmed beach. Overhead, low clouds raced toward the distant mountains, as if to hurry away from the imminent rites.

As soon as a yellowish-gray horizon in the west gave way to darkness, the bellow of a *carnyx* sounded and the wood pyre at the ritual shaft lighted. Rising flames threw out circles of orange light on the rocky ground and hurled sparks dancing on the wind toward Aventia. Shortly after, pinpoints of yellow-orange began to dot the bleakness below. Farmstead families had followed the example on *Benn Samain* and lighted their own new year bonfires.

I backed the wagon nearer the flames so Dividiac could keep warm and look out. After I jumped down to unhitch the mares from their traces, I was surprised to see Ollam Fodla standing under the shaft's pavilion. *How did he get up to the summit before us?* The druid wore a dark tunic decorated with silver skulls. His green cape billowed out in the wind with such force that he seemed on the point of being carried off with the sparks into the void below. The effect was to turn his sallow face into one of the skull-apparitions set on the posts.

Dividiac had not noticed him, but Cluvios whispered to me, "The silver crescent on his head is an arch-druid's *mina*. Fodla has elevated himself to that rank."

"He's holding a decorated shield."

"Yes, to ward off spirits of the dead."

When I turned back to look at Fodla, he was gone. I went to see how Dividiac felt. Mother watched him sit hunched in a chair at the wagon's back, staring at the fire and fingering the silver disc that had determined our future at Bireg. Uncle was oblivious to everything except the blaze and

I wondered what hazy shapes of phantom warriors he saw in the pyramid of flames, what images of legendary gods and heroes his mind conjured up out of the brightness?

On a high place sat Conal in the company of the spirits of the dead, waiting for Cernunnos, waiting to enter the Land of The Living... .

Peredur strolled in the enchanted valley and saw a tree on the riverbank—one half of it blazed in orange fire and the other half had green leaves, smooth, uncharred bark.

The three daughters of Airitegos disguised themselves as she-wolves and slunk out of the cave in search of sheep prey. But Corach sat on top of the cairn and played sweet music until evening came, and he persuaded the wer-women to change back to their human form, whereupon Caolite hurled his spear through all three of them, and cut off their heads....

It was full dark now with the fiery stacks of other bonfires visible on the crest making silhouettes of the druids and spectators. In the darkness, the slabs of tents, the posts and skulls, the shadowy forms of horses, wagons and sacrificial animals all seemed suspended in a black liquid in which there was not an up or down. On the plain below, many points of orange light twinkled into the distance. Some reflected into the lake, others were scattered, glimmering dimly toward the distant foothills of the *Benn Vindos* range. The largest fire glowed on the island in the lake directly in front, but only a patch of blackness marked an ancient village where the sorcerer, Tergwath, had cast his curse.

While I watched, the distant fires below took on shapes. Outlines of animal forms—a horse, a boar, now a deer, shimmered in the connecting orange dots. I had made out a human figure, when I heard Cluvios's raspy voice.

"I was here once for Samain, but forgot how easily the shapes can be seen."

"What do they mean?"

"Each clan is under the protection of an animal or human god that might shape-shift and cause harm. The people hope their god will see the clan totem fires and be pleased at being honored."

I recalled, "Dividiac once told me about the importance of Samain while we were waiting for sunrise. This is the end of the year's old cycle and the beginning of a new one. Tonight marks the edge of the empty space between us and the world of spirits."

"He believes that the normal balance between the two worlds can be upset and the dead may cross over into the Now-world." Cluvios coughed, spit, and pulled a fur cape tighter around his shoulders before continuing. "Our people believe that the passage can be forced by the dead unless druids prevent them by ritual fires and sacrifices. It must be done properly, just as when we pour metal into a mold. We make sure to wrap the hardened clay with bands, heat it, then pour in molten metal at the right moment so the mold will not shatter and the casting be ruined—"

A blare of trumpets followed by the bellowing of cattle and bleating of sheep interrupted Uncle's explanation. The sacrifices had begun. By the circles of flickering firelight, golden blades slashed the beasts' jugulars. Clan members gathered around the druids to watch the slaughter and be ritually sprinkled with the animals' blood on sprigs of mistletoe picked six days before the new moon.

"Thus we believe at Samain." Fodla's voice came from behind us—he evidently heard Cluvios's explanation. We turned to confront eyes that were points of reflected orange in his sallow face. "If the rites are not observed, the proper animals slain, the ancient dead may cross the abyss to harm us."

I had turned seventeen the day before, so felt bold enough to ask Fodla about the death of Acos. Before I could, he clapped his hands as a signal. Moira and Sabia came out of a nearby tent wearing long wolf pelt coats. Their faces were painted blue with isatis dye. Each woman carried a pitcher of hot liquid, which they poured into a silver bowl decorated with a horned Cernunnos holding a neck torc and serpent and accompanied by forest creatures. They went among the nearest tribesmen, offering their families sips from the bowl.

Fodla continued, "This is the dark half of the year when Belenos has been driven further and further away by the Spirits of Cold, who try to make the Mother barren." He beckoned a druidess. "Moira, these are friends from the village. Offer them drink."

With her expression masked beneath the blue-painted patterns on her face, Moira held up the steaming contents of the bowl to Cluvios and asked in a voice deeper than I expected, "An offering to the spirits of the dead?"

Cluvios, as numb from cold as I, accepted. She then turned to me with the bowl and trace of a smile. The liquid smelled like wine. After taking a sip, I felt that the sharply scented steam seemed to eat up through my nostrils and into my head. After a longer drink, the hot, sweet/bitter potion flowed in a relaxing wave through my body. Moira let me gulp down more, but when she pulled the bowl away, her smile was gone, replaced by a sneer of contempt.

After she moved to another group, Fodla said, "The ice spirits would destroy us, but our new fires warm the Mother and beckon to the sun god. Their light signals to Belenos that sacrifices to him have begun."

To me, the druid's final word, "b e g u n," sounded distorted, stretched and distant in the way his voice had sounded in the grotto. I felt dizzy, yet pleasantly so: an orange and black scene undulated before my eyes. I was aware of a rocking sensation, as if the stony ground under my feet were moving. I remembered Boccus. *Is some giant buried beneath the earth, heaving it upward in an effort to break out?*

I sat on the ground, leaned against a wagon wheel and felt as if I were in a boat on the rolling ocean that Lucius had described at Liscos's banquet. A sea god agitated the watery expanse with nauseating regularity. The many bonfires rotated in wheels of brilliant colors.

Surely the gods will be pleased with this fine display of lights. I laughed like a child at the turning brightness. In my mind the druids and animals they slaughtered grew to an enormous size that engulfed my vision until they wavered and dissolved into blotches of white, crimson, gold, and orange against the black cloth of night.

Finan's harp music sounded from somewhere nearby. He stood up wind, his melodic strumming seemed to join the wind and enter the bonfires, to be carried high to the gods on the billows of curling smoke and sparks.

The sound was added to the spinning in my mind and to the lights until the three merged and the empty space between the dark vault of sky and the points of light on the plain became a solid filled with a touchable substance resembling milkweed fluff, and the image became a revelation, like Belenos burning off the morning mists on the mountain, and in my new awareness I felt fear, a sensation of fright that became panic, and I wanted to cry out that the spirits of the dead had a medium on which to catch hold and force their way into the Now-world, and I wanted to join the sacrificing to prevent them, grasp a golden blade and slash smooth, white throats beneath innocent, pink eyes, heap wood on the fire until the pyres blazed as hot and brightly as Belenos and the god in jealousy would return to take up his daily journey across a familiar blue sky. I tried to raise my arms but they felt heavy as iron loaves I bought at Chondix, and when my legs would not move, my panic deepened for I was in the grip of some force that was unseen, yet had the power to restrain me. I tried to cry out at my nightmarish impotence, yet only a raven-like croak sounded from my throat and I thought I was shape-shifting into the Babd, the bloody raven of battle, as a hundred images spun into my mind: Alar, our wooden clan god, came to life and mocked me; the silver image of Cernunnos sitting cross-legged in horned majesty on Moira's bowl grinned at my helplessness; all the forest animals with him that I had encountered conjured themselves out of the smoke boars, foxes, elk, deer, a she-wolf, and when I forced myself to look away my head turned heavily as if I were under water, and it was the red eyes of Moccus the boar that glinted in the distant fire points down the slope. I closed my eyes against the images, but they had taken over my mind and the darkness became the gloom of the cavern where the head of my father was joined by those of Dividiac and Fodla, darting through the blackness with an eerie, white glow, and inside the congealed stone formations, sleeping giants stretched and groaned as they freed themselves from the retraining mass and tried to push through to the surface, and the putrid stench of the grave came to my nose as generations of our dead warriors with their women and children strained to surge out and span the abyss to my world. One immense figure did break out, and I whimpered as Boccus the African groped for support, holding a lamp, and I tried to hide behind one of the twisted-stone towers while his yellow eyes in a dark face as rough and scarred as the cavern walls searched the gloom for me, and he held his lamp high as his nightmarish figure approached. I was discovered—

I gasped out a scream and forced my eyes to open. The bobbing yellow flame of Boccus's oil lamp resolved itself into a distant blurred disc. Through my terror, I realized that it was the ruddy face of the rising moon, three nights from fullness, appearing and disappearing behind the racing clouds. My fear lessened a bit, yet my sense of time was so distorted that I did not know if it was still the night of Samain or not. I shivered from cold, realizing that now the smoky crest was dark and silent. My ears again caught the melodic strains of Finan's harp. His skilled fingers had slipped gently into the soft strains of sleep to imitate the magic instrument of Dagda, The Good God, The Lord of Perfect Knowledge, whose soothing rhythms penetrated and neutralized the unbalancing effects of the hallucinogenic drug Moira had blended into her wine.

The crisis was past. I felt nauseous, yet recalled forgotten things I had heard Dividiac say when I was a child. Morigan, the evil female counterpart of Dagda, who introduced fear and irrational behavior into the world, the goddess, who delighted in creating panic and whose time was Samain eve, would be lured back to the Other-world by the music. The gap between the worlds had closed and made secure once again.

The earth slowly stopped heaving under me. The swirling in my head lessened. I staggered up and crawled into the blackness of our wagon, where warm furs and soft bolsters engulfed my body and my consciousness. The final image in my mind was of being cold and naked in the rain outside Lucius's tower, as if I had shed a part of my Celtic past in the forest of Arduinna and Moccus.

Chapter XVI

When I awakened in the chill mists of dawn, lying on the furs of the wagon, my head ached and my eyes throbbed in pain. I wasn't sure what drug Fodla had put into Moira's wine to alter my senses, but it had caused my mind to conjure up horrifying images that seemed so real I thought I experienced them. I sat up, thinking of my mother and uncles. How were they after the long night? I saw Cluvios asleep near me, his open mouth exhaling steam in regular gasps. Mother slept, leaning against the chair in which Dividiac had slumped to face out of the wagon's back. He sat upright, seeming awake, although I couldn't see his face. Feeling nauseous, I winced at dull pain in my head as I crawled forward to lean out of the wagon, if I vomited. A thin yellow band of light brushed across the eastern horizon and threw the smooth curves of the Jurassos range into flat undulating outlines, with no dimension in depth. On the summit of *Benn Samain*, this cold flush of dawn revealed a deathly scene gloated over by the blanched human skulls on the ritual posts.

Bonfire ashes smoldered in the center of blackened circles of burned grass. The the mute carcasses of slaughtered beast offerings lay around the edges of fire pits. Jugular blood stained the white hides of sacrificed calves and the fleece of dead sheep, or lay congealed in snow-filled crevices slashing through ochre grass. Around the perimeter of the carnage, black shapes of vultures and ravens quarreled over the slain beasts. Several bolder scavengers had torn open animal bellies to feast on their livers.

Standing tethered among the bodies of the sacrificial victims, oblivious to the carnage, draft horses and mules nuzzled through dry weeds, searching for edible stalks.

Most of the pilgrims were asleep inside tents, but a few lay under the wagons, where they had crawled during the night in a drugged stupor.

The cold wind had died down to sporadic gusts that riffled grasses in bursts of wavering motion. I climbed over the wagon's front seat and jumped down to see if Dividiac was all right. As I came around to the back, a shaft of golden light broke free of its mountain silhouette and shone onto a group of druids clustered together, hands up-raised, chanting a prayer of praise to the newborn Belenos and urging him back to the north again.

I turned away to look at Dividiac. His eyes were set in a fixed gaze that seemed to stare beyond the limits of the Now-world, a world again set in balance by the return of a sun god, whose brilliance promised reincarnation to the desolate landscape. For a moment I thought Uncle was dead, that his mouth, fixed open in what looked like a last scream of terror, had sounded across the abyss and into that Land of the Eternally Young that he yearned to visit. As his stiff lips began to move, I strained to hear his distorted, mumbled words.

"I have...not seen. Over two-twenties of years did I serve the gods...sacrificed to them...and yet I did not find them. They...they were not there."

Dividiac's voice sounded listless, broken. After a lifetime of teaching and conducting rituals, of enduring difficult pilgrimages to distant nemetons, of bargains made with Lugos of the Long Hand, in pacts with the Three, he felt that he knew less now about the nature of the gods than he had as a child. The truth came to me as abruptly as the ray of dawn light that illuminated our wagon: the shocked expression on Dividiac's face was not from having caught a glimpse of the Other-world for which he was prepared, but from the void—that black, awful emptiness over which he had called to Celtic gods. They had not answered. They had not been there.

Cluvios and Mother awoke shortly afterwards. Other clan families stirred and in an eerie silence prepared to leave the sacred height. Nor did anyone in our family speak. While Mother settled Dividiac as comfortably as possible in bolsters and furs on the wagon bed, I helped Cluvios check the wheels and the mares' harnessings. Uncle let me steer the team along the winding road that led down from the summit and back to Sego. As I braked the wheels, ahead of me and low in the sky toward Gallia, I saw the translucent disc of the last-quarter moon settling over a renewed land.

ଔଓ

The days following the lighting of the new hearth fires at Samain passed slowly. Wrapped in furs, Dividiac sat next to the warmth, his numb face twitching while he tried to unravel the tangled skein of his mind and find an answer for his inability to penetrate the Other-world. I overheard anxious conversations between Mother and Cluvios about taking the old man to the healing springs of Sequana, in a sacred grove at her river's source in Gallia. There, shrine druids attempted to cure the physical and emotional ills of pilgrims who came to the goddess for help.

In the difficult journey to reach *Benn Samain,* and the confusion at the summit, the day of my birth had gone unnoticed. Yet I was a warrior's full age now, subject to the duties and privileges of manhood. I spoke to Cluvios about the frightening images brought on by whatever drug the druidesses had dissolved in the wine. Uncle thought it might be a lettuce-like leaf that he had heard Dividiac mention, yet not name. To describe the unsettling effect, he said that druids used the Greek word *narkotikos,* and also *aluein,* which meant "to wander or be confused."

I was brought up in a town so had no idea about how a rural village prepared for our winter months. Food was a prime concern. On market days at Arialbinnum, I had gone with our slave-servants to buy supplies. At Wermaros, for a month before the snow came, swineherds went into the forests with their pigs, letting the animals root among rotting leaves and fatten up on oak-corns and wild mushrooms. Well-off villagers like Liscos, who could afford the services of butchers, paid them to come to their lodges and slaughter the porkers. After the blood was caught in a basin, boiled barley was poured in to make a pudding. The carcasses were singed in cone-shaped burning straw tents, and then disemboweled. Lard was gathered. Some of the meat was salted or pickled, but most went to the smokehouse to be cured and sold as a Sequani specialty.

Slaughtered geese were plucked of their feathers to fill the bolsters that Mother said were cheaper than woven blankets. Cluvios showed me how to use goose fat, which did not harden as did lard, to lubricate wheel axles, keep rust off iron fittings, and water-proof our winter boots. Mother used the clear oil as a base for poultices and ointments.

I went with hunters to the backwater ponds of the Dubis and snared wild ducks. The men also waded through these swampy areas to catch boar. If the beasts' long-legged, suckling young were caught, the piglets were raised in a sty built behind a lodge.

Woodcutters stacked logs under the overhanging eaves of lodges, and no man, woman or child came into the village without carrying a load of dead branches for kindling fires.

I continued to work at the forge with Cluvios for my fourteen-day period, and alternated with an equal amount of time at the *Castor* tower. Although Dividiac had not agreed that I could go there, he was too ill to teach me, and did not find out about the arrangement between Cluvios and Lucius. I looked forward to my time at the tower. Since Liscos now had forbidden the garrison's men to come into Wermaros, I usually brought meat, onions, and dried beans to sell them. This supplied food and avoided trouble between legionaries and husbands and fathers of village women.

Under Marcellus, I trained five hours a day alongside his legionaries with a heavy wooden sword and shield. The added weight gave us an advantage when we used the actual lighter weapons. Lucius said he was surprised and pleased that I caught on so quickly, but I reminded him—a bit haughtily—that my father had been warrior-chief of a Celtic clan. War was in my blood, if not my yearning. Marius worked with me in speaking more Latin and in writing the language by using letters that sounded out words.

After I told Lucius of the conversation I had in the cave with Fodla, about the threat of Ariovistos encroaching on Sequani lands, he had Tribune assign Germanic slaves to teach me and four of his men their guttural language. Although Roma had an alliance with the Germanic king, Lucius felt it would be wise to have legionaries who could communicate well with all the area's tribes.

Despite Liscos's order that legionaries be banned from Wermaros—which I felt was Fodla's doing—Lucius was still a frequent visitor to our lodge. I knew that Cluvios was aware of his growing affection for my mother. He tried to keep them apart as often as he could find an excuse to do so. It was not jealousy: the evil in Uncle's body was relentless—he had lost his sense of taste and smell and now his hair was falling out—but as Alrix's surviving brother, Cluvios must bind Briga to himself in a marriage contract. Even Liscos hinted as much, every chance he could.

Cluvios had not yet told Mother about Alrix's death, but he agreed with me to do so a year from the day of the raid.

❧❧

At the tower, I had watched the men celebrate some of their festivals. In our month named Elembiv, which Lucius called Sextilis, they celebrated their twin gods Castor and Pollux. The day did not occur during my half of the month there, so I missed it. In his September, two festival days were dedicated to the sky god Jupiter. He is like our Taranis. In the next month, two celebrations were for his wife, Juno.

Not much celebrating took place during our month of Samon, but Lucius told me that one of his longest feasts would be in the second half of the next month, Decembris. "Saturnalia," he called the festival. Gifts were exchanged during seven days and so was the social order, when masters might wait on their slaves as part of the festivities.

❧❧

Lucius came to our lodge on the first afternoon of Saturnalia. When I watched him give Mother a present, she laughed in pleasure for one of the few times since we had arrived in Wermaros.

"What is this Sat-ur-nala... and this gift?" she asked, fingering a pendant's image carved in a cream-colored stone.

Lucius said, "It's ivory and shows the head of *Roma*, a woman symbolizing our capital."

"Beautiful, Lucius. Where did you get it?"

"The cameo belonged to my mother. It's the only thing I have left of hers."

Briga looked up, shook her head, and handed the pendant back. "Then you should keep it."

"No"–Lucius closed her hand over the pendant–"I...I want you to have it–"

"Lucius," I interrupted to relieve the awkward moment. "Tell us about this Saturn-god you honor."

He looked at me with a grateful nod. "I shouldn't admit it, but that's another thing we Romans borrowed from the Greeks. They named the god Kronos, but we call him Saturn. On my farm, we used his planet's position in the sky to mark the end of the winter planting season. Greeks connect him with some past golden age of theirs they believed was all beauty and peace."

Cluvios, who had been listening, taunted, "And you could never accept that. Your legions are stationed in our Celtic lands to the south."

I was disturbed at my uncle's belligerent tone, but Lucius brushed it aside.

"Cluvios, no offense to your work, but some of our poets think of the present as an inferior 'Age of Iron.' Quite a step back from that golden time."

He retorted, "You would have a hard time of it if you fought with swords forged of gold."

"A golden sword would be for the better," Briga interposed. "Warriors might find their weapons too valuable to risk fighting with them."

"Enough, Woman!" Cluvios shouted at her in the angry tone he used lately.

"Lucius," I said quickly, "I've been telling Uncle about the different names you have for your months. Do you reckon time by moon phases, as we do?"

"In a way. One of our months has twenty-nine days, others thirty or thirty-one. It's an imperfect system by which to calculate the length of a year, and some Greek natural philosophers had different ideas about the moon. To them it was less mysterious and quite understandable."

We had finished a supper of roast duck, cheese, and bread and now sat by the hearth fire, sipping the last of our *cervisa*. I wanted to know more about these...what had Lucius called them...Fila-soph-ers? I asked him to explain more.

"Well, A Greek named Aristarchus thought that the moon didn't produce its own radience, but that it shines by reflected light from the sun."

"But the sun is gone during the night," I countered. At Lucius's shrug of uncertainty, I asked, "Why does the moon change shape over a month?"

"According to Aristarchus, it's a globe moving across the sky. Half of it is lighted up until its full face is toward the sun, then it starts to move back and repeats the process in reverse."

Briga admitted, "I'm not sure I understand."

"Well then, there's another explanation by Berosus."

"Who's Ber-o-sus?" I felt a bit giddy from the effects of drinking.

Lucius explained, "I think he was Chaldean, from a country that's about as far away as you can imagine. Berosus believed that the moon was a ball and that half of it is luminous and half of it blue all the time. Because light attracts light, and the moon travels in a circle around the sun, the bright side is attracted by its rays. Then, as the ball moves to the east, away from the sun, Apollo—"

"Ap-ol-lo?"

"Our name for the sun god, Alberix. When Apollo releases his hold on the moon, it turns its bright side to the earth. The cycle repeats itself every twenty-nine and a half days."

"And so we have the lunar month," Briga said.

"Exactly. Another Greek named Erastothenes"—Lucius chuckled—"don't try to pronounce his name, Alberix, but Erastothenes declared the earth like the moon to be a globe suspended in space."

"Ridiculous," Cluvios muttered. "Any fool can see that it's a flat disc."

Lucius did not contradict the craftsman. "Perhaps, but he calculated its circumference by observing shadows cast by the sun."

I was getting tired, yet fascinated. Lucius went on to describe the voyage of a native of Massilia ,from where Celts bring in wine. I didn't catch his name, or every detail of his voyage, but he sailed north in search of tin and amber and discovered an ice-filled land he called Thu-le. He said he had entered a sea of floating ice-mountains that were as big as the rock cliffs along the Birsa gorge. The region was so remote that he thought it to be the hibernating place of Belenos, because the sun did not appear there for half of the year.

To help keep myself awake, I stood up and added wood to the fire. Lucius was talking about actual men, not legendary heroes that went on those magic adventures in our bards' songs. He had a name for the sun, and did not mentioned hidden gods like Cernunnos, or supernatural forces and shape-shifters, only the familiar elements we could see every day.

I recalled my impulsive undressing in the forest after I fled the horror I had seen in the grotto. Was the act a stripping away of beliefs about the gods that I had been taught? The idea left me empty, yet eager to be filled with more knowledge about the world of which Lucius spoke.

Despite Cluvios's irritability and taunting, I hoped the day would end pleasantly. I saw mother yawn. When Lucius apologized for staying late and got up to leave, Uncle ordered Briga to give him back the pendant.

The Romans celebrated their new year and five other festivals in the first half of the month of Januarius—our Rivros—so I missed them because I was at the forge. Dividiac still felt weak, but seemed to have improved in the two moons since Samain. A few outlying farmsteads raised sheep, but no one in Wermaros did, so Mother decided not to tell him when the first day of Anangatios came, our lambing festival of Imbolc.

During those two weeks with Cluvios, I worked the forge on days when weather permitted. Mother stayed indoors, but Trauna came over with a portable loom and taught her how to weave shawls.

Ollam-Fodla and his followers remained out of sight in their requisitioned lodge. I wondered if the druid was there at all. Boccus, too, seemed to have disappeared. Not even the twin druidesses came to the marketplace, yet Liscos made sure food was sent to their lodge every week.

A Roman festival in the same month as Imbolc was celebrated on its thirteenth day. Lucius had told me that it commemorated the rescue of twin infants—I forget their names—who later became the founders of Rome. Celebrants sacrificed dogs and goats at a cavern near a river that flowed through the city, believing that a she-wolf had suckled the newborns at that spot and saved their lives. Later in the day, he said, naked youths ran through the streets with thongs cut from the sacrificed animals and whipped any woman they could catch with them. This was supposed to make females more fertile.

When Lucius came to our lodge on the evening of his festival day, Dividiac was sitting near the fire. Uncle felt stronger and had begun to display his old crustiness, yet he hadn't spoken of continuing my training as a druid. He had not talked to Lucius since the parley last year, but I was pleased that he seemed willing to discuss the celebration.

Uncle spoke slowly and slurred the words a bit after Lucius sat down with a horn of *cervisa*. "Alberix tells me you have a festival today. What is this occasion?"

Lucius explained the story without naming the commemoration, then tactfully commented on our lambing festival. "Your Imbolc seems a gentler feast than our Lupercalia—"

"Lupercalia?"

"That's what we call the festival I just described. The whippings are harmless and the women do come to believe that they will conceive more easily."

"The mind, man, the mind!" Dividiac retorted, animated once again. "Power is in what the mind is made to see. Your priest-augers are too involved with the Now-world. They should predict more than the outcome of business ventures or battles."

"We do deal in ideas," Lucius replied. "I've told Alberix about our Twelve Tablets of the Law and our system of justice."

"We Men of the Oak mediate justice."

"No offense, sir, but we've found that those in power often interpret laws to their advantage. With the Tablets, Fortuna is given a free hand."

"Fortuna!" Uncle abruptly shouted. "You mean Tyche, another of your thefts from the Greeks."

Feeling the *cervisa*, Lucius responded curtly to the accusation. "And you druids stole their alphabet to write down your nonsense."

I knew he regretted his comment, and Mother went over to calm the old man. "Dividiac, perhaps you should sleep now. I'll help you to your room."

Lucius apologized to him. "Sir, I...I'm sorry,"

When Mother touched his sleeve in understanding, he caught at her hand, but she pulled it away.

After Briga took Dividiac to the far end of the lodge, Lucius turned to Cluvios. "Have you told her about her husband's death?"

"Not yet."

"You must."

"Not for your sake, *centurio*." Uncle looked at him with eyes leaden from his illness. "Briga is Celtic, you are Romani. A lamb does not run with a wolf."

Lucius barely suppressed his anger. "Crafter, we're talking about people, not animals. No matter what you think of us, our Gallic province enjoys a peace that you Celts never achieved there."

"By destroying our shrines..." Cluvios began to cough violently.

Lucius looked toward the darkened end of the room. Briga had not come back so he stood up to leave. "I'm sorry, *carantos*...friend. I should be getting back to the tower. Alberix, you'll come in two days?"

I nodded and watched him leave, saddened that both of my uncles were against my friend. I knew that soon I would have to choose between them and Lucius.

Chapter XVII

Despite his reluctance, early on the following evening Cluvios told my mother the truth about Father's death, nine days short of a year since the deadly Harude raid. He said nothing about Dividiac's possession of his relic, even though the old druid sat hunched near the fire pit. His numbed vision of ever meeting the gods had turned as gray and cold as the ashes at which he stared.

I watched my mother go with Dirona in silence to her sleeping room.

Briga removed the golden pins from her hair, letting its copper cascade tumble free. She took off a brooch that Alrix once had given Dirona, which her sister had let her wear as a token of hope. She put on the plainest tunic that Liscos had brought from Vesontio.

As a sign of mourning, Trauna put out the hearth fire and asked me to bring the harper, Celtillos-of-the-Milky Eye, to the lodge.

The old bard came in with his harp to sing poems of praise and revenge for the dead chieftain. I caught the words of his first one.

"Alrix's death, the death of a great champion,

Leaves me a walking corpse without a soul,

Without strength, without power,

Without a zest for life.

Germani have killed him, and now

My hatred will come against them,

And follow them to the ends of the Two Worlds."

Yet when he began to improvise other verses that spoke of Alrix's deeds and likened them to the magic exploits of heroes in bardic songs of old, Briga came out to stop him.

"Bard," she told him gently, "my husband was not one of your legends, although his life was cut short like a tale before it is ended. His was a warrior's calling and he suffered a warrior's death in the Now-world." She looked into the dead ashes of the fire pit a moment. "But Alrix changed. He died building a village of peace, not a new oppidum, a stronghold from which to carry out raids. As a woman I had little to say about the affairs of warriors, but I bore him only one son. This I could control. I may hope that Alberix learned from what happened to his father."

Mother did not glance at me and I knew she expected no comment, no affirmation of her wish. She turned and went back to her room, where she would seclude herself and speak to no one for an entire moon period.

Our spring month of Ogron was mild this year. Moisture from the winter's snow and the warming smile of Belenos made the trees bud early. Forest ferns were coaxed into yellow-green fronds that curled amid bright speckles of wildflowers growing in the compliant body of the Earth Mother.

While I was at *Castor*, two mornings after the day that Lucius said was the Ides of Martius, his war god, he told me he wanted to visit my mother. Her absence had left his spirit empty, yet he had honored our Celtic custom of her month-long seclusion after a death. He did not mention that Father died over a year earlier, but we both understood.

Liscos had relented and now allowed legionaries from the towers to come into Wermaros, as far as the marketplace shed to buy supplies. After Lucius left four legionaries there to purchase food, he trotted his horse toward Cluvios's forge.

As he passed the small crossing lane that led to the bake ovens, he spotted Briga's familiar green tunic among the other women. Turning his horse onto the path, he felt his heartbeat increase as he neared the group. At the oven, after knowing smirks and glances at each other, the women gave way to the Romani chief. Each knew the reason he had come, and it was not to buy bread. Nor had they reasons to dislike the newcomers—there were boastful threats against the tower garrisons by a small clique of warriors led by Epananctos, but no trouble. The Romani had spent welcome copper and silver coins in the village before Liscos ordered them to stay away. They were doing so again.

"Briga," Lucius called out, hoping that she would attribute the flush in his face to spring sunshine. "It...it's good to see you out again."

As she looked up at him, Briga knew that the other women watched both her face and his—Celts always read emotion in a person's features. A "price of face" mentioned in contracts dealt with intentions—honorable or otherwise— that could not be masked and revealed a person's truthfulness.

"You...you look well," she replied, aware that her companions were observing words and gestures that would be told around supper boards that evening. "I...I was just returning to my lodge."

"Climb up behind me, I'll take you there," Lucius offered, feeling as nervous as before his first battle.

After a moment of hesitation, Briga extended a hand, held up her tunic hem with the other, and by a graceful turn swung up to seat herself side-saddle behind him.

Nodding farewell to the other women, Lucius turned the horse back up the lane, conscious that the supporting hand Briga held around his chest could feel his rapid heartbeat.

When they reached the main road, Briga ordered, "Turn right, toward the river gate. Go up into the mountains."

Lucius felt that his heart must sound as loud as his horse's hoof beats. The animal trotted past surprised sentries, across the Dubis bridge, and up the gentle rise of road opposite. When they arrived near Dividiac's observation shelter, Briga pointed to it. "Stop over there."

Lucius angled his mount off the road, into a field of stumps, grasses, and newly grown field plants. He helped Briga dismount, holding her under her arms, conscious of a musky scent of her perspiration. She shook off his hold, which had lingered a moment, then walked to a fallen log, where she knew Alberix recorded daily sunrises. Briga sat down and looked across the valley. On the opposite mountain crest, the uncompleted stone *menhir* stood high inside a clearing.

"Dividiac's *menhir*," Briga remarked. "The spring equinox will be in three days."

"I did promise Dividiac that we would have the marker ready."

"I'm grateful...Lucius."

"You mean 'Shorthair' don't you?"

Briga's laugh at his jest was musical as a harp chord. "Dividiac is too ill to conduct the equinox sacrificial rite. I...I'm very worried about him."

"Alberix thinks he's getting better. He seemed his old self when I talked to him on Lupercalia."

Briga disagreed. "His mind is bewitched by Danach."

Lucius sat down next to her. "Alberix told me about his uncle's former pupil. Why do you say he bewitches Dividiac?"

"At Beltaine last, before you came, Danach wanted to sacrifice a person, not a heifer. In an evening ritual, Alberix said the druid went through a shape-shift, changed into the antlered god, Cernunnos—"

"Ridiculous," Lucius interrupted, "a conjurer's illusion."

"I know, but spectators had been drinking all day and were tired. Alberix told me about Finian's harp music...the druidess's dance."

"What does your son think?"

"That the druid put on stilts, a deer pelt, and headdress. The two women threw mind-altering herbs on the fire..." Briga's voice trailed off and she shivered despite the warm day. When Lucius unfastened his cloak and tucked it around her shoulders, she nodded thanks. "Now, Danach is always around Liscos, whispering poor advice to him."

"There is a change in the man's attitude toward us," Lucius affirmed. "He no longer is friendly, even though he allows us to buy at his marketplace again."

Briga wiped a tear away. "Liscos drinks too much. Dirona told me that lately he's even irritable with Arduinna."

"And you think this Danach is responsible." Lucius's closeness to the woman had become an aching urge to hold her that took all of his discipline to control. He wanted to pull Briga against him, kiss her eyelids and hair, nuzzle her graceful throat, yet only said, "Alberix told me about the druid's ambition, when he went inside a cave with Dividiac."

"Cave?" Briga's eyes widened in surprise. "What cave is that?"

"Ah...just some cavern..." Lucius glanced away from her. *Hades, I forgot. Briga doesn't know about her husband's head...or Dividiac's attempt to use the relic to enlist Alberix in persuading Raurici clans to fight against Germani.*

Briga said, "Druids are such a political force in Gallia that Danach wants to enlist Liscos in his schemes. Dividiac was never interested in power, only in serving our people through the gods."

"I believe you. Liscos has done well here, but this village is not Vesontio. To me, the man seems overly ambitious...too eager to be more than he is."

"'Our Celts say, 'Better to be the head of a mouse than the tail of a cat'.'"

"Or, as we put it, 'First in a village, rather than second at Roma'.'"

Both laughed at the similar proverbs. Briga reached down to pluck an early Sunblossom and toyed with the closed green head. "Alberix likes the time he spends at your tower, but doesn't say much about it. That would upset Cluvios."

"He's doing well. Your son has a natural ability with a sword."

At his remark, she threw down the blossom. "His father could have taught him that!"

Lucius flushed. "Ah...swordplay is just part of it. Alberix is learning to read Latin. Germani slaves teach him words in their language."

Briga recalled, "When we came here, my sister Dirona seemed to think that our gods had a special interest in Alberix. I didn't want it to be by Caturix, our war god."

"My idea of the gods is different, Briga. Alberix is realizing that we're all responsible for our lives. As for training him in war, I would prefer to see this fighting stop and go back to Italia. Buy myself a farm."

Briga looked at Lucius with eyes that reminded him of the color of wild chicory blossoms. "You are very much as my Alrix was, a man of war who desires peace. You both are like animals with two different heads, not sure of its nature."

Lucius put his hand on her arm. "I believe that it's Roma's destiny to bring peace to what your people call the Now-world. Our legions brought that and prosperity to the Narbonensis—"

"At what cost to our Celts there?" she interrupted. "Lucius, you Romani control your warriors like Cluvios does his forge fire. He steps on the bellows treadle and air blows in a dependable way. Alrix complained that Celtic warriors blow when and where they want..." Briga touched a scar on Lucius's cheek and studied the weathered creases in his face. "Poor man." She eased her arm away from his hand and stood up. "It...it's gotten cool, Lucius. Take me back to the village."

No, please, not...not yet." He faced Briga and pulled his cloak tightly around both of them. She stood motionless. He knew she felt his warm pressure, yet did not pull away. When Lucius stroked her hair and kissed her eyes and face, he felt Briga wince slightly at the rasp of his beard stubble. She did not otherwise respond, yet he held her to him, not daring more intimate touchings—It was enough to enfold the woman with his eyes closed and breathe her musky scent. Her voice, quiet near his face, came too soon.

"Lucius, your duty here can't last much longer. There is always renewed fighting with the arrival of warm weather—"

He shushed her lips with a rough finger. "Hispania is taken," he said as softly as she had. "Italia is quiet and Pompeius has made peace in Asia."

She slipped out of his embrace. "Have you so quickly forgotten Dividiac's prophecy? 'The future of our people is with the birds of death'."

Lucius nodded remembrance. Like the ache from an old wound, the druid's warning had troubled his mind. He grasped Briga's shoulders. "Surely, you must believe that men can control the future much better than the thrashings of a dying animal."

"So my Alrix thought, yet look what happened to his village, and to him. Will...will you take me back now Lucius?"

"All right."

After he helped her onto his mount, they rode down from the crest with Briga's head lying against Lucius's back. The wind splashed a welling of tears across the sides of her face. *The feel of a man is good, yet...a legionary of Roma or the warrior from a Celtic tribe...only the clothing is different. They kill each other and are killed.*

Briga had not lain with a man since Alrix, and the physical—even emotional—emptiness was even more acute in a village that was not of her tribe.

Liscos's unmarried warriors had eyed her as early as the first Beltaine festival, but if she followed tradition in contracting another marriage, it would be with Cluvios.

"Alberix is right," she affirmed to herself. "Our laws bind us too firmly to the Wheel."

"Did you say something?" Lucius asked, leaning back to hear.

Briga shook her head. She held herself away from Lucius's back as the horse canted across the bridge, past smirking sentries, into the village. Alrix's widow went into her lodge without a word, but with dried tears caked hard in the corner of her eyes.

⇜⇝

The warm spring weather made the Helvetii tribal leaders impatient. Four days after the full moon of Ogron, rumors reached Wermaros that their druids had declared the auspices favorable for beginning the planned migration to the west.

Because Cluvios was too ill, I had gone to Chondix alone to pick up a load of ore. When I looked down from the heights above the Sorna Valley, I saw many dark shafts of smoke scattered across the plain. They reminded me of the ones I had seen earlier near Aventia. Were some of our Raurici clans also burning their villages and joining the Helvetii?

Iron workers at Chondix confirmed the migration rumor and torching of clan villages. Families not involved in mining ore had joined other Raurici going toward Aventia. To keep clansmen from returning, reports told of Helvetii chieftains destroying four hundred villages and twelve strongholds, including Aventia, their capital.

Other catastrophic rumors told of Germani warriors to the east crossing the Renos River at Brigantium and swarming into Tulingi lands. They were reported to be moving rapidly toward Raurici farmsteads to the northeast of Wermaros. Yet another report was that a Roman legion at Genava had defeated advance contingents of Helvetii, as they had Allobroge warriors two years earlier. Everyone feared that the whole land was about to burst into unquenchable flames of war.

I bought the ore and returned to Wermaros as quickly as possible. When I arrived, the river gate was closed, the first time I had seen it so barred in daylight. Sentries recognized me and opened the portal, but I headed the mares directly to our lodge without answering shouted questions about what I had seen at Chondix.

When I pulled up at our lodge with the wagon, Cluvios sat in the shade of the forge shed. His face was the color of raw lead. What hair on his head had not fallen out grew in unkempt tufts. His once-tawny mustache, which he had kept trimmed, was all but lost in a growth of white-flecked beard. The silver torc hung loosely around his neck. The forge fire was not alight.

"Uncle," I cried as I jumped down from the wagon seat, "the Helvetii are on the move and burning their villages. Some of our Raurici are joining them—"

"Your news is cold as our forge ashes," he interrupted gruffly. "After you left, a merchant came from Vesontio. Casticos and Dumnorix of the Aedui knew all along the route that Marcios would take, yet kept the information from Liscos. Your towers have kept watch over a route that was never intended to be used."

I felt a chill of anxiety. "Is Mother inside?"

"No. Briga left yesterday with Dividiac and some villagers. They will take him to the shrine of Sequana in Gallia."

I felt my skin crawl with renewed alarm. "But that's in the path of the Helvetii migration."

Cluvios showed no emotion at the danger. "Your *centurio* is gone."

"Lucius? To where?"

"He'll join his legion at Genava, but the Shorthairs can never stop Marcios and his tribe—"

"Uncle," I blurted. "I...I'm going down there to find Lucius."

Cluvios had anticipated my decision. "I thought as much. Look inside, near the fire pit. I made up a bundle of supplies you'll need along the way. I added a pouch of Sequani coins."

I thanked my uncle, but my eyes teared up as I went inside, knowing I might never see him again. After getting together a bearskin covering and other small things I wanted to take with me, including the knife Tribune had given me at the parley, I brought Derka around to the lodge door and secured the bundle. Cluvios did not help, but after I tightened the last saddle strap, he stood to embrace me.

"Your father became a man of peace," he reminded me in a hoarse whisper. "His son can be no less. Yet...yet you should find a leader among your own people, not the Romani."

"Uncle..." I choked, feeling that I abandoned the dying man who had raised me, a person I knew better than my own father. I could only hold Cluvios tightly, nod dumbly in agreement, and stain his tunic shoulder with tears.

When I finally pulled away, my throat was tight with grief. I mounted Derka and turned her toward the river gate, glancing back at Cluvios. He waved feebly to me.

The sentries opened the familiar portal with its array of grinning skulls nailed above that I might be seeing for the last time. No guard spoke, so I surmised they saw me as one less mouth to feed. Should war break out and the village put under siege, supplies would no longer come through from Vesontio.

A sense of reality hit me once I directed Derka along the road I had taken with Cimbris to Aventia. Dread, really. *Would I ever see Wermaros again? My mother? Dividiac or my aunt Dirona?*

A little more than a year earlier, I had envisioned the village as a wheel that held the spoke of my destiny. How could I know that the gods...or what Lucius called "Capricious Fortuna"...would steer me along the spoke of a possible war against my own mother tribe, the Helvetii?

Chapter XIX

At a place where the road forked to the south, the branch I had taken with Cimbris to Aventia, I continued on to the southwest. To avoid the gorges of the Dubis River, the roadway entered a valley, the same route Lucius and his legionary comrades had taken in coming up to Wermaros from Genava.

Not to overtire Derka, I stopped early at a mountain hamlet for the night. I had seen many people on the road, groups of armed warriors and carts or wagons holding entire families, heading away from the Renos—they were taking no chances that rumors about invading Germani might be false.

Rather than spend even one of the coins Cluvios had given me, I decided to eat food he had packed for me and sleep in the nearby woods. Before that, I went to the common room of the hamlet's only inn for whatever information I might find out about the migration. I left Derka in the care of a boy to whom I promised a copper coin.

As the men watched me come in, I knew they were trying to determine my tribe. They soon ignored me, but drinking had made them talkative. Despite the different dialects, I was able to understand that the Helvetii were the topic of both defeatist and defiant conversations. I learned that the tribe would have to pass into the far northwest corner of the Romani Narbonensis Province. Speculation about what Marcios might do, either ask for permission to cross or fight his way through, dominated the arguments. Bets wagered that the massive number of Helvetii—some estimates put them in the hundreds of thousands, a number I could not even imagine—would overwhelm any legions sent to oppose them. Our people seemed quite well informed, reporting that there were only two legions in the entire Narbonensis, a total of about six or seven thousand men. Only one unit was at Genava.

I felt elated. That had to be the legion that Lucius rejoined.

Those who bet against the Helvetii pointed out that the sheer size of the migration—men, women with children, wagons, carts, and livestock—would force the tribe to move slowly, giving the Romani time to bring in reinforcements from Gallia Cisalpina.

When the innkeeper came around with a cups and a pitcher, I felt I had to buy his *cervisa*, and paid with one of Cluvios's bronze coins. The innkeeper looked at the Sequani inscription, then went to show it to a warrior at a nearby table. When both glanced back at me, I realized that a Sequani would not be part of the migration and that I might be accused of spying. I gulped down the sweetened brew and left as casually as I dared. No one followed me out. Still nervous, I gave the boy too large a coin, then mounted Derka and canted her off to a forest clearing, where I would sleep.

❧❧

Because of near-trouble at the inn on the evening before, for the second night I stopped at a lake that was just past a series of rapids in the Dubis. At that point the road crossed over a bridge to the river's left bank. Fellow travelers told me that the source of the Dubis was about a day and a half's journey away, and that the springs were in the center of an extensive nemeton. That made me think of Mother and Dividiac at the shrine of Sequana, farther to the north. Beyond the source, I was advised that the road turned and twisted up a ridge of the southern Jurassos, then descended to the village of Gex, which overlooked the southern end of the Lake of the Allobroges. The tribe's fortress at Genava was about ten Roman miles beyond Gex.

❧❧

Late on the afternoon of my fourth day of travel, and despite listening to talk at another inn about the great number of Helvetii in the migration, I was unprepared for the incredible sight that lay before me from the pass above Gex.

More people than I thought existed, tens of thousands of members of clan families, were spread out, preparing to camp for the night on a plain that fronted the crescent-shaped Allobroge lake. To the northeast, I saw immense clouds of dust still hovering over the route these clans had taken from Aventia.

The dark-blue surface of the lake sparkled through the dust and haze. I guessed that a concentration of wood smoke almost directly south marked the location of Genava. Across the water, the nearby snowbound summits of the White Mountains, colored by a low sun, stood out in golden relief. When seeing them from atop *Benn Samain*, I had never imagined the sheer mass of this mountainous barrier.

The shortest route to the Allobroge fortress-capital seemed to lie ahead, along the north shore of the lake. Reasoning that I would not be challenged in the confusion of camping warriors and their families, I started Derka down the twisting road from the head of the pass. Shortly afterwards, low northeast clouds, which had threatened rain all day, opened up in steady downpour. I put on a leather hat and hunched into my cloak.

Once I was on muddy, flat land, I threaded Derka between carts and wagons, sodden tribal members, sputtering campfires, caged chickens, and cattle or pigs being herded in for the night.

After I reached Genava, soaking wet, I found the Allobroge stronghold situated on the heights of a triangular island that was set between the Rhodanus and another river. Massive stone walls protected the city. A gate at the far end of a bridge over the Rhodanus looked barred. When I went there, a group of frustrated tribesmen told me that despite earlier agreements with the Helvetii, the Allobroge over-chief, Viridios, had ordered the gates closed. None from the migrating tribes was allowed inside the citadel.

Nevertheless, some of the city's merchants had come across the river to barter with tribesmen willing to part with cumbersome possessions for the gold and silver coins they could more easily carry. A few intense arguments over trading suggested that these city bargainers were more than willing to take advantage of the migrants' desperation, but the presence of several thousand armed warriors in the vicinity convinced other sellers to keep their prices reasonable.

I dismounted and led Derka past the vendors' stalls, then along the right bank of the Rhodanus. A short distance beyond the triangle where the rivers joined, a bridge made of new wood spanned the waterway. The broad river, which I estimated at about eighty-five paces wide, was swollen with water from melting alpine snow packs. Its current surged against piers beneath the boards with a force that made the span tremble.

Barring the roadway's nearest end was a double row of supply barrels, topped by a log barricade studded with sharpened tree branches pointed toward an attacking force. Sentries patrolling in front of the makeshift defense were equipped much like the legionaries at *Castor*. I realized they were not Allobroge, but Romani, and sure I would find Lucius among them!

When I approached the nearest guard, he warned me in Celtic to halt, then added in Latin, "No one is allowed to cross over."

I called back in Latin, "I'm looking for *Centurio* Lucius Velcanius. He's my friend."

Hearing the request made in his language, the guard lowered his weapon. I surmised that Helvetii spies were testing potential crossing points over the river by probing enemy strength.

After a conversation with his mates, the sentry told me," The *centurio* is downstream with the Tenth Legion, but no one is allowed through."

"I must see him. I've come all the way from Sequani territory."

A man down near the water, stooping to inspect the bridge pilings, evidently heard the exchange and stood up. He looked my way and clambered up the slippery bank. Incredibly and with relief I recognized Marcus Marius!

"Alberix!" he called out, as astonished as I. "What in the name of Vulcan's Shield are you doing here? Did I hear you ask for Velcanius?"

"Yes. I returned from Chondix and found out that Lucius had come here."

"Hold on..." Marius climbed over the bridge railing and ordered, "Sentries, pass him through. He's one of our allies."

The guards scrambled to lower a tree trunk and roll barrels far enough apart to let Derka pass.

Marius walked through with me explaining, "The legion is building a line of defensive works along the left bank of the river to strengthen shallow parts, where the Helvetii might try to force a crossing, but"—he glowered at the sky—"if this rain continues, it will slow construction."

"I was fortunate you were here, Marius. What were you doing at that bridge?"

"Trying to work out the quickest way to dismantle the span, if need be. What did you see of the Helvetii north of Genava?"

I responded that I couldn't count the vast number of those camped there. "It looks like the clans burned their villages and brought along everything they owned. I'm sure some of our Raurici are with them."

"I should report that to Titus Labienus at the legion praetorium tent. The legate has just taken over command."

"Legate? I don't understand that word."

"Like an over-chief of the legion."

As we walked to the camp Marius told me that Julius Caesar was in Gallia Cisalpina, desperately trying to raise enough recruits for two new legions. He said he had also sent for three units that were still at Aquileia. That quickly would give him seven legions, perhaps twenty-five thousand men.

The Rhodanus looped away to the north, but we picked up the river again where the first makeshift fortifications were being constructed on bluffs above the riverbank. Fortified watchtowers and guard posts set along a rough barrier of split tree stakes over-looked the river's right bank and several low islands in the stream's center. A contingent of mud-stained legionaries strained at cutting the smooth bluffs down vertically, to make them more difficult for attackers to climb.

Marius remarked, "Lucky the Rhodanus has high banks at this point. The Tenth alone could probably hold this position until Caesar returns with reinforcements."

Three thousand men against perhaps five times that number? I pointed to some strange-looking devices that legionaries were assembling and positioning on the top level of the towers. I asked what they were.

"We call them '*Scorpiones*,' after a nasty creature we have in Italia that stings with its tail. The device shoots bronze bolts at an attacker with incredible force. Narbonensis Galli were terrorized even if not many of their warriors actually were hit."

Marius's scoffing chuckle that followed reminded me that friend though he might be at this moment, Romani had little mercy for anyone who became their enemy. Now I understood a little better what had disturbed Dividiac about the"Shorthairs."

We walked further along, toward where the embankment again sloped down to the level of the water. More mud-spattered legionaries, stripped to the waist despite the cold rain, dug another broad ditch and stacked the slick earth away from the river's side. Other men raised a palisade of logs into position on top of the dirt barrier. To provide stakes for the wall, the opposite side of the Rhodanus almost was stripped of pine trees. Legionaries also destroyed protective brush cover that might conceal an attacking force. The main road led west along our bank of the river, yet I realized that if the Helvetii decided not to force this defensive wall, the tribe could use the cleared area on the other side as an escape route.

We had reached orderly rows of leather tents, a vast duplicate of the small camp outside *Castor* tower. The rain stopped. At the same time the sun dropped behind the far western horizon and colored a distant bank of low clouds a blazing red, an unsettling effect that made it seem to me as if all Gallia were aflame. I wondered if Marius recalled Dividiac's prediction of war at the bungled treaty sacrifice. If he had, he did not comment, but told me, "Cornelius is further downstream, staking out locations for more trench-works. About ten or twelve miles away, those distant mountains drop down to the right bank and leave a narrow pass into Sequani territory. It's the only route the Helvetii can take that doesn't go through our province." He stopped at a crossroad in the center of the encampment and pointed to a large tent surrounded by legion standards and banners. "I have to go in the praetorium and report what you saw to Labienus. Walk straight on toward the river and you'll find Velcanius..." Marius grasped my arm. "May Fortuna be with you."

"*Gratias.* And with you."

I found Lucius supervising a detail of legionaries fortifying a shallow bend in the river. On the far bank a band of Helvetii warriors watched the preparations. They taunted the men by shouting and rattling swords against their shields. Some threw an occasional lance that fell short. A few tribesmen were naked, the blue-dye war designs on their bodies now blurred by rain.

"Alberix!" Lucius exclaimed when he saw me. "How in Jupiter's Name did you find me?"

"After I came back from Chondix, I heard that you'd left." I ran to grasp his arm.

He returned my grip. "Sorry, I didn't have time to wait. Just as you found out at Aventia, the Helvetii are on the move. We were able to stall their leader, Marcios, and arrange a parley for the ides of Aprilis. Meanwhile, Caesar is raising legions in the Po Valley area."

"Marius told me."

"You found him, too?"

"He told me you'd be here."

Lucius wiped a neckerchief across his mud-stained face and glanced across at the blue-painted warriors. "The enemy already is here, and we only have nine days to complete these fortifications."

"Why are they coming this way? What about the Vesontio road? The watch-towers?"

"That's Sequani land and north of a route I believe they planned on using all along. Julius Caesar talked with two Helvetii leaders, Nammeius...you told me about him...and a Verucloetios. What he understood, if the translation was correct, is that they wanted permission to take their tribe through the northern corner of our province. Caesar refused, of course, but the Helvetii think the Allobroges will help their migration. We defeated them two years ago and they don't much like Romani."

"And now?"

Lucius said, "If the Helvetii use the two bridges or boats to cross the Rhodanus, that will be considered an invasion, an act of war. One of the two consuls at Roma is Caesar's father-in-law. He'll give the commander all the backing he needs to resist."

"Lucius, I want to stay here, but haven't brought any equipment."

He chuckled in answering, "All you'll need is a shovel. Right now every man in the legion is a mole chaser!"

"I'll dig, or do whatever I must to stay with you."

"What about Cluvios and Dividiac? Briga...your mother?"

"Dividiac went with Mother to a healing site. You remember how ill he became "

"We could use people who know Celtic and some Latin if we go into—"

Lucius didn't finish, but I knew that he meant "into Gallia." I thought the idea absurd. There was one Roman legion of about three thousand men on the frontier, and a reported quarter-and-a-half thousand Helvetii across the river. "What can I do after I'm through digging?" I asked, trying to dispel my anxiety. "I work with metal."

He laughed a little, but still put me off. "We can talk about that later, Alberix. It soon will be dark, so I'm calling a supper break."

I watched Lucius move among his men, ordering them to put down shovels, go back to their tents, and bring mess pans to a tent where cohort butchers prepared meals.

After returning, he explained, "Eight man squads usually prepare their own food, but with everyone digging trenches, Titus Labienus ordered the legion butchers to serve as cooks. Bread and a stew made from vegetables and the meat of sheep we bought at Genava." I repeated to Lucius that I wanted to stay with him. "Certainly not to fight." He thought a moment, then said, "We *do* have legionaries who are non-combatants… medical orderlies, surveyors, smiths. Ranks such as those. I could assign you to repair equipment in a Gallic *auxilia* unit. Actually, I may need you as an interpreter next month, when Caesar talks to that Helvetii delegation." He looked at the palms of my hands. "Good, toughened from your forge work. You'll have to wield a shovel in the morning, Alberix. As I said, every man in the legion is chasing moles right now."

"I'll dig."

Lucius put an arm around my shoulder and squeezed. "It's good to see you. Now, let's get some of that stew. The men will work by torchlight through the night, but you had better sleep. I'll have someone take care of your horse."

I *was* tired. After a quick supper, Lucius took me to a cot inside a field tent he shared with nine other legion centurions, then returned to his men. I immediately fell asleep. Not even the excitement of finding Lucius or the nightlong clanging of iron shovels against rocks kept me awake.

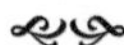

Toward dawn, I experienced the same dream about the she-fox that I had in the forest, where dogs had destroyed the fox's pups as they tried to escape across a river. Surely, the vixen, her pups, and the pursuing dogs were symbols of imminent action, perhaps even the predication of a Romani victory, and yet one could never be sure that shape-shifters had not deceived a dreamer about its true outcome.

Chapter XIX

At Wermaros, a report of the truth about the long-rumored Helvetii migration elated Ollam Fodla. Acting as the agent of Verocloetios, the druid had continued urging Liscos to allow his village to be a rallying point for tribesmen wanting to join what would be an inevitable battle against outnumbered Romani—one that the Shorthairs would be certain to lose. Epanactos, the head of Licsos's bodyguard, had caught Fodla's attention. The warrior was intelligent—certainly younger and stronger than Liscos—and Fodla realized that the man was eyeing the position of chieftain. Once Liscos was drained of usefulness, Epanactos would be grateful for an opportunity to succeed his one-armed lord.

Despite the fact that the moon had entered its inauspicious phase, Fodla summoned Liscos and Epanactos to his lodge. With the Helvetii migration a reality, the druid wanted to discuss advantages for them in that tribe's action.

Moira served the men sweetened wine and honey cakes, then sat further off with Sabia.

Epanactos glanced back at her. "Fodla, your druidess is quite beautiful. Does her dedication to the Oak forbid bedding? Wood must be a companion that is hard enough, yet not in the right place."

Annoyed, Fodla coldly reminded him, "I called you here to speak of the Helvetii. Moira and her sister are part of my plan, but it won't do to have a rutting elk disrupt them with his lusting."

Epanactos shrugged and took a gulp of wine.

Liscos drained his cup in a single instance, then slammed it down, boasting, "Th' Romani are finish'd!"

Fodla agreed, "There can be little doubt that the Helvetii will overwhelm them. This Caesar has only one legion at Genava. With Orgetorix dead, and Marcios in Aedui lands, the leadership will go to Dumnorix and your own Casticos at Vesontio. We are here to plan our part in this and obtain our reward for recruiting warriors to the Helvetii cause."

Epanactos objected, "Dumnorix's plot against Marcios has been uncovered. How will those still loyal to him turn the Helvetii north toward Bibracte, the Aedui capital? The tribe is heading west to reach Santoni lands."

Fodla replied, "Bibracte is ruled by Diviciacos, and Dumnorix is his brother. The old over-chief will protect his kin. Even before the Romani are defeated, Dumnorix must convince the Aedui to join with the Helvetii in smashing Ariovistos and his allied Germani. No single Gallic tribe is strong enough to challenge them."

Epanactos understood and chuckled. "With Ariovistos no longer a threat, Dumnorix should be able to dispose of two old men."

"Marcios an' Diviciacos?" Liscos barely followed the conspiracy.

"Yes. Your own over-chief, Casticos, will expect to regain his northern lands, but the Helvetii will need to be resettled." Fodla smirked at his own cleverness. "We can force the weaker tribes...Mandubi...Lingones...to occupy their vacant lands and thus buffer our frontier with Germania."

"Casticos an' th' Sequani will protest."

"Liscos"—Fodla squeezed the chieftain's good arm—"it is common knowledge that Casticos took his father's place illegally. A clever chieftain such as you with the backing of Men of the Oak might yet avenge this wrong."

Moira arose to bring more wine, but Fodla waved her off and stood up. "I travel to the shrine of Sequana in the morning. One can always learn about the latest events in Gallia from pilgrims arriving there. Liscos, while I'm away you'll continue to recruit warriors to join us against the Germani."

Epanactos asked, "What can I do?"

"Keep watch on the garrisons still in the towers, their routines, such as when hunting parties are away. Anything that might help in planning our attack." Fodla grasped each man's hand in a cold grip. "When I return, may the gods grant that this Caesar's head and those of his officers will decorate the walls of Bibracte!"

After a final leer at Moira, Epanactos left. Liscos lurched toward his lodge with muddled images playing in his mind of being over-chief at Vesontio. Inside and down the ramp from the entry, he found the large room strangely empty of people.

Dirona came out of her room. "Husband, I heard you come in. Briga has just returned and told me that Dividiac has died."

"Dead? How?"

"Near Divonese, on the road to Sequana's nemeton."

Liscos stared at the floor, mumbling to himself. When Briga came from her room, he looked up at her with bleary eyes. "Dividiac...is...dead?"

"Our uncle was old. His mind had gone to the Other-world long before his body."

"Then Fodla is druid of th' village now."

Briga said, "Not if Cluvios has any say in the matter—"

"Th' crafter hasn't. *I'm* chief'tain here!" Liscos stood up to stagger off to Arduinna's room and sleep off his stupor.

'Churl!" Briga spat after him. "Dividiac helped make you rich and gave you prestige."

Dirona predicted, "With Dividiac gone, Fodla *will* have control over Liscos."

"And I come back to find that Alberix has joined the Romani." Briga went to a table near the cook-fire, sprinkled chamomile leaves into a sieve, and poured hot water over the herb into two cups. She handed one to Dirona. "After we arrived here, you said that you thought the gods had an interest in my son... a destiny, if you will."

"Sister, I still believe it."

"With Dividiac dead, Alberix won't become a Man of the Oak. He's with his *centurio*. Do the gods wish my son to fight his own people?"

I...I don't know," Dirona admitted. "The gods' minds are not always revealed in the obvious. And our people have always fought each other."

After a sip of herbal, Briga commented, "Only the clothing is different. They kill others or are killed. There will be no answer to my question until I am either rejoicing... or mourning...for my son." She studied the pale liquid in her cup a moment, than looked up at her sister. "What can we do about Danach and Liscos?"

"We're only women," Dirona shrugged. "What have we ever been able to do that was not governed by our laws? Perhaps I can speak to my husband, try to balance Fodla's influence. What of Cluvios? How is he?"

"You wouldn't know him when the evil takes over his mind. I haven't talked with him yet, but he may think the Romani took Alberix away with them."

"Lucius seems an honest person. Do you like him?"

Briga stood up from her chair, hiding a blush with one hand. "I...I must talk with Cluvios."

"And I'll pray to understand the gods," Dirona promised, embracing her sister. "You must trust that Alberix knows his own mind. Remember, Father used to say, "The sun is not dishonored by shining on a dunghill.""

"A saying I never really understood."

"It means in this case that Alberix will not do anything to dishonor himself or his family."

Briga smiled wanly. "Father did have a precept for every occasion, didn't he? Farewell, Sister, for now." *Father's words usually gave me a measure of assurance,* Briga thought as she walked back to her lodge. *I won't trouble Cluvios about Danach. I'll talk to the druid myself. Perhaps I could convince him to follow Dividiac's middle path of dealing with problems.*

❧

Ollam Fodla left Wermaros at dawn without seeing Briga or learning that Dividiac had passed over to the Other-world.

❧

By the ides of the month of Quintilis, Legion X Gemina had been pulled south to Viennadorum on the Rhodanus River, the northernmost town in the Roman Narbonnesis Province. The unit was joined by three other legions recalled from winter quarters in Aqueleia on the Adriatic Sea: VII Dalmatia, IX Hispania, and a yet-untitled Legio XIII. Julius Caesar had arrived on the upper Rhodanus after an incredibly rapid, six-day march from Ocelum, in Cisalpine Gaul, with two legions hastily levied in that province, then moved north to Viennadorum. The raw units had been numbered XI and XII, but had yet to distinguish themselves in battle and receive an honorific title.

Viennadorum was a long day's march from the triangle formed by the confluence of the Rhodanus and Arar Rivers. Now, its wharves were cluttered with supply barrels and bales unloaded from river barges by slaves and legionaries, sweating in the spring sunshine. Teams of mules shuttled the provisions to the legion camps that had been set up around the town.

On flat drill grounds, from sunup to sundown, centurions and tribunes bawled out their training commands into the ears of Cisalpine recruits. The raw men drilled in formation, erected fortified camps, and were ordered on eighteen-mile forced marches in a hurried effort to have them quickly toughened by army discipline.

The cream of the Gallic auxiliaries were cavalry, experienced horsemen in Romani service who were assigned to each side of legion formations as *alae*—protective wings—and were sent into battle to drive in enemy flanks.

Most of the men only caught glimpses of their commander, Gaius Julius Caesar, easily identified by a distinctive scarlet cloak both in camp and on the field of battle.

❧

About a month later, Gallic scouts reported that the Helvetii again were on the move. Roman fortifications along the left bank of the Rhodanus River had prevented the tribe from crossing there, yet with the connivance of Casticos at Vesontio, the main body of migrants had passed through a narrow defile on Sequani territory along the river's right bank. They had entered Aeduan lands, allies of Rome, and already pillaged the countryside for fodder and grain, commodities they would need in their long trek across Gallia to the lands of the Santoni near the Western Sea.

Aedui and Allobroge envoys went to Caesar with an urgent plea for assistance. They protested that their villages were being destroyed, their children sold off into slavery, and their strongholds attacked all under the eyes of Roman armies. Each day messengers from other neighboring tribes came to complain to Caesar and Labienus that an immense Helvetii army pillaged their lands on their trek toward the sea.

Subsequent reports indicated that one of the four Helvetii sub-tribes, the Tigurini, were acting as a rear guard and protecting the main body of their countrymen as they crossed the Arar River. Further alarming Roman commanders was a report that three-quarters of the tribe already had managed to cross the river.

Caesar immediately ordered three of his legions to break camp and marched them north to intercept any enemy warriors remaining on the east bank of the Arar.

Chapter XX

"Don't tell me you're gettin' 'army back' already?" I heard someone say. "Frog shit! You'll never last twenty years!"

I looked around for the voice, wincing at the stiffness in my body. A lanky youth with a shock of unmanageable red hair, the beginnings of a like-colored mustache, and a prominent hooked nose, extended a hand. I slowly reached over to grasp it.

"Myself, I'm Brunix, but they call me Becco, 'Rooster Beak,' on account of this nose. You?"

"Alberix. What do you mean, 'twenty years'?"

"Didn't you sign up for that long?"

"I took the oath as an auxiliary, Brunix, but—"

"Call me Becco," he interrupted, and went back to frying dough for his supper in a pan sizzling with too much olive oil. "So, where you from?"

"Wermaros." I settled my buttocks into a hollow I had found that helped support my sore back. I had done fairly heavy lifting at the forge, yet nothing crippled me like the backbreaking work of digging ditches during the past thirty days, then another eight or so marching along the Rhodanus to this place. I had lost count of the actual time.

Becco jiggled the pan and broke the recollection of my misery by asking, "Where in Lugos's Lance is Wermaros?"

"On the Dubis River, at the big bend."

"Me, I'm from Vesontio..." Becco lifted the soggy edge of his dough with a knife blade to test its crispness. "You join th' auxilia like I did to get away from pig shit on your father's farm?"

"My father is dead. I worked at my uncle's forge, then Lucius came with—"

"Who's Lucius?" Becco didn't look my way, intent as he was on flipping over his disc of soft dough.

"A *centurio* at a watch tower built near my village. I came here to find him."

"And ended up digging frog-shit ditches!" Becco laughed, but it sounded more like a cackle—evidently his beak wasn't the only reason for a poultry nickname. "T' do that," he went on, "Romani got a legionary rank called *Fossor*...'Ditcher'...but everybody was ordered t' help."

I shifted position in the hollow, flinching at new aches. "Becco, where exactly are we? Since leaving Viennadorum, I feel like I've walked across half of Gaul."

Becco cackled again at my complaint. "Me, I've hunted these parts. Below that ridge over there you can see where th' Rhodanus and Arar rivers come together." He indicated the hill with a toss of his head, while scraping salt onto his fried bread from a crystalline chunk. "That's Aeduii land over there, and th' Hels are somewhere t' th' north of us." He opened a leather bag, sliced off two pieces of hard goat cheese, wrapped his soggy bread around them, and tore it in half. "Here, Wermaros, eat this. You look too tired t' cook."

I nodded thanks, but even that hurt my spine. "I just may fall asleep eating." Brunix-Becco had gotten my name mixed up, but I chewed in silence a moment before asking, "If the Hels...Helvetii...are nearby, do you think there might be fighting tomorrow that involves us?"

"Frog shit there will! Romani don't much trust us auxilia, so we'll be pretty safe back here with supply wagons. What's your job when you're not digging?"

"Weapons repair. I told you I've worked at a forge."

"Me, I'm a muleteer." Becco spit out a rind of cheese that sizzled in the fire. "Driving mules isn't for me. I'd rather fight."

"Have you ever been in a battle?"

He hedged, "Cernunnos's Cock, out here there aren't even any 'does' to mount, like there was back at Genava."

I winced at his irreverence. Dividiac had taught me to honor the gods' names, but Becco sprinkled them into his speech like salt on his food.

"You got a 'doe' in your village?" he asked with a lewd wink.

I nodded that I had a girl, wondering if I was lying to keep up with Becco's boasting. Despite his brashness, I liked him. I washed down my last bite of bread with a swig of sour wine from a leather bottle he passed to me. "Thanks for the food," I said, handing the bottle back. "I'm dead."

"Myself, I'm rolling in early, too, 'case there's action tomorrow." He yawned and unfolded a gray army blanket while continuing his thought, "Will be if we sight any Hels. They weren't allowed in parts of Vesontio...too frog-shit rough...swaggering around like they owned th' place."

Becco wrapped himself in his blanket and lay down, leaving his pan to char in the dying fire. I pushed it off with my foot. Soon, my new friend's regular breathing told me he was asleep. His talk of girls had reminded me of Pixtila, but I was not far behind him in falling asleep. My last ridiculous thought, surely brought on by fatigue, was to wonder if Becco would sit up at dawn and crow like a rooster.

❧

It was full night and cold when the harsh, brassy call of a signal *cornua* startled me awake. I threw my blanket aside, painfully stood up, and looked toward watch fires in the nearby legion camp. Officers were shouting to awaken their men.

In moments, a legionary holding a torch, whom I recognized as our cohort prefect, stumbled over Becco's sleeping form, muttered a curse, then bawled, "Everyone up! The Helvetii rear guard has been sighted. All up! Prepare to move out!"

Beccos' sleepy reply grunt went unheeded. The prefect was followed by a tribune, who adjusted a sword belt around his chain mail shirt while spewing out frustration to the gods of the Roman underworld. I had come to know a little about Tribune Fufius Trebonius. He spoke a fair amount of Celtic with an accent I couldn't identify, and had been assigned to our supply unit because he knew the language. Trebonius wanted to be in a cavalry wing, complaining that there was no glory in merely being in charge of wagons.

"Armorers and reserve weapons carts only!" he shouted, to clarify the prefect's order. "Get those mules hitched up and into the camp double-quick, or by Pluto's Prick you'll be assigned to digging latrines for the rest of your service time!"

After Trebonius ran past, I rubbed frosty dew on my face to force myself awake. My clothes were clammy from sleeping on the ground. My back felt only a little less sore than a day before.

I bent down to shake Becco. "Get up. We've been ordered to move out."

"Go 'way, Frog Shit, or I'll split your skull open," came his muffled threat.

I pulled off his blanket. "Trebonius's orders, Becco. The Helvetii are somewhere near our area."

"What?" He sat up and rubbed a hand through tousled hair. "You say th' Hels are *here*?"

"Their rear guard was sighted up ahead." In darkness I harnessed my mule to a cart loaded with leather bundles of the slender iron spears the Romans call a *pilum*. "Becco," I yelled to him, "I've been ordered to the legions' camp with these weapons. You'd better get to your assignment."

"Epona's Tit I will. I'm not staying back here coddlin' mules. I'm goin' with you."

I had no authority over the red-haired youth. He rolled up his supplies in the blanket, tossed it into a cart next to mine, and then helped me finish tightening my mule's harness. It was still dark. I heard muttered, confused curses as men tried to match up horses and mules to traces on the proper wagons.

Becco climbed up and sat next to me. Guided by the legions' campfires, I drove the short distance to a gate bridge that spanned a ditch surrounding the palisade. Here there was none of the auxiliaries' confusion. Well-disciplined legionaries were lining up on the streets outside their tents in marching ranks of ten men each. Camp slaves struck their tents. Some already had been loaded onto wagons in the baggage train. I might have been digging ditch works, yet had many chances to observe and admire legion skills. I wondered where Lucius was at that moment, then thought of Dividiac. *Perhaps it's good that he was gone when I left. What would he think of me in the service of his hated Shorthairs? Uncle was already upset because I wouldn't join him and Fodla in their plot against the Suebi, but that was sheer madness. Fodla took over his mind.*

Fufius Trebonius rode up, demanding to know the cause of delay. A tribune of the guard told him that there were three legions preparing to move out. If they were close to full strength, I figured them at over ten thousand men. It would take time, and reserve weapons carts were to merge into the advance baggage train.

While we waited, Trebonius talked nervously about what was happening, as if the telling relieved his anxiety. It seems that Julius Caesar had met with his legion commanders, tribunes, First Centurions, and Sequani and Aedui guides to plan out strategy. Although no actual contact had been made with the Helvetii, many signs of their migration had been seen in the discarded belongings strewn around abandoned campsites. There had also been a gruesome discovery of bodies of tribal oldsters, who had slipped away to commit suicide rather than impede their families.

The night before, scouts had been sent out from our Gallic cavalry allies to establish the exact route of the Helvetii by tracking the location of their campfires. Orders were issued that if contact were made with the enemy rear guard, two of the three legions brought up from Aquileia, VII and VIII, would move out after them led by Legio X. Trebonius added that Julius Caesar hoped his key tactic, *celeritas*—"swiftness"— would catch his enemy Marcios, by surprise, as it had many of his adversaries in the past.

Nervously fussing with his sword hilt, Trebonius told us that, shortly after the midnight watch began, Aedui scouts rode in with a report that they had sighted the Helvetii eleven miles to the north. They attempted to cross the sluggish Arar River on boats and makeshift rafts. After the scouts determined that most of the tribe seemed to have crossed to the river's western bank, Caesar made an instantaneous decision to attack those still on his side of the waterway.

Trebonius pointed at us and reverted to his gruff command voice. "You two get in advance of the baggage train when those wagons come out. Take a center position. We'll need those weapons in your cart, so keep up or you'll be grubbing latrines when we get into winter quarters."

I heard Becco mumble, "Frog shit, Tribune," but the officer was gone.

The camp gate swung open. Legionaries identified by their banner as LEGIO X GEMINA quickstepped through, setting the pace in a rhythm of tramping hobnailed boots and soft rattle of metal equipment. Aedui cavalry fanned out ahead of them to harass enemy stragglers. I thought I caught sight of Lucius at the head of his century of men, but the darkness and massed units made me unsure. I did recognize Julius Caesar on horseback because of his red cloak. I saw him from a distance at the Rhodanus fortifications, but never close enough to know how he looked.

Another wing of cavalry rode out in front of the next legion. I caught the number VII on a banner, and the name GEMINA, a twin to Legion X. I noticed that the riders were dark-skinned, like some of the slaves I had seen at Arialbinnum.

"Numidians," Becco commented. "Living close to Belenos burnt their skins t' a crisp, but, Epona's Tit, they ride horses even better than Celts or Germani!"

After the final legion, VIII Dalmatia, passed through the gate, followed by covered medical wagons, Trebonius shouted for the armorers to follow them ahead of the baggage train. A camp slave thrust a torch into Becco's hand as I turned the mule into the ruts of the roadway and choking dust that thousands of legionary boots raised. Word passed back that it was halfway into the third night watch and that Caesar hoped to make contact with the enemy in the flush of pre-dawn. Prisoners had reported that the rear guards were Tigurini, one of four enemy sub-tribes.

Some way on, as carts lurched along by torchlight, I noticed the fluttering drop of ravens and heard their coarse rasps, abruptly realizing that what I thought were boulders alongside the road were crumpled human bodies. Emboldened by the torchlight, the carrion birds ignored passing wagons and men to peck at the dead and quarrel, like those I had seen massed around the sacrificial victims at the New Year rites on *Benn Samain*.

"Know who they are, Wermaros?" Becco asked me, sounding strangely hoarse. This unexpected sight of death seemed to have tempered his boasting about joining battle.

"Tigurini stragglers," I guessed. "Cavalrymen must have caught up with them." I remembered that some of our Raurici had joined Marcios, so it was possible that a few of the dead might be our former neighbors from Arialbinnum.

❧

A pale greenish light brushed the eastern horizon when Trebonius ordered the baggage train to halt. I made out the fishy smell of a river that reminded me of the Renos and Dubis. The tribune rode on ahead, then returned shortly and ordered only weapons carts to move further on.

When Becco and I came upon the first field hospital, it was light enough to make out distinct forms. Beyond the road, tents and trestle tables were set up at the edge of a wheat field. Amid the incongruous, soft chatter of awakening birds and a distant crowing of roosters, surgeons in bloody aprons worked over injured men by the light of oil lamps and torches. Acrid torch smoke, dissipating in the cold air, overpowered the scent of hay plants that I so liked at Wermaros. I shuddered at the nerve-shattering screams of badly mutilated men and heard the moaning of those less seriously hurt, who lay on the wet grass awaiting a surgeon's attention. Other men from cohorts of Legio X and Legio VII lay unconscious, or had died in bloody pools from spear thrusts or sword slashes they had not been able to treat by themselves. *Capsari*, medical orderlies carrying bandage pouches, reached them too late.

I was sickened at the carnage, a vast magnification of the dead and wounded I had seen after the Suebi raid on Wermaros. Becco, pale as a dead person himself, leaned over the cart's side to vomit.

Although ghastly, Roman casualties were not overwhelming. Most of the legionaries had received spear thrusts to the groin, where the chain mail of their lorica ended, or deep, long-sword slashes that had hacked past shields and into arm muscle and bone. Working frantically, the surgeons tried to staunch the flow of blood and sew gashed tissue back together. Medics moved among the seriously wounded, giving out pain-numbing potions that would prepare luckless men for limb amputations.

On nearby rise of wooded ground, oblivious to the grisly scene below them, I saw legionaries lounging on the grass near a banner of Legion XII DALMATIA. Caesar had kept them back as a reserve force. The men were not young, obviously veterans of other battles and not Gauls from Caesar's two hastily recruited Cisalpina legions. Despite casualties around them, I heard some of the men complain that in the unfolding battle the cohorts of legions VII and X would take not only the glory, but whatever enemy trophies they could hide for themselves before captured loot went into legion funds.

I had dropped the reins to let the mule wander into the grass, when I saw Trebonius ride up, white and shaken. Beyond the officer, a low, rumbling sounded like the rush of rapids in the river I had smelled. The noise resolved itself into distant shouting.

Becco, recovered from his nausea, asked the tribune, "Wh...what's goin' on in front of us?"

"The Tigurini are about a half mile off beyond those woods, still trying to cross the river. You two dump those javelins on the ground and take your cart down to bring up our wounded. I'll go back and order others to help."

As Trebonius reined his mount away, I jumped down to help Becco unload the javelins. When I walked around to lead the mule by its bridle, the animal balked and would not move.

Becco snorted, "That mule's got more sense than t' go down there, a *lot* more than that tit-ticklin' tribune."

"We were ordered to go."

"*Frog shit!* We're not even armed."

"Becco," I reminded him, "we were issued leather helmets and swords, but in the confusion this morning I left mine with the supply wagons. So did you." The sheathed dagger that Lucius had given me at the parley was attached to my belt, yet too small to defend myself. "We're sure to find weapons on the field. Help me unhitch the mule and we'll just pull the cart."

"You...you goin' down there?"

"Didn't you hear the tribune? Leave the cart here. We can help the less seriously wounded men walk back. Are you coming or do you want a lashing on the *furca* for insubordination?"

After a momentary pause, in which Becco thought about the cross-shaped beams on which he had seen legionaries punished, he gave me a weak grin. "Myself, I'm with you."

I grinned back, yet apprehension had begun to hollow out my stomach the way it had that day with Pixtila when the Suebi appeared, or more recently in the cave with Boccus. Yesterday, my new friend had boasted about wanting to fight, yet now he felt as frightened as I did.

I led the way thorough dense woods along a crude pathway the Tigurini had hacked out to reach the Arar. After walking a short distance, we came upon several of the tribe's supply wagons pushed off to the side. Their axles had broken and bales of goods tumbled out onto the ground. The noise of battle that I had mistaken for rapids sounded louder now. I tried to recall Marcellus's training exercises, worried that Becco, as a muleteer, probably had received little instruction in handling weapons.

Soon the woods thinned out and followed a gentle slope that led down to the sluggish river. At the far edge, nearer the waterway, stumps of trees dotted the ground, and tangles of withering branches hampered footing.

"The Hels cut those trees to make the rafts that Trebonius mentioned," I said, then sniffed the air. "Smoke that smells like burning grass?" Several fluffy black specks floated down on the morning breeze. "These are ashes, Becco. What do they mean?"

He did not reply. *Is Becco thinking of what was happening down below us?*

We had walked a short distance into the stump area, when we came upon the first casualties on the battlefield itself. Bloodied enemy torsos, parts of arms, hands—even decapitated heads—were strewn among disabled wagons, food bundles, and casks of supplies. Most of the victims were Tigurini, including children and women. Becco suppressed a retch, then found the courage to reach down and take a long-sword from a mortally wounded warrior. Unable to resist, the man gazed at him with still-defiant eyes that were glazing over in death. Just beyond, he found a bent pilum still impaled in an enemy shield and pulled it free. Becco looked over at me and held up the sword and javelin with the trace of a victorius grin.

I needed a weapon. A short way further on, I found a dead Roman pinned to his shield by a spearhead. The legionary still clutched his short-sword. I pried it from his grip and tugged off his bronze helmet. My hands shook as I adjusted its padded liner to fit my head, again trying to recall the defensive lessons of Marcellus.

Stunned and sickened at the sight of the sprawled bodies and limbs, neither Becco nor I spoke as we picked our way through the carnage and toward the river. The smoke was thicker now and ashes fell like black snow, coating both corpses and ground. After I picked up a legionary shield, I found the glued-together boards to be lighter than the practice one with which I trained.

There were no wounded men for us to take back—all the fallen were dead— but the shouting was closer now. I saw the riverbank ahead, a confused mass of wagons and carts, some burning. Terrorized horses and cattle were being herded onto makeshift log rafts. A few wagons were afloat in the water, buoyed up by logs lashed to their sides or skin bladders filled with air. The Helvetii had prepared well for their migration, yet had not counted on much resistance, or greatly underestimated the capability of the legions to intercept them.

A crash splintered a cart on one of the rafts, sending the men who were steadying it diving into the muddy river. Splashes from other missiles threw up geysers in the water around them. After I heard a whoop of triumph as a bolt head smashed into a wagon, I looked around. At the far edge of the field of stumps, four-man legionary teams reloaded a row of catapults, the *"scorpiones"* I had seen along the Rhodanus fortifications. Their deadly bronze boltheads induced panic in the fleeing Tigurini.

Now I saw our cavalry in the far distance, slashing at men and women, who fought back from shore with swords and spears, even tree branches and stones. Others tried to swim across the river. Where the Gallic and Numidian cavalrymen maneuvered their mounts in after them, the muddy water was dotted with floating bodies and tinted by bloody streaks, a color intensified by reflections from a red disc of sun that had risen in the east. Fanned by a light westerly breeze, more whitish-gray smoke and clouds of ash drifted toward us from across the river. Our cavalry had crossed over and torched grain barns and wheat or hay bales lying in harvested fields. Buildings and sheaves were ablaze. We had adequate supplies, yet in the event that Helvetii contingents managed to hold us off, or drive the legionaries back, their forage parties would find no food crops or animal fodder for continuing their journey.

At the riverbank ahead, groups of Tigurini warriors, most of them naked, fought off a line of legionaries, harassing them as they tried to gain time for tribal members crossing on boats and rafts. Most warriors had designs painted on their bodies in blue plant dye—spirals and symbols that druids said protected them from enemy weapons. I had watched the confusion of the Suebi attack on Wermaros, yet never could have imagined anything like the bloody fighting happening ahead.

As Becco and I made our way forward in a kind of horrified stupor that impelled us toward the fighting, a band of legionary stragglers looting the bodies of dead and dying warriors, glanced over at us. When one man stood up as if to challenge our passage, I hoped our auxiliary tunics and my helmet and shield would explain our Celtic features. I suddenly recalled the password the prefect had brought the night before, Julius Caesar's motto.

"'*Celeritas vincit*'," I called out. "Swiftness conquers'."

The man grunted, then turned and went back to twisting the bloodied neck torc off a dying warrior.

We were close enough to the river now to hear the metallic clash of weapons, the bellows of the wounded, and even pick out shouted words. The Romani line facing the Tigurini was a solid wall of interlocked shields and jabbing short swords, which moved forward in unison, dropping enemy warriors and driving survivors back into the shallows of the river.

"Becco..." I stopped, sweating despite the cool air, wondering what to do. "Becco, wh...where should we help?" He looked over at me, and shrugged a helpless gesture. "If only I could find Lucius, he would tell us."

Cowardice had not made me halt. As the looters implied, anyone with Celtic features and not wearing a legionary uniform was in danger. If Becco and I forced our way into the legionary line and tried to help them, harried men might turn on us in the confusion. I realized now even more clearly why my father had come to hate war.

We were about five paces away from the base of a sandy knoll overgrown by stunted sumac bushes. Without warning, the body of a legionary slid around the edge of the bushes and down the slope, his mail lorica run through by a spear. Eyes wide with shock, the man grasped the ashwood handle and struggled to stand, but fell back in spasms, then lay still.

"*F...Frog shit,*" Becco stuttered. "H...he's dead too!"

At the same moment I heard a familiar voice call out a command.

"CENTER. Back...Quick step! Flanks. On my command, PIVOT IN!"

"Lucius!"

I ran through the tangle of sumac and stood at its far edge. Lucius, a few paces beyond me, flashed down his vine-wood baton to initiate the maneuver. My friend could not see me since he and perhaps twenty of his men faced the opposite way. Beyond them, a mass of desperate Tigurini warriors tried to hack through the wall of shields with longswords and spears. Some, unarmed, threw their bodies against the deadly barrier.

As Lucius's command was obeyed, the center of the Roman line, with shields still interlocked, swung backward, like twin doors opening. So swiftly was the movement completed, that the foremost Tigurini fell headlong into the unexpected gap. They quickly recovered: teeth clenched in rage, bellowing war cries, the warriors slashed recklessly at they charged past the Romans.

I barely heard Lucius's command to pivot in, but the legionaries on each side of the gap shoved their shields against the warriors on the flanks of the breakthrough, their swords jabbing out from the wooden barrier. Tribesmen went down, tripping the men behind them in a tangle of fallen bodies and weapons. Becco came alongside of me. We stood motionless, too stunned to react, aware only of the howling blur of men ahead.

As the center legionaries struggled to close in again, Lucius ran behind them to supervise the maneuver. In doing so, he glanced up and saw me. Distracted, he slightly dropped his left arm, in which hand he gripped a small cavalry shield. The instant was enough for a wildly slicing blade to catch him on the shoulder, just below his protective mail doubling. Lucius's reflexive jab with his sword caught his assailant in the abdomen. The man dropped to his knees, writhing on the sand as a crimson trickle spread over the upper part of his trousers.

I left Becco, dropped my shield and sword, and ran to pull Lucius away, into the screen of sumac.

"Why aren't you...in the rear...with the weapons?" he gasped, stumbling to the ground, his face white with shock.

"We were ordered to bring back wounded..." I tugged off my neckerchief and wrapped it around his arm to staunch the bleeding. "Can...can you walk back to the medical area?"

Lucius glanced at his men through the bushes. The flanking counterattack had happened so rapidly that the Tigurini had had no time to turn and defend themselves from the side thrusts of legionaries. The Roman center had closed in again and the men moved as a single organism, forcing surviving warriors back down the far side of the knoll and into the bloody shallows of the Arar.

"I should be down there—"

Remembering the night my father was killed, I screamed, "Lucius, you've got to get to the medics!"

Dazed, he looked at me a moment, then nodded agreement. I didn't know where Becco was, but helped Lucius stand. We made our way through the massacre of fallen bodies and abandoned supplies, toward the field hospital.

Chapter XXII

When we reached the medical station, the surgeon-in-charge glanced at Lucius's emblems of rank, a red horsehair helmet crest and twin silver torcs attached to his neckerchief, then motioned for an assistant to finish treating a legionary's slashed ear and cheek.

"*Centurio*, I am the surgeon, Psen-Ammon," he intoned softly, almost as if the butchery around him existed only as dream images. "Sit here. If you will let loose of that cavalry shield, I shall examine your wound."

Lucius seemed as surprised as I to realize that his fingers still were tight around the handle of the shield he had carried back. After he relaxed his grip, I threw it aside and sat on a nearby bench.

I wondered about the origin of the smooth-faced, dark-skinned man with a strange name and accent. He was slightly built, with a clean-shaven head that revealed an oval of blue-veined skull. I watched him unwind my scarf from Lucius's arm and select a flat-bladed probing instrument from several set in a pitcher of wine. The bleeding started again. Lucius winced as clammy sweat beaded his forehead.

"*Centurio*, tonight you can offer a libation...even a sacrifice...for whatever god you prayed to before this battle," the surgeon murmured. "Another finger width in depth and that arm of yours would have been the god's offering." He paused to sip from a silver cup on the instrument table, then added with a thin smile, "That kind of fortune ought to be worth a goat or two." When Psen-Ammon turned to look at me, I noticed that the pupils of his eyes slightly dilated. "You are this officer's slave?"

"*Slave?* No, a friend," I said, resenting his question. "My name is Alberix."

"Ah, one of the barbarian *Keltoi*. 'White King', is it not in your language?"

I wasn't sure if his comment was meant to translate my name or mock me as a Celt. To cover my anger, I demanded, "How will you treat Lucius?"

"Treat? For a day, White King, I shall apply fresh cattle meat to the wound, then bind it with oil and honey."

"What will that do?"

When the surgeon paused to look harder at me, I felt he was pleased at my interest and replied, "You ask about what boils in another's pot. As the ancients knew, in such an open wound heat may come forth. Its two lips become red and its mouth gapes open." In a language I did not understand, but thought was Greek, he gave orders to his assistant, then told me, "Before I close the wound, your *centurio* will drink the waters of Lethe."

I didn't know what that meant. Before I could ask, Psen-Ammon went to examine another injured legionary. I watched Lucius drink a potion the assistant poured from a jug, then asked about the surgeon.

"Egyptian," Lucius replied. "Caesar probably found him as a senator's physician-slave and possibly educated at medical schools in Alexandria. Nothin' but the best for th' Tenth Legion..." Lucius's words became slurred and he closed his eyes to accept what might be the similar feeling of weightlessness I felt on *Benn Samain* from Moira's drug.

When Psen-Ammon returned to close the wound, Lucius was asleep, breathing in heavy rises and falls of his chest. "After your *centurio* awakens, tell him that when he sacrifices that goat, to pray that whatever Long-hair did this had no evil on his blade." He sipped from his cup. "You, White King. Have you a god of healing to whom you pray?"

I thought of our tribal god, Alar, but he was not a god of healing. Not wanting to seem ignorant, I told him, "Druids say that Lugos of the Long Hand is very powerful."

The Egyptian put down the cup and took up a threaded golden needle. "And you have seen helpful results from this Lugos?" He motioned for his assistant to hold the two sides of the wound together with a small clamp.

"Perhaps not personally—"

"But others have told you?"

I remembered that Mother had taken Dividiac to the shrine of Sequana. "There's a healing shrine in Gallia not far from here."

Psen-Ammon nodded, but did not question me. *Does he know that or not?* I stayed with Lucius, watching the surgeon deftly sew together the gash. He spoke as he worked, not directly to me, but described the thread as having come from a land called Sinae, where the sun rose. I realized it was the same shiny material from which the case that encased our tribal god, Alar was made.

After he finished, the Egyptian turned to me. "Do you fear death, White King?"

"Death?" His question caught me by surprise. "I...my...my uncle teaches that this life is merely the spoke of a wheel and that we may return in another form—"

"Our ancients have a poem," he continued as if not listening, "'Death stands before me today like the departure of a storm. Like health returning to the sick. Like returning home from the wars'."

"They saw death as pleasant?" I asked. "Something worth looking forward to?"

"Stay with your *centurio*," he ordered abruptly. "I have much work to do."

I watched Psen-Ammon go to a badly injured legionary, than sat near Lucius, wanting to be there when the drug released him.

❧

As the sun approached its mid-summer zenith, reports came back to our camp that the surviving Tigurini warriors had broken off the flight and escaped into woods along the riverbank, some on horseback. Those who had managed to cross the Arar now stood on the west bank, shouting exhausted defiance before setting out after their families. It had taken the tribe twenty days to ford the river on rafts and in small boats, and I guessed they thought they had time to regroup before the Romani could follow. They would try to attack us with thousands of warriors at a place of their choosing, and not be caught with their backs against a wide river.

Order gradually replaced battlefield confusion. As *Cornuae* sounded recall, exhausted legionaries trickled back to the baggage wagons. Some tried to conceal neck torcs and bracelet in their cloaks, willing to risk a punitive lashing if discovered.

Simmering waves of heat withered the fields of maturing grass. Men of the reserve legions, who had not fought, set up leather awnings against wagons to shield wounded men from the sun, or formed burial parties. As the surgeons finished their grisly work, the groans of the wounded merged with a renewed song of meadowlarks in a bizarre counter-melody.

After I was sure Lucius would sleep longer, I returned to the armory area, hoping to find Becco. He was not there when prefects ordered armorers to drive their carts to the battle site. We were to salvage damaged and discarded weapons, bringing back spears, swords, shields, daggers and helmets. Unusable ones would be smelted down to forge new weapons.

Walking among grotesque corpses littering the field, most of them Helvetii, I picked up armaments, unclasping stiffening fingers from a sword hilt or shield handle, and helping to pull spears from legionary bodies. Swarms of flies crawling on bloody wounds buzzed around my head as I disturbed them. Ravens preened nearby, waiting for the human scavengers to leave.

I found Becco just below the knoll, near the sumac bushes. My new friend was split open from throat to navel, with the bent javelin still clutched in his hands. His eyes were open in a final stare of terror and disbelief. The slash was typical of a Celtic sword wound—the frenzied charge of the Tigurini had cut down anyone facing them as they burst through the Roman center. A boy from Vesontio had been in their path, and my run towards Lucius surely had saved me from a similar fate. I recalled Psen-Ammon's verses: Death *had* stood before Becco and he returned home from the wars in a shroud. The red-haired youth from Vesontio would be buried in a mass grave with legionary strangers as companions. Becco loved to hunt. I hoped, yet doubted, that he would find a bow and quarry in the Land of the Eternally Young.

With that thought, I vomited.

๛

In the morning, tribunes were anxious to question Helvetii and Tigurini prisoners. Fufius Trebonius and an unsteady Lucius brought me to the field where they sat, guarded in sullen groups. As the defeated warriors huddled half-naked in dew-wet grass, iron manacles secured their hands. Slave collars chained the prisoners together. None wore gold or silver bracelets and neck torcs.

Lucius indicated a prisoner whose stained trousers were more elaborately checkered than those of his companions. "I think that man may be a chieftain," he told me. "Find out who he is. Where his tribe is going."

The warrior was bare-chested, with dye designs on his body blurred by sweat and blood. Not sure the man would understand me, I touched him on the shoulder and asked, "What is your name? Your tribe?"

Looking up, he evidently saw an opportunity for a final defiant act. "Tigurini!" he spat out. Noticing Lucius, he repeated in Latin, sure to be understood. "*Pagus Tigurini.* What does that mean to you, Shorthair?"

"So you *are* from the Tigurini tribe," Lucius confirmed. "Rumors said as much. Nemesis, divine retribution, joined hands with Fortuna. Caesar must be told at once."

I recalled the trading fairs at Arialbinnum. "Are these the Tigurini that Cluvios talked about?"

"The same," Lucius nodded. "About fifty years ago they and two other tribes left their territory to raid farms and villages in our southmost province. In an ambush, they captured Cassius Longinus, commander of a legion sent to intercept them. The Tigurini killed him and took his head as a trophy. Before legion survivors were put up for ransom, they were humiliated by being forced to pass beneath a yoke of spears "

"And this Caesar will suffer the same fate," the man boasted.

Lucius bent down as if to slap him, but taunted, "Not today, warrior. It is your tribe that Fate has summoned."

Despite the Tigurini's bravado, I saw that his fellow prisoners were far removed from the swaggering tribesmen at the Arialbinnum fairs, who wore Romani loot that their grandfathers and fathers had taken from defeated legions. *The Wheel of Destiny has rolled in an unexpected way to put the old Romani enemies under their sword. Perhaps this Julius Caesar has been especially chosen by his gods.*

I had only time to question a few more prisoners before they were prodded to a standing position by javelin handles wielded by a guard detail that arrived to take them back to the main camp.

The centurion in charge, a stocky, bull-necked man with pig-like eyes, ignored Lucius and saluted Trebonius. "I'll be taking these animals off your hands," he rasped, "They've a habit of committing suicide when captured. Pity more of 'em haven't done it here. Save th' cost of feeding 'em."

I immediately disliked the man. Trebonius, who had little good to say about Celts, seemed taken aback by his coarseness. "Yes...as...as you will, *Centurio*," he stammered. "Get on with it."

"'Right, Sir. Guards!"—he turned to his men and flicked a leather whip at the prisoners—"Don't be taking any slop from these red-haired pig butchers. Quick step....MARCH!"

As the prisoners jogged off to the jangling cadence of neck and hand irons, Trebonius mounted his horse and followed them.

Lucius frowned to explain, "That was Publius Silanus. The man literally hacked his way to the centurionate in the Hispanic campaign. I've known gladiators with softer hearts. You see how he's replaced his vinewood baton with a whip? That's contrary to regulations, but even tribunes are afraid to cross him. Trebonius acted like a frightened rabbit. Fortunately, Silvanus is not with us, he's assigned to Legio Twelve, new conscripts from the Cisalpina. I suppose he'll make decent legionaries out of the ones that don't desert back to their farms, or he doesn't kill in training."

Psen-Ammon, standing nearby after bandaging the wounds of those tribesmen who would accept medical help, overhead Lucius and commented in his soft voice.

"*Centurio*, in my country there is a saying that a wasp comes to honey, not to sour wine. Your Caesar has opened a wasp's nest these past days. Is this the sweetness he brings?"

Although the Egyptian was clearly insubordinate, Lucius did not reprimand him. I guessed his throbbing shoulder wound made the matter of little importance. This was confirmed when Lucius said he wanted to return to his tent and rest. He refused my offer to go back with him.

Psen-Ammon remarked, "White King, your *centurio* fears to hear the truth."

I didn't want to hear any criticism of Lucius, so I diverted the surgeon's attention to the distant line of prisoners. "What will happen to them?"

He shrugged an emotionless response. "Slaves in the mines, perhaps, where the fortunate ones will die. Yet how much value does a man put on his life, who does not seek revenge?" He fell silent, and I wondered if he was thinking about his own fate. "White King," he said at length, "I must tend to the wounded. Come, you may help."

⋙⋘

Despite the fierce resistance of the Helvetii and their allies, Roman casualties were relatively light. The burial parties dug a mass grave for the dead Tigurini, and Celtic auxiliaries salvaged weapons from the littered Arar battlefield.

Sextus Tullius Tilius, still *quaestor*, was in charge of the legion fund. The officer was annoyed at having to revise his burial club accounts, grumbling that crossing out the names of dead legionaries destroyed the symmetry of his columns, even as he coughed at smoke drifting in through his tent flap from funeral pyres. Tilius was forced to deal with sutlers arriving daily—merchant-scavengers whom he likened to vultures and jackals, whining to buy barbarian loot at the lowest price, and sell legionaries wine and food at the highest cost.

As I half-heartedly sorted through the stock of captured weapons, separating those that were repairable from those that should go to smelting furnaces, I thought of the red-haired youth I had not had time to know well. Brunix, too, had been trying to escape the Wheel of Destiny. I wondered what kind of rebirth Dividiac might have prophesied for him, yet I was too heartsick to look into the signs.

⋙⋘

During two days of rest, Caesar again enhanced his reutation for swiftness. When I was not with Lucius, I saw Marius, Cornelius, and their fellow engineers near the river, felling trees and building rafts onto which they lashed a log roadbed that would span the slow-moving river. I had watched lodges being built, yet marveled at the men who could bridge a river so quickly.

On the third morning, the order came to break camp. Our legions and auxiliaries tramped across the undulating causeway to the western bank of the Arar, completing a maneuver that had taken the Helvetii twenty days to accomplish by ferrying themselves over on small rafts, boats, and floating logs.

The following day, the eleventh one of the month Lucius called Sextilis, rumors swept through our camp that Gallic cavalry under a Lucius Aemilius had encountered a delegation of Helvetii chiefs. They said they wanted to parley with Julius Caesar. Incredibly, their leader was the aged Divico. Lucius explained to me, that he was the chieftain who had led the Tigurini a half-century earlier and humbled the legions.

I realized that the strategy of the Helvetii was obvious—to frighten legion commanders with the man who once defeated them in the field. When Caesar heard the proposal, he quickly agreed to meet. Once Divico saw the strength of his legions, he would consent to a peaceful return to tribal lands. Caesar also wanted to confront the tribe with their most recent transgressions into Aedui territory and demand restitution. I was sure that he also was eager to meet the legendary conqueror of a Roman army.

Lucius's shoulder wound was not responding to treatment as well as Psen-Ammon hoped, yet, as was usual whenever Caesar made a strategic decision, he called his tribunes and First Centurions to his tent and listened to advice about the enemy's offer of a parley. Lucius was invited because of the time he had spent among the Sequani, neighbors of the migrating tribe. He also commanded the towers built to report Helvetii movements. Lucius insisted that I accompany him.

Julius Caesar faced his officers with confidence, although most of them were new to him. My first impression was of a lean, tanned face that reflected days and nights in the field, during his recent campaign in Hispania. Deep creases on either side of a somewhat prominent nose accented a small, sensitive mouth. One barely noticed the commander's thinning hair. As he spoke to each of the men, penetrating eyes beneath square brows seemed to look into the inner being of each officer. I listened as Caesar confidently addressed them.

"They send us their old men to remind us of old victories," he began with heavy sarcasm in his voice, and to laughter from officers. "Let us show them that Romans do not easily frighten! I firmly believe that the gods have delivered Divico's tribe into our hands... into *my* hands...for redress. The same Tigurini killed the consul, Lucius Piso, great grandfather to my wife, as well as the legate sent after them, Cassius Longinus. Surely Nemesis, the goddess of retribution, and my own ancestors, the goddess Venus and Trojan Aeneas, watch our response, along with the Senatus and People of Roma."

I didn't know any of the names, but could feel Caesar's enthusiasm ripple through the officers as they discussed the inexorable workings of the gods and Fortune. More practically, now being backed by five legions, they unanimously agreed with the decision to meet Divico.

Before dismissing his men, Caesar threw out a problem for his staff's response. "My translator, Valerius Trouvillus, has not arrived from Provinica. Whom do we have in the Gallic auxiliae that I can trust?"

Lucius raised a hand. "Commander, my young friend here, Alberix, translated at the questioning of the prisoners. He is Raurici, yet understands both Helvetii and Sequani dialects, as well as a fair amount of Latin."

"The youth standing next to you?"

"Yes, Commander."

"Is he enlisted in the auxiliae?"

"Blacksmith-armorer, sir."

Caesar nodded agreement. "Good. If we can have confidence in your friend's Latin, we may, perhaps, defeat the old one with legalisms instead of legions."

The commander gave me a half-smile, obviously pleased that there would be no delay at meeting with the Tigurini. I know that I flushed with pride at his offer, yet noticed that Caesar was cautious in completely trusting me.

◈

The following day of Sextilis, our Celtic month of Middle Summer, *Mean Souree*, was agreed upon for the meeting. The fields were fragrant with the sweet smells of timothy and alfalfa, and jeweled with white and blue blossoms of clover and wild chicory. Insects buzzed or chirped as they whipped in and out of the warming meadows, setting the cavalry horses' tails swishing in agitation. The horse smells, too, were at home here, yet instead of mingling with the scent of the fields and perspiration of farm laborers, they joined with that of the legionary auxiliaries.

Although the sun was hot, the Tigurini chieftains wore the full splendor of their rank, including furs and clan staff-totems. From a distance I noticed that their right shoulders were bared in our sign of peace, yet the chieftains sported arms and as many items of equipment from Cassius's defeated legion as would fit over their woolen tunics and checkered trousers.

Divico himself wore what was probably the dead legate's helmet. Its crimson crest plume was tattered to a few strands, but the bronze was recently polished to reflect the bright sun. I judged the old man to be in his seventies, yet his full beard and shaggy hair were still tawny-colored. He sat tall and erect on his stallion.

The Tigurini delegation stopped in the road a short distance from us. A bodyguard next to Divico leaned down from his mount and scratched a line in the dirt with his spearhead. The gesture was understood: both Celts and Romans dropped their weapons on either side of the mark, and the horses were cantered to the shade of a nearby grove of trees. I went ahead with Lucius to arrange for good-faith hostages that would be sent back to our camp during the talks. Divico became angry after he heard me tell him of the request, countering that it was Helvetii who *took* hostages, they did not *give* them. After I translated for Lucius, we returned to tell Caesar that the over-chief had rejected his hostage proposal.

"So the old one chooses to be defiant?" Caesar remarked. "An incredible affront, wearing Cassius's helmet and his legion's equipment, but I'm willing to shield my anger to assure success. Tell him, 'Let us talk together as chieftains'."

Divico agreed, yet when the two men were face to face, the Tigurini chief repeated his refusal. "We will exchange no hostages, yet speak here as men of honor."

I translated, noting that the wily over-chief had added the word "exchange," which was not part of the original request for only Tigurini hostages. Caesar nodded agreement to me. It was not an important point.

After both sides had called upon their gods to witness the truth of their words, Divico opened the council. "Caesar Romani, we are here in these lands without your permission, because we do not need it. They are not your lands. You say that the Aedui are your friends and they called for your help against us, because we harmed their people. I say that the tongue of their over-chief is harnessed to lies!"

I saw Divico glaring at me during each translation. It was not unusual for Celts to enter Roman service, yet the old man signaled his contempt for me without attempting to hide it. Lucius had told me that the parley could avoid a repetition of the bloody fighting that had just taken place. On that account, I was eager to translate. My voice occasionally faltered from tension as I tried to put Divico's words into their accurate meaning and avoid a tragic misunderstanding.

The old chieftain spoke slowly, his voice taking on an ingratiating tone. "But no matter, these lies. I am not here to haggle like an old woman over the price of her eggs." I stumbled over the metaphor and translated it twice before Divico went on. "Helvetii are an honorable people. We will settle on whatever lands you see proper to give us in Gallia and are willing to live in peace as neighbors of the Romani, even until the moon be no more."

After the translation, I realized how clever the old man had been, and presumed that Caesar also did. Divico was asking the Romani to award him land that belonged to other tribes, a move sure to alienate their Aedui and Allobroge allies.

Julius Caesar was as clever in his amiable response. "You speak the truth, Divico, these are not our lands. Thus we cannot offer you even a sword point of earth."

When my voice dropped in translating the commander's counteroffer, Divico snapped at me to speak louder. Embarrassed, I repeated, "But they also are not your lands. You and the Helvetii have the territories of your fathers that are to the east of the Jurassos Mountains. You must return to them at once if you truly wish for peace between your nation and ours."

After they heard my translation, derogatory laughter and murmurs of defiance broke out among the Celtic delegation.

Divico ordered me, "Tell the Romani they misunderstand. I am offering *them* the terms of peace, or has their Senatus forgotten so quickly the shame of their chief, Cassios, and the consul Piso?"

Even before I finished translating, I realized Caesar had caught the gist of the reply by recognizing the two names. He reddened almost to the color of his scarlet cloak. His officers shifted uneasily on their horses. "The man's insolence is unacceptable," he muttered, then turned to me. "Translate this carefully. Ask him how many Tigurini did not live to cross the river four mornings ago and cannot continue their empty boasting."

Seeing the taunt, anger-contorted faces of his sub-chiefs, Divico raised a hand to calm them. He looked directly at the commander as I translated his reply. "Be you not boastful, of your legions, Caesar Romani. You have five, have you not? Your legions took a small number of women, children and old warriors by surprise as they slept. The Tigurini learned from our ancestors to fight in the open, not by ambush or treachery. Take care, that your own name not be chiseled on a stone next to that of Cassios and Piso, and that this place not be remembered in mourning by your people."

Divico's companions laughed. Caesar's officers instinctively reached for swords that were not in their scabbards, but the commander signaled for restraint. He told me to repeat the Roman position and remind Divico that the attack long ago against Lucius Cassius was inside a Roman province, where the Tigurini had no claim, and that Romans had never done the tribe any wrong. He cautioned that the latest insult against the Aedui and their neighbors was not forgotten, that the cup of Divico's insolent boasting had turned bitter at the Arar. The final vengeance of the gods of justice would prevail. Even so, Caesar was willing to accept hostages as evidence of a Helvetii guarantee to return to their former lands. If they reimbursed the Aedui for burned crops and homesteads, and the Allobroges for a new bridge at Genava, he was willing to sign a peace treaty with Divico in the name of Rome.

I shortened what Caesar's told me, yet knew Divico would reject the humiliating terms. He did so in anger. "Tell the Shorthair that it is the Helvetii custom to dicatate treaty terms, not receive them." With that, he called out orders for his sub-chiefs to pick up their arms and go back, then flung out a warning to me. "And, young Celt, your accent is Raurici, is it not? Beware that when you no longer please your Roman masters, they do not replace the silver of your neck torc with one of iron, and forge chains of steel onto your heart that shackle your spirit."

Chapter XXII

The old Tigurini chieftain's words stayed with me as I rode back to the legion camp with the others, yet his intended rebuke did not trouble me as much as the condition of Lucius's arm. My wounded friend rode alongside, but his flushed face betrayed fever. He swayed unsteadily on his saddle from time to time.

"Lucius, I feel responsible for your injury," I called to him, wondering if he did not feel the same way. "I distracted you at the wrong moment."

"There is no right moment in war," he said. "Only favorable or unfavorable circumstances of fortune that are acted upon. The wound took me off the battlefield. I might have been killed."

I felt pleased that he wasn't resentful. "You could look at it that way."

"Then stop worrying and that's an order! Psen-Ammon is an excellent surgeon or he wouldn't be serving Caesar's pet legion." After I promised I would, Lucius managed a grin. "Good! I'll recuperate more or less at leisure, but you must go on with your assigned duties."

"Salvaging weapons?"

"You can scoff, yet that's important work. We'll not be finding state armories for awhile."

I fell silent. Lucius's implication was that we would be going deeper into unknown parts of Gallia, in pursuit of the Helvetii. If I felt any guilt in attacking my mother tribe, their leaders' subversive attempts to dominate neighboring tribes, and eventually all of Gallia, justified my decision.

❧

Over the next few days, I continued to sort and repair spears and swords that were constant reminders of Becco's bloody fate. I slept fitfully at night —dreams of my dead friend and Divico's warning merged with nightmares of warriors sprawled in death and hearing bellows of pain from horribly wounded men.

Lucius was foremost in my mind. I hadn't seen him since returning to camp after the parley, so it was with relief that, one afternoon, I heard his voice among our tents asking for me. I ran to find him.

"Lucius. I didn't know where you were. How...how is your arm?"

His reply disturbed me. "Could be better."

I noticed an angry swelling that puffed up part of his forearm and hand that showed outside a sling. I didn't want to tell him how bad it looked, so asked, "What's been happening with the Helvetii?"

"Our cavalry scouts were out searching for them, but let themselves get caught on low ground. They took a few casualties and that made the enemy bolder. The tribe seems to be heading north for Bibracte."

"The capital of the Aedui?"

He nodded. "Caesar is looking for a site that's suitable to our way of fighting. Meanwhile, our cavalry is harassing the tribe's foragers to keep them from getting more supplies..." Lucius winced and gently rubbed at his shoulder through the sling.

"Your arm isn't healing well, is it?"

He ignored my question. "I came to tell you that Caesar is going to talk to his officers in a little while and reassure new men. The commander is quite an orator. Come hear him."

"I would like that."

"Then walk with me to the praetorium."

I was glad to get away from my salvage duties. While we walked toward the headquarters tent at the center of the camp, Lucius explained that Caesar was well aware that the present dangerous situation could destroy his five legions. He was pursuing an enemy force ten times the size of his. If the Aedui should betray him, he would be in the territory of a hostile tribe and totally surrounded by enemies. The Aedui leadership, supposed allies, had been withholding grain they had promised. Caesar was desperate to convince his inexperienced men that Fortuna would not desert them.

When we arrived at the open space before the praetorian tent, legion and cohort flags and standards were set up alongside men privileged to carry them. Liscos had displayed his clan banners and animal-headed war trumpets along his palisade, but Celts had nothing like the impressive array before me. The Legio X banner and a gilded eagle rose above the others—unit symbols that depicted open hands, what I supposed were various gods, and particular identifying emblems for each hundred-man unit. I didn't understand them all, but Lucius had explained at the tower that the standards were used on the battlefield to signal the men about tactical movements, or rally them to one point if they became disoriented in the confusion of battle.

I saw Julius Caesar standing alongside a raised platform, calmly watching his tribunes and centurions assemble. An older man, whom I assumed to be Titus Labienus, the senior commander of Legion X, was next to him. Officers wore parade uniforms and decorations they had earned. I noticed a few men with torcs and armbands taken as trophies from slain enemy warriors.

After the nervous officers gathered around the rostrum, a loud blast of circular trumpets sounded. The men fell silent. Caesar moved to the front edge of the platform, looked his officers over for a moment, then began speaking.

"Citizens of Roma, the Republic is threatened in a way that has not happened since the sedition of the gladiator, Spartacus, and his army of rebellious slaves, twenty years ago. Yet at that time, Consul Marcus Licilius Crassus, whose own son is one of my *quaestors*, defeated these renegade insurrectionists.

"I hear that some of you newer tribunes are preparing your wills. To you I say that Romans have faced and defeated Gallic armies before. In the memory of every man here, the Arverni and Allobroges were humbled. In our fore-fathers' time, Gaius Marius vanquished the Cimbri and Teutones. Yet not all Galli are enemies. Our senatus has recognized several of their leaders formally as 'Friend of the Roman People.' The Aedui in whose lands we stand are allies, because Diviciacus asked us here to help turn back Helvetii invaders.

"It is true that we recently suffered casualties, yet we shall wait patiently to act. *We* will be the ones to choose a field of battle that is advantageous to our tactics. Meanwhile, we remain vigilant. We show Diviciacus that we trust him, yet also that we expect him to honor his obligation to supply us with grain."

Caesar then summarized the success of Romani armies wherever they had fought in the past. Except for Greece, I hadn't heard about any of the places he mentioned—Asia, the Carthaginian and Macedonian campaigns, and his own recent victory over the tribes of Hispania. The City of Roma, he reminded the men, had a destiny, which was to institute a universal *Pax Romana* under the laws and gods of the Republic.

Once Caesar felt he had inspired the officers by reminding them of Roman victories, he began to address them individually.

"I see officers here I do not yet know." He pointed to one man. "*Centurio*, what is your name and legion?"

"Marcus Petronius, Sir. Eighth Legion."

"From Aquileia, then. I dragged you from your sunny Adriatic beaches to the gloomy forests of Gallia. A fine welcome, eh?"

After laughter from the men subsided, Petronius saluted, "Sir. A privilege to serve with you."

Caesar nodded and called to a man next to him. "And you, *Centurio*?"

"Sir, Lucius Fabius. Also the Eighth."

"Good. You, Tribune, there?"

"Gaius Volusenus, from Dertona, Commander. Twelfth Legion."

Caesar smiled recognition. "My new Cisalpina unit. Tribunes and centurions, glance around at the decorated veterans surrounding you. All may one day earn a *corona*, like those that some of my officers wear. I asked them to put on their awards to show you new men the rewards of battle won by your comrades."

Caesar stepped down from the platform and walked among his men. I heard him asking about the names and places of origin of those he did not recognize, and trading campaign incidents with those he knew.

"Many officers here requested assignments to Caesar's command," Lucius confided to me. "His political star is on the rise and this is a chance to impress them by his confident manner. I imagine he's promising each one a land allotment after they're discharged from service—"

Just then, the commander reached us. Lucius straightened and tried to salute, but winced in pain at the effort.

Caesar warned, "Easy, *Centurio*, let that arm heal properly. Where were you wounded?"

"By the river, Sir, pushing back the Tigurini rear guard."

"A bloody action..." Caesar turned to me. "And this is the young Celt who translated at the parley with Divico."

"Alberix, Sir," I reminded him.

"Son, I don't mean any disrespect for your efforts, you did very well, but I've sent for Valerius Troucillus to be my interpreter."

I flushed, but replied, "I'd be pleased to learn from him."

He looked at me a moment, glanced at Lucius, then grinned. "Son, you'll go far with that attitude."

As I thanked him, Caesar looked over my shoulder. "I see Labienus gesturing to me. Fortuna be with you both."

"And with you, Commander." After he left, Lucius remarked, "You said the correct thing, Alberix. I'm sure you *can* learn from this new interpreter."

❧❧

Gaius Valerius Troucillus received Julius Caesar's summons on the ides of Sextilis at his villa outside Arelate, upsetting the merchant's plans to travel to nearby Massilia. The commander, an old family friend and now governor of the province, had sent a message that he needed a trustworthy interpreter because of some trouble with Gallic tribes.

Troucillus had many business contacts at Massilia, the Greek port city on the Mediterranean coast, about thirty miles east of the nearest mouth of the Rhodanus River. On the day the request arrived, he was hosting a dinner for Nikomaxos, a Greek associate with whom he jointly owned an importing business at the port. The guests were in the villa's garden, where his partner's son, Simonides, had been reading them an account of a war in the 119th year of the Roman Republic against the Celtic chieftain, Brennos.

"A coincidence, Nikomaxos, that your son should be reading about Celts just as this message arrives?" Troucillus commented, waving the papyrus sheet.

Simonides asked, "Poor news?"

"Perhaps. The Governor has summoned me to eastern Gallia to act as his interpreter in some confrontation with one of the local tribes."

"That's history in the making!" Simonides exclaimed. "Zeus, to be there like Herodotus and write about it."

"You're an accountant," Troucillus recalled. "Aesop tells of a lion who let go of a hare within in its grasp for the hope of catching a passing deer. It lost them both."

"Nikomaxos was noncommital. "History amuses my son, yet as long as he keeps our account scrolls in order I suppose it's a harmless pastime."

Troucillus now was interested in Celts. "Son, you say this Brennos was threatening the Etruscans from the north?"

"At Clusium, sir." Reading silently to the end of the account by Polybius, Simonides unrolled another section of the papyrus, which he had bribed the city's librarian to lend him for several days. "Here. The Etruscans appealed to Rome for help against Brennos, yet, instead of an army, the Senate sent a delegation to deal with the invading *Keltoi*."

"And what happened?" The question came from Thuccydia, the dark-eyed sister of Simonides.

"Well, it seems the Romans had killed a *Kelt* chieftain and the Senate refused to punish those responsible. Brennos defeated an army sent after him. Just the savage look of the *barbaroi* evidently terrified legionary recruits. Three days later, Brennos entered Rome. Citizens who hadn't fled barricaded themselves on the Capitoline Hill—"

"And these are the Celts that Caesar wants me to talk with?" Troucillus interrupted, clearly apprehensive. "I hope to be wise enough to avoid danger, just as that fox in Aesops's tale of the old lion."

"My dear, Julius Caesar will watch out for you," his wife, Semne, chided, then frowned. "And *please*, Gaius, don't quote us any more of your insufferable Aesopian fables. Continue, Simonides."

"It seems Brennos stayed at Rome for seven months, yet the citizens managed to hold out. After the Senate voted the chieftain an enormous ransom, he headed back north to meet a threat from another tribe."

Nikomaxos predicted, "That lust for battle will be a *Keltoi* undoing." He watched his son roll up the papyrus, then asked Troucillus. "Gaius, does Caesar mention the kind of trouble they stir up now?"

"I suspect I'll know before the next *kalends*, but it's something about the Helvetii trying to migrate through the extreme northeast corner of our Narbonensis province." Troucillus laid aside the papyrus and reached for his wife's hand. "My dear Semne, I suppose I should leave as soon as possible for the commander's camp."

"I'll burn incense to the gods each day for your safety—"

Simonides unexpectedly blurted, "Gaius Valerius, take me with you! This is an opportunity for me to study the northern *Keltoi* at close range. I...I could teach you more Greek...read to you. Sir, it would be at least fourteen, uncomfortable, boring days on the road. Alone, that could seem an eternity."

Troucillius glanced over at Nikomaxos, who made a helpless gesture with both his hands.

"Perhaps, Simonides, you have a point," the interpreter agreed. "Even half a month in the company of an illiterate legionary escort would be a punishment. If you agree, Nikomaxos, I would probably have your son back for the September games."

"He could write about his adventures," Thuccydia added, grasping her brother's arm in excitement. "I'll save all your letters."

"And become a female Polybius!" Nikomaxos chuckled and looked at Semne. "What do you say, wife of my friend? Were dear Ariadne alive, would my son's mother approve?"

Semne thought a moment then nodded. "Niko, let him go along. Perhaps he won't be so restless at his abacus once he returns. You're always complaining about that—"

"*Efharisto!* " Simonides broke in, before anyone could change their minds. "Thank you, Father. Dear friends."

Semne insisted, "My kitchen slaves shall prepare food. I do admit to some apprehension, yet I wish to make your journey comfortable."

Simonides asked, in an uncharacteristic, sheepish tone, "Uh, Father, if you'll advance me a few sesterces on my salary, I'll go out early tomorrow to buy travel clothes and writing materials." Nikomaxos mumbled something in Greek, as he unlaced his purse and counted bronze coins into his son's open palm. He was about to close the drawstring when the youth added, "Perhaps, Father, a denarius or three for travel expenses?"

"No doubt about it," Troucillus quipped, watching his partner give out additional silver coins, "as a Greek, Simonides, you've inherited all the cunning and impudence of the wily-hearted Odysseus!"

Troucillus's wagon was a heavy, traveling dormitory pulled by four draft horses. Along with bunks that could sleep three persons, its bookshelves held the reading material that the merchant brought with him. Simonides added a few scrolls of his own, and requisitioned a folding desk as his property, by opening it and positioning his inkstand and pen box at the top.

The two men and an escort of ten auxiliary cavalrymen left through Arelate's north gate, the *Porta Avennio*, on the Via Rhodani, a stone-paved roadway that led north along the left bank of the Rhodanus to Viennadunum, the northernmost town in the province of Gallia Narbonensis.

Simonides and his father had made the journey many times, accompanying imported merchandise—bronze pans and cups, kegs of olive oil, or the sweet Greek wines and stronger Italian Falernian for which the northern Celts were willing to pay dearly. A single barrel of wine could be exchanged for a slave worth several times that of the vintage. When not traveling by barge, they would stay overnight at a friend's villa at Avennio, then at inns near mile markers XXXXIV, LXVIII, and at Valentia. A day-and-a-half further upstream was Viennadunum, a former fortress-capital of the Allobroges. Thus, even under ideal conditions good weather and no break-down of the wagon or mules it would take six days just to reach the edge of Aedui lands.

The weather turned rainy at Viennadunum, where Troucillus learned from the garrison commander that Julius Caesar pursued the main Helvetii force near Bibracte, the Aeduan capital. Simonides studied a crude military map of the area and estimated that the fortified town was ninety miles to the northwest, over undetermined roads of poor direction and condition. The wagon would be fortunate to make twelve to fifteen miles a day, and that would put Caesar still at least a week off. He felt pleased that his original estimate of fourteen days travel had been accurate and only slightly exaggerated to convince Troucillus that he had needed a traveling companion.

Leaving a frontier river port now clogged with army supply barges and carts, the wagon jolted inland toward the Liger River in the company of a supply detachment—the mens' escort of auxiliary cavalry had defected somewhere in Viennadunum. Continual heavy rains had turned the roadway into a rutted streamlet in which wheels bogged down and hampered progress.

At a fair-sized hamlet less than a day's journey from Caesar's camp, the two men hired a peasant family to guard the wagon and leased horses from them on which to continue. Julius Caesar's letter and the fluency of Troucillus in Celtic passed them through Roman and Aedui patrols. Finally, later that afternoon, the two men were led into the camp of Legio X.

Late on the afternoon of the twenty-fifth day of our month of Equos, which the Celtic calendar considers an unlucky month, I was with Lucius when we saw Tullius Tilius coming toward us.

Despite his obvious pain, Lucius jested, "I wonder what the *quaestor* wants? Surely not to pay us, as legionaries haven't seen a lone sestercius since leaving Genava."

"*Centurio*," Tilius ordered, "the commander wants you and Alberix to meet Valerius Troucillus, his interpreter who arrived from Arelate. He's made the praetorian tent available."

The three of us made our way along mud-churned streets, past rows of legionary tents, to the camp's center. The rain had let up, so Troucillus sat on a folding stool outside the praetorium, his face soaking up the feeble warmth of a setting sun.

After introductions, I was the last to enter a tent that smelled of leather and a lingering incense that did not quite mask the rancid odor of goose fat worked into the hides to waterproof the shelter. Inside were several stools, a portable field desk and chair. Ironbound trunks were covered in calfskin. These made up the commander's sparse furnishings. At the tent's far end, lamps and candles flickered at a shrine to small figures of Romani gods.

At our entry a black-haired, swarthy youth stretched, yawned and slowly rose up from Julius Caesar's own cot. His features reminded me of the Greeks I had seen at Arialbinnum's trade fairs.

"This is Simonides, my partner's son, who came with me," Troucillus explained, then grumbled an aside to him, "Does Caesar know you're in here?"

Simonides replied with affected seriousness. "The commander is chasing down a rumor. I guard his property while he's gone."

Tilius shook his head in exasperation, then turned to me. "Troucillus, this is Alberix, a young Celt Caesar wanted you to meet. He's done passable interpreting, so the commander felt you might work with him while you're here."

"Son," Troucillus commented to me without humor, "Caesar's family and mine are old friends, yet if I could teach you good Latin by cock-crow tomorrow, I would return to Arelate from this mud hole. It's obviously has been forsaken by all the Olympian gods!"

Simonides extended a hand. "Your name is Alberix? That means 'White King,' doesn't it?"

"It does," I replied curtly, recalling the Egyptian surgeon's mocking tone.

"I like it. What's your tribe?"

"Raurici."

"Never heard of them. Where"–Simonides paused to scribble notes on a wax slate like the one Lucius used–"Where is it located in Gallia?"

Tilius protested, "*Graecus* that's about enough! We didn't come here for a lesson in Celtic geography."

I noticed Troucillus reddening, but Simonides remained unaffected. "Sorry, *Quaestor.* Uh...why *did* we come here?"

Tilius glared at him, but Troucillus repeated the question. "You're to meet with supposedly loyal Aedui leaders tomorrow and demand to know why our requisitioned grain hasn't been supplied."

"*That's* the big problem?" Simonides questioned. "A trivial loaf of bread?"

Tilius ignored him. "They tell us that the grain is being collected from storehouses, or that it's in transit. They don't understand why it hasn't arrived, and so on. It's almost time to issue the legions' grain allotment."

"The Aedui, you say?" Troucillus asked. "Who are their leaders?"

"Diviciacos, and a *vergobret* named–"

"*Vergobret?*" Simonides interrupted. "What does that mean?"

"Our chief magistrates," I told him. "An office of power."

Troucillus sighed at the interruption. "*Quaestor,* go on,"

"Caesar suspects that a number of influential Aedui have prevailed on farmers not to supply grain, because they said they would rather be ruled by Celts than by outsiders. If Romans are victorious, Aedui and other Gallic tribes will lose their independence."

Simonides glanced up from notetaking, his stylus poised in midair. "And will they, Sir, just as happened to the Narbonensis Gauls?"

Flushing at the implication, Tilius reached for his sword. Troucillus pushed his hand back, then reprimanded Simonides. "Hold your tongue! This isn't something you're reading in Polybius and know the outcome ahead of time."

Tilius relaxed his grip. "No, and Caesar suspects a conspiracy on the part of Dumnorix, the brother of the Aedui over-chief, Diviciacus."

"Conspiracy to do what?"

"Take over Bibracte–"

The flap of the tent opened as two sandy-haired slaves, obviously from a Gallic tribe, entered with trays of *bucellatae,* hard army biscuits, chunks of smoked pork, and three cups of wine. Alberix saw them glance at him and Troucillus as they slid the trays onto Caesar's field desk, then turn to leave.

While handing a cup to the interpreter, Tilius explained, "The men ate supper early and I thought you'd be hungry. Help yourselves."

Simonides took a sip from his cup, made a sour face, then spat the wine behind the cot. "Vinegar! And those biscuits look moldy."

"*Graecus,*" Tilius told him brusquely, "they're field rations the same as Caesar eats. We're down to watered 'vinegar' and bottom-of-the-barrel *bucellatae.* That's why that grain ration is so crucial."

"The men could mutiny," Troucillus reasoned. "Fine, *Quaestor.* Show us to our quarters and I'll prepare for this meeting tomorrow with the Aedui. Simonides—"

"No, you go, sir. I'll stay here awhile and talk to Alberix. But...you were going to ask about my request."

Troucillus sighed impatience. "*Quaestor,* the young man is interested in history and wants to write about it. Think you could arrange for Julius Caesar to take him on as one of his secretaries?"

I saw Tilius flush again and guessed he felt that he hadn't been with the commander long enough to warrant asking for favors.

Troucillus noted his discomfort. "Of course, I could speak to Caesar myself, as our families are close. But if you could keep an eye out for Simonides... shield him from harm...I wouldn't forget your help."

After Tilius mumbled words I took to be agreement, Simonides leaned toward me to whisper, "Sounds like they're talking about a stray pet!" He stood and faced the officer. "I'm truly grateful, *Quaestor,* and I *will* convince your Julius Caesar that I'll earn my moldy biscuit and vinegar ration. Teach him proper Greek, or something, and I do *promise* not to eat too much. We *Graeci are* known for moderation."

Troucillus tactfully added, "My partner's son *is* clever. Simonides, tell us a fable that fits this situation. Watch, *Quaestor*...he'll have one faster than a strike from Jupiter's thunderbolt."

Simonides searched his memory a moment. "Well, it's said that apes give birth to twins, but the she-ape lavishes attention on one, while neglecting the other. Result? The one clutched to her breast is usually smothered to death, but the neglected one survives. He paused to let the point of the story sink in. "You see, if I'm to make a monkey of myself, I'd rather do it without too much supervision."

Troucillus was not amused at his sarcasm. "Simonides, you're to obey the *quaestor's* orders!"

"May I stay here and talk to Alberix?"

Tilius fumed, "In the praetorian headquarters? Follow me to your tent, *Graecus,* or tonight you'll sleep outside near the latrine ditch."

"I don't think he likes me," Simonides muttered as stood up and clasped my arm. "White King, I'll talk to you later."

I learned on the following day that Caesar's suspicions about the reason for grain being withheld had been correct. Furthermore, the conspiracy of Dumnorix to gain control of Bibracte had been uncovered. Caesar had wanted his ally, Diviciacus, to punish his brother, but the older chieftain had prevailed on his friendship with the commander to plead for Dumnorix. Caesar relented, but warned the conspirators not to make further trouble.

Early on I learned that rumors in a legion camp ran as swiftly and as dark as the Dubis River in springtime. Yet that also was true of our Celtic tribesmen: either the Leuci to the north of us were preparing to attack, or the Arverni had massed their cavalry for a sweep to capture Aedui slaves. Perhaps the Allobroges were in revolt against their new masters, the Romani. Stories like that. At Arialbinnum, Germani had been the main subject of talk and all too often the reports had been true. Soon after Troucillus arrived, word spread around the camp that the Helvetii had halted their wagons at the foot of a hill. They were about half a day's march away from us.

Later that night, I found out that Lucius, despite his festering wound, had been ordered to the praetorian tent to confer with Julius Caesar, Titus Labienus, and First Centurions of two of our legions. The officers were to help the commander determine how to handle the new situation either as an opportunity to take the Helvetii by surprise, or that it would be foolhardy to attack them on their fortified high ground.

I was not allowed inside the tent, where the meeting was just ending. A guard in the Tenth Legion, who knew I was a friend of Lucius and may have wanted to impress me—confided that scouts had come back with a report that the backside of the hill was undefended. The height could be climbed undetected! He added that he overheard that Libienus and the two legions, maybe six thousand men in all, would attempt to take the hill's summit that night. The plan was that, before dawn, Caesar would march toward the site along a route the enemy had taken, signal to Labienus, and stun the Helvetii with a coordinated, two-pronged cavalry and foot attack. They would strike the enemy as I would a piece of iron between a hammer and an anvil.

I waited until the centurions came out of the tent, speaking quietly among themselves and gesturing tactics with their hands—the plan was not without risk—but I didn't see Lucius. As a trusted centurion with Caesar's Tenth, he was part of the commander's inner circle and still in consultation.

Tired, worried about Lucius's arm, I went to my tent.

❧

It seemed that I had barely fallen asleep, when I was awakened and told to quietly harness my mule to the salvage cart and prepare to move out when the order came. To not alert the Helvetii, Caesar wanted the least amount of noise. We were not to kindle new campfires, only to work by embers of the previous night's. Outside, when I glanced overhead at the broad swath of brilliant star points, I thought of Dividiac. What might I be doing had I decided to take up Uncle's offer to train as a druid priest? His world seemed so small and relatively secure, yet locked into inflexible rules that had little in common with the larger world as I experienced it these past months.

Hours before, Titus Labienus's two legions—I heard they were the Eighth and Ninth—had moved out silently with metal weapons wrapped in cloth neckerchiefs to muffle sound. Shields were in their canvas covers. Only the lingering smell of dust, which hobnailed sandals had raised in the night air, betrayed the fact that several thousand men were on the march, hopeful of taking their objective—and surviving.

❧

The pale light of pre-dawn began to silhouette the surrounding hills when Julius Caesar ordered all but one of his new Cisalpina units, Legio XII, to move out as silently as had Labienus's men. I was alongside the camp gate, waiting to take my position at the end of the column, when I noticed a dark figure slip nimbly between the gap in two centuries and approach me. I thought it might be Lucius—yet surely he would not be part of the action?

"*Kalimera sas*...Good morning, Alberix," a voice called out and I realized that it was Simonides. I had forgotten about him. "I finally tracked you down," he said, climbing alongside me on the cart's seat. "Where are we going?"

"Should you be here? I mean, did the *quaestor* agree that you could come along?"

"I've been here five days now. That's enough time to learn Tilius's habits and when to ask about doing what I don't care much about, and when to simply do what I want without asking. I understand we're trying to surprise the Helvetii?"

"Trap them in a hammer and anvil situation."

"Exciting. I have my slate ready to take notes."

I didn't reply. Becco, and even I, had felt that kind of naïve excitement just before our first encounter with Tigurini warriors. *Has Simonides seen even a dead legionary?*

"This hammer-and-anvil maneuver," Simonides continued. "Give me details. How am I to write history if I don't experience it?"

"You may experience more than you want to write about."

"What does that mean? What's *your* assignment?"

"Armorer. I collect weapons from the field and repair them to be reused."

"Necessary, I suppose, but not too—"

"Exciting?"

Simonides retracted his comment. "Alberix, I didn't mean it that way. Hades, my mouth bit off one tough piece of meat! Sorry. What do we do now?"

"Wait for orders to move up and scavenge the battlefield like the Babd's ravens. If we're fortunate, the weapons we collect will be the enemy's." I dreaded the possibility of becoming involved in another massacre, as at the Arar.

Chapter XXIII

I had fallen into an exhausted doze when the approaching sound of horses' hooves awakened me. A cavalry patrol sent out in advance clattered past my cart, shouting that the Helvetii were alerted and taken the hilltop. As proof, they said they had seen their distinctive Gallic helmets, shields, and longswords from a distance. This meant that the fate of Titus Labienus and his men was unknown, but the risky ambush had failed. Caesar's two legions would be quick-stepping back to their camp in retreat.

I looked around for Simoniades. He was not in the cart. *He's gone off with his note slate to watch the battle, as if it were like cheering for the games at our Lugnasad festivals.* As I turned the mule around and went back toward camp, I recalled Becco's fate. Had Simonides been captured or slashed down in a frenzied charge, like the one at the river by Tigurini? I realized the last was a more logical fate—Helvetii would not take prisoners who had to be fed from their meager supplies. Despite the Greek's brash manner, I had begun to like him. I vowed never to let myself get close to another person as long as this war lasted.

When I came to the camp, I decided that I couldn't bear to tell Lucius the news myself. Cavalrymen probably had done that near the gate outside the palisade,

Later in the day, I saw Caesar coming in the distance. Identified by his red cloak, surrounded by staff officers, he trotted his white horse toward the gate. When the commander passed me, he sat rigid in his saddle, staring ahead, obviously brooding at an unexpected turn of events. If he felt that victorious Helvetii might press their advantage and attack his camp, I thought they would only stay and loot the battlefield of weapons and supplies. Then, with relief, I recognized Simonides immediately behind Caesar's contingent. He was mounted on a shaggy pony, his feet almost touching the ground as he rode ahead of one of the two returning assault legions.

I stood in the cart and called out to him. "Simonides! Over here! I...I thought you might have been killed."

He grinned and clucked the pony toward me. "Why would you think that?"

"It was a Helvetii victory—"

"*Lanthasmenos*...wrong! That cavalry officer...what was his name, Publius Considius? It *was* dark, but this Considius and his scouts panicked, saw what they feared most, and didn't wait to confirm who it was they thought they saw. Labienus had taken the hillock and waited for Caesar's two legions to close the trap."

"How do you know all this?"

"It's written in here…" He held up his slate with an understandable smirk. "I climbed that hill and spoke with the Roman sentries on duty."

"But Caesar looked defeated just now."

"No, *thimomenos,* just angry. Wouldn't you be, if your opportunity had been lost because of false information? Once the commander heard that the Helvetii were at the crest of the hill, he pulled his men back to high ground and formed a defensive line."

"Instead of attacking. You saw all that too?" When Simonides grinned as an answer, I demanded, "You're telling me that *you* went and told Caesar the truth?"

"Well, in all modesty, men from Legion Eight brought in a few prisoners. They confirmed what I learned."

I burst out laughing. "I guess this tightens you as the commander's secretary like the iron rim around the felly of a wheel!"

"That's good to hear." Simonides looked around. "Where are the cooks? *Pinao* … I'm starved!"

❧

Although it was well past midday, Caesar overcame his disappointment with Considius, a fine cavalry Decurion, who had fought in the legions of both Lucius Sulla and Marcus Crassus. He ordered the camp palisade dismantled: Aedui scouts reported that the Helvetii had moved on and Caesar wanted to be no more than three miles from them at any time, in case he encountered terrain favorable to his tactics.

Then the commander changed his plan. The distribution of legionary rations was due in two days. Since our allies were still offering excuses instead of grain, he decided to bypass the Helvetii and march straight to Bibracte, the well-stocked Aeduan capital eighteen miles to the north. Unfortunately, a few *auxiliae* deserted and reported this to the enemy, who evidently thought the Romans were no longer interested in blocking their migration, or they had effectively terrorized our legions into avoiding battle. After Helvetii *vergobrets* voted to change the direction of their march, warriors began to harass our rear guard in an attempt to destroy supplies.

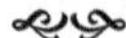

Each evening after camp was secured I had gone to visit Psen-Ammon at the field hospital. Now Simonides joined me. Despite my vow not to get too close to him, we were becoming friends.

We listened to the Egyptian speak of immense structures he called pyramids, and ancient temples that he said were built at a time when Celts were still without horses. That was his way of counting a time far beyond the memory of living men. I found out that shape-shifting was known to Egyptians. Psen-Ammon spoke of cat and ram-headed gods, deities with cow and bird faces. A falcon sun god that we would have identified with Belenos changed shape three times a day, into beetle, hawk, and human forms. Some of the animals he described were so fantastic, such as giant scaled lizards that lived in rivers and ate humans, that Simonides and I exchanged mocking glances of disbelief. We once caught Psen-Ammon suppressing an occasional smile, yet I sensed in the Egyptian a mystical understanding of the powers of the Earth Mother that might be superior to what druids knew. I wanted to tell him about my dreams, because I now believe it foretold the defeat of the Tigurini at the river, but held back. Besides, my new Greek friend asked the Egyptian most of the questions.

Today, while I curried my mule, I looked out at a field speckled with yellow sunblossoms and noticed Psen-Ammon bend down to crush the plant stems and taste the bitter juice that he used to treat patients. Afterward, he stood, stretched out his arms, and offered the small flower heads to the sun, much as Dividac had done at the Birsa with his silver medallion when asking Belenos to point the way to a bright future for our people.

On the morning of the day we went towards Bibracte, our rear guard contingents found themselves hard-pressed to fend off Helvetii attacks. Caesar ordered his cavalry to scatter the pursuers. Then, hoping to lure the main enemy force into a battle, ordered his four lead legions to turn off toward a hill on the right side of the road and form triple ranks halfway up its slope. Legio VII and the two Cisalpina units were to continue on with their auxuliae and position themselves on a hill a mile beyond. The men formed an arc facing the route the Helvetii would follow.

I was with Simonides in front of the baggage carts, near the center of the long marching column, when the legions forded a small stream. We were surprised to hear the sound of trumpets up ahead, but I was not sure what they signaled. The column halted. Something had happened in the front.

Even Simonides was silent for once, aware that we were deep into Gallia, pursued by an enemy that vastly outnumbered our six legions. I had paused at the waterway to wait, when I turned to see Fufius Trebonius riding toward us from the rear. He shouted for the cart and baggage train drivers to turn up the nearest hill, but reined up when he saw me.

"The *brachatae* are behind us, massing to attack," he shouted, using the insulting term, "breeches-wearers," to describe Helvetii. "You're to drive with the baggage wagons into a defensive circle behind the nearest legion, up on that hill to the right."

Simonides asked, "Tribune, what is happening ahead? Why are we stopped?"

"Caesar is angered by attacks on our rear guard and decided to make a stand here."

"May I go with..." Simonides's request was lost in the clatter of hooves as Trebonius reined his horse toward the head of the column. "Zeus take it! I was going to ask him if I could watch the legions form ranks."

"You'll see them from up there." I pointed toward the hill and turned the mule off the road to where there was no path. I knew the animal had a more sure sense of where it could walk safely than I did.

"Look!" Simonides exclaimed, pointing ahead. "Thousands of legionaries are running up the hillside! Listen...more trumpet signals. Do you know what *those* mean?"

"At the tower near my village, Lucius used wooden blocks to show me how a legion forms into a triple battle line, the *acies triplex*. That must be what's happening."

Simonides flipped open the wooden cover of his wax slate. "Go on," he urged, poised to write.

"If you wait until we stop, I can use sticks to show the position of the ranks."

"Alberix, in the name of Zeus start telling me now!"

"All right. The first rank is made up of *hastati*, younger recruits who kneel behind their shields and throw two javelins when the enemy comes into range. Then they fall back behind the *principes*, more experienced warriors who move up and use their short swords to take advantage of the confusion,"

"Speak more slowly, Alberix... 'short swords...advantage...confusion.' Good, then what?"

"The veteran legionaries in the third rank are called *triari*, reserves in a sense. When they see the *principes* weakening, they move in."

While I waited in the sultry air for Simonides to finish writing, I looked along the undulating line of men, which I estimated at being about a mile long. If I recalled Lucius's lessons correctly, Legion Ten would be on the far right, facing the enemy left wing. A strong right front could shatter an enemy's left and send it reeling against its own center.

By midday, when the legions were almost in position, the Helvetii arrived in force. Tribesmen used the bellowing tones of their animal-headed trumpets to signal the wagons to form into a circle on two heights to the left of the road. The baggage, women, and young or old members would shelter inside the tight barricade. A camp for the warriors was set up nearby. On the plain between the hills—a narrow gap in the mountains—our cavalry fought off poorly coordinated enemy attacks. In the haze of dust and shouting, it was difficult to see who had the advantage, yet it gave the legions time to finish their deployment, and even for Caesar again to inspire his men with a speech. I couldn't hear what he said, but it probably was similar to what I had heard on the evening of the failed attempt to outflank the tribe.

At the base of the hill, facing the Roman line, many warriors, whose custom was to stiffen their hair with lime paste and pull the strands into spikey points, had not finished the ritual. Most were working themselves into a furor, gesturing with their weapons and shouting curses at the enemy. Others performed twirling dances that renacted the fury with which they would destroy the enemy. Some were naked, except for torcs and weapons. A few painted themselves red to disguise bloody wounds. Sweat sprayed from their bodies as they jumped and danced in frenzied movements.

Watching the action unfold, I thought that the legions assembling on the hill resembled a busy anthill, while the wild antics of the Helvetii preparing to attack were more like a horde of angry wasps knocked from a nest. I thought of Psen-Ammon's similar remark at the Arar, when, abruptly, I heard the surgeon's voice behind me.

"Once again, White King, the ants and wasps prepare to battle. Where is your *centurio?*"

"Lucius is somewhere to the far right with the second cohort of the Tenth."

"Ah, he would be. Your *centurio* has not separated duty from folly, yet when his arm is a stump, legion recruiters will do so for him."

"His wound isn't healing well, is it?"

"When I last examined the injury, flesh was black and odorous. Evil entered with the metal and your *centurio's metu* brought in the breath of death."

"Metu?"

"We believe that ducts bring noxious substances to parts of the body. There are twenty-two—"

"Will Lucius heal?" I demanded, too concerned to listen to medical explanations.

"It is in the hands of Khensu...in his will."

Frustrated, I protested, "Khensu is one of your animal gods!"

Psen-Ammon's reply was soft. "White King, you have much to learn. Do your people not have gods of healing like Khensu-nefer-hotep? Or the Asklepios of the Greeks?"

"We...we have Sequana."

"Sequana? A goddess like Isis. Where is her temple?"

"I've never been there, but I don't think Sequana has a temple, only a nemeton, a sacred place in the forest. My uncle told me about a well in the center of an oak tree clearing. He goes every year to preside over healing rites."

"This uncle is one of your druid priests?"

"Yes. Dividiac has fallen sick, so Mother took him to the shrine of Sequana."

"I should like to meet this priest-uncle—"

Psen-Ammon's request was interrupted by the arrival of Fufus Trebonius. "Th...the *brachatae* are attacking our...our lines in strength," he stuttered in a nervous voice. "Egyptian! Get...take y...your medical wagons down closer. You, Celt, help him!"

After he reined his horse away to warn others, Simonides and I strained to see what was happening.

Urged on by the bellowing of animal-headed trumpets that added to the clamor, a horde of wild-eyed, painted warriors naked and half naked, some without shields, all wielding long-swords and shouting hoarse battle cries had almost reached the first ranks of *hastati*. The Romans shifted nervously, then, on command, leveled their javelins. A flash of brightness rippled through their ranks in a metallic wave. Even as far away as we stood, we could hear the labored breathing of warriors who had run hundreds of paces up the hill, a charge that carried them almost to their enemy's front line. When the Helvetii were ten paces off, the *hastati* shouted in a combined roar that sounded like a distant waterfall. In unison, the first of their javelins hurled forward, a swarm of glittering points that arced into the massed warriors. Men screamed and fell to the grass. Some writhed in agony, others were killed on impact. After the maneuver was repeated with a second javelin throw, the first line melted back into the second rank of *principes*. The sword-carriers, protected by shields, loped forward to engage surviving warriors.

As he ran up the slope, Celtios, youngest son of Nammeios the Helvete, heard the Shorthairs shout above the yelling of his fellow warriors. His breath came in hoarse gasps. Salty sweat stung the flesh of his knee, where he had scraped it raw in a fall. He had gotten up again and continued forward in a half-limp, but found that he was no longer in the front rank. His comrades had surged up the hill ahead of him.

Sweat burned his eyes as Celtios paused to look towards the noise, now intensified by the screams of warriors, felled when the Shorthairs' javelins tore into their ranks. Wiping his brow with the sword arm, Celtios saw that thin, iron shafts of javelins bent when their points imbedded themselves in wooden shields. Warriors on the ground struggled to pull out the now-useless weapons, some of which pinned adjacent shields together. As the furious men tried to work the angled heads loose from bulky shields, a second volley of the deadly lances glittered down, impaling more warriors. Men ahead of him fell. They half-resembled the straw practice figures outside Aventia, yet the agonized screams and contorted bodies writhing on the ground were those of flesh-and-blood humans.

In his brief stop, Celtios was aware of the beating of his heart, already quickened by the uphill run, but also hammering in his chest from fear. Other warriors ran around him, their glistening bodies jostling his, rubbing off blue and red dye onto his skin as they joined the attack. He wondered where his two brothers were—Nammeios ordered them placed at wide intervals in the attacking ranks to lessen their chance of all being killed at once. Despite the throbbing pain in his knee, he started forward again. Incredibly, the line of Shorthairs had fallen back! His fear abated somewhat, thinking that the enemy had retreated under the pressure of his massed tribesmen. As he limped into the tangle of dead and wounded bodies, he wanted to stop and help wrench javelins from the shields of those still alive.

The illusion of an enemy retreat was abruptly shattered: where the javelin-throwers had been, a new row of shields appeared, locked side by side into a wooden wall. The painted designs formed a garish fence. Sword-carriers moved up to replace the javelin-throwers, then started forward. Stabbing at wounded men on the ground as they advanced, the Shorthairs moved in a smooth unison that Celtios had never seen in charges by his countrymen. His sword hand was slippery from perspiration. His shield arm ached from carrying the heavy wooden oblong on his uphill run. He was aware of men falling backward, coughing blood and clutching at belly wounds. Then, all at once, the wall of shields was upon him.

Hacking in terror at a painted design, he was able to back-step away, but the blade of his iron sword clanged onto a circular bronze boss in the shield's center and stung his hand. He recalled the words of an old chieftain, who advised warriors to climb up the wall of shields and slash down from above at their adversary. Throwing himself upward, in a desperate lunge, he heard his sword clang against a metal helmet, moments before the sudden, sharp pain in his abdomen was deadened by a soft blackness that slowly enveloped his mind.

If legionaries in the third rank of *triari*, who stepped over Celtios's body, thought about him at all, it was only to hope that they themselves might live and come back to collect the bronze arm bracelets and sliver torc that banded his bloody corpse. Moving in relentless ripples down the hill, the Roman line gained momentum and outmatched the desperate attempts of Helvetii warriors to hold it back. Under the unyielding attack of the Tenth and its three supporting legions, the enemy left flank slowly gave ground.

I learned this information later and shared it with Simonides: Julius Caesar had set an example for courage and boldness by dismounting his horse and ordering his officers to do the same, thus equalizing the danger to all ranks. Those who could do so saw the commander in his red cloak, seemingly everywhere along the line, encouraging legionaries in the fighting. Caesar noticed that the Roman right had thrown back the Helvetii attack: the undulating line of his men's shields pivoted to the left, almost at a right angle to their original position. Surviving tribesmen were forced across the road on which they arrived. At this point, the men broke ranks. Desperate warriors struggled up the hill behind them, toward the relative safety of their barricade of wagons. Legionaries were ordered forward at quick-step, to prevent the enemy from reaching them or gaining the advantage of the rise if they decided to turn and resist.

Even though his men were tiring, Caesar had sensed victory, when unexpected shouts and the sounds of fresh fighting caught his attention. He ran toward the site. Waves of Boii and Tulingi warriors, who had been the Helvetii baggage guard, now pressed on the exposed Roman right flank. They threatened to overwhelm exhausted cohorts and break through their lines. The escaping Helvetii, encouraged by the help, turned to renew their attack. Forced to risk a double front, Caesar ordered his first and second legion ranks to fight against the Helvetii. The commander's third, most experienced veterans, faceed the newly arrived tribesmen.

Eventually, one part of the Celts retreated to a hill, and another to the wagon barricade and camp. The latter were captured, after hard fighting that lasted into the night. Orgetorix's daughter and one of his sons became prisoners.

❧

When the fight had moved on to hills over a mile away, I went looking among the dead and wounded for Lucius. An hour before sunset, I found him collapsed in a ditch next to the road. His wound, and a final effort in rallying his men to meet the new threat, had drained any remaining strength.

The littered field around us was a massive repeat of the carnage by the Arar River, with Celtic and Romani dead lying in uneven ridges. Injured men on the ground twisted in shock and pain.

Simonides had gone with me but, at the first screams of the injured, his eagerness to record the battle had evaporated. He stood in white-faced terror with his unopened slate and unused stylus held limply in one hand.

I placed Lucius on a litter, assisted by frightened recruits from Legio XII, who were ordered to help with the dead and wounded. Two men carried the centurion to the medical wagons that Psen-Ammon had brought down to the road. Before I could follow them, I had to prod Simonides out of his stupor.

I told him, "That was terrible to see. Perhaps you should go back to Arelate."

"What? Arelate...?" He turned to stare at me a moment, then slowly shook his head. "No. I...I begged to be allowed to...to come with Troucillus. I won't dishonor either him or my father."

"Then come with me to make sure the Egyptian knows that Lucius was brought to him."

Psen-Ammon worked on the seriously wounded like an apparition, staunching the flow of blood, stitching gashes, and ordering the application of poultices, even as he sipped a narcotic from his silver cup. After medics and *capsarii* separated the men sure to die, from those who seemed to have a chance at recovering, the Egyptian worked on them first. I overheard him ordering assistants who spoke Latin to treat the Helvetii wounded, if the warriors would allow it.

Simonides overcame his shock and helped me do whatever I could. We bandaged wounds and gave out opiates until our bloody leather aprons and those of the medics resembled the gore-stained apron of Fluvius at his butcher shop in Arialbinnum.

A mile and a half away, a battle still raged at the Helvetii camp and barricade, but distance muffled its furor.

Gradually, the medical area grew still as men died or opiates took effect on the wounded. Campfires were kindled. Oil lamps threw out a soft glow inside tents. The area became almost eerie in its quietness. Legion cooks came to say they had prepareda stew from the flesh of horses killed in the battle.

Psen-Ammon motioned for us to walk with him among the casualties. I thought he wanted to talk, but the only comment he made was that it would take three days to tend to all the wounded and bury the dead.

❧❧

The battle ended in a Roman victory, yet many of the surviving Helvetii, 130,000 by the estimate of prisoners—unless they were boasting—managed to slip to the north and enter territory belonging to the Lingones. Caesar decided not to pursue them, but warned the Lingone over-chief not to give the fugitives help. Otherwise, he would consider him to be an enemy of the Roman people and act accordingly.

Over the next few days, burial parties undertook their gruesome duties. Simonides helped me salvage weapons off the battlefield. I went to see Lucius whenever I could. The last time, I found out that he had been moved to a tent with other men who would die.

When I found the place, a brass censer on a table gave off sweet-smelling, bluish smoke. Lucius was half-asleep, lying next one of the Numidian cavalrymen I had seen leave the camp. The black man's thigh oozed pus from a sword wound, and his lower leg was swollen and red.

I was on the edge of tears at the thought of Lucius being near death. After I decided to go out and find Psen-Ammon, the surgeon pushed aside the tent flap. A burly Celt was with him.

"Ah, White King. I thought I would find you here."

I blurted out, "You can't let my friend...can't let Lucius... die!"

"Your *centurio* will die, like this Numidian next to him and the others I cannot help."

"I don't believe you," I shouted. "There must be something—"

"White King"—Psen-Ammon took a scroll from his Celtic companion and held it up for me to see—"this man, Amatos, is Aedui and brings a map of land around Alesia. Is he correct in saying that the shrine to your goddess Sequana is here?"

He pointed to a red mark on a road curving to the northeast of Bibracte. "Yes, that's where I told you my uncle would be."

Psen-Ammon nodded. "I have Caesar's permission to go there with your *centurio* and the Numidian. It seems he is son of an allied king in a northern part of Africa. It would not be good politics to allow this prince to die."

In my grief and helplessness, felt my anger rising and lashed out, "Your remedies are useless, so you'll leave a cure to the whim of a barbarian goddess?"

Psen-Ammon seemed not to resent my criticism. "White King, there is healing there. Your druid uncle knows that."

His calm answer convinced me. "Then for the sake of Lucius we must go."

The Egyptian rolled up the papyrus with a smile hovering on his lips. "We go for the Numidian, who is of more importance. Yet it seems your *centurio* caught Caesar's eye at the Arar and at the parley with the Tigurini."

I looked at Lucius. Barely sedated by the drug, his half-open eyes were glazed with fever. A nauseating smell that incense smoke could not mask came from his wound and that of the Numidian. Rather than praying to Sequana, who had not helped my little cousin at Wermaros, I felt more like cursing Cernunnos for wanting to take another of my friends.

Psen-Ammon told me, "My medical wagon is being readied. We leave within this Watch, with Amatos and an escort of his people."

Chapter XXIV

A wash of yellowish light, thrown from torches held by Aedui guards riding ahead of our wagon dimly illuminated shapes lining the roadside. As we came closer, I realized they were barrels, bundles of supplies and overturned carts abandoned by the Helvetii. Families had scrambled up to what they thought would be the safety of the circle of wagons on the hilltop. It had not been so.

Dusk retained the day's heat that was accompanied by the trill of night insects, distant hoots of *cavannos* the owl, and the faint barking of scavenging dogs roused by our passing. A line of orange-red sky edging the horizon of black mountains to the west reminded me of my premonition, when the red sunset at the Rhodanus made it appear that all Gallia was afire. The moon was new, the fourth day of growing into its light phase for the month. It was *Mat*, the lucky half, a good omen for Lucius, yet the thin crescent was tinted dull orange.

We followed the course of a large river. I lay between Lucius and the Numidian. A putrid smell came from their wounds. Flies buzzed around the two patients, who lay on straw mattresses set in a wooden frame. Psen-Ammon slept at the wagon's back.

We had gone perhaps ten miles, now dark enough for the familiar pattern of stars to appear in the sky, when I felt the wheels jolt off the road and into a field. The wagon stopped. Amatos looked back and handed me a lighted oil lamp.

"We sleep here," he said in a clipped Aeduan accent, "and continue on at dawn." He mimicked sleep, eyes closed. "Your Greek friend snored before he hit the ground!"

"Simonides came with us?" I hadn't had time to tell him where I was going, but should have realized he would find out.

Amatos boasted. "Paid me well for a horse."

"I'll talk to that *ambaxos* in the morning—"

"Indeed, he's a wild man," the guide agreed.

Psen-Ammon roused himself, opened a leather flap at the back to let in air, and noticed the setting moon. "The blood of battle is still on its face," he mused, then turned around toward me. "White King, my people have made Khensu lord of the moon."

I was not reassured knowing that an Egyptian god of healing also ruled the night. "Can you do anything for Lucius?"

"And for the Numidian prince? The breath of death has entered their wounds through their *metu*" I recalled that he used the word once before.

"Vessels in the body through which evil may enter. Twenty-seven are described in the vessel book—"

I cut him short. "Lucius's wound isn't healing. Can you do something until we reach Sequana's nemeton?"

"Hold your lamp closer." Psen-Ammon opened a wooden chest decorated with strange human figures and took out a sealed jug, basin, and strips of cloth. "Soak these in the extract of sorrel, cover the wounds. Sponge their fever."

I had collected the bitter-tasting sorrel plants with Dividiac. They helped in relieving fevers, also as a poultice to lessen redness in deep cuts. The men groaned as I wiped their faces, yet the *shepen* narcotic that the Egyptian had given each still held its power over them. After soaking their wounds with the sorrel solution, I lay back into an exhausted sleep.

❧

I awakened at the sound of Amatos's voice, cursing out his Aeduan companions. Dawn had broken in a dull yellowish light to the east. Low clouds threatened rain. Stiff from lying on boards covered with thin straw, I crawled over the wagon's seat and asked the guide what had happened.

Amatos fumed, "Those spawn of she-asses left during the night. Your Greek friend, too."

"Our escort deserted and took Simonides with them?"

"With the coins I paid them. Some may have been Dumnorix's men. They fish with two spears, not ready to catch either side until they see how strong the Helvetii faction is. Or perhaps they just went back to whore in Bibracte."

Psen-Ammon appeared, his shoes and the hem of his tunic soaked by dew. He held up young mullein leaves. "We apply these to *webnu,* to wounds. My medicines are almost gone."

I told him that our escort left during the night.

"We are without protection?" When I nodded, he said, "Ask the Aeduan how far we are from the goddess's shrine."

Amatos told me we would arrive at the nemeton on the day after tomorrow. Groans from the wagon brought us around to the back. When I opened the leather flap, the Numidian, half sitting up on an elbow, squinted and turned away from the light.

"Adherbal eye hurt," he complained in broken Latin. "Leg hurt."

At the voice, Lucius stirred and also held a hand up against the glare as he gazed around the wagon. I saw his confusion and told him that we were going to Sequana's spring to heal his arm.

"Sequana?" Lucius's drug-numbed mind struggled to understand. "But Caesar...the legion."

Psen-Ammon said, "*Centurio*, you have a victory over your enemies. Now we seek victory over an evil in your wound. Your friend will change the bandages."

The Egyptian watched me as I began to ease off the damp sorrel dressings from the previous night. I gagged at the smell and at the sight of both wounds, now crawling with maggots. I started to brush away the creatures, but Psen-Ammon held my wrist. "No, *anaret* are good. They feed on dead flesh, clean the wound. And yet—"

I finished the sentence he did not, "Yet they are not a cure."

"Your speech is true, White King. Cover the *anaret* with damp linen until we arrive at the shrine, then flush them off with salt water. Tell the Aeduan we must be underway. You must eat."

I wasn't hungry, but forced myself to down army biscuit soaked in wine and a bit of salted pork. A light rain came down almost as soon as we left, which pleased Amatos because it would limit the number of warriors who might stop us on the road.

Towards mid-morning, a group of six armed Aedui passed us. After Amatos shouted out jests to them about taverns in Bibactre, they laughed and kept on. Shortly afterward, the guide turned the horses away from the river, onto a smaller road at a ferry crossing marked by a shrine to Lugos, protector-god of travelers. The flatboat was gone and the ferryman's hut abandoned.

The road led northeast, passing through a landscape timbered with beech, maple, chestnut, and oak trees that were far different from the pine and fir forests I knew.

Distant mountains were hazed gray by the drizzle Rain had let up, but the road was a stretch of mud, where our horses strained to pull the wagon wheels through mired ruts.

At a stream that flowed from a dense stand of beech trees, Amatos turned the wagon toward the grove and drove in far enough to hide them from sight. "We water the animals and rest them here," he said. "Eat again."

It was probably good advice, but the picture in my mind of fat white maggots feasting on the dead flesh of Lucius and Adherbal curbed my appetite.

Amatos had gone somewhere. I was watching the horses, when I saw the guide hurrying toward me. He looked uneasy.

"More warriors, and from their shields, mounted Mandubii," he whispered hoarsely. "If we've entered their territory, there will be a toll hut ahead."

"Can't we pay them?"

"Your friend and the Numidian wear legion tunics."

I understood the danger. We could be captured as slaves or held for ransom to supporters of Dumnorix. Having seen all the abandoned farmsteads along the way gave me an idea. "Amatos, I could take one of the horses and go back to that last empty house we passed. Celtic tunics or jackets might be left behind."

The guide shook his head. "Risk. We wait until nightfall and travel then."

I protested, "And lose the rest of today?" I worried about Lucius, but hoped Amatos would let me take a horse if he thought the Numidian was in danger. "Should the prince die because of delay, Caesar will not be pleased. He trusted you with his life."

"The boy reasons well," Psen-Ammon added, holding a net bag of plants he had gathered. "We cannot risk time."

Amatos grunted assent, but told me to leave my knife in the wagon and go investigate unarmed. I set off, murmuring a prayer to Lugos, and reached the farmstead unchallenged. The main house was stripped of everything by brigands, but I found worn tunics, breeches, cloaks, even straw hats, strewn on the floor of the slave huts. Had they escaped in the confusion and left their meager belongings behind?

With Lucius and Adherbal dressed in ill-fitting tunics and hats at the wagon, we continued on. Road mud gradually hardened under a spring sun. Soon, other ill pilgrims joined us, walking or riding toward the healing springs. No one challenged us, and the toll hut was abandoned. We spent that night again hidden in woods, then started out before first light. We had almost arrived at Sequana's shrine, when Amatos pointed to a flat-topped hill, about two miles to the west. He said it was Alesia, a great fortress-city of the Mandubii. Because of its location, I thought it an impregnable stronghold.

It was late afternoon. Daytime heat and restless nights worrying about Lucius found me half dozing, when Amatos called out that we had arrived. I looked out and saw the first tents and wagons of Sequana's pilgrims surrounding the trees of an oak grove in which the healing spring was located. To the right was a cluster of huts and booths set up by crafters who sold silver, wood, or stone votive figures carved hands, arms, legs, feet, as well as of the goddess herself. Even stomachs, lungs and internal organs that needed a cure were displayed. Some booths sold food and drink. It was like a trade fair, with only offerings to the goddess available.

Amatos pulled into an empty space between two tents. Psen-Ammon was the first to step down from the wagon and beckoned me to follow him. He handed me a gold coin showing the image of a curly-haired man, or god, on one side, and a standing eagle on the other, inscribed with what resembled

Dividiac's Greek letters. "Purchase a leg carved of new green wood and also one of an arm. Be prompt, White King."

I took the coin and walked along the line of booths. At one that displayed superb carvings in walnut, a gray-haired craftsman worked on the figure of a woman. I ran my fingers over two small statues of children, but the man did not look up. I finally called to him that I needed a leg and arm carved of new wood. He motioned with his head in the direction of limbs hanging from a rod to the side. I had experience selling our forge items, but wondered whether I could bargain with the maker of healing images. What was a sick person's recovery worth?

"A leg votive," I repeated, "and an arm."

The man put down his chisel and limped over. "Left or right leg?"

"Ah...right. Left arm."

"You have coins?" he asked before taking the carvings down. "Or something to—"

"I have gold," I answered quickly. "Nothing else to barter."

"A hundred Roman sestercii...each," he said, avoiding my eyes.

I was in no mood to argue price and handed him the coin.

"Ptolemaic," the craftsman muttered, then looked up. "This will do. Take your offerings to Sequana and may the goddess grant a cure."

When I returned to the wagon, Amatos had hired stretcher-bearers. Lucius and the Numidian already lay on litters. Psen-Ammon had put on a white linen tunic that reached to his ankles and draped the pelt of a spotted, cat-like animal around his shoulders. He wore gold-trimmed reed sandals, and a golden amulet around his neck that I imagine pictured his god. The surgeon noted my interest and held up the disk.

"Yes, it is Khensu-nefer-hotep. The god wears the lunar disk encircled by two sacred cobras and holds the *ankh*, a looped cross representing Life."

The unusual clothing made the fragile surgeon seem taller, more imposing. As he ordered the porters to follow us, he handed me a small leather box with a shoulder sling. Curiously, I had not seen him sip from his silver cup since we left the battle site.

While we walked, Amatos commented that many older druids were at a shrine in Gallia called Carnutum, for the annual mediation of major disputes among tribes. As the Egyptian led the way to the spring, priests and the ill paused to stare at the bizarrely dressed foreigner. He was not a druid, yet brought with him one supplicant with short, black hair and a dark beard. Another was a burnt-skinned companion. None dared challenge his authority to do so. A few of the ill even followed us out of curiosity, or hope that the stranger might possess healing powers that druids did not. I wondered if Dividiac and my mother were still at the shrine.

The sacred spring of the goddess welled up in a clearing shaded by oak trees, its black water reflecting the crippled petitioners gathered along its edge. Psen-Ammon ignored their stares and ordered his porters to carry the two men further down a stream that flowed from the spring. He stopped where a mud bank lay exposed in the water's shallows. Water beetles scurried away at our approach, and mud flies swarmed up to circle the glistening ooze.

The Egyptian scooped up a handful of the black mud, felt its grit, then held the sticky lump to his nose. He sniffed several times, then patted the mud back into place, rinsed his hands, and called me over. "White King, the *qah* is good, much like the Nile's. Do you know the achillea plant?"

"Yes, Dividiac and I gathered it—"

"The druid I hoped to meet. No matter, bring me two handfuls of the plant's lower leaves. I shall be further down this stream."

I easily found the achillea and brought what Psen-Ammon wanted to another mud bank, a short distance away.

"Tell the porters to bring the wounded men here. I shall tear the leaves into fragments and knead them into this *qah*."

I imagined that was the word for 'mud' in his language. When I returned, the surgeon ordered the porters to place the two men under a willow tree with branches growing over the stream, then for Amatos to pay them and return to the wagon. He searched in the box he had me carry and pulled out a shiny glass phial. After opening the beeswax stopper, he leaned over his two patients and passed a pungent aroma from the vial's contents under their noses. As they stirred to consciousness, the first object they saw was the Egyptian's golden pectoral of Khensu. The glittering pendant held their attention.

"Adherbal...Lucius...you are awake now," Psen-Ammon intoned. "You must believe that you will be cured." He turned to me and pointed to his mound of mud on the shore. "Cover the leg and arm wounds with *qah* to the depth of three fingers. After I had done so, he waded into the stream's edge and called out the names of the two men. "Adherbal! Lucius! Listen to my words! You will receive the healing you seek from Sequana and Khensu. I hold up his image. Look upon it, look upon the image of Khensu-nefer-hotep, 'He-who-can-banish-the-evil-spirits-of-earth-sea-and-sky!

"The time of Khensu is with that of the first gods, with Ra, Osiris, Horus, Set, Isis and Nephtys. Khensu, who was with Atum when,

"The sky was not—

The earth was not—

The gods were not—

Men were not—

Even Death was not.

"Adherbal! Lucius! You will be as asleep now, yet you will hear and obey my words."

The hypnotic effect of the swaying pendant and monotonous prayer had its affect. After the eyelids of the two men fluttered shut, the Egyptian ordered me to bury the wooden leg and arm carvings in the riverbank. Then he placed the medallion of Khensu over drying mud on the Numidian's leg and stepped further back into the ooze.

"Homage to thee Khensu, Lord of Healing, and to Sequana, goddess of this place," he prayed, loud enough for Adherbal to hear. "Adherbal, Prince of Numidia, knoweth thy names! Deliver him from the evil that possesseth his leg.

"Spirit of Evil! Khensu is known to you and he knoweth your name.

"I, Psen-Ammon-Khensu am pure. I have power over the spells that are mine.

"This is my first bidding to Khensu: Come down and swallow up the spirits of Adherbal's sickness."

The surgeon's eyes were closed as he stood in shallow black mud that held him in its oozing grip. *Is he imagining Adherbal's limb as whole and healthy, trying to transmit his mind image to that of the prince's mind?* I heard him pray again.

"Divine Sequana, Adherbal buries the incorruptible leg-form of living wood in your spring as an offering of thanks. May Adherbal arise again in the forms of health! Khensu! Sequana! Destroy also the faults that are within Adherbal since he came forth from his mother's womb, even as was done to the Seven Shining Ones.

"Deliver thou Adherbal from the spirits that inflame his leg. Draw them into the *qah* of Sequana's sacred spring and cast them off from his presence..." The surgeon paused to let his words be heard by the two gods, then called out, "Adherbal! Adherbal! Know that it is so!"

The Egyptian, at one with Khensu the Healer, repeated the ritual with Lucius, substituting his name and the corrupt shoulder wound.

Afterward, Psen-Ammaon stood in the water without moving for a time, his eyes shut. Then he waded out and slumped down against the trunk of the willow tree, as if part of his life force had drained out of him.

"We await the pleasure of the gods," he murmured in an exhusted voice. "Lie here, White King. Sleep."

I did as he said and fell asleep immediately. I had been without solid rest for several days.

Cold drops of rain spattering my face wakened me. I shivered. In the dull light, I could not tell if it was evening of the same day or sometime during the one following our arrival. Wind driven sheets of the downpour undulated across the surface of the stream in graceful waves. The air reverberated with crashes of thunder that followed flashes of lightning in the dark sky. Psen-Ammon was awake, soaked by rain, yet pulling away a section of dried mud around Adherbal's leg. I came to watch: the flesh underneath was still swollen, but the redness had lessened and the Numidian slept without fever.

Above the wind, I heard Egyptian say, "The rain god, Min, adds his power to the water of the spring. It is good."

A peal of thunder awakened Lucius. When he complained that his mouth felt dry and rancid, I turned his face to the rain. The mud on his shoulder was softening under the wetness, when the surgeon ordered me to peel it away. To my astonishment, I saw that the suppurating wound had almost cleared and was filmed-over with scar tissue.

Just as the storm abated, Adherbal awoke, weak and perspiring. He sat up and tried to explain his experience of the ritual in hesitant Latin.

"I heard your words, surgeon, yet I...I was not here. It was in my own country ...on hot sands. My leg felt... blazing...like the sun. How long this was I do not know. Then, I was tempered in water like a steel blade. My leg...hissed like the metal. I heard your words...saw the leg of wood. It shone like the sun... then it was in flames...burned up. I...I felt cool. It was in my garden...under palm trees... a breeze from the sea. I was cool and I slept..." The Numidian paused, grinned, and patted his stomach. "There is to eat, yes?"

Chapter XXV

Psen-Ammon continued the achillea-mud treatments for three days. When I asked him about the healing effects of mud, he said ooze from a great river in Egypt was used as a cure since the time of great over-chiefs called 'pharaohs.' I asked about them.

"A name for our ancient kings. It is recorded that forty-two papyri of human knowledge were written. Six concerned medicine...diseases of the body, remedies, and surgeon's instruments."

"What happened to them?"

"The language was forgotten and superstitious fools believed the written documents to be magical. They burned some and mixed their ashes in wine to drink, hoping to effect cures." The surgeon thought a moment before adding, "You ask about river mud? White King, we are ignorant of why *quah* is an effective agent of healing."

I recalled something else he had said. "You prayed that faults inside the Numidian since birth be destroyed. What did you mean?"

He looked at me with a thin smile. "You have the curiosity of the cat, Bast. Man is composed of mind and body. One can observe the body healing itself after a wound, but the mind is locked inside the heart. I can only surmise what mischief is imprisoned there that cannot escape. My words open locks, to relieve minds of guilt that may be the cause of illness." I told him I was still confused. "White King, the mind is the seat of understanding, yet may hide what it understands. Let us say that Adherbal has a brother who is older and thus will become king of Numidia before him. If consumed by envy, our black prince may become ill. As a false cure, his mind may suggest his brother's murder. I prefer to purge a body of worms, as an act that allows a person to believe his illness is cast out."

It was something I had not considered and asked if his land had nemetons like Sequana's?

"You speak of a sacred place that possesses healing power? Indeed, many, but, just as here, how they are effective we cannot yet know."

"Or *yet* know? Will we find out someday, Psen-Ammon?"

"If it is the will of Khensu."

"Do you believe in gods of yours who shape shift into animals?"

The Egyptian looked at me for a long moment before answering, "One of our pharaohs taught that there was only a single god, yet even he thought it was Aton, the life-giving sun disc. He could not conceive things hidden beyond the gaze of this world."

"Celts believe in an Other-world."

"As did our ancients, yet they saw the place as a reflection of this world, just as that willow tree is reflected in the river."

"What do you believe, Psen-Ammon?"

"White King, can a Being powerful enough to create earth, sea, the sky, and stars be clothed in flesh and blood?"

The Egyptian again was answering my question with another. He left a solution up to me and went see his patients.

❧❧

By the fourth day, Lucius was strong enough to take short walks with his shoulder cased in a sling. In the afternoon, while Adherbal rested in the wagon, we went to see the sacred spring and observe ill patients hoping for a cure. I didn't see Dividiac or my mother—perhaps they already had returned to Wermaros—but Psen-Ammon came with us to watch white-robed druids recite incantations over votive offerings before dropping them into the pool. Its dark waters were believed to hold a passage to the Other-world of our Celtic gods.

"Why river mud, surgeon?" Lucius asked the Egyptian, echoing my question of a few days earlier.

"I told your young friend it is done in my country. Hapi, god of the Nilus, as your people call our river, is thought to be the Father of Life. How the mud cures is a mystery." The surgeon looked away. "At times, *centurio*, the truth is that it does not."

I added, "Psen-Ammon believes that disease often begins in the heart and mind."

"White King, you remember well. What is imagined can have power that affects the health of a body. My spells, my words and actions, as those of druid priests, may counter what the mind has caused."

We strolled along a path among oak trees that opened up into a clearing and revealed a square temple building with a surrounding porch. Several families lounged in the front courtyard with their ill lying on stretchers. Other pilgrims waited in a line to enter the temple one or two at a time. I noticed all were more richly dressed than those at the pool.

"A temple for the wealthy, "Psen-Ammon surmised. "An image of the goddess must be within."

I heard astonished murmurs at the Egyptian's unusual appearance. Several among the ill came to touch him and ask for a blessing. He laid his medallion of Khensu on them, closed his eyes, and recited a barely audible prayer in his language. Afterward, he shook his head in pity. "Poor shadows of themselves, if only they realized that a cure often lies within."

I was still confused. "Then why petition Khensu and Sequana? The medallion, those votives—"

"Externals, White King, visible signs for words and thoughts." Psen-Ammon paused to touch a man whose withered arm hung uselessly at his side. He recited a brief incantation, then continued, "Our traditions speak of a god who needed only to utter a thing's name and it was done."

Lucius had said nothing more, but remarked, "The Hebrews have such a god. Their temple is said to have no statue or image of him."

"Yes, my people know of the Habiru, a stubborn race who insist that their god is an invisible, spiritual entity who is above all other gods." The Egyptian pointed to posts carved with human features sunk into the ground. "Even these are symbols that people cannot understand."

The wooden shafts were like those I had seen on *Benn Samain*. Hung with mistletoe or holly, some had bronze or silver votives nailed on. Dividiac believed that the posts made contact with earth spirits, from which they drew up powers and transmitted them to the ill person through the metal images.

When I suggested going into the temple, Lucius said he would wait on a bench under a tree until we came out.

A young druid guarding the doorway looked at us with suspicious eyes. After Psen-Ammon spoke to him in Greek, he bowed and motioned us inside.

Dusty rays of light angling down from small windows set high in the walls, reflected from a central pool. A gurgle of water that fed the pool welled up between the feet of a life-sized statue of Sequana. Like Klega's small image, the goddess's hands spread out in welcome. Crystal eyes looked down in pity on those who came for a cure.

A voice from near the statue broke the silence. "Sequana bids you welcome."

It sounded like Ollam Fodla. He materialized from the gloom, seated to the right of the goddess. Moira stood beside the druid, ripples of reflected light playing over her white tunic and blue-painted face. I dropped my head lower, hoping my shorter hair and light beard stubble would hide me in the dim light.

"What is your petition to the goddess? What cure do you seek to…?" Fodla's words trailed off as he leaned forward to examine Psen-Ammon more clearly. "Priest, you come from a far-off land. Shall we speak Greek or do you know the tongue of the Celts?"

"I am poor at it, yet you shall understand. I am from Alexandria, a surgeon-priest of Khensu."

"Ah, an embalmer of the dead," Fodla scoffed. "As your writings have it, 'You have not gone as one dead, you have gone as one living to sit on the throne of Ausar'."

Psen-Ammon masked his surprise at hearing the funerary text and completed the line, "'In life he sits in Amenta. He has eaten of the knowledge of every god. His existence is for all eternity and everlasting in his spiritual body'."

"Well quoted, priest," Fodla remarked, yet without masking a sneer. "I would like to exchange spells with you, should I have anything of value."

The surgeon ignored his request and opened his purse. "It is the leg of my patient that is in need of healing." He selected a gold drachma and handed it to Moira. She gave it to Fodla, who scrutinized the image. "You offer *cavannos*, the bird of night?"

"To druids a sign of evil, yet one of wisdom to ancient Greeks. And, priest, worth a thousand Roman sesterces."

Fodla half smiled and threw the coin into the pool. "May Sequana grant your request."

The Egyptian bowed slightly. "May Ausar grant you eternal life."

I kept my head low as we passed by Sabia, the other druidess. Once outside, I told the surgeon about Ollam Fodla.

"He showed up at Beltaine, one of my uncle's former pupils. Now he's scheming to take Dividiac's place in our village."

Psen-Ammon said, "Your words do not surprise me. I saw an aura of evil around the man. No matter. Let us return and see how our Numidian prince fares."

❧ ❧

Later that day, Ollam Fodla left the temple, puzzled by the strange visitor he had seen. "The clients of the Alexandrian must be very wealthy to afford his services," he mused aloud as he walked back to a hut at the edge of the shrine.

He was met by Moira, who had taken Sabia back to their hut an hour before. Her anxious expression came from a face stained by smudges of the blue dye. "Sabia is ill. The child in her womb is restless."

Annoyed at her report, Fodla screamed, "It is too soon...too soon! See to it that she does not give birth before the equinox."

"Sabia should rest and not stand in the temple all day."

"So be it. Is Triccos here?"

"Inside."

When Fodla entered the hut, a sallow-faced younger man greeted him. "The day's offerings," he said, pointing to a leather sack placed on a wooden chest. "Our pilgrims were generous today. That drachma alone—"

"The money is of no concern," the druid interrupted. "What did you think of the Egyptian who gave the golden coin?"

Triccos shrugged. "A foreign priest commands a high fee."

"Exactly, and did you see how his companion was dressed?"

"Simply, and not as a wealthy landowner. Another outside wore a slave tunic, yet had a shoulder wound not unlike those suffered by warriors."

Fodla said, "No Celtic chieftain would know to hire an Alexandrian physician. What does that suggest to you?" Triccos frowned in thought, but could not come up with an answer. "Fool!" the druid mocked. "Romani legions have Egyptian surgeons. Today we may have healed Caesar's man."

"Caesar's man," Triccos repeated in a mumble, half understanding the druid.

Sabia's loud moan behind the curtain changed Fodla's mood. He hissed at Triccos, "What is this about my druidess?"

"The child is early."

"You mounted her when?"

"Th...the new moon of Rivros, as...as you ordered," he stammered. "You... you watched me."

Fodla slumped in a chair and called for Moira to bring him wine. "Mark the day, Triccos, it must be an equinox child. Keep a record of the woman's time. If not this year, when will we rise against Ariovistos and the Romani?"

"Have you found a leader yet?"

"To lead our wolves against enemy sheep?" Fodla forced a smile to cover his failure. "Sequana's spring is an ideal place to collect information and meet with clan chieftains who are not too timid to plan sedition."

"But the Helvetii plan failed," Triccos pointed out. "Word comes daily of Romani successes. Even the daughter and son of Orgetorix are taken. Gallic chieftains rush to thank Caesar for punishing the tribe—"

"Enough, you fool!" Fodla screamed, his sallow face reddened to an even less healthy hue. "Talk like that will soon have all Gallia in the hands of the Shorthairs. Moira! My supper."

The druidess went to a pan to dish out leeks boiled with pork into clay platters, then broke chunks of bread into a basket. Fodla motioned Triccos to sit opposite him, yet ate in silence, brooding. *All has not gone well. The Helvetii conspiracy has failed, as has their plan to migrate. Casticos fled Vesontio despite being an old ally of Ariovistos. His Germani already have a third of Sequani lands. Thinking this Caesar distracted, surely they will demand more. Aeduii loyal to the Romani watch Dumnorix. Verucloetios might well be dead. At Wermaros, Liscos has not recruited a single warrior fit to even be a sub-chieftain. Dividiac is ill and powerless, yet Briga will be a problem. She'll try to counter my influence over Liscos through her sister.*

Fodla abruptly pushed his plate aside, resolving that Briga would suffer for criticizing him at Wrmaros.

❧❧

Adherbal's leg retained only a slight inflammation as the sword gash filled in with live flesh. I whittled a crutch for the prince and helped him get used to it by hobbling from the wagon to the spring. His Latin was not very good, but we were able to talk. He drew a rough map in the dirt of what Celts call the Middle Sea and showed me where the Italia of the Romani was located, as well as his country of Numidia on the African shores of that sea. Belenos shone there every day, and land was fertile, even though rain was scarcer than in Gallia. They had no snow. A vast sand desert beyond imagining stretched across the entire south of his country. Our Celtic auxiliaries had named him *Dubnogetorix,* "Black Warrior."

I was not too concerned that I had not seen my mother and Dividiac at the shrine. Perhaps my uncle had been cured as quickly as Lucius and Adherbal. Lucius suggested that they might have gone on some business for Cluvios, twenty-five miles further north, to the great Celtic trading center at Vix.

❧❧

A day later, a Latin-speaking cavalryman, who knew Lucius, arrived with orders for us to report to Vesontio, the Sequani fortress-capital that Caesar's legions now occupied. Lucius was unbelieving at first, but the Celt said that several clans of Ariovistos's Suebi, along with thousands of Harudes, were preparing to cross the Renos and join the Germanic king. Alerted to the migration, Julius Caesar had moved with his customary swiftness to capture Vesontio before Ariovistos could reach the stronghold.

❧❧

At Wermaros, Briga learned from bakeoven gossip that Fodla had returned from Sequana's nemeton with a younger druid named Triccos. She decided to confront the two men before they again had time to influence Liscos. With the Helvetii defeat known to Sequani, she hoped the chieftains' ambitions would blow away like wheat chaff in the wind. Dirona told her that the unexpected Romani victory had stunned Liscos. His dejection was not helped by quantities of cervisa he drank to drown his frustration.

Ollam Fodla's lodge was not far from the Acantos quarter in the town. As Briga approached by a back lane, the unmistakable stench of pig wallows pervaded the area. Moira answered her rap on the door.

"I wish to see Danach," she told the druidess.

Without speaking, Moira led her into a dim room where a spicy smoke scent overlaid the foul smell of outdoors. Fodla and Triccos were hunched over a papyrus sheet on a table. The druid covered his surprise at seeing Briga by rising off the bench and forcing an insincere smile of greeting.

"Ah, the crafter's woman."

A clan chieftain's widow," Briga corrected him. "Cluvios is yet my brother-in-kin."

Fodla seemed friendly, "Yes, you were *bena*, wife, to the warrior, Alrix. May Succellos strike the Germani with clouds of blood for their murdering! I heard about Dividiac's death. May he return as one loved of the gods—"

"Danach, bury your flattery," Briga interrupted. "I remember it only too well with a bitter taste. I've come to speak of Liscos."

Fodla's tone turned cold. "Your sister's husband. What have I to do with him?"

"Now that Casticos fled, you've made him believe that he'll be over-chief at Vesontio. That Epanactos is recruiting warriors for him. You've twisted his mind."

Fodla feigned innocence. "Woman, it is drink that clouds his reasoning. Even so, it is the Germani of Ariovistos who threatens here. More warriors would help Liscos be over-chief."

"Lucius says that the king is a friend of the Romani over-chiefs."

"The *centurio*." Fodla's mind made the connection. *The woman's voice betrays that she has feelings for the man. That could be useful.* "Woman, misfortune makes enemies of friends and Germani are pressed for land. This Caesar will oppose them. After his victory, the ignorant of our people whisper that the Romani commander is Lug Lamfota reincarnated. If only your Alberix had sworn vengeance on his father's head in the cave and joined us!"

Briga paled and sucked in a breath. "His...his father's head? Danach, of what do your speak? What do you know of Alrix's death?"

Fodla glanced at Triccos. *Is it possible the woman does not know about Dividiac's relic?* Briga grasped his sleeve for an explanation. "Lucius mentioned a cave once. Did that have something to do with what you just told me?"

Fodla pulled away, concealing a gloat in his question. "Your son must have told Cluvios, yet the crafter never mentioned it to you? I bought Alrix's head in Arialbinnum after the raid, when I searched for Dividiac in your lodge.

Germani know of our people's veneration of the head and the Harudes recognized Alrix's rank. The barbarians would sell their old seeresses for a high enough price."

As she listened in horror, Briga felt nausea rising. She wanted to run from the druid's words and his lodge. Recalling the box with a cedar smell that Dividiac kept in his sleeping compartment, Briga bolted from the dim room and up the earthen ramp into the brightness outdoors. She ran past startled villagers; only the contents of the cedar box was in her mind and imagination.

Inside her lodge, nothing of Dividiac's had been touched since his death. Among the tunics in his storage chest, Briga found the container, smelling of cedar oil and decay. She fought an urge to pry off the cover, but wrapped it in her best shawl and carried it outside. Passing beyond the mountain gate, Briga half-stumbled across the common meadow to the forest's edge, where Klega's grave had been marked with a white stone carved in the crude likeness of a child.

Tearing away grassy turf, Briga scooped out dirt underneath until her fingernails were broken and fingers scraped raw in the doing. She set the cedar box into a hole above Klega's bier, then pushed back earth and grassy clods with tears of resentment... There would be no elaborate chieftain's funeral, no vast pit lined with wooden planks that sheltered a chariot and slain horses, a sword, shield, and chieftain's armor. Neither funeral food nor wine. No stone marker. Not even another mound would indicate the grave's location. *There, Alrix. Your remains in the Now-world will disappear as finally as your plans to begin a new town in which to sign treaties with Renos Germani. Their enmity cost me a husband and your son his father.*

As Briga walked into the forest to be alone for the rest of the day, she realized that Cluvios and her son had not told her about Alrix's fate in order to spare her feelings. Still, she resented a presumption that she was a woman and should not be told, until men decided... .

Chapter XXVI

Amatos and I arrived at Vesontio by late afternoon, with the wagon carrying Lucius and Adherbal. At this point, the Dubis River made a great loop that surrounded the fortress on three sides. Legionaries guarding a wooden bridge across the waterway challenged us. It was true, then, that Caesar had reached the Sequani capital ahead of Ariovistos. *Celeritas Vincit!*

Lucius identified himself as a centurion with Legio X. We were allowed across, just as a foraging detail commanded by Fufius Trebonius returned. Recognizing us, the tribune said that Simonides had been gathering information for his journals and was in one of the legion camps. He pointed out the main camp area set up within the loop. We followed him toward that of Legio XII, located on a wooded plain facing a bend of the river. Most of the trees had been cut to make a palisade that was higher and sturdier than one assembled from wooden stakes each legionary carried with him. In passing along an unpaved main street of Vesontio, to reach the camp, I sensed the near panic that gripped households. There still was a threat of a renewed attack by Germani. A few families had returned to unload carts of belongings and bring them into their lodges, but many houses and shops were vacant and shuttered. Amatos thought owners had fled northwest to Mandubii lands.

At looted dwellings, broken room furnishings and bundles of clothing littered muddy side streets.

When I arrived inside the camp, the same sense of anxiety seemed to affect our new recruits from Cisalpina. The legion had seen battle only once in the recent assault on the Helvetii. Dividiac had warned me that uncertainty bred fear.

I found Simonides in the praetorian tent, lounging on a cot and reading notes he had transcribed to papyrus. I scowled at him, recalling that he had deserted along with our Aedui guard escort, yet he seemed pleased to see me again.

"Alberix! *Thavmassios*...wonderful!" he greeted, jumping up to grasp my arm. "I hope you understand why I had to leave that morning. *Meghalos Zeus!* I couldn't pass up a chance to see Bibracte, could I?"

I admit that I liked his spirit, but hid a smile. "That's a question only you can answer."

His own grin faded into an anxious look. "Why are you here? Is Lucius—?"

"No, he didn't die. In fact, Psen-Ammon cured him at Sequana's nemeton. Adherbal also is recovering."

"*Kalos*. Tell me about them while we eat supper. I've had enough of moldering legion rations and that vinegar they call wine. Let's celebrate your return at an inexpensive tavern that I discovered in an older part of Vesontio."

"I suppose I could—"

He anticipated my hesitation. "You're worried about Lucius? He'll want to greet his men, see how they are. Your *centurio* will be fine without you, and I want to hear about those marvelous cures."

"I *am* hungry."

"Let me get a cloak." He grasped my arm again. "Alberix, it's good to see you so well!"

Old Vesontio spread out from the base of a high bluff on which the Sequani *oppidum* and residences for the tribe's noblemen were built. I found myself thinking like a legionary: from the plain, the fortress had looked impossible to capture.

It was nearing sunset when we followed a new path that led from the camp to a gate on one side of a well-constructed stone wall similar to the one I saw at Genava. The ramparts enclosed log and stone lodges and shops, but in a quarter that seemed largely deserted, except for boisterous legionaries on the prowl for diversions from battles of the previous weeks. I assumed that Liscos's sons lived in the wealthy upper quarter, yet they may have fled with Casticos.

Simonides's tavern was an open lean-to room set against one side of a stone rampart. The pitch of the straw roof reached to the ground. Inside, both legionaries and Celts crowded a smoky common room. The two groups separated themselves on each side of a central cooking pit. A greasy pig carcass glistened on a spit turned by a boy slave. Where the Romani sat, we found two empty bench seats on the opposite sides of a trestle table stained by food, wine, and beer dregs. As we sat down, I heard snatches of anxious conversations about the possibility of an attack by Ariovistos and the invincibility of his warriors. The half-drunken men at our table were Legio XII recruits, resentful at being sent to fight warriors other than Helvetii, their reason for enlisting. Tension in the room was thick as the greasy blue smoke swirling up from the cooking pit.

'Sorry," Simonides apologized. "This *taberna* has deteriorated in the last few days."

I reassured him, "That pork does look good and it won't be moldy."

He laughed, then ordered local wine from another boy slave. I had just begun describing the healing mud at Sequana's nemeton and the strange ritual of the Egyptian surgeon, when one of the legionaries caused a commotion by refusing to pay for his meal. I recognized Publius Silanus, the brutal *centurio* who had taken charge of Tigurini prisoners at the Arar River.

"Y'ought t' be grateful we saved your stinkin' asses from the Helvetii," he growled at the tavern owner. "You'll not get a single sestertius from me."

The proprietor responded in angry Celtic, then snatched up an iron poker from the cooking pit and shook it at the seated officer. Silanus unsheathed his dagger and half-stood, crouching unsteadily to defend himself. His companions rose to back him up with their own weapons. The room was quiet for a moment before Sequani warriors, sitting at their tables, slowly stood and brandished eating knives or belt daggers. A few shouted threats in Celtic at the Romani.

"Great Zeus," Simonides mumbled, "I've got to do something to avoid a massacre. What was your tribe again, Alberix?"

"Raurici. Why?"

"Men!" he shouted, climbing onto the table. "Legionaries, listen to me!" After they turned to look at him and the room quieted somewhat, Simonides continued, "This Raurici with me has just come back from the Renos. He'll remind you that Ariovistos is the enemy, not Romani against Sequani. You all act like those unwashed *barbaroi*. If you fight each other, Ariovistos will be the victor."

Simonides was trembling as he finished, but his ruse released tensions. A few Celts even laughed. Silanus's companions sheathed their daggers, threw a few coins on the table, and hustled their drunken centurion outside. The room quieted again as drinking and dice or board games resumed.

Perspiring, Simonides sat down to finish his wine in one gulp. I told him, "You took a lucky gamble. If one of the Sequani had thrown his knife instead of laughing, the others would have followed his lead."

He nodded feeble agreement. "Wars are started by a foolish act of *hubris*... pride...or some such misunderstanding."

"This ended well, so let's order that pork. You did promise me supper."

"My stomach needs to stop churning first," he complained with a weak smile.

We ate in silence. I did not finish telling him about Sequana's cures.

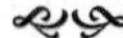

Despite his legions' recent victory, Caesar realized that the morale of his men was deteriorating through an irrational fear of Ariovistos's warriors, and being in an unfamiliar land. To dispel rumors and restore confidence as he had before the Tigurini action, he decided to address all the legions' centurions, some three-hundred sixty officers.

Next day, at the beginning of the second morning watch, Caesar ordered legionaries to remain in camps and summoned their centurions to the front of his headquarters tent. By working in his father's business, Simonides told me he had learned to do what he wished without being much noticed. He wanted to listen and take notes. I was to come with him.

We stood, half-hidden in the shadow of a tent near the praetorium and watched them come: gray-haired veterans, who, Simonides whispered, probably served as recruits in Africa under Marius, then with Sulla and Pompeius. They had signed on far beyond their twenty-year tour of duty. Younger men came, Lucius Fabius and Marcus Petronius bearing scars from the recent Hispanic campaign. I would learn that both died six years later in the siege of Gergovia.

Lucius Velcanius walked with Publius Baculus, who would survive wounds the next year in battling the Nervi, and then be sent with Legio XXII to find a shorter route into Gallia through the White Mountains. Behind them, Titus Balventius and Quintus Lucanius chatted quietly as they reached the forum. They would be killed in an ambush of Legio XIV by warriors of Ambiorix, king of the Eburones.

Publius Silanus came alone, bleary-eyed, flicking the whip he carried instead of a vinewood cane.

For his talk, Caesar again ordered the legions' standards set up. In front of the praetorium tent, silver and gold totems reflected morning sunshine. An array of cloth and fur flags or pennants caught a light breeze. When a trumpet sounded a change of watch, the commander strode out of his tent.

"He's wearing the violet-bordered mantle of a priest augur," Simonides remarked. "Great Zeus...his hands are steaming with fresh gore! Caesar has sacrificed some animal or other."

I recalled the first day of Giamon's sacrifice at Wermaros. "I helped my uncle Dividiac sacrifice at our Beltaine festival—"

"Just watch."

Two orderlies followed Caesar. One carried a bronze bowl, the other a pitcher of water and a towel. Centurions watched in silence as their commander rinsed and dried his bloodied hands. Caesar mounted the rostrum, glanced over his officers a moment, then announced in a strong voice, "All the auspices are good!" After spirited applause, he continued, "When I arose this morning, a wild drake was sitting before my tent, as if summoned there by Jupiter himself. It made no effort to escape and I swear by the god that it presented its breast to me as an offering that would prophecy victory for us. Indeed, its entrails were whole and without disease."

An aide appeared, carrying the limp body of the mallard, its metallic blue-and-copper sheen stained with gore. He placed the sacrificed bird at the foot of the rostrum.

Caesar nodded approval. "My brave centurions, you are the *fasces*, the combined rods that give strength and order to your legions. You administer discipline and transmit orders from your legates through their tribunes. You do not question these orders, but trust that they are based on strategies to which you are not privileged. Is that not so?"

After murmurs of agreement came from the men, Caesar frowned and continued in a voice that had lost its friendly tone. "Why, then, centurions, do you question my decision to pursue the Germani? During my consulship, Ariovistos was eager to seek the friendship of the Roman people. Why should any of you think that he would be so foolish as to cancel his obligations to us? I am convinced that when the king sees the fairness of what I ask of him, he will not reject my friendship or that of the Senate."

Caesar went on to chide the men for their lack of trust in their own courage and his competence as a commander. Asking the group why they feared the Germani, he pointed out that the Helvetii had defeated them on most occasions. Roman legions had just beaten an immense army of that tribe, the greatest yet assembled in Gallia. It was by cunning that Ariovistos defeated Gallic forces, not by pitched battles. Still less, he stated, would the king attack the disciplined legions of his friend and ally, Gaius Julius Caesar.

One *centurio*, who Caesar recognized, raised a hand. "Publius Baculus. Speak."

"Commander, we're short of supplies. A legionary may march on booted feet, yet his stomach tells him for how long and how far."

"Well said, Publius," Caesar replied, to chuckles from the assembly. "Tell your men that Sequani, Leuci, and Lingones now bring in grain requisitions."

I noted a few of the younger centurions glance down and shift uneasily. Like our warriors, most were promoted to their rank through acts of bravery, yet some might have been influenced by fears about the legions' "Two-Year Wonder Warriors"—short-term cohort tribunes. I hoped that as they heard Caesar recall his own successes and good fortune, they would regret their fearfulness.

To conclude his appeal, the commander ordered that the *vexillum* standard of Legio X, surmounted by its golden eagle, be brought forward, along with the insignia of the various cohorts. Raising his voice so that even those in the rear ranks would be sure to hear, Caesar ended with an unexpected announcement.

"I will do something I had intended to postpone for several days. I will order all the camps taken down during the night, because I want to know whether your shame and sense of duty are stronger than your fear. If no other unit follows me, I shall march out only with Legion Ten. I have no doubts whatsoever about the brave men in the Tenth. They will be both my bodyguard and vanguard."

For a moment, the men stirred uneasily, murmuring among themselves, then Marcus Petronius shouted out, "Caesar! Caesar! Lead us to victory as you did in Hispania!"

The cry was taken up. Other centurions pressed forward to pledge their loyalty. In the rush to reassure their commander of support, the eager officers trampled underfoot the body of the hapless mallard duck.

The first tribunes to thank Caesar for his confidence in them were those of Legio X. A few who had made wills burned the condemnatory papyri in his presence. Tribunes from other legions came forward to repeat the ritual, or swear assurances of loyalty.

"That fox!" Simonides marveled. "I don't think Petronius was put up to his spontaneous cheers, but Caesar's rhetoric molded him and the others to his wishes, like...like a lump of clay is turned into a useful object. Beautifully done!"

I agreed that not even my father might have been able to convince hundreds of desperate Raurici that he was right about Germani weaknesses.

Once the assembly was dismissed, the centurions returned to their units with the new orders. The balance of the day was spent striking tents, securing equipment and supplies in carts, and loading baggage wagons with the belongings of officers and men.

By the time legionaries were cooking evening meals, the camps had been dismantled and the wagons ready. Cohorts were ordered to move out at first light.

Simonides seemed to be able to discover everything. He told me that Caesar had met with the Aeduan, Diviciacus, to draw up maps of a northern road through open country, an easy route for the legions to take. My Greek friend went back to the praetorian tent for supper. I ate bread and cold sausage rations with other auxiliaries, then spent an uncomfortable night in a sudden rainstorm, wrapped in a wet cloak and sleeping on the ground. I was almost glad when the blare of trumpets roused me for what would be the first of several twenty-five-mile-a-day forced marches. Swiftness might conquer, yet why did it always have to start on foot at such an early hour!

❧❧

On the seventh day of the march, Sequani scouts reported that they had sighted advance cavalry units of Ariovistos's warriors. The Germani were about a long day's journey ahead of us, heading in our direction.

Simonides realized that he was with Julius Caesar only because of Troucillus's influence, so was careful to keep out of the commander's way. He told me about a man with a name that sounded like Hertios, who was Caesar's secretary. This Hertios had appeared in camp a few times and sent frequent dispatches to Roma by couriers.

๛

Caesar gained a victory over Ariovistos and his allies. Simonides had promised to send his sister letters about his experiences in Gaul, through his father. He read me his latest about the successful campaign.

Land of the Sequani in Gallia Comata.

Month of September, Consulship of Lucius Piso and Aulus Gabilius.

My esteemed Father Nikomaxus, from your loving son, Simonides.

As I write to you there in Massilia, the dreadful cries of the wounded and dying still assail my ears, in the same way Roman legions attacked the phalanxes of the Germani king, Ariovistos, a few days earlier. I have witnessed my second battle, this one at close enough range to have been thoroughly frightening. It is an ugly sight when you are almost in the midst of fighting and not just reading about it in Thucydides! I must say that it has given me a new respect for the courage of our ancestors long ago in opposing the ambitions of the Persians under Darius and Xerxes. Yet if there is any glory to fighting, as at Marathon and Thermopolye, it is entirely in the bravery of men in a fearsome and bloody battle line. Here I must say in the equal bravery of both the legionaries of Rome and barbarian warrior allies. I admire the skill of Julius Caesar, but then I do not know any other commanders. Perhaps they are all like him. He gave a talk at Vesontio, after he found out that almost all his tribunes were about to desert their legions, because of rumors about the Germani that had taken on a fearsomeness rivaling that of Polyphemos.

They say that Caesar studied oratory at the School of Apollonios on Rhodes, so there was a clear logic in his presentation. Yet, beyond that, his words were alive with a belief in himself and his men. I have notes to his speech, which I will send once I've organized them into a proper grammar that does the commander justice. When you realize where we are in the middle of foreign territory that is as rotten with intrigue as an over-ripe melon, with only six under-strength legions and auxiliae of doubtful trust, you can appreciate the boldness of Caesar. It was reported that over three hundred sixty-five thousand Helvetii migrated, of whom about a third were warriors under arms. The Romans were outnumbered almost five to one! Those are not odds that even the bravest gladiator would take in our arena. Personally, I believe the numbers to be exaggerated, yet this does not detract from a brilliant victory for Rome. I wanted to research this more by speaking with Helvetii prisoners, even though they may lessen numbers to excuse their defeat. The truth will be more readily ascertained if I inquire from several sources. I was unable to do so because of Caesar's dictum 'Celeritas Vincit.' He rapidly moved to engage Ariovistos.

If they have fewer men, it is the discipline of the Romans that makes the difference. Moreover, each legionary is a specialist at construction, repair, or supply tasks. At Vesontio, Caesar began his speech by reprimanding centurions for questioning his decision to set out after Ariovistos, because they did not know all the facts concerning the matter. Not that he doesn't keep his officers informed; Lucius, the centurion I first met, told me that the commander confers with his staff officers and asks their opinions beforebattle. Once a decision is reached, he demands total obedience.

There was a parley with Ariovistos. Caesar wouldn't let me come with the nego tiators—too dangerous he said—yet I think he doesn't fully trust me or he doesn't want me to have access to certain information, since his own secretary, Aulus Hirtius, is helping him write an account of the war. The parley with Ariovistos failed, largely due to the hubris of the king, who arrogantly ordered Romans out of Gallia, even though he himself is an invader. Caesar refused the second offer of a meeting, but sent Valerius Troucillus and Marcus Metius, who had ties of hospitality with the Germani, to see what Ariovistos had to say. The king arrested the two men as spies and put them in chains! When Caesar heard this, he realized the Germani were not serious about desiring peace, and ordered a fortified camp set up, facing the enemy position. Since I've written about the ensuing battle, in which Troucillus and Metius were rescued, thank Zeus, and the Germani completely routed, I won't give all the details here.

Troucillus left for home soon after his release. I had hoped to give him a rough manuscript about the Helvetii defeat, but, as I said, Caesar moved too swiftly. We scarcely stay in camp for more than a day or two, and I've been on the move continually since about the ides of Sextilis. At the end of the day I'm too exhausted to write much! I've met a young Kelt, Alberix by name, the son of a Raurici chief who was killed by Germani. He was at the parley with Ariovistos and told me the king was unbelievably insulting, by challenging Romans to attack whenever they wished. Hadn't the fool heard of the Helvetii defeat? Ariovistos had been declared 'Rex et Amicus' by the Senate, recommended by Caesar when he was consul. But the king was so arrogant and sure of himself that the honor meant nothing. Yet the Fates will have their sport. It wasn't only this blatant hubris that led to his downfall. Caesar found out from prisoners that Germani, like Keltoi, have a superstition concerning the phases of the moon. Their crones prophesy by consulting marked twigs from fruit trees, and had warned that the warriors would lose any battle fought before the appreance of a new moon. Caesar lost no time in taking advantage of the information and immediately ordered his legions deployed. He cleverly placed the auxiliae in front, to give Ariovistos the impression of a greater number of regulars. The commander opened the battle with Legio X attacking the enemy left wing, which he correctly considered their weakest flank. The Germani rapidly gave way, yet if it had not been for reserve legions brought in by a cavalry decurion, Publius Crassus, our own right might not have held. I'm sitting at the portable table and stool that you sent me, Father, about two hundred and fifty paces from what was the main battle line. Ahead of me I can see the carts and wagons that the Germani set up as a barricade to prevent their warriors from falling back. Some reserve cohorts are still searching for survivors among women and children. Caesar has gone with his cavalry in pursuit of Ariovistos and the remnant of his army, which is trying to get back to its own territory at the Rhenos. That fabled river, about fifteen miles away, marks the boundary of Germania and Gallia. I hope to see it while here.

Medical teams are helping the wounded and sorting men who might live from parents, wives, children, and amores, who finally might comfort those who are sure to die of their wounds. It is the pitiful cries of the injured that makes me want to stop up my ears with beeswax.

I came intending to write of glorious ordeals, like the adventures of Odysseus, but all I have seen are fallen legionaries and enemy warriors, whose bodies lie tangled in a ridge of horror, their last blood coagulating into each others' wounds, each a man who was alive three days ago. They look less than glorious now, and if the reward of their bravery is in their concept of an Underworld, that is only a small consolation for the dead. The men's new life with Hades is no substitute for flesh and blood companionship. What Roman poet wrote, 'Dulce et decorum est pro Patria mori'?

In traveling here, I have realized how large is this kosmos, this world, how much land there is for all tribes to settle peaceably if they would. What compulsion to war, then, is there in man? Is it a matter of training or nature? We sometimes say that men behave like animals, but I know now that animals are governed by different natural appetites. There are no terms to express what I am trying to say, for no animal of which I know creates the wanton destruction that does man.

I end now. The dispatcher will leave shortly for Vesontio with news of Caesar's victory, and has agreed to bring this to Calenus, if he has returned. Your agent will see to it that it is brought to you on one of the supply barges.

To my dear Mother and Sister, and to all friends in Massilia, greetings!

Chapter XXVII

A few days later the legions' men took time to shackle barbarian prisoners together. Burial parties dug mass graves for the dead on both sides.

As I repaired a damaged shield, while wondering if Dividiac's illness was helped at Sequana's shrine, and worrying about how Cluvios and my mother were managing, Lucius came into the stone shed where I had set up a rude workshop.

"Incredible!" he exclaimed in an agitated tone. "Caesar is ordering his legions to stay in Gallia during the cold season."

I put down the shield and wiped my face on a sleeve. "Is that not done?"

"Normally, legions go into winter quarters at their base camp like one at Aqueleia, or at least to some closer location such as our Narbonensis province."

"What is the commander's reason for staying here?"

"Seems he'll go back to his Cisalpina province and tend to judicial matters. Caesar trusts Titus Labienus to keep watch on the Sequani from legion camps at Vesontio."

I said, "The men can't feel too happy about that."

"No Roman army ever wintered north of the Narbonensis. I heard muttering from tribunes and centurions, but they were stung by Caesar's reprimands before the battle with Ariovistos. Most feel bound to honor their promise of loyalty, yet there are certain to be desertions. It'll be barley bread and water rations for those caught, and you can wager that the *furca* will hug a lot of company!"

"*Furca?* That cross-shaped beam where legionaries are tied as punishment?"

Lucius nodded and looked around. "Do you have water?"

"In that skin hanging on the peg." I watched him unstop the leather container and swallow a deep gulp. "You're not feverish are you? How is your arm?"

He shook his head, then pulled up his left tunic sleeve. "Look for yourself."

The terrible festering wound I had seen at Sequana's nemeton was a white scar. Lucius almost had full use of his arm. "How did Psen-Ammon heal it? Was it mud from the spring or his strange prayers?"

"Perhaps your Celtic goddess helped. The cure was at her shrine?"

I thought Lucius jested, but his look was not one of amusement. "You're serious?"

"Alberix, there are things beyond our understanding. By the way, Tullius Tilius had expected to go back to Aqueleia or Roma. He confided to me that he'll resign rather than spend another miserable winter in Gallia."

"Will Caesar allow him to do that?"

Lucius pulled down his sleeve. "Tilius is smooth as marble. He bragged that he'll plead that he can be of more use to the commander at the capital, extolling accomplishments that he personally witnessed while tribune. That he could support legislation the *populare* faction wants passed. The *quaestor* may be right. With other tribunes up for discharge, Caesar would have substantial new support in the Senate."

I was almost afraid to ask, "Do *auxiliae* stay with the legions?"

Lucius shook his head. "They're disbanded and go back to their villages until spring."

"That's good." I formed a plan that long had been in the back of my mind.

We took a slow-paced march back to Vesontio, which lay several days south. Legionary cohorts herded chained Germani prisoners in front of them. They would be auctioned as slaves. Lucius told me that some of the sub-chiefs were more fortunate—they would be sent to Roma as bargaining hostages.

The first distribution of loot from Ariovistos's camp was made at the site of the battle. Each legionary received over a year's extra pay in Celtic coins and captured items. The remaining weapons, supplies, and clothing—along with women and children—were loaded into the enemy's wagons and brought along in our baggage train.

At a crossroad village about two days from Vesontio, the legion's cavalry vanguard was met by a group of men driving wagons and coming from the direction of the Sequani capital. Lucius told me these were sutlers, *lixae* in Latin, who bought the men's loot and sold or traded with them for supplies of wine, olives, smoked meat, and other foods unobtainable during the campaign. At the unexpected encounter, Caesar called for a three-day halt so his men could sell what they did not wish to keep, and at the same time have the baggage train lightened of seized goods. Since building the fortifications along the Rodanus at Genava, the legionaries had been continually on the move. The action against Ariovistos had made them miss the September *Ludi Romani*, ancient games that Lucius told me were an important part of military life. By stopping here and allowing trades with the sutlers, Caesar knew how to shore up popularity with his men.

Although the threat of an enemy attack by surviving Germani warriors was remote, we set up camp palisades on the east bank of a river on which this village was located. I watched sutlers examine the legionaries' merchandise and look over prisoners they might buy and auction off. After hearing some merchants coax the men with promises of higher prices for dealing with them, rather than competitors, I realized that Romani waged war with an efficiency our Celts could not imagine. After a successful battle, our warriors collected loot and sold prisoners, but then they feasted, drank, and quarreled among themselves about which man had been the bravest, or who was responsible for the victory. A new chieftain might be elected, yet after a few months the cycle of deadly raids would continue.

Caesar had seen to it that the Helvetii tribe was no longer a threat and Ariovistos would never again lead warriors into battle. I wished Father had been able to talk to me, and this year he would have done so. Did he know about the Romani way of fighting, from learning of the victories that gained them their Narbonensis Province? I would never find out from Father, but resolved to one day continue his work toward treaties that might ensure peace, not continual war.

Adherbal, the Numidian prince, came to visit me from his cavalry unit and again talked about his country and his cure. His wound had healed, but he walked with a limp. The man was curious and intelligent, wanting to learn more about our Celtic ways. I was equally interested in hearing about his desert kingdom, which seemed like a land of perpetual sunshine, like the Isles of the Eternally Young about which old Celtillos sang.

On the afternoon of the second day of bargaining, Adherbal was with me when we heard a spontaneous cheer come up from the men of Legio X. Sentries had spotted three large house wagons crudely painted with scenes of women engaging in sex with men. The legionaries hurried to the gate or lined the palisade wall to watch the arrival of what the prince termed *Lupae—* women who accepted money for their bodies. I later learned from Lucius that by working their way north from Viennadunum, the prostitutes had missed the legions at Vesontio by only a few days. After learning of our victory, these "She-wolves" joined the last of the sutlers traveling to meet the army. Although I was curious, even aroused at the prospect of visiting these woman, Lucius had warned me of the terrible diseases he had seen that resulted from such sexual encounters. I didn't go, but remembered how close I had been to having Pixtila on that day of the Suebi raid.

It was now past the middle of the month we called Edrin, the Roman September. Late on the day before we struck camp to move on toward Vesontio, Lucius and I climbed a hill opposite the village. We wanted to escape the stench of camp latrines and enjoy mild evening air. The heavily forested hills around us already displayed autumn russet and orange colors that brightened a countryside green with pine and fir trees.

We watched sentries pace the stone bridge to the village, and the activity of a few persistent *lixae*, who tried to barter with drunken legionaries. Lines of men still formed at the doors of the prostitutes' garish wagons. Flush with coins now, and free of the anxieties of campaigning, the men's jokes carried on the air across the river to us. Lucilius seemed preoccupied with other thoughts and was hardly aware of them.

"Legions wintering this far north," I heard him mutter. "I doubt the Senate would have agreed to it if Caesar's father-in-law wasn't consul this year."

To distract him I asked, "Lucius I won't stay here during the cold season, will I?"

"No, I told you you'd go back to your village until called up again in spring."

That's good." I turned to look toward the southeast, where the blue-green outline of the Jurassos Mountains undulated across a distant hazy horizon.

Lucius followed my gaze. "You're thinking of Wermaros."

I nodded, recalling the thought that had come to me earlier. "You're on medical leave, aren't you?" In answer, he moved his arm, still in a sling. "Then you could come to Wermaros and—"

I was interrupted by the sound of the approach of a man on horseback, riding up the hill. I recognized Adherbal. The prince dismounted near us.

"Alberix. I see you go to here," he said, then asked Lucius, "*Centurio*, what happen to me now? Battle all gone."

He replied, "I was just telling Alberix that *auxiliae* are disbanded for the winter and can return home."

"Home? My home in Afric."

I said, "That's far away, Adherbal, and I was asking Lucius to come with me to my village. Why don't you come with us? Do you like snow?"

"Snow?"

"I forgot. You probably don't have a word in your language for a kind of... of frozen cloud."

"Adherbal like to come."

"Good. And if Simonides doesn't return to his family, he could stay there and work on his notebooks."

Lucius toyed with his scabbard a moment. "Alberix, your proposal isn't bad and, in truth, I'm still assigned to the towers." He looked toward distant mountains, about fifteen miles away. "I...I'm quite fond of your mother. It's insane, I know, I'm Roman. Perhaps in the Narbonensis, I could...."

I said nothing as his voice trailed off. I was aware of Lucius's feeling and the opposition of Cluvios to a marriage. Nor would Dividiac allow our tribal laws to be broken. Lucius picked up on my silence.

"I know something of your legal codes," he said without looking at me. "As her husband's brother, Cluvios is the one who would marry Briga, yet she might—"

"No, Lucius," I warned. "If Mother went against Dividiac, he would banish her from our clan."

"I know that, and I've argued with him that the law should be a live organism. Some traditions are...like...like dead bones. From time to time they need new flesh to restore the whole body." Lucius put an arm around my shoulder. "But I like your idea about going to Wermaros. Let me talk to Caesar before he leaves for Cisalpina."

The prince said, "You ask for Adherbal, too?"

Lucius laughed. "I will, but some morning when you wake up to cold snow drifts that are past your knees, don't complain to me."

"Adherbal like new things. Will like snow."

⁂

Lucius told me that when Caesar heard of the plan he approved. The two watchtower garrisons would remain as a Roman presence on the edge of Helvetii territories and a condition of the tribe's defeat was that the remnant would rebuild their burned villages. The new tribal leaders hoped to reach their old lands and start work before the cold season. Caesar also reasoned that the Numidian king would be grateful to learn that his son would be recuperating from his wound with friends in a warm village lodge, not in the cold drafts of a legion field tent. As for Simonides, the commander jested that, away from Legio X, the brash Greek would not be able to pester the staff of Titus Labienus for details about recent campaigns.

I was to find out that winter what Lucius did not tell me: Caesar's plans for Gallia included recruiting strong supporters among the Celtic tribes, as he had done with the pro-Roman Diviciacus of the Aedui. After studying the new maps of Gallia-above-the-Narbonensis, which his staff was compiling, the commander proposed a bold mission for me in the spring, after I returned with Lucius to rejoin the legions. I would be past eighteen years old at that time, the same age at which Caesar had outwitted those pirates in the story that Marius had told at the treaty parley in Wermaros.

Caesar also sent two Suebi prisoners to go with us. Rotlar and Baldig had a good knowledge of our Celtic language and agreed on an oath to their sky god that they would serve for seven years as teachers of their native tongue.

After that time, they would once more be free men. The alternative was that they would be sold on the Vesontio slave market. The choice was not hard to make, yet it was difficult to tell from the men's expressions whether or not they were grateful, would fulfill the promise, or try to escape across the Renos and back to their tribe.

Sequani scouts, who knew the area northeast of the Dubis River, reported that Wermaros lay along one of the roads that led from this village and through the Jurassos. Mother, Dividiac, and Cluvios were less than a day and a half away!

❧

The road we followed was clogged with ragged Helvetian families and individual warriors, driving whatever horses, mules, and wagons they had been able to salvage. The despondent tribal remnant slowly moved back to lands they themselves had devastated in Marcios's ill-advised migration plan.

Three days after what Lucius said was the Roman calends of Octobris, Lucius, Simonides, Adherbal, and I halted our horses on the upper forest road in sight of Wermaros, the wheel-shaped village where I had had that vision of my destiny.

I was home!

Chapter XXVIII

My first sense that not all was well came as I rode down to the mountain gate and looked up toward the crest where Dividiac's equinox menhir was located. The stone shaft was to be completed for the past Beltaine, yet the marker was not even half-finished.

The village's gate was open and without sentries. Puzzled, I canted my horse through the unguarded portal toward our lodge. On the outcropping of the Acanthos quarter, stone huts still clustered together, yet looked abandoned. No one was outside our lodge. The forge was cold. Where was Cluvios? Dividiac? My mother?

Without waiting for the others riding behind me, I dismounted and ran through our entranceway, down the ramp, and into the common room. Mother was seated at a table with Cluvios, and saw me enter. She uttered a pitiful cry I had never heard before, stood, and seemed about to embrace me, but held back and only wiped her tears away with a sleeve. Managing a smile, she stammered, "Alberix...y...you look thinner. Taller. And...and is that the beginnings of a beard and mustache?"

"Mother, I'm a man now."

"So I see... " She hid her smile of relief behind a hand.

"Uncle..." I went around to clasp Cluvios's arm, shocked to see his drawn and sallow face. More ill than when I left, much of Uncle's hair had fallen out and saliva drooled from his mouth.

Cluvios stared at me with lusterless eyes. "So our Romani lover has returned."

Briga warned, "Cluvios, don't—"

"Mother, where is Dividiac?" I asked to avoid an argument. "Did Sequana make him well enough to ride off into the woods again?"

Briga replied softly, "Your...your uncle died on the way to the goddess's shrine."

Cluvios snorted, "The old fool always wanted to visit the Other-world. Well, he's there now. Let him come back and tell us how wonderful it is."

I glanced at Mother. The hateful comment was unlike Uncle's, who kept criticism of Dividiac to himself. "Cluvios," she reminded him gently, "he was very ill."

"I never believed in his druid spells."

I touched his arm. "Uncle, Dividiac did not practice destructive magic. The Earth Mother was his teacher—"

"Like the Romani are to you!" Cluvios jerked his arm away and fell into a spasm of coughing that left him retching. I moved back as he stood and shuffled to his sleeping ledge. Mother tried to help him, but he shook her hand off his arm and went behind the wicker screen.

"I'm sorry for him," Lucius remarked from the top of the ramp.

Mother flushed when she looked up at him. "Lucius...."

He had watched the tense encounter and came down into the room. "Briga, it...it's so good to see you again."

She nodded and went to a bronze kettle simmering on the hearth fire. "I...I'll bring Cluvios a hot linden and honey drink. It helps his cough."

The light from the fire revealed how tired Briga looked, how the lines around her eyes and mouth were deeper. I said, "Mother, I've brought two new friends. Lucius, are the others outside?" After he confirmed they were, I told her. "Simonides is Greek, like the Kephestos brothers. He's writing about the war. Adherbal is a prince from across the Middle Sea. Africa—"

"It's time for supper," she broke in. "Cluvios doesn't eat much, but all of you must be hungry. Perhaps I can get two ducklings from my sister."

"How *is* Derona and Liscos?"

Briga began to sob, and turned to hide her face in a towel.

I touched her shoulder. "What is it? Has something happened, other than with Dividiac?"

"Everything is changed since he died. Danach controls Liscos." Briga wiped her eyes and reached for a net bag on the shelf. "I can't talk about it now. I'll see if Derona can spare food and ask Liscos if your friends can stay in the guest lodge."

Ask Licos? Does Mother, the wife of a clan chieftain, now need permission from her sister's husband for what she wishes to do? I glanced around the cooking area. Only a few storage jars were ranged on the shelf. When I looked into grain barrels along the wall, most were less than half-full, even though the harvest was brought in only a month earlier. Where was enough food for a long winter?

Briga returned with two ducklings, bread, and a skin of wine. Liscos had allowed Mother one servant, Sueba, a sullen Germani woman named after her tribe. Once I realized that the middle-aged slave could utter only guttural grunts, I realized that her tongue had been cut out by her people for some offense. Perhaps even by Liscos to keep her from repeating what she might overhear in his village.

Sueba roasted the ducklings on a spit, while Mother cooked the last of the summer greens—leeks and beans—in a pot of water. Liscos was away, so Derona had given us more food than her husband would have allowed. She would visit us tomorrow.

While the food cooked, I decided that I would settle Simonides and Adherbal in the guest lodge without Liscos's permission After I returned with them, we sat at the table, drinking Dirona's wine and finishing the dried, now-slightly-green, salted meat we had brought along as rations. The wine *was* good, better than any we had gotten in Gallia, and we refilled our drinking horns a little too often.

While Sueba brusquely served our meal, Mother said she would see if Cluvios wanted anything to eat.

While drinking we had told stories about the campaign against Ariovistos, but now ate in silence. Simonides finished his portion of duck, wiped his fingers on a cloth, and decided to question the Numidian prince.

"Adherbal," he said with a slight slur in his voice, "your land is across the Mare Intern'm f'om Massilia. but I don' know anythin' about it."

"It has beauty," the prince replied, frowning as he tried to think of words to describe Numidia. "Beauty, but like pretty woman can be cruel. Much sand. Many mountain. By sea is nice. Thabraca has good river with palm tree..." Adherbal reached over and patted Simonides on the head in jest. "You come some day, Si-mon-idees. My father king there."

I heard my friend mutter slurred thanks and guessed he had realized that a drinking bout was no place to gather information. From what Adherbal had said, I tried to picture Numidia's wild people amid their sand and mountains, and compare them with the beauty of women. I had been filling my wine cup often, and his mention of women again made me think of Pixtila. Had I done enough to try to save her? The Acanthos village looked deserted, but I resolved to go up and find out what happened to the people. I thought of Dividiac, not yet reconciled to the fact that he was dead. Would he return in some animal form like the bird he predicted for Klega?

I suddenly blurted out, "How can all the dead we saw crowd in to meet Cernunnos all together?"

Simonides straightened up, belched, then took on a serious look of authority and announced, "Alb'rix, th' dead are like shadows. They don' take up space and they don' come back—"

"Dividiac said my little dead cousin would come back as a bird."

"Y' seen her yet?" he scoffed.

"No."

"An' I just told y' why."

"Never argue politics or religion with friends," Lucius added, grinning foolishly as if he had discovered some great truth.

"Or horse or woman!" Adherbal exclaimed, pounding a fist on the table.

Mother returned from Uncle's room and sat at one end of the table, near Lucius. He asked how the crafter was.

"Asleep now. The evil in him comes and goes like spring winds."

The centurion glanced around the room. "Briga, where's that Germani slave of yours. She should bring you food."

"No. I...I'm really not hungry."

I said, "Mother, there's enough for everyone. Here, take some of my duck."

She shook her head. Lucius filled his cup to pass over to her. In his eagerness it tipped and wine sloshed onto the table.

"Sorry..." He watched as Briga blotted the stain with a towel.

She smiled for the first time. "A little spilled wine is worth it to have you"—she caught herself—"have *all* of you back."

"Yes, "Lucius remarked, "Gallia is at peace."

Briga's hand stopped. "Peace? Have our chieftains stopped fighting each other?"

I quickly intervened, "Mother, what exactly has Liscos been doing since we left? You mentioned Ollam Fodla's influence over him."

"I'll speak of it later..." Briga pushed away her cup. "I wish to sleep now." She touched my arm. "Alberix, it's good to have you home. Your friends are welcome."

Lucius lurched to his feet. I knew he wanted to talk to Mother alone, but he only took up the wine cup he had given her and managed a solemn farewell gesture. The others imitated him.

"I'll stay at *Castor*," Lucius said. "I'd better go and see how the men have fared since last spring."

Lucius rode back to the tower, fantasizing a life with Briga in one of the veteran's colonies the Senate was authorizing in Italia and Roman Gallia. He had more than enough service time for retirement. If Briga did not want to leave Gallia, they could even live in the Narbonnese Province. Rich farmland was available around the colonies of Narbo and Aquae Sextae, and they would be under the *Lex Romana*, away from druidic rites and her constraining Celtic tribal laws.

When Lucius arrived at the tower, the men greeted him enthusiastically. They were eager to hear about the battles he had fought, about his wound, about Julius Caesar, but he put them off and went directly to his old sleeping quarters.

Tossing on his rustling straw mattress, unable to sleep, oblivious to a new throbbing in his shoulder wound, he repeated over and over words that he had rehearsed, telling Briga of his love, of his plans for them. In his mind he pictured the happy moment of her acceptance—as he had hundreds of times in muddy camps and on field campaigns.

The recent battles, his brush with death, were far from his thoughts. Only the bright face of Briga filled his mind.

☙❧

Wermaros prepared for winter in the brilliance of shortening autumn days. At first, Arvos and a few charcoal makers jested about Adherbal's blackness, but the impassive Numidian merely offered to stuff the men into their charcoal stacks, "To make whole body black like Adherbal, not just face."

Most villagers were too occupied with the threat of war and autumn tasks to take much notice of the newcomers. Pigs were let out of the common pen to forage in the woods for oak corn. The porkers would be slaughtered and their meat smoked or salted in barrels by the winter solstice. Only a sow or two and her sucklings were kept to provide fresh meat at Imbolc. Lard used for cooking and in making *sapo* cakes was stored in bladders. While smokehouses cured pork carcasses, woodworkers coopered new barrels for storing the meat.

Farm homesteads took their final growth of hay plants off drying racks and brought them into barns. Well before Samain, herders had brought cattle down from their highland meadows and stabled them for the cold months. Plots of barley growing in the light soil near the river, and wheat and rye on stonier land, were sickled down and bundled for threshing. Even the smallest children helped by carrying pails of sand and pots of olive oil to field hands for honing sickles. Older children lugged skins of water to slake thirsts.

Women brewed vats of foamy *cervisa*. They sprouted wet barley kernels, then dried them in kilns. Scalding water was poured over the sprouts and the mash boiled. After yeast-water had been added, and the cooled liquid strained off, the pulpy dregs were fed to pigs. A special broom was used to stir the vat. When fermentation was complete, the beer was sweetened with honey and stored in barrels.

When Liscos returned, he did not come to visit me, but I observed him from a distance supervising activities. He would jest with some *vassos*, and without apparent cause, flare up at others. The chieftain always brought Ollam Fodla with him and a full wineskin of his Falernian. As Mother said, the druid from Inisfail had taken over Dividiac's priestly functions, yet so far presided over only one ritual. This was at the month-long harvest festival of Lugnasad that marked the transition from a hot to a cold season. Dividiac had performed sacrfices to Lugos, the festival's patron god, but the dark druid included two goddesses, who were personified by Moira and Sabia. Fodla's continual harangues against the villagers' faithlessness confused them. When they complained to Liscos, he defended the druid.

In searching around the village, just before Samain, Simonides discovered that survivors from the Helvetii tribe were held under guard in one of Liscos's storage sheds. While they straggled back to their lands after the defeat, Fodla had ordered several warriors and their families detained. Liscos assigned three of his *vassos* to oversee the fugitives, but Briga insisted on helping the defeated tribal members.

In order to visit them, Simonides bribed Liscos with one of his gold Ptolemaic coins. Afterward, he came to see me. "White King," he began solemnly.

"Just calling me Alberix, will do," I told him, not sure if he mocked my imaginary status with the title.

"Fine, Alberix. Did you know there were high ranking Helvetii prisoners kept at your in-kin's barn?"

After I said I did not, Simonides asked me go with him to speak with them. I asked him why. "Because I need more than rumors to confirm the tribe's conspiracy."

"For writing your history?"

"Exactly."

I was curious about who the captives were and agreed. A guard passed us through to a smoky interior with a scent of herbal medications that did little to mask an odor of offal and festering wounds. I was surprised to see Mother and another woman bathing a child. Briga noticed us and came over.

"Alberix, what are you doing here? Liscos will be furious."

"I paid the oaf," Simonides told her. "We have his permission."

I would question Mother at the lodge later about why *she* was here. "Who is this detained Helvetii leader? Anyone of rank?"

Briga pointed toward one of several crude sleeping compartments. Nammeios and his wife. He is a *vergobret*."

"Wounded?"

"Only in spirit. Three of his sons were killed."

"Mother, I would like to see him."

She objected to the intrusion, "Let them both grieve in solitude."

"I must speak with the man," Simonides insisted.

Briga shrugged and went back to finish bathing the child.

Inside the compartment, a low sleeping ledge was strewn with furs and clothing. Nammeios's wife, Alisana, leaned against a wall, staring at the floor. Although the sub-chief looked older, I recognized the man at Aventia who had averted a confrontation between the followers of Marcios and Orgetorix.

He glanced at Simonides, who spoke to him in Celtic. "Greetings, *vergobret*. I am Simonides from Gallia Narbonensis. My friend is Alberix, a Raurici." When Nammeios did not reply, the historian told him softly, "I'm not a Romani. I...want to find out what caused this war."

"What caused the fighting?" Nammeios reacted in anger at the question. "We were betrayed! Orgetorix...Dumnorix...promised an easy victory over the Romani. We would humble the Arverni, then rule Gallia with the Aeduii and Sequani."

The *vergobret*'s wife spoke to him, words I didn't catch, yet they calmed the old man. "After our defeat at the Arar," he continued softly, "many wished a return to our old lands. Divico would not hear of it. Because a thousand moons past his Tigurini ambushed a legion, he thought he could destroy this Caesar as easily."

I asked him why they didn't go on to the Santones, where they planned to settle.

Nammeios gave a spiritless laugh. "That was a diversion of Dumnorix, who always intended to take power from Diviciacus at Bibracte. We never thought the Romani could strike so quickly."

A commotion at the entrance distracted us. After angry words with the two guards, Lucius brushed past them and strode into the room.

"I learned that Helvetii prisoners were being held here, yet this is a Roman matter, not Sequani. Liscos should decide from which cup he'll drink." After Lucius noticed Briga, he lowered his voice in calling to her. "What...what are you doing here?"

"I help with the wounded. You may remember Helvetii are my tribe's father nation?" She put down a towel and started for the entrance. "It...it is time for me to go."

"Briga, wait..." He turned to Nammeios, "Tomorrow I will have you and your tribesmen moved to the tower camp. You will be well fed, your wounds treated." He walked to the entrance with Briga and asked her to tell the guards what he had said. "Make sure they understand the Helvetii are Roman prisoners." Once outside, he held her back by the arm. "Could...could we walk by the river? I haven't eaten."

Briga hesitated, then agreed. "There's a food vendor at the river gate."

Lucius bought bread, goat cheese and a small skin of wine. Across the bridge, Briga turned onto a woodcutter's path that bordered the Dubis before angling into the forest. The woman walked with Lucius in silence until she pointed to a fallen tree, where they could sit on the trunk to admire autumnal tree colors on the opposite slope.

They sat in silence until the harsh call of a jay broke the stillness to warn of their presence.

Lucius chuckled and tossed a piece of bread toward the sound. "Foolish bird, we mean you no harm." He glanced at Briga, who clutched her tunic around her knees and stared at the trees. He cut the bread and cheese into small pieces and offered her some. When she shook her head, he said, "You're thinking of those Helvetii. They will be better off with us."

Briga reached over to touch his arm. "It isn't your doing, this war. Just as do our warriors, you follow commands."

"Roma has a destiny," he contended, but immediately realized it was the wrong thing to say.

Briga pulled her hand away. "Do not speak to me of destinies! Who decides, Lucius? There were four destinies in the Helvetii balance. *Vergobrets* chose to follow Divico."

Lucius clasped her hand firmly in his. "I didn't come here to fight with you, Briga, not even with words. Caesar did give the Helvetii a chance to turn back."

"Will he first cut off the captured warriors' right hands?"

"What? No...no! We want them on their old lands as a buffer against Germani. Clans were sent back to rebuild their homesteads and towns. Don't they know that here?"

"Liscos tells us nothing."

"The Sequani chief puzzles me. Why didn't he tell us at the towers about the Helvetii migration?"

"His mind is Danach's now."

"The druid again?" Lucius surmised. "At Sequana's shrine our legion surgeon, an Egyptian, saw an aura of evil around the man."

Surprised, Briga asked, "You saw Danach there?"

"Alberix told me who the druid was."

"Then Danach wants to involve my brother-in-kin with some scheme of his, yet Liscos won't talk about it."

"Can you find out? Liscos did respect Dividiac when he was druid here."

"Lucius, will the wolf now listen to the hare?"

Briga squeezed his hand, then freed herself and walked to a pine tree. Lucius moved behind to embrace her, conscious of the woman's scent. She leaned back against the warmth of his hold to block out thoughts of Danach and Liscos. He kissed the reddish hair at the nape of her neck, then gently turned her to face him. She started to return his kiss, but abruptly broke away.

"I can't Lucius, not...not now. Not yet."

"Because of Alrix? Briga, your husband is dead."

She shook free and started back down to the village. Lucius left the food and followed a step behind her on the path. At the bridge he let her continue on, then leaned over the rail to look down at the dark water. He kicked a pebble into the river, unsure of whether to curse Venus and her son, Eros, or his own inexperience with women.

That night, while thinking of Briga, for the first time he regretted his oath of service. It bound him to the legions for twenty years, yet now the war might extend longer than that time.

❧❧

Liscos refused to allow his Helvetii prisoners turned over to the Romans. Lucius did nothing rather than force an action that would pit his outnumbered men against the growing number of warriors filtering into the village.

Under Fodla's influence, the Sequani chieftain's vanity and insolence grew, as well as poor judgment brought on by too much drinking.

❧❧

Just before Samain, Liscos and Fodla came to the forge to have Cluvios craft a wooden arm with a silver hand. Fodla pointed out that Nuada, an ancient Celtic king, owned such a limb. I told them my uncle was ill and to go to Vesontio for the votive. They stalked back to their lodge, where I'm sure both vowed to avenge the insult.

While Simonides stayed inside to write his journal, I became a companion of Adherbal. The Numdian was expert with a bow, and taught me how to make one of ashwood reinforced with sinew and horn. By the new moon of Imbolc I could hit a straw column set up in the snowy meadow with every feathered shaft I loosed...even from the back of Derka at full gallop.

Since the forge was shut down during the cold season, Cluvios's health improved a bit. Adherbal promised him a deer for the Imbolc festival that marked the early return of the sun god to the north. We brought one down from the forest. Our stag would provide enough food, so I asked Uncle to invite Lucius and Marcellus from the Castor garrison to celebrate Imbolc with us. Because of Liscos's hostility toward the Romani, the chieftain and Dirona stayed away, yet he allowed Nammeios and his wife Alisana to attend the meal. The *vergobret* could prove useful: some of the returning Helvetii men had joined other warriors that Liscos recruited as they passed through.

At dinner, Adherbal told the story of how I had brought down the stag, but after that, conversation lagged. My glance at Simonides confirmed that former enemies, a more or less occupied village, and an absent, hostile chieftain did not foster pleasantries. Lucius stared at Briga a number of times, but she rarely looked his way. At one point the centurion did not realize that Nammeios spoke to him. Marcellus elbowed him into awareness.

"...Caesar is unlike other chieftains," the *vergobret* was saying. "All considered, his policy of repatriation is a wise one." When the old man reached over to squeeze his wife's hand, tears trickled from his eyes. "Alisana and I will return to Aventia to help rebuild. We will adopt other sons."

Lucius remarked, "Caesar will be pleased. The commander rewards loyalty and magistrates will have to be appointed."

Adherbal, not following the conversation or names, digressed, "How your story comes, Simon-id-ees?"

"Very well, although speaking with the Helvetii here, I find Caesar's estimate of their numbers far too high. I calculate it would have taken forty thousand wagons to hold the supply of rations the tribe reportedly took with them. Hades! They would still be filing through that pass now!"

I saw Lucius flush and slice into his meat, but Cluvios intervened before he could contradict the Greek. "We are here to celebrate Brigantia's festival," he reminded them. "Let any talk of war slip behind us."

Mother glanced at me. "Yet each drop of melt-water marks an interval before you must all return to Vesontio."

No one replied as each person thought about the future. After pushing his plate aside, Lucius abruptly stood up. "Briga, put on a fur," he ordered in a strained tone, "While we have daylight, show me the colts foaled last year. My men may need horses."

It was an odd request. Mother looked toward Cluvios, then asked Lucius, "You wish to...to see horses now?"

"Yes, for...for the garrison." He said to Cluvios, "We...we'll only be gone a short time."

He nodded to Briga. "Go with your Roman."

The winter air outside was cold, with a western sky lightly rouged above the horizon. Lucius walked beside Briga to the common pens in silence. They watched the animals prance in the twilight, steamy breath exhaling from their flared nostrils. Standing next to the woman, Lucius's excitement returned: he wanted to bury his face in the smell of her wolf-jacket and body scent.

Reaching down, he covered her hand with his. "Briga...I...I have served more than twenty years in the army. I could retire and we—"

Briga long had surmised his thoughts. "You wish to marry me, Lucius? Is that it?"

"Yes."

"It is not possible." She touched his face, then looked back at the horses again before saying, "At...at Beltaine, Cluvios is to contract me as wife."

"The man is dying in front of your eyes!" Lucius blurted out.

"It is our tribal law."

Lucius had seen cattle sledge hammered by army butchers and knew how they died; his own legs sagged from the force of Briga's words. He wanted to ask her how she felt about him and about marrying Cluvios. An empty ache spread through his body unlike any he had felt before a battle or from a wound. As a welling of tears blurred his vision, Lucius turned away. His horse forgotten, he walked, then jogged up the road toward *Castor*. If Briga called after him, he did not hear. *Fool! You should have kept your feelings shut up behind a mental wall and ditch, where they belong. Cluvios is right. These are alien tribes and you've intruded into a life that existed before you came, one where you have no place as a Roman.*

A dim orange square appeared through the trees, marking the high window of the tower. Lucius stiffly greeted the men in the camp, then climbed a ladder to the doorway. He went to his room determined to retreat into the emotional safety of a self-constructed, mental palisade.

Briga returned to the lodge and walked directly to her sleeping compartment without speaking to Cluvios, her son, or the other men. As she twisted her hair into a nighttime braid, tears dropped to stain her night tunic. Briga was surprised: she thought she had shed all of them these past months for her dead warrior husband, Alrix.

❧

On a windy day just before the ides of March, two army messengers rode into Wermaros from Ocelum. A late snowstorm had stalled them for several days at the Mons Genvris pass and their delay confirmed a concern that still preoccupied Julius Caesar: it was imperative to find a shorter route over the Alps into Gallia, perhaps through the upper Rhodanus valley.

Alberix, Simonides, and Adherbal were rehearsing new Germanic words from Rotlar and Baldig, when Marcellus arrived at the lodge to summon them to *Castor*.

"Lucius is promoted to *primipilaris*...First Centurion..." he reported. "There also are orders for you, Alberix, Adherbal. You're both to meet Lucius at the tower."

"Back to Gallia, men!" Simonides called out. "I sense it will be a difficult year."

"Adherbal go, Adherbal not sick. Need to be with fellow Afric horse-men now."

Simonides asked, "What of me, Marcellus? Did Lucius mention my name?"

"Get your horses, all three of you," he hedged as he turned to go. "Leave as soon as you can."

As I rode with my two companions up the familiar trail to *Castor*, a warm, gusty wind foretold the promise of early spring greening. When I climbed the ladder into the barracks room, legionaries were packing their gear. Were the watchtowers to be abandoned? When we reported to Lucius, he said little by way of greeting. The centurion had not seen Mother since Imbolc. I was conscious of a hurt in my friend I had not caused, nor could prevent. His voice was officious as he read from a parchment.

"Adherbal, after Psen-Ammon examines your leg and clears you for duty, you'll rejoin your cavalry wing. Rumors reached Titus Labienus that the Belgae are conspiring with neighboring tribes to attack us."

Simonides asked if the towers would be abandoned. Lucius ignored him and read on. "Two new legions have been recruited from the Cisalpina and will move to the Narbonensis as soon as forage permits. Their commander is Quintus Pedius."

"Pedius?" Simonides muttered. "Caesar's nephew by his aunt Julia."

"*Graecus*, that's not your concern!" Lucius snapped, then turned to ease a vellum sheet from its leather case and hold it up. "Alberix, you're not to return to Vesontio. This map is crude, yet shows a pass that some merchants use to go more directly into Gallia than by taking the Genvris Pass. We need to draw up an accurate chart and determine the mood of tribes in that area."

I protested that I had never done anything like that.

"Nonsense, "Lucius responded irritably. "You scouted out Aventia."

"I had a guide."

"Perhaps Cabirios, from the Nuantes, a friendly alpine tribe, will do?"

I caught his sarcasm, but it was Simonides who asked, "Where do *I* go?"

Lucius said. "I was coming to you. Caesar suggests that you accompany Alberix to record what you find and draw up the new map."

"And keep me out of Gallia? Is it because we haven't agreed on the reports he sends to the 'Senatus et Populi Romanus'."

Lucius ignored his sarcasm. "Of course, you're not a legionary. Caesar can't order you to go, but you have his permission to publish a narrative of the journey. The Greek historian, Polybius, is all they talk about at the capital."

Simonides mumbled that he *might* consider going, but I knew he concealed the excitement he felt at the prospect of this alpine adventure.

Lucius rolled up the scroll. "I'd ask you to supper, but the garrison is being rotated with men from the Eleventh. These are packing up and I'll take them to Vesontio in the morning. Adherbal, you can ride with us."

The prince grinned. "Adherbal will go."

"Dismissed, then." Lucius looked at me. "Alberix...stay a moment."

While the others waited near the ladder, Lucius toyed with the map case a moment, then said, "I...I had intended to draw up adoption papers that would have made you a Roman citizen. But now with Cluvios and your mother marrying, that seems presumptuous." He clasped my shoulders and handed me the case. "*Fortuna tecum.*"

My Roman friend turned away quickly, but I caught the glint of tears.

Chapter XXIX

Octodurus, a village of the Veragri • XII dies ante nonae Maius.

To my father, Nikomaxus from Simonides, his son.

I write from far up the Rhodanus Valley, among mountains that are the most spectacular I've seen. You no doubt received my winter letters. Since then I have traveled the length of Helvetii lands with Alberix. We are on a mission for Julius Caesar, to scout a pass into Gallia that lies beyond both Mons Genvris and Cenis. The circumstances of why I am with him are best related when I see you again, as I would rather use my dwindling supply of papyrus to tell of this journey. Our guide is Cabirios, of the mountain Nantuate tribe, whose face looks as weathered as the limestone crags that are his home. His raven eyes miss nothing – the fellow has all the instincts of an animal combined in his humanity. Rather than the checkered brachae and bright tunics of the Keltoi, Cabirios wears a brown leather blouse and trousers stained with greenish plant juices. This makes him invisible in forests and mountains. I was surprised that he uses a gastrophtes as a weapon—the kind of crossbow that our Greek ancestors invented three hundred years ago! It is cocked the same way, with an upper diostra that slides forward to engage the bowcord by an iron claw. When the diostra is pushed back, it locks into place for shooting feathered bolts that go forward with tremendous force and accuracy. Cabirios saved our lives, when we were attacked by brigands who tracked us to a high point above Lacus Lemannus. Without our guide's quick reflexes, I would certainly be writing to you from the House of Minos!

Hidden by forest trees, Bithus the Dacian scanned the dirt road below for travelers who might become an easy prey for his band of renegades. Soon tiring of the vigil, Bithus motioned for a companion to stand watch, then leaned against a pine trunk and thought back on the previous few weeks.

It had been a bad winter for brigandage. Raids into Sequani lands resulted in little plunder, but much quarreling among his men about dividing the loot. The unexpected arrival of Romani legions across the Arar and their decisive victory over the Helvetii had put Gallic tribes on alert. Peasants armed themselves to keep watch against foragers. Food and coins were hidden or buried. Armed merchants banded together in caravans that were too well protected for the ambush tactics he used with his men. Because of the unsettled countryside, even pilgrims going to healing shrines became scarcer.

Bithus lay back to doze and let spring sunshine bathe his face. The Dacian's mother had been a slave, an Asiatic from the Yue-Chi peoples, captured and sold on the slave market at Sulina, on the Danuvius River delta. The slaver had brought his human cargo upstream and bartered with another dealer at Sarnuzgetura, capital of the Dacian kingdom. Intrigued by her exotic beauty, the second owner had placed the woman in his harem of concubines and fathered her son.

When Bithus was old enough, he was sent with the man's other children to rob strangers in the city bazaars. After authorities arrested the slaver, his fortune and life were forfeited. At age fourteen, Bithus was left to survive by his own cunning. At Dierna he fell in with a company of Thracian archers and learned the bowmen's art before being sodomized and put in their male harem. The youth murdered a eunuch guard, escaped, and moved westward along the Danuvius, picking up outcasts and criminals. The predator band lived by raiding merchant caravanss or pillaging isolated farmsteads.

The lookout awoke Bithus: below, on the road leading south, three travelers rode in the afternoon sun. The Asiatic's almond eyes squinted against the light and saw that their horses were good. They would bring a high price from the Helvetii, who needed mounts. The trio led no packhorses, which meant they probably had sold their goods and had money. He wondered why the men were not armed better, then shrugged. He would know the answer to both puzzles when his victims' bodies were searched.

Bithus signaled with a birdcall for the five lounging men in his band to mount horses and begin moving parallel to the road. They would keep out of sight at the edge of the woods until an opportunity for ambush presented itself. It always did. Although his companions preferred longswords in an attack, Bithus utilized his composite bow—the feathered shaft could transfix a man before he came close enough to use his sword or hurl a spear. The Dacian shook his head as he maneuvered his horse through the pines. Why did these blond westerners not take up a weapon as efficient as the bow?

Cabirios had bought bread and a skin of beer that morning, allowing the three men to eat while riding. Now, in late afternoon the guide led the way along a trail that led to the heights overlooking the Lake of the Allobroges. Stopping short of bushes growing beyond the line of trees, where the woods ended, the trio caught a glimpse of sparkling blue water. Haze veiled the lake's surface and a distant outline of mountains in Gallia.

Once we had tethered our horses out of sight among the trees, further back than I expected, Cabirios motioned for Simonides and me to lie at the edge of the overlook. The cliff dropped almost vertically into the lake, except for a flat strip at its base barely wide enough for a road the Veragri had built as a passageway. Opposite, I saw a fortified village standing on a rock island that jutted out of the water. Workers replaced a wooden palisade with stone ramparts.

Cabirios whispered to Simonides, "Say this when you write. The Veragri and Seduni will fight if your Caesar tries to seize this road. There is no other way north and toll coins are their only wealth. Say that the garrison has been strengthened." The guide shaded his eyes from a sun that was on a line with his and elbowed his way to the right.

Cabirios heard the swoosh of an arrow just before he saw its feathered shaft slide into the flattened grass where he lay an instant before.

"*Attentio!*" he shouted as he rolled into bushes and unslung his crossbow.

Bithus loosed another shaft.

At the guide's warning shout, Simonides had turned and in a reflex motion held up his writing board to shield his face: the Dacian's iron arrowhead passed through the plank in a crunch of wood fibers and stopped a hand-width away from his forehead.

I stood, fumbling for the sword Cluvios had given me. One of the brigands lunged toward me with a broadsword, but crossed Bithus's line of vision as he leveled his weapon at me. He cursed the man away, then gaped in astonishment as Cabirios's bolt tore through my attacker's chest in a spray of blood. The brigand's sword fell from his hand as he dropped to his knees, eyes wide with shock.

Bithus lowered his bow to stare: there was no arrow's shaft in his companion, yet he lay foaming blood at the mouth as if from an arrow wound. The Dacian felt an instant of panic, then sent his arrow flashing into the bushes from where he thought the invisible missile had come. A scream of pain sounded in the greenery. Bithus grinned as the promise of another kill overcame his fear; he deftly notched another arrow onto his bowstring.

Simonides lay on the ground, trembling and staring in disbelief at an iron arrowhead protruding from his board. I was twenty paces from the bandit, could see his smirk as he slowly drew back his arm and aimed at me. But his grin of victory stretched into a muted gurgle as Cabirios's second bolt ripped through the Dacian's neck. A final breath, which Bithus had drawn and held, at the moment of aiming, escaped from his throat in a bubble of crimson froth. His arrow swished over my head in an erratic arc and splintered on the stones of the roadway below.

We followed behind Cabirios as he crept back to the horses. As he expected, the other brigands were searching through our saddle bags. In moments, only two of the four were left to run in panic from their unseen devil-assailant and to their own mounts. It was clear now why our guide had tethered the horses at a distance—a lure to any bandits we might encounter. We went back to look at their two dead companions.

"A death they made for themselves," Cabirios remarked as he picked up the composite bow. "Better had they died with their mother's milk still on their lips." He glanced toward the cliff's edge. "Let us move away before Veragri come up and look for the sender of that arrow."

♋

I tell you Father, Herodotus never mentioned that sort of adventure! Yet I admit to being so frightened that my fingers had to be pried loose from the writing board. I became ill with a fever that same evening and have no memory of traveling through the valley to reach Octodurus. Because of my illness, I was unable to climb to the pass. In fact I am still recuperating after Cabirios sent a seeress to bring me back to the land of the living.

♋

Cabirios led us higher along the ridge for the night. We sheltered in the lee of a hillock and ate the last of our rations. Once the sun dropped behind the mountains, darkness came on quickly. Patches of snow glowed dimly in the hollows, seeming to lurk as ghostly apparitions of the dead bandits. Despite a thick cloak, I shivered in the cold. My near encounter with death and the faces of the brigands filled my mind. I dozed briefly, but awoke chilled and stiff as the victims of Cabirios's crossbow. A thin crescent of moon had arisen, but without enough light to identify a creature that scurried past me into underbrush. I thought of Ollam Folda and the shape-shifting illusions of my bizarre visions on Samain Mountain.

The sound of a harsh cough roused me. Shortly after the attack, Simonides's throat had begun to feel raw. Now his head ached and fever ravaged his body. Later, he told me that in his delirium the shapes of dark shrubbery seemed to rise and crush him, then turn into bundles of black wool that rolled harmlessly over his body. Some forms were his parents, especially the stern face of his father, scowling disapproval. When the phantoms in his mind eventually gave way to exhaustion, he slept fitfully.

With the warming rays of the morning sun, Cabirios led us down to the level of the nascent Rhodanus and its wide valley. When I entered the vale, I gaped at the wild grandeur around me. A broad spread of bottomland and immense snowy peaks dwarfed the narrow hollow of the Dubis and the modest rounded heights of the Jurassos range. By the time we reached Octodurus, almost a day's journey south, the weather had turned cloudy, with a smell of rain rolling down from the surrounding peaks.

Simonides could barely sit his horse during the long journey. At Octodurus I helped Cabirios lift him from his mount and carry him into a log house at the far edge of the village. Our guide greeted an old woman with eyes filmed over by an opaque membrane. After he spoke to her in a Nantuante dialect I didn't understand, she pointed toward a sleeping ledge. Cabirios laid the Greek historian down and covered him with furs, then motioned me outside.

"Your friend cannot continue with us. Magha will treat him while we climb to the pass tomorrow."

I recalled the feverish face of Lucius at Bibracte. "Will...will he recover?"

"If his fate is only in the hands of Magha, he will be well. Gods are not as predictable. Come inside to eat."

I ate hot food for the first time since leaving Wermaros, a stew of venison flavored with early mushrooms and mountain herbs. After the meal, I sat by Simonides. His face felt hot, dry. He stared with vacant eyes at the hearth fire flames. Several clay bottles and sprigs of dried herbs were arranged on a table next to his ledge. A short while later, a young woman perhaps a year or two older than I, came in from another part of the lodge carrying a small bowl. After the girl noticed me, she looked away and spoke to Magha, who motioned toward the table. When she bent to put down the bowl, her loose, tawny hair fell in a tumble around her face. I thought of Pixtila, but this girl was more lithe and graceful. When she glanced at me again before leaving, I noticed a frightful loneliness shadowing her blue eyes.

Although almost blind, Magha deftly spooned a honey remedy from the bowl into Simonides's mouth, murmuring incantations as she did so. I moved aside as she faced him in my chair and put herself into a trance state, to struggle with evil spirits that had taken hold of my friend's throat and body.

I gave the crone privacy by going outside and climbing a path behind the village limit. Although clouds were low on the mountains, there was no rain and the late afternoon light held. I could see into the direction from which we had come, but a stand of pines blocked my view up-valley. Cabirios had told me that three days travel in that direction a great mass of ice clogged an adjacent valley. Its melt water became the source of the Rhodanus. Swollen by other linking streams, the great river turned south at the Allobroge lake and eventually emptied into a salt sea that Simonides had called the *Mare Internum*. I thought of how I had found another new spoke on my wheel that reached out from hub to rim.

❧

Early in the morning, as Cabirios and I prepared our horses for the climb to the pass, the young woman who had brought the bowl to Magha approached us. She was dressed in furs and led a white mare by its halter.

She told the guide, "Magha told me to go with you to the summit and gather the first Snowgold blossoms."

"Apsa, you are her eyes," Cabirios replied in a kind voice. "How else could she get her healing plants?"

So her name is Apsa, and named after the Aspen tree. I helped Apsa onto her horse. When seated, she drew away from my touch and said nothing.

The sun had not yet broken above the peaks when we turned our mounts up a trail to the pass. Snorting in steamy gasps, the animals struggled through red, algae-stained snow layers and splashed through pools of icy water to avoid rocky outcrops. We followed alongside a stream until we reached an area of the pass. Stunted Areole pines no longer grew here, and only a lake, frozen beneath its sheet of surface water, reflected the flat, stony land. Three log buildings for sheltering travelers stood on the shore. Cabirios went to stable the horses, while Apsa and I waited by the glittering lakeside.

After we spent an awkward interval of silence, watching the wind ruffle the layer of water, I asked, "Is Magha your grandmother?"

Apsa shook her head without looking my way. "She owns me."

I was stunned; the woman was a slave. "Are...are you Veragri?"

"I was told my parents were Raurici. They sold me here after losing their trade goods in an alpine storm."

"Raurici?" I was surprised again. "I'm from a Raurici tribe. We lived at Arialbinnum."

"I was small. I remember only Octodurus."

"Will Magha be able to cure my friend?"

"She must heal his inner spirit first. The fever is there because of a recent imbalance between his mind and body."

I recalled that Psen-Ammon had spoken the same way. "We were attacked by bandits just before Simonides became ill."

"It could be that. Magha will know."

I was astonished at her sensitivity, a slave girl who had the Egyptian physician's intuition and much of Dividiac's understanding, about how a body became ill.

Apsa still had not looked directly at me, and barely glanced my way to say, "We call the earth, 'Mother', because she nourishes us in all things. Yet we must learn to trust her, just as when a child asks for food."

Cabirios returned and beckoned us to a steep path that led higher along a gale-swept limestone upthrust. At the summit, a stone shaft leaned away from the wind, its near surface carved with the crude likeness of a man holding a wheel. The image was of Taranis, Lord of the Sky. I felt that I had entered the realm of the god himself: jagged white peaks surrounded me, some pushing into clouds that masked their crowns. Others were faint, almost lost in the hazy distance. Toward the west, the largest mountain I had yet seen rose like a gigantic mass of snow heaped up as if by Celtic gods at play. Cabirios sensed my awe.

"*Benn Albion*," he explained. "A half day's journey off, even for eagles."

Apsa came to us, holding a flower with spiky white petals and a cluster of golden globes in the center. "Mountain Snowgold. The plant brings healing and good fortune."

I turned the blossom in my fingers, thinking that Dividiac would have a story about how the flower came to be made of snow and gold.

Cabirios told me that Romani who had been here named this summit after Jupiter, their chief god. I hesitated a moment before asking, "Why did you agree to guide us here for Caesar, the legion's commander?"

The guide thought a moment and then swept his hand in a wide arc toward the stunning scene. "The pine that bends has no fear of being uprooted by the wind. Romani challenge our tribes with their way of fighting and their laws. They have the Narbonensis and that province sleeps in peace. Gallia must bend or be broken."

When he did not elaborate, I looked around me once more. Behind stretched the white mass of the inner Alps; to the northwest, a haze-tinted sparkle marked the crescent of the Allobroge Lake that Simonides called Lemmanus. Even the distant Jurassos were bluish folds on the farthest horizon. *Surely this must be the top of the Now-world.* Holding Apsa's flower, I walked closer to the rock-bound edge. Hawks circling below were dark specks against the soft greening of the valley. I felt slightly giddy, almost nauseous, and began to imagine that I could soar with them into the vastness.

Cabirios knew the sensation and warned, "We must go down now. There are dangerous visions when you stay in the high places too long."

He led the way back to the lakeside lodge, where we would spend the night.

❧ ❧

Whether from Magha's magic or her plant remedies, Simonides recovered so rapidly that he could jest about King Minos undoubtedly having no use for his writing talents in the Underworld.

We waited another day so that Simonides would be strong enough to draw his map and travel back to Octodurus. Cabirios took apart the bandit's composite bow to see how it had been made. I spent time walking with Apsa along the heights above the village, helping her collect herbs and plants for her aged owner. She said little at first, but gradually relaxed enough to laugh musically at stories Dividiac had told me about the origin of certain plants. I wondered about the possibility of taking her back to Wermaros with me.

Would she agree to leave Maghda? My idea was foolish: under Celtic law, I must pay the old woman a ransom price I probably didn't have.

My fantasizing came to nothing. Simonides finished his map and journal. Cabirios prepared our horses for the return journey to Wermaros.

Before I left—yet knowing it unlikely—I stammered something to Apsa about one day coming back to Octodurus. I rode away, distressed by a return of the despairing look I had first seen in her eyes, an aspect that had softened in the few days we spent together. That night I tried to induce a dream that might predict my future with a young woman named after the aspen tree. None came.

When we entered the territory of his Nantuate tribe, Cabirios invited us to stay with him for the balance of the summer. Simonides justified the delay by saying he would chart the south shore of Lake Lemannus for Caesar's engineers. While he consulted Herodotus on how best to note the geography of the land, and the legends and customs of local Celts, I accompanied Cabirios on hunts. The guide taught me the habits of mountain creatures, how to track them, ways of trapping smaller ones, and to release unharmed those not needed for food.

Cabirios finished a crossbow he had begun making that winter and gave it to me. Even before I could do much practicing with the weapon, I unexpectedly fired a bolt at a living target: a bear surprised the guide as he constructed a willow-reed fish trap in a river. The black pelt was a constant reminder that I had saved the mountaineer's life.

❧❧

In early September, I decided that Simonides and I should return to Vesontio. Along the road that passed Aventia, signs of the devastation caused by the Helvetii when they burned their villages, still scarred the countryside. Many homesteads were charred timbers because too few survivors returned to rebuild them. Fields, where stalks of grain had rippled two seasons ago, now were speckled with the blue blossoms of wild chicory. Deer and elk nibbled at meadow grasses where tribal cattle had grazed.

When we reached Vesontio, we learned that, except for a small garrison, the legions would not winter in the area this year. The campaign against the Belgae and northern tribes had been such an astounding success that Caesar decided to quarter his legions further north. After the camp praefect opened orders left for me. an exception was made clear, On the basis of Simonides's report that the Rhodanus tribes would fight rather than accept a Roman presence at the new pass into Gallia, Caesar decided on a surprise winter campaign to secure the height. Legio XII was to undertake this task under the command of Servius Sulpicius Galba. I was assigned to one of his tribunes as a guide and interpreter.

A wing of cavalry under Adherbal was to join the legion, but there was no mention of Simonides in the orders.

I wondered where Lucius would be, and if he was safe.

October / 57 BCE — December / 55 BCE

Death comes to touch you abruptly, unannounced;
who can know his features;
how many can escape the sound of his step approaching?

Chapter XXX

When I reported to Gauis Volusenus, the cavalry tribune with Sulpicius Galba, who was assigned to lead Legio XII to Octodurus, I found the unit in disgrace. That summer the Cisalpina recruits came close to being destroyed in an action against the Nervi tribe.

Charged to hold the right wing, pushed back by the Gallic warriors, the men cramped themselves so closely together that they had no room to fight back. Julius Caesar placed himself among the milling legionaries, shouted out names of centurions still standing, and ordered the officers to open the ranks. Two other legions guarding baggage were ordered in to rally the men. Titus Labienus, commanding Legio X, saw the near disaster and moved his legionaries at quick-step to finally turn the situation. Kept on as commander, Galba was determined to restore luster to the Legio XII eagles by redeeming its reputation.

I was disturbed to see that Publius Silanus, the centurion who had caused a near riot in that tavern at Vesontio was leading men in Volusenus's cohort.

I used a copy of Simonides's map to retrace the route we had taken four months earlier with Cabirios as guide. Harrassed and ambushed, Adherbal's cavalry scattered an ineffectual resistance by the Veragri. Cohort counterattacks won skirmishes with other warriors. At Bex, about ten miles from Octodurus, where Galba wanted to set up camp, a delegation of old men from the Veragri brought five boys with them and asked for a parley. Claiming to be chiefs, they offered the youngsters as hostages to seal a peace proposal. There were no men of warrior age in the group, which made Galba suspicious of their motives, yet he accepted the offer. Since a river bisected the the village of Octodurus, it was agreed that the Romans would occupy lodges on one side, while the residents would move to the opposite bank for the duration of the cold season. Perhaps falsely reassured, Galba sent two cohorts back to winter with the Nantuantes.

Once at Octodurus, legionaries began construction of a ditch and palisade to isolate and protect their half of the village. I tried to find Apsa, but Veragri guards turned me back. The agreement stipulated that the Celtic enclave was closed to legionaries and *auxiliae*. After I found that the village's common lodge would be a hospital, I went there to see if I could learn more about medical practices. Nikos, the Greek surgeon's slave assistant, told me he was a deaf-mute named Aristides. Nikos was friendly and knew Greek, Latin, and enough Cisalpina-accented Celtic to speak with me.

A day later, I was helping Nikos unpack medical supplies, when Adherbal came to the hospital with two legionaries. They carried in a wounded cavalryman from a Numidian patrol ambushed by Veragri warriors. The tribe was determined to keep control of the road to the pass and had attempted to prevent a Roman detachment from returning to Octodurus after foraging for grain and fodder. Adherbal said that other warriors hidden on the slopes around the village saw the action as a signal to begin an assault on the Romani half.

Barely forewarned, Galba summoned a council of his officers. Most presented him with two conflicting suggestions: some tribunes and centurions favored breaking out and fighting their way back to Nantuante territory. Others wanted to utilize the almost-completed defenses and hold off the Veragri until they tired of the siege. Galba, conscious of his brush with disaster, was reluctant to be disgraced as a commander who abandoned a fortified position without fighting. He would defend the village.

Joined by Seduni allies from further east in the valley, the Veragri attacked in a furious mass. After our javelins thrown at short range from the wall parapet inflicted terrible casualties, the warriors fell back to regroup and bring back dead and wounded.

While helping cart javelins to the wall defenders, I recalled the most vulnerable section of the camp defenses, an unfinished barrier on our bank of the river that separated the two sides. Because legionaries might need help, I took the crossbow Cabirios had given me and ran toward that section of the palisade.

The wall was small pine trunks implanted into sandy ground. Working from each end of the unfinished barrier, the men wove stripped-off branches between the trunks to make a screen difficult to penetrate. Branches and thorny brush blocked an incompleted center—a temporary barrier that engineers hoped would stall any attack. I watched from the edge of a lodge and saw that the brush pile could easily be set afire. When Veragri realized this, they might burn their way through and into the village.

I climbed to the roof of the lodge for a better view of their warriors. They would have to cross the river in boats to reach the ditch and wall, and the makeshift barricade concealed them from our defenders.

Lying on the roof thatching, I felt the same tension I had experienced at the Arar. I clung so tightly to the crossbow that its wood and metal parts embossed themselves into my palm and fingers. As I watched, a band of Seduni carrying good-sized tree trunks ran from between the lodges. While others distracted our men by throwing a barrage of spears and stones near the end of the wall, the other warriors tried to lay the trunks across the waterway as a bridge. Exploiting the confusion, three warriors swam the river and crouched at the far edge of the brush barrier.

I slid back out of sight. My hand shook slightly as I reached into my leather bag of bronze bolts and slipped one into the crossbow slot. I peered over the ridge; one warrior had climbed to the top of the barrier, almost on a level with me, some twenty-five paces distant. He was out of sight of legionaries at each end, who concentrated on finishing the pine barrier, but I saw the man pour liquid from a jug into the dry, withered branches. *Olive oil, to make setting fire to the brush easier.* A second warrior carrying a spear climbed up next to him. I'm not sure why, but I shouted a warning for them to go back down. The spear-carrier bared his teeth at me in rage and hurled his weapon. The loose brush made his footing unsteady—the pointed shaft arced across and slid into thatching below me. He called down to a third red-haired warrior, who handed him a spear for another throw.

I don't recall aiming, but released the bow-cord trigger just as the man straightened up: the bolt shot into his rib cage, through a lung and out his back. He toppled sideways and rolled down the matted branches until his body caught in a hollow. I slipped below the ridge again, sick to my stomach. I had shot at straw targets, and dropped large animals, but never before killed a man. Yet, as Cabirios had taught me to do after releasing a shot, I cocked the weapon and fit another bolt into its groove. I glanced over the ridge again, knowing that the two survivors would be puzzled at the lack of an arrow in their dead companion. They had seen me and felt my magic must be countered.

The two swam back across the steam and ran to a nearby lodge. Moments later, they came out with an older person I guessed was a druid priest. After pointing to the barrier, the two warriors re-entered the house and came out again holding torches. They would burn the brush as planned and destroy any evil lodged in its branches. As a red-haired warrior loped forward to throw his firey brand across the waterway, I aimed at his upraised arm. The force of the bolt spun him around and sent the torch rolling to the ground. Shouting in astonishment and fear—they saw no arrow in the man—his companion and the druid backed away from him and back to the lodge's safety.

As I watched the wounded man crawl away, I rationalized, *The dead warrior and the other two would have killed me had they been able.* In a way I could not explain, the excitement I felt on hunts returned. Now I was the prey and yet could kill as easily as hunters. It was as if the warrior blood of my clan flooded out reason in this remote valley and asserted its ancient power to assure the survival of Alarian men. Gripped by the sensation, I sent my deadly bolt against the figures creeping back to the log bridge, dropping the dark shapes as if they were straw targets. I had no awareness of time passing, only of releasing my bronze missiles until my arms ached from the strain of pulling back the cocking mechanism. I fell back onto the roof thatching in exhaustion.

◈

Well into the third watch, Galba realized that his men were tiring, while the enemy constantly renewed attacks with fresh warriors. The shock of the first javelin barrages had passed. Now, savage assaults were thrown against the palisade from all sides by yelling tribesmen, running down the slopes to replace their dead and haul away wounded. Several warriors crossed the river and hacked at the wooden stakes with axes.

Tribune Volusenus and his *primopilaris*, Publius Baculus, decided it was time to execute the emergency plan suggested at the war council. They found Galba brooding outside his tent and guessed that he might contemplate suicide once the enemy breached the palisade and swarmed inside.

"Sir," Volusenus counseled, "you must attempt a sortie. It will be dark in two or three hours and we can't hold out if fighting goes on after that."

Baculus elaborated. "Order the men to stop throwing javelins, let them rest awhile. Then use cavalry to lead a charge through all palisade gates with the cohorts close behind. We'll spread out and take the enemy from behind."

"I...I don't know," Galba replied, indecisive. "As you say, the men are exhausted. We are under strength. It...it could be a massacre."

"Mars help us, I don't believe so," Volusenus contended. "A sortie is just what the enemy is not expecting."

Baculus added, "Sir, it's a tactic worthy of Caesar himself!"

Caesar, again. If I lose the legion, my political future ends here, along with my head spiked on a Gallic spear. He looked up at his two officers. "Inform our centurions, then. Have the men rest, but make it clear that our only hope is to break the enemy. Courage and discipline will determine success."

Volusenus grinned. "Sir, they won't let you down."

After the two left, Galba went inside his tent and unsealed a small amphora of Falernian. He had saved the wine for celebrating when the palisade was finished, but poured it all out on the ground as a libation to Mars and Fortuna.

◈

Evidently, the two gods were pleased with the offering, as the unexpected sortie resulted in an incredible victory.

At a signal, Numidian cavalry charged through the four gates with legionaries quick-stepping on foot. Providently, at that moment the Fourth and Ninth cohorts returned from foraging as if Mars had warned them of the impending action. The Veragri and their ally thought the maneuver somehow coordinated. Not sure of the size of the relief force, the warriors broke the siege and tried to escape up the surrounding slopes. Adherbal and his Numidians ran them to the ground until it was too dark to see. Legionaries killed any stragglers or wounded they found.

Despite the victory, a subdued meeting was held that night in Galba's praetorian tent. Tempered by the reality of his situation—the Veragri could regroup and surely had sent messengers to the neighboring Lepontii about the Roman presence. If more tribes helped in resisting, the legion could not sustain itself. Once snow fell to block the road back, an orderly retreat would be impossible.

Galba issued terse orders. "Officers, in the morning we burn Octodurus and return to the Narbonensis."

At dawn, I helped pack medical supplies onto carts in an icy wind that swept down the valley from the surrounding snow-laden peaks. The poor weather hampered burial parties stacking bodies on funeral pyres made from dismantled palisade stakes. Other cohorts had stripped weapons, shields, gold or silver neck torcs, brooches, and arm bracelets from Veragri and Seduni corpses. The killing of tribesmen the previous evening, and now the indiscriminate looting of corpses repelled me.

Volusenus asked that I help him search the village for survivors still hiding in lodges. He wanted to question them about concealed stores of grain that we could take with us. I walked with him to a brush barrier now torn down and used as a bridge over the sluggish river. In the village across the waterway, legionaries ransacked enemy lodges and prodded out slaves who had hidden inside during the fighting. At the far end of a street, I recognized the lodge where Magha had nursed Simonides back to health. I jogged to the house. Perhaps Apsa was there with the old woman!

Just inside the entrance, I recognized the coarse voice of Publius Silanus.

"She's mine!" he gloated to himself. "Time I had another slave, an' what a beauty this one is."

Silanus came out of the doorway, pulling Apsa by her blond hair. I flushed in anger and reached for my sword. Volusenus had caught up with me and gripped my arm.

"I know that woman," I protested. "She's from my own tribe."

"A freewoman?"

"No, she's the slave of an old woman healer."

"Then she's property like anything else, and the *centurio* is within his rights. He can own her after he pays whatever Galba decides."

Apsa's look of terror changed to surprise when she saw me. She tried to wrench free, but Silanus grinned and grabbed her wrists. "Spirit. I like that in bed."

I started forward again, but Volusenus's hold on my arm tightened. "Harm him, and if not crucified you'll be flogged senseless on a *furca* as an example to *auxilia* units. Easy there, *centurio*," he called out. "Galba won't tolerate abuse."

Silanus ignored him to pull Apsa and a burlap sack of loot between adjacent lodges.

Volusensus followed me when I twisted my arm free and ducked through the lodge's doorway. Magha, the old woman who had saved Simonides, lay sprawled on the dirt floor among pottery shards. A torc-like flow of blood seeped from her slashed throat. Her filmed eyes were open in a sightless horror at a fate her divinations had failed to predict.

"Silanus...mur...murdered her," I could only stammer.

"And without witnesses," Volusensus said quietly. "He would claim that he found her dead and rescued the girl."

The tribune pulled me to the doorway, saying that we still had to finish our preparations and safely reach Nantuante territory.

Later, as the legion moved back down the road to the Rhodanus valley, the acrid smoke from flaming thatch and weathered pinewood seared my nostrils. The smell was identical to that of my father's burning village on that long ago February night.

Chapter XXXI

In the territory of the Lexovii.

Cluvios, my uncle, and my mother.

I have more time to write my Latin now that we are in winter camp. Simonides helps me, but he is often with Caesar getting information for the manuscript of the war in Gallia. Are any Romani left at the towers who can read this to you?

I am so far from Wermaros that I see new stars at night. Artos is higher at night than there. It is said around camp that we are near the sea of the Island of Blue Warriors. Not far away is the mouth of the river Sequana. More rain is here than I have seen before. The poor weather ended our campaign to punish the Morini and Menapii for not sending vergobrets to discuss peace with Caesar.

My hand is cramping. I must stop now. Alberix.

∾∾

I write again. I try to keep from killing as I did Veragri at Octodurus. I was in a kind of trance I learned from Dividiac. I wanted to keep shooting my bow, although I do not remember much of that afternoon. I did feel revulsion at the killing of unarmed Veragri stragglers, before we left the village ruins. Simonides is the only friend I have talked with about this, so I will ask him to write of my feelings. Instead of fighting, I repair weapons and help Cornelius and Marius, who are here.

I write farewell for now. Alberix.

∾∾

Simonides greets you, Cluvios.

Alberix asked me to help him put his confused feelings into words, since there is little chance that he will see you for at least a year.

I start by saying that he cannot deny that he has the blood of his Alarian clan in his body. By that I mean the blood of warriors that is attracted to violence and thereby rises to the surface of the skin. It can suffuse the mind to the point of overpowering reason. Our Greek physicians call the tendency παράλογος —"irrational" as opposed to λογιηος—"Rational," although to our ancestors fighting was considered a noble action. When it comes to your people, the Keltoi, we must look at the phenomenon in overview. In Gallia Comata there is little of the security the Romans have in Provincia. The tribes, clans, and even families, are broken into so many warring factions that an overall peace among them seems impossible, given their system of tribal dominance as a basis for governing. I use the example of Julius Caesar as "overchief" of all the Romans—and I believe he will be that one day. Under the Roman system of governing, there is one entity that would be above him, a principle greater than any one man, whether he be ruler or ruffian. I speak of the universal law that binds citizens and the republic together. A citizen of Lusitania in the Ibernian hinderland has the same rights as one at Roma itself, or of someone in a stony hovel at a remote corner of the Asian Province. It is this sense of communis, of belonging to one state that you Keltoi lack. One need not be an auger to prophecy that if some leader of your own does not soon attempt to join the tribes together, then Caesar will surely accomplish it under Roman eagles. Two years ago, the Belgae were correct to be alarmed, when they heard that legions wintered in Vesontio.

Alberix is no coward, rather he is intelligent enough to see that to choose the sword as his instrument of destiny is to die by it and thus accomplish nothing of lasting value.

If your druids teach that the Other-world is a glorious reward for dead warriors, then it suits their purposes to continue. In this they are no different from any Egyptian, Greek, Roman or Hyperborean priest, who wishes to control thoughts or ideas and petrify tradition. I must speak of Caesar again. Assuredly, he is ambitious for power, yet I must be fair. I believe he envisions a vast Pax Romana. He agrees with many in his Senate that it is the destiny of Roma to institute that peace through the imposition of law, then trade, and finally culture. I think that Alberix could be a leader of warriors, yet he realizes that he might be able to lead only a battle or two before being killed. His service to the legion, unlike the majority of men in the auxilia, who are out for plunder, connects him with a cause he believes could show the way to a peaceful and lawful future for the tribes. If this sounds like a philosopher's ideal world, let us pray to whatever gods we still honor that he is never betrayed in this belief.

Alberix is well, as his letter to you indicates, although somewhat despondent over the fate of a young slave woman we met at Octodurus. Her name is Apsa, and she was taken from her lodge by Silanus, a brutal centurion, whose duty should be in the halls of Hades. The man plainly abuses her, but auxiliae are kept out of the main legion camp—fortunately—or Alberix might kill Silanus and himself be executed. I shall keep a watch on him for you

When the letters arrived at Wermaros, Briga and Cluvios, now her husband, listened to words read to them by a cavalry auxiliary who returned home for the winter.

Afterward, Briga lamented, "Like his father, Alberix has taken up the sword. It was not what I wanted for him."

Cluvios was not in better health despite heavy rains that hampered work at the forge. He bitterly criticized Alberix for another reason. "My nephew uses my sword against his own people. Better it had been ruined in the forging!"

Briga told him, "The Greek youth speaks of a Romani peace that would bind the tribes together. Alrix wanted that."

"We need no strangers to impose peace on us!" Cluvios ranted. "Our *vergobrets* are capable of making such treaties."

"And why have they not?"

"They... they need only a leader to follow."

Cluvios's agitation brought on a bout of violent coughing.

Briga went to prepare a hot chamomile drink for him. In crushing the dried leaves, she thought of Lucius. He was in a different legion, so none of the letters mentioned him. Briga realized that if she had defied tradition and accepted his marriage offer they could be settled on a farm in the Narbonensis. Her son might be with them, away from the killing.

Cluvios never mentioned the Roman he had looked on as a friend. The contract marriage had ended bake house gossip, but because of the evil in his body it was suspected that he had not been able to consummate the marriage. Women tattled about rumors of the crafter's impotence. Men jested about it. Because the irrational behavior of Liscos and the dark influence of Ollam Fodla had made villagers suspicious, even of each other, many focused their uncertainty and anger on anyone who showed weakness. In soggy tents on the outskirts of town, Fodla's warrior recruits were increasingly restless at their inaction, adding yet another simmering cauldron to the already tense atmosphere in Wermaros.

❧❦

While Julius Caesar stayed at Ravenna during the winter to administer his Cisalpina province, he placed his trusted friend, Attius Titus Labienus, in command of the legions in Gallia. The legate reported frequently to his commander.

A. Titus Labienus salutes you, Caesar Imperator.

I write this on the ides of Januarius. In spite of heavy cold and bitter winds that come from Oceanus, I constantly send out patrols to keep watch on tribes living around my camp. Lutetia, an oppidum of the Parisii tribe living on an island in the Sequanna River, is four days march from here. Since rumors as well as merchandise are exchanged there, I report the common talk our scouts pick up.

Last summer you displayed foresight in dispatching Legio X to the Treveri, who dwell near the Rhenus. You were successful then in discouraging Germani from crossing into Gallia, but now two specifically named tribes, the Usipetes and Tencteri, have crossed the Rhenus near where the Mosa empties into the sea. As far as I can determine, this is not an invasion, nor even a raid. The tribes are harassed by more powerful neighbors, the Suebi, and seek asylum.

I brought Tencteri tribesmen into camp, fugitives discovered at Lutetia. They claim the Suebi raise some one hundred thousand warriors each year by alternating an equal number of men between military service and agricultural work—the same total working the land while a comparable number train as warriors. I blame their druids for this aggressiveness, because these priests constantly urge them to press on into Gallia. Yet the agricultural ineptness of the Germani, as well as their cold climate, makes crop-growing a small part of their food supplies. They spend much time hunting, since the greater part of the land is forested and inhabited by all species of wild animals. It is said to take nine days to traverse this forest at quick-step!

An animal I learned of that might be exhibited in the arena is called an auroch. It is the size of a young elephant, very hairy, and with the demeanor of a bull. They are extremely fierce, attacking anything that moves. The gladiator named 'Invictus' might provide a great attraction if pitted against one!

To summarize: Germani are even more undisciplined than Celts, since from childhood they are never restrained from doing what they wish. Thus, in battle men are immature and reckless in the same way that Gallic warriors display their 'furor.' I have no hesitation in saying that Roman legions can deal with them.

I report on my new primipilaris, Lucius Velcanius. Some illness afflicts him. He is irritable with the men and has become generally apathetic about his duties. I talked with Psen-Ammon and insisted that he examine the man. The Egyptian found nothing physically wrong with Velcanius, but prescribed snake-root to alleviate his depression. Fortunately, we are not in battle this season or I fear Vulcanius might be killed as a result of apatheia, as Greeks call his affliction. If the situation warrants, I may give him leave to visit his native Campania. I have a pouch of letters from tribunes and other dispatches that I will send to Lutetia, to be barged up the Sequanna to the Arar and over Mons Genvris pass to Ocelum.

SPQR A. Titus Labienus, Legatio, Legio X.

Here in northern Gallia the past two winter nights turned fairly warm. A soft wind from the south brought rain that tried to coax a thaw in the frozen ground. Most of the legionaries adopt our Celtic clothing for the cold months—wolf-fur boots, woolen trousers, and hooded cloaks—but this rain has churned camp roads into quagmires. Mud clings to boots and spatters clothing with grayish, caking gobs. Much of the time between watches is spent brushing loose the hardened clods.

This morning, hunched in my cloak against a dawn drizzle, I went to the horse pens to choose a mount. Galba chose me as a go-between with merchants at Lutetia. I'm to hire barges for transporting supplies between there and camp. Rivers in Gallia rarely freeze over in winter, thus are easy and dependable roadways. Mucky ooze sucks at my boots as I pass the shelter stabling officer's horses. The buildings are a series of *vinae*, long, narrow sheds used by legionaries as protection from enemy missiles while attempting to breach the walls of a town. When we are on the march, we dismantle the sheds and carry their parts in the baggage train.

I'm not sure why, but I decided to turn into the shed where the commander's horse and those of senior tribunes are stabled. Unlike Celtic animals, which often are of haphazard breeding, these Romani mounts are sleek horses, well-bred and spirited. One of them reminds me of Derka, so I bring that mare an occasional chunk of salt. None of the stable slaves is up yet, because discipline is more relaxed in winter camp. When I entered, horses nickered softly, anticipating that I'm bringing them fresh fodder. The dim interior smelled of manure strong enough to overpower the fragrance of hay plants. I'm not surprised that slaves have put off the unpleasant duty of dunging out the stalls.

I had almost walked the length of the shed when I heard animals at the far end struggle at their tethers and whinny nervously. The sound made me recall a time when Derka had reacted in the same way. A serpent sunning itself on a rocky ledge had surprised her and she panicked. I clucked soft, reassuring sounds as I eased my way toward the horses. At first glance, a limp shape I saw hanging on the end stall resembled a white blanket draped over a harness peg. But, as I came closer, the horror returned that I had felt in the cave at Dividiac's showing of my father's head.

Apsa's body slumped forward from the board wall, suspended above an overturned wooden bucket by a halter that passed around her neck. Her stomach curved noticeably in pregnancy. I must have cried out as I sprang forward to lift the weight from her throat. My sudden movement further alarmed the animals. The stallion reared back and frantically pulled at its short tether. I was able to support Apsa's sagging body with my left arm, then reach back for my sword with my right hand. I used the blade to saw though the leather strap above her head. Released, her weight fell forward, catching me off balance. We both fell to the straw-covered floor. I shielded Apsa's body and ducked my head low: the hoofs of a wild-eyed stallion towering above narrowly missed me.

Finally roused by the commotion, two slaves stumbled through the end door, while rubbing grimy faces to wake up. I shouted in Celtic for them to help us.

One of the youths scrambled to hold the horse's tether and calm the animal. The other helped me slip the halter length from around Apsa's throat. She was unconscious, but breathing. I picked her up and ran toward the hospital tent, cursing both myself and the gods for allowing this to happen. *I should have confronted that brute of a centurio.* At the entrance, I shouted for Nikos to open the flap. He appeared eating barley porridge.

"Alberix...what?" he mumbled, then realized who I held. "Silanus's slave girl... Zeus! Take her to that table at the far end."

My boots dropped muddy clods the length of the tent. Aristides was in back, finishing his cereal. When he saw me with the woman, he snatched up a fur to place on the wooden table.

Apsa's lips were blue, her arms and feet as cold and white as snow drifts on the north side of the tent. A wet tunic clung to her small breasts and swollen abdomen.

Aristides examined her head and neck while Nikos rubbed briskly at Apsa's arms and asked me what had happened. I said that I found her hanging by a strap in a stable pen.

Nikos signed to the surgeon, but he already had found the welts on Apsa's throat. He eased back her eyelids to check the pupilsand felt gently along her neck. After running a thumbnail along the soles of her feet and noticing a reflexive wiggle, Aristides cut away the wet tunic.

Nikos placed heated stones in fur bags and arranged them alongside Apsa's body. "I had heard she was with child," he muttered. "Silanus was about to throw her out because she was too ill to do his cooking."

"I'll kill the bastard!"

"And end up decorating the camp spiked to a cross?" Nikos warned. "Anyway, Silanus isn't here. I heard him request a month's leave because of winter inaction. We are all glad to be rid of him."

Apsa coughed and I came to her side. Nikos told me to carry her to the mattress on a cot in the nearest cubicle. I laid the warm bags alongside her and covered her body with blankets. Nikos came back with a pot that smelled of camphor oil

"Rub her body with this to induce heat and bring blood up to her skin."

As I knelt beside her, Apsa's shivering subsided, but tears formed at corners of her closed eyes. I brushed them away gently as I could.

Nikos went back to eating his porridge and called to me, "Pull that blanket away. The medication won't work if it's not directly on her body."

I folded the blanket down to her bulging navel and poured oil in my hand. Apsa pulled back at my touch and opened her eyes to stare at me, a blank look beyond fear.

"It's Alberix," I told her softly. "You're with friends, Apsa."

She closed her eyes again without acknowledging my words.

As I smoothed the pungent oil over her chest and breasts, I tried to temper my rough hands with lighter strokes in working the balm over her rounded abdomen. I was grateful when Nikos came to cover her upper body again; my manhood had reacted to my touch on Apsa's body.

"Rub her legs and feet. When Apsa can swallow, I'll give her a hot drink." Nikos touched the welts on her neck. "Zeus, another few moments and we would be putting Charon's coppers on her eyes."

"Coppers?"

"They're for Charon, a boatman who ferries the dead over the river Styx to the Underworld. Coins are placed on the corpse's eyelids as payment for his service."

"Simonides mentioned your land of the dead, but not the coins."

"I think she'll be fine..." Nikos tucked the blanket tight against the woman. "You probably haven't eaten. Come and have some of this '*horridulus*' as I call it, a kind of perverse pun on '*horedum*,' the word for barley. After Nikos spooned the mush into a bowl, he watched me eat. "Off the subject, but you haven't had much experience with females, have you?"

I shrugged, glad that my mouth was too full to answer.

"No wonder...I've seen your fat village women..." Nikos let his comment speak for itself. "Where did you find this slim beauty?"

I swallowed, then told him, "I met Apsa at Octodurus before Galba came. When she's well enough, I'll send her with my mother at Wermaros to have the child."

"Hold on friend. She's not yours. Silanus paid for her."

"I'll buy her back from him."

"He doesn't like you, remember? If he even suspected that you wanted Apsa, he'd sell her to a brothel before you needed to piss again."

I ate another spoonful of porridge before asking, "Would you—

"Take care of her for you? I...I can't afford to make an enemy of the *centurio*. If I wanted to fight, I would not have been a surgeon's apprentice."

"Then I'll take her." I pushed my bowl back and stood up.

He quipped, "Still intent on being a camp decoration? Of course, if it could be proved that Silanus abandoned her—"

"He did. You said as much."

"I know that a runaway slave is considered a thief for stealing his owner's property, but abandoned slaves may be the property of anyone who claims them. Get advice from a tribune who studied law."

I looked toward Apsa, asleep now. "Take care of her, Nikos. I'm riding to Lutetia in the morning with the dispatch troop."

"Mercurius be with you." He clasped my shoulder, knowing that even routine assignments could turn deadly.

I grasped his arm. "Don't let Silanus get near Apsa or the fight will be with me."

Nikos laughed, but I was sure my eyes warned him and my grip bordered on painful. "She's under medical law now. Trust me in that."

≈

That afternoon I went to the praetorian tent. I found Simonides and asked him to add a message to the next letter to Cluvios, telling my mother that I was sending a young pregnant woman to Wermaros. I would explain when I returned for the winter.

≈

Silanus returned from his furlough to find the girl gone and me waiting for him. There was no angry confrontation and his friendly manner baffled me. He said the poor girl should not have gotten pregnant, but if I paid him what he had given Galba, plus a bit more for the child—another potential slave, after all—then Apsa would be mine. He invited me to drink together and seal the bargain. I refused that part of his offer. Simonides, whose father still sent him a regular allowance, lent me the balance of a ransom price I didn't have.

Later that day, Titus Labienus assembled the legion's tribunes and centurions to tell them that Caesar would arrive early, within a month, to meet his legions. In drinking circles that evening, rumors about an imminent campaign against the transrhenus Germani poured out as rapidly as the wine. A foolhardy thrust across the Rhenus was the last thing we could imagine. Many besotted legionaries tried to predict their future by the cyrystalized dregs in their wine cups.

Publius Silanus drank late with a single companion, Petrosidius, a standard-bearer. He boasted of his agreement with Alberix as part of other plans that were on his mind. He had the Celt exactly where he could make use of him. The trusting fool actually had come to him—all because of a female slut!

Chapter XXXII

Julius Caesar enhanced his reputation for accomplishing the unexpected, even the reckless, by ordering his legions to attack Germani living on the Gallic side of the Rhenus. After catching a main force of Usipete and Tencteri warriors off guard, the legionaries drove survivors into the river. Cavalry auxiliae hunted down women and children joining the retreat.

While the legions regrouped, Caesar negotiated with the Ubii, a tribe across the Rhenus, friendly to Rome. After deciding to cross into Germania in a show of power, Caesar rejected an offer of boats and ordered a bridge constructed by engineers to span the waterway. He would impress local tribes with the ease by which he crossed to their side of the river. Camps were set up and details sent to cut trees. Engineers assembled a bridge model. All went well until a week into construction, when rains began.

Poor weather forced *Optio* Gnaeus Cornelius and Marcus Marius to stop outdoor work on the span. Feeling like soggy prisoners in their leaking tent, the two engineers became increasingly irritable. A constant downpour added to the psychological effects of being near the mystical river that Germani called "Father Rhenus" The ongoing gloomy weather affected the nerves of everyone in camp.

One dismal, wet afternoon, Cornelius and Marius passed the time reminiscing about the towers at Wermaros and the village girls who had welcomed them in such an erotic way. I entered their tent to tell them of a puzzling request by Publius Silanus.

Marius asked, "What did the *centurio* want you to do?"

"Cross the unfinished bridge into Germania."

"Dangerous," Cornelius warned. "I thought he was being civil to you."

"Yes, I don't understand. I don't see Silanus often, but he seemed to have sheathed the sword."

Marius quipped, "Reminds me of the story of a farmer who found a half-frozen snake, warmed it in his tunic, and received a fatal bite for his trouble! Kindness won't change another man's nature. Even a silver piss-pot was made to hold piss."

After we laughed at his jest, I asked, "When will the entire bridge be completed?"

Marius stood to show the model. "The roadway here shouldn't take over two days. Even of the rain doesn't let up, no more than four, wouldn't you say, Cornelius?"

He nodded while dripping honey from a comb into a bronze flagon set on coals at the edge of brazier. "That ought to make this vinegar more palatable."

"I'd like to get over the bridge and back in three days," Marius said. "Those dark hills...that black river water. If I believed in sorcerers I'd say they lurked around here."

I asked, "Will we winter in Germania?"

"Not likely, at least not with all the legions." Cornelius stirred the heated wine and tasted it with a finger. "Not bad. Supply problems, for one thing, Alberix, yet if Caesar decides to do so, the good old Tenth will have the honor."

The tent flap opened. Simonides came in bringing a gust of air that smelled of wet earth and rotting fish.

"Greetings, historian, and close that opening," Marius called out. "This place feels like a *frigidarium* as it is. Attis's Balls, *Graecus*! You look like a Lucanian who fell into a muddy manure heap."

He replied, "Friend, that's a compliment considering where I have been. This cursed rain..." Simonides shook out his leather cape and stood near the brazier to absorb warmth. "I've been slogging through a pig wallow for days. Those Germani don't have barns worth a copper lepton."

I said, "You obviously haven't stumbled upon another Vesontio. Where *have* you been?"

He clasped his hands around a cup of heated wine Cornelius poured out. "I...I was across the river."

"Across the Rhenus?" Marius affected disbelief. "So what's holding your head in place, *hubris* or *stulticia?*"

"That's just the point. I'm not stupid and can't see much difference between the Germani over there and the Keltoi on our side. Villages look poorer and farm tools are more primitive, but I understood the language...a sort of guttural Celtic. I even ran into a couple of Roman merchants who winter there."

"Romani?" I repeated in surprise. "I had to translate for Caesar with the envoys of Ariovistos."

"It is confusing," Simonides agreed. "That king was Suebi, and there are tribes that don't understand Celtic, but the river is not a frontier which absolutely divides Gallia from Germania. At least not linguistically."

Marius recalled, "Caesar seems intent on making it one."

After a sip of warm wine, the historian nodded. "That's what bothers me. Before I went over, I organized some of the commander's notes. Alberix, when was the last time you had to translate?"

"Not in a while."

"Exactly! I think Caesar is making a political issue of the Rhenus 'frontier'."

"Hold on," an irritated Cornelius protested. "Mere legionaries don't question strategies."

"No offense, *optio*, but even if I look like one of you mud-eaters, I'm not exactly military." Simonides laughed to ease the tension he felt in the engineer. "Hades, Cornelius, be loyal to your oath of service. I just want to know the real situation."

Marius intervened. "No offense need be taken."

Simonides asked, "Cornelius, do you have that map of *Terra* I let you keep?"

He nodded toward a field desk. "In that leather cylinder."

After he took the papyrus from its case, Simonides pointed to the center. "See, Germania is directly north of Italia. It borders Caesar's Cisalpina province in a direct line with Aquileia."

Marius wondered, "If it's as poor as you say, why bother to conquer the place?"

"To establish a limit?" Simonides suggested. "Finish off Gallic tribes, then protect your Roman flank with a show of force."

I began to understand. "That's one purpose of this bridge."

Cornelius flushed. "Let's hope you two make better a engineer and historian than you do political philosphers!" He snatched up the map and pointed to where they were. "Ariovistos started all this by inviting more and more of his barbarians into Sequani lands. The two tribes we've just beaten crossed over to attack the Menapii. I'll place my sesterces down on stopping the unlawful settling of Gallia right here. Great Jupiter! There are four hundred-thirty thousand Germani!"

Simonides corrected him. "Come, Cornelius, perhaps a tenth that number."

"Look, *Graecus*..." He walked toward the tent opening to peer out. "Stopped raining. I'm going to the mess tent and see what we have for supper."

None of the three cared to continue the conversation, but a legionary courier ducking into the shelter interrupted a short interval of quiet.

"What's his trouble?" the man asked, jerking a thumb at Cornelius. "I only asked if he's seen Alberix, not for a loan."

"What is it?" I asked.

"*Centurio* Silanus wants you over the bridge right now. Some Germani are trying to tell him something, but he can't make out what they want."

Marius said, "I thought he knew their language."

"Don't know, sir. My orders are to tell Alberix to come at once."

I put on my still-damp cape. "Simonides?"

"No, no, *grates*. I've had enough of Germania for awhile, and could sleep 'til the new moon. Tell me tomorrow what the *barbaroi* wanted."

Marius said, "Come back here afterward. Cornelius will be over his sulking and we'll teach you how to win at dice."

I grinned at him and left with the courier, a recruit from Ticinum who said his name was Nonius. We slogged through a muddy camp street, where receding rainwater puddles reflected an apricot-hued sunset sky. Outside the camp gate, we passed piles of soggy construction timbers and then descended the river bank to where men of Silanus's century were on guard. I saw that the bridge pilings were driven into place and brush-covered sapling branches extended about a quarter the distance across as the roadway. I picked my way past its end on side beams, noticing posts set in the murky water as barriers to boats loaded with burning brush that might be sent to lodge against the supports.

When I reached the east bank, I saw Silanus standing with four legionaries around a group of Germani horsemen. One of the mounted warriors pointed in my direction.

The centurion came to meet me and indicate a rider and his two bodyguards behind him. "That there is Ogerth. He's got information th' commander should hear."

Ogerth wore a fur jacket, woolen trousers, and heavy boots, but did not dismount to ask, "Kelt, you learned our language, where?"

I was in no mood for conversation. "Prisoners taken from Ariovistos. What is this message for Julius Caesar?"

Instead of replying, Ogerth signaled to one of his bodyguards, who had maneuvered his horse behind me. It was the last thing I remembered before a blow on the back of my head stunned me. I had a vague sensation of being lifted onto a horse and feeling the animal gallop away.

Silanus and his companions mounted horses that Ogeth had hidden among the trees and followed the Suebi chieftain. The band rode a few miles south along the Rhenus before turning east along a small tributary of the river. Here they followed a trail until it was almost dark, then halted in an oak grove for the night.

When I regained consciousness, leather thongs bound my wrists and ankles. Rather than struggle, I decided to conserve my strength and find a reason for my abduction. We had nothing to eat. I eventually fell asleep on the cold ground.

At first light, one of the Germani roused me and untied my feet. Two of the legionaries hoisted me in front of the same horseman, and we continued northward along the stream. Later I found it named the Lagona. Since the men did not stop to rest, by midday we arrived at a small settlement I estimated was twenty-five miles from the bridge.

A flimsy palisade surrounded a cluster of mud-and-wattle huts. Weed-grown plots of root vegetables and stunted barley stood in gardens alongside the dwellings. I recalled the poor agricultural methods described by Simonides.

Ogerth said, "We get new horses here and eat food."

His men bathed in the icy river, but put on the same sweat-and mud-stained clothing, before sitting on the ground to eat. Three women brought out rye bread and a rabbit and barley stew, which the warriors gulped down as if rapid meals were a habit. My right hand was untied, but the left bound to my leg. Between bites of the thick, meaty mush, I questioned Silanus.

"What's your purpose in this, to obtain ransom money? Romani don't pay to get *auxilia* members back."

"Ransom? That's a good one," the centurion rasped. "Oh, I'll be rich all right, an' you'll get your share, too."

"My share? What does the money pay for?"

Silanus ate without replying, then pushed his dish aside. "I'll show them fancy officers. They still can't piss without their mommies holdin' it. Wanted me out of th' Twelfth, did they? They'll regret that. Where do y' think I went last winter? T' make a deal with old Ogerth. He's Suebi an' wants me t' teach his barbarians how t' fight like us. Discipline an' all that. He'll pay...pay well! Don't let these latrine-villages fool you. Ogerth gets tribute from other tribes. Gold an' silver. I seen it!"

"Where will you spend all these denarii? You can't go back to Romani lands."

"Ogerth promised me a holding of my own further east. I'll be a chieftain." Silanus's voice became conciliatory. "Look, Alberix, these Germani are just now tastin' what you Kelts have an' they like it. They'll take it all some day, an' we'll be on the winnin' side. Not all furcin' Roman commanders will be lucky as Caesar."

When Ogerth signaled that the rest was over, his warriors and the legionaries mounted fresh horses to continue on. No one bothered to tie my free hand and I was pushed up in front of another warrior whose river bath had done nothing to sweeten the smell of his clothing. Silanus had said they were Suebi, and I recalled the two warriors who had climbed up to signal the attack on Wermaros. Could Ogerth have been there?

In the lead, the chieftain strained his shaggy, short-legged mount to the limit. He knew about Caesar's reputation for doing the unexpected, and would not want to chance an encounter with cavalry sent out to find me or the missing legionaries Silanus had persuaded to desert. Ogerth knew the unfinished bridge was in his favor and that Suebi would be suspected of abducting the men. Search parties would range south, toward the Moenus River, not north.

The Lagona narrowed as we rode into its upper reaches. By late afternoon, the outline of a larger village appeared on a rise of cleared land. We left the river trail and soon encountered a pack of hounds that came yelping at us in greeting.

Ogerth's holding was more substantial than the miserable huts where we had gotten horses and eaten. The palisade was similar to the one at Wermaros, but the gate lacked metal hinges. It was secured at the lintel and pivoted upward on heavy oak pegs. No guards were on duty at the open gate. Did this lack of discipline prompt the Germani chieftain's strange alliance with Publius Silanus?

Slowing their mounts to a trot, the warriors turned onto a path alongside the lodges. Windows closed with sliding shutters. *Germani have no crafters skilled in iron-working, or no iron.* An open doorway emitted a stench of manure from animal stalls attached to the dwelling. *Livestock and humans share a common roof.* Although muddy paths connected the houses, a central road was laid with logs to provide a jarring, but more solid roadbed.

The hounds lost interest and loped off to beg meat scraps from women preparing evening meals. Ogerth led the way to an open area where a substantial lodge stood at one end. I guessed that a hundred persons and a third that many slaves lived in the village enclosure.

"My *buthlaz*," the chieftain said, after he stopped in front of the lodge. "You *centurio*, you Kelt, and Nonius will live with me," he ordered, then shouted for his men to house the others and station guards at the gate.

A cluster of curious villagers gathered to watch. When a door at the end of the lodge opened, a young woman stepped out. She dressed in the same woolen trousers and fur jackets as men, but had long wheat-colored hair twisted into twin braids.

"My daughter," Ogerth said, grinning with pride. "A pity she was not born a man. She has the spirit of a warrior. Frieda! We have been without food since sun up."

She called back in Germanic, "Food awaits you and your guests, Father."

Frieda ignored the iron-helmeted strangers; the blond-haired youth with eyes the color of field chicory interested her.

"Kelt," she asked me, you know our language?" I nodded that I did. "Good. You will tell me stories of your people."

Ogerth chuckled as he dismounted. "Frieda is a bold girl, who always has her way. Come, come. Tonight you are guests. There will be time enough tomorrow to sort out your places here."

I thought it a subtle way to put it, for a man who held our lives in his sword hand.

The lodge entrance opened into a large open room with four timber roof supports. Eight other columns receded into the hall and formed braces for partitioning off sleeping rooms. At the far end a stable provided a measure of insulation from westerly winds, but the entire space stank of manure. River rushes were strewn on the dirt floor. A trestle table large enough to seat eight to ten warriors was placed at right angles to the south wall. A fire enclosure similar to those in Celtic households was on the opposite side, near the center of a crude kitchen. From there slaves helped Ogerth's wife, a short, plump woman younger than her husband, bring in heaping wooden trenchers of food.

Ogerth and his bodyguards gorged themselves without speaking, except when the chieftain paused to urge the Romani to more helpings of beef and pork from a central platter. He jovially pushed horn serving spoons on them and told his wife to bring more dark, brank-barley bread.

Frieda seated herself opposite me, elbowing aside warriors too intent on the food to notice. As slaves filled our drinking horns with poor quality sweetened brew, Ogerth held up his horn. The curled, black rams-horn was decorated with a hunting scene.

"This is *Medu*," he said. "A beer like the Keltens'."

"You know much about us," I remarked to him, trying to avoid Frieda's look as she stared at me.

Ogerth boasted, "I was two years with Ariovistos. I saw the richness of Sequani lands, the Kelten way of life. Then my father died, so I came here to inherit his lands and this village."

Frieda interjected, "Father, you saw the Romani fight."

"True, daughter. I saw them protected like the tortoise, stinging like a hornet with short swords. I saw the warriors of Ariovistos fade away like field mists."

Emboldened by the drink, almost feeling like a guest, I asked, "And you, Ogerth? Did you run?" Silanus choked at my question. Nonius paled.

The chieftain paused before replying, then nodded his head in admission. "I, too, fled across the Rhenus to fight again."

After his guards finished rapping their knife handles on the table in tribute, I asked, "To fight Romani hornet to hornet?" I felt reckless and gave my neck torc a decisive tug.

Frieda clapped in delight. The Kelt youth's spirit matched her own.

Ogerth slammed down his horn and scowled at everyone in a signal for quiet. "Ah, no, you misunderstand. Only tribes in the east, at the rising of the sun god, will feel my sting." After his men had rapped the table again, the chieftain looked into his horn, trying to interpret a pattern in the foam. "Enough!" he weaved slightly and slurred his words. "We sleep now, to be up for a dawn sacrifice to Tiwaz."

Frieda tongued the lip of her cup as she watched Alberix walk into the dimness of the corridor, to a compartment where he would sleep. She pushed away the groping hands of Gurther, head of her father's guards and decided she would lie with no man again until it was with the Kelt youth.

❧

Ogerth and an assembly of sixty lien warriors were to meet at dawn at the shrine of his war god, Tiwaz. In the chill morning, mounted on a stolen white horse with the brand of Legio XI, the chieftain led his hirelings and me, a possible hostage, along a forest trail that led to the sacred oak grove. The woods gave way to a clearing, where a stagnant pool reflected the pale dawn light. I was reminded of Sequana's sacred spring, but this nemeton was smaller and more enclosed. Mist hovered over the ground, yet I could make out the dim forms of Ogerth's warriors standing motionless around the pond. Their painted shields were a ring of color in the muted sanctuary. On the far side of the pool, crude wooden cult figures guarded a gnarled and twisted oak tree. Frayed ropes hung motionless from a low branch of the tree. A sapling ladder reached the top of the bough from which they dangled.

I gradually saw three older women wearing ragged tunics. The seeress's matted gray hair fell in disheveled strands around thin shoulders. On the ground in front of a younger priestess lay a bronze cauldron. Judging from the shape and decoration, I thought it Celtic workmanship.

Ogerth halted us a short distance from the edge of the trees and dismounted. He looked over his massed warriors, grunted approval, and turned to speak. "We begin by offering to Tiwaz, our god of war. May he be pleased with the sacrificial victim."

At his guttural command one of the women led two white oxen pulling a cart from the forest. It was light enough to see an old warrior in the bed, his shoulders covered by a bearskin cloak. Three of Ogerth's guards moved to escort him to a sacred oak tree. Once there, they pulled the frail oldster off the cart, unfastened the bearskin, then half-carried him to a branch where ropes dangled. Tiwa's victim swayed from senility or a narcotic he had been given. While two warriors supported the oldster by his shoulders and head, another tied him by his ankles. In moments, the old man hung suspended four feet above the ground, like a chicken in a market stall.

Two of the crones came to him. One dipped a yew branch into the pond and sprinkled water over his emaciated body. The other walked forward to hold the cauldron beneath his head. The youngest priestess cluched a bronze knife and climbed a few rungs of the ladder. The old man's final outcry ended in a liquid gurgle: as the blade slashed across his throat, warm jugular blood spurted into the bowl, steaming in the chill air.

Even Silanus reacted with horror to the aborted scream. I realized that it had been the only sound around the pool. The chirp of awakening birds was silenced by the macabre ritual. As the victim's convulsions ended, his rigid body twisted slowly at the end of the halter. I turned away in disgust.

Ogerth's sword pricked the back of my neck. I turned to look into eyes that were the same gray as his steel blade. "Kelt, you will watch from fear that you might become one of the privileged of Tiwaz before your time."

When I looked back, the third crone had spilled blood from the cauldron into the pond water. The first dipped her yew branch into the gore and smeared it on the idols.

Ogerth remounted and trotted his horse to the line of warriors and pointed his sword at the oldster's body. "Fohrden, son of Thurgo, was a warrior without fear, brimming with courage. If any man disputes my words, let him come forward." Grunting approval when none did, he ordered, "Take Fohrden down."

Two men lowered the pliant corpse to the ground. The women wailed as the body of the aged warrior was carried to the pool's edge and laid on a reed mat. The victim's sword was placed at his side and a painted shield lain over his body. His bearskin was arranged on the shield. Each warrior walked past and placed a pine bough on the still form, then the crones bound the greenery with rushes. Flat stones secured on the boughs with willow withes made sure that the funerary bundle would sink.

Without further commands from their chieftain, the men slid the bier into the water and watched it bubble down into the chill blackness. I caught a glimpse of Fohrden's gray hair sinking from view.

After the pool's surface was still, the crones ceased their wailing. Ogerth ordered the priestess to pass around the cauldron of blood. "Taste!" he commanded. "Taste the blood of Fohrden that you may drink in his courage!"

I felt sickened. The nervous legionaries glanced over at Silanus. Even he went pale when Ogerth turned to them. "You, my Romani, have no need of Suebi courage. Our bravery did not pierce through your wall of shields."

Ogerth's stare rested on Publius Silanus. "Begin now, *centurio*. Begin your training of my warriors."

❧

The rains ended and the weather turned colder, hardening the mud into clods that were hard as marble. The snow held off. Ogerth's seeresses told him it was a sign: Tiwaz had accepted the offering of Fohrden's body.

Silanus, Nonius, and four legionaries struggled to organize their arrogant and peevish Suebi men into some semblance of a disciplined formation. The tedious translation and explanation of his commands irritated the recruits. They chafed at the orders and snarling reprimands of the short-haired strangers.

In the second ten days, the warriors balked at digging a ditch-and rampart defense. Ogerth, watching, ordered his slaves to do the work, but the frozen ground resisted their poor digging tools. The project was abandoned.

When their Roman instructors tried to train the Germani to move in unison behind their shields, the ragged line of warriors fought each other. Men rushed ahead to be the first to engage an enemy and reap glory. They complained that they were horse-warriors, not *schlammesser,* foot troops, who ate mud clods thrown up by horses in front of them.

By November, the men refused to drill during the unlucky dark phase of the moon. Many went off to their farmsteads to help with the winter slaughter of pigs and cattle. Others disappeared into the forest and resumed hunting animals that would keep their families fed during the long snowbound days to come.

Silanus ordered me to translate his commands, but on days when training was suspended, I started fashioning a bow like the one I made with Adherbal. Gradually, I hid a crude weapon and small cache of bone-tipped arrows in the straw mattress of my sleeping space.

Frieda came to the training sessions, correcting my words so that the unfamiliar battle orders would be less confusing to the warriors. She laughed at my pronunciation of new words, but always reassured me that I had done well. I thought of Apsa, of course, but also found myself looking forward to the Suebi girl's presence. If she was absent for a day, I understood a little more the pain that Lucius felt at Mother's rejection.

❧

By the moon before the mid-winter solstice, Ogerth's plan was in disarray. With growing frustration, he watched his band of warriors dwindle. The chieftain began to believe what his old seeresses whispered: the Romani were bewitching his men into the precise formations that Ogerth remembered seeing on that autumn day, when Ariovistos was defeated *and he had fled!* After Ogerth told Silanus, the centurion laughed at the notion, but the chieftain's face remained grim. At meals, he no longer spoke to us. He drank too much and muttered vague threats each night before lurching off to his room.

At times when I looked at Ogerth from a distance, his mannerisms seemed vaguely familiar, as if I had seen him somewhere. The few Germani I knew were slaves, or the three at Wermaros who taught me their language. I stopped trying to place him.

Frieda told me that she was concerned, not for the hired legionaries, who did not interest her, but for me. Her father might be more reasoning than most Germanic chieftains, yet his blood heated easily. She had seen his knife flash out to avenge an insult and feared that he was losing patience with his Shorthair instructors.

❧

One mid-winter afternoon, when the air was cold and the evening sun still a handspan above the frozen horizon, Frieda took me to the nearby Lagona. The river was unfrozen, with only its sandy edges rimmed by thin sheets of ice. On either side, the landscape was brownish ochre, tinted in low places by white pockets of snow. A soft violet of skeletal trees framed the evening sky.

After we sat awhile on a fallen tree trunk near the shore, she reached for my hand. "I love the river. Is your homeland like this?"

I said, "There are more mountains around my village and the river is deeper. I did live awhile on the Rhenus, at Arialbinnum, across from Germania. That's where I learned a little of your language."

"I...I want to go where you live," she said, looking into my eyes and squeezing my hand. "I want to leave here with you."

I had not expected that from her. "What about your father and mother?"

"They don't matter, I've decided. Father is angry with the way his plan to train warriors is going. He sees now that his idea was no more than an ignorant dream. Every day Ogerth grows more furious. He won't act until the solstice, but after that—"

"He'd kill us?" I hadn't thought of that possibility until I blurted it out.

"As an offering to Tiwaz, like that old warrior..." She tightened her hold on my hand. "Kelt, there will be snow within this moon phase. The old ones have thrown their twigs and predict it."

"There is always snow this month."

"*Heavy* snow," she emphasized.

"Then we won't be able to train the men."

"And my father will become even angrier."

I eyed the low sun. "When is the solstice?"

"In two nights." Frieda explained, "My father will be at the sacred grove with the old women and warriors who are still here. They will light bonfires and stay the night, until the sun returns in the morning."

Frieda abruptly stood and pulled me along the river's edge. A short distance away, over a low hill, she pointed to a stone hovel thatched with rye straw and fitted with a wattle door. "A boat is in there. It was hidden when you Romani came."

I pulled open the door and looked inside. A shallow-bottomed skiff much like the ones I rowed on the Dubis leaned against the wall. Its oars were stacked with a clutter of farming tools that would not be used until spring planting. I realized this would be a safer place to hide my bow, and I might have a chance to escape downstream in the boat.

Frieda pressed against me in the small room, reaching under my cape to pull my body to hers. I bent and found her mouth with mine. In the cold air, our warm tongues touched with a pleasant wetness that sent shivers through my body in a way the chill evening air had been unable to do.

She whispered, "Then, Kelt, you will take me away?"

I nodded and searched for her tongue again. We kissed, caught up in a release of tension. My hardness pressed against her thigh until she broke away; this frigid hut was no place to take off clothing. Frieda took my hand again and led me back along the river to the village. Before we reached the gate, she stopped to look into my face and trace the outline of my lips with a finger.

"Father has gone with his liensmen to cut trees for the solstice celebration and give them gifts. Tonight, when the others are in the grove, come to my room."

After we tongue-kissed again, she walked alone into the village.

After supper, I could only think of Frieda. When I heard her and the slaves go to their compartments, I waited until the only sounds in the longhouse were those of winter sleep.

At my hesitant rap, Frieda opened her wicker door and let me in. Coals in a brazier warmed the air. A bronze lamp I guessed was loot from a ransacked villa gave a flickering orange light to the small room. She had put on a green, embroidered tunic and loosened her braids. In the warm light, her tumble of golden hair gleamed like burnished metal. "You look so...so beautiful," I stammered, feeling excited, yet awkward.

She smiled and touched my mouth. "Help me," she whispered and started to pull the tunic over her head.

I fumbled as the bodice caught in her hair. In a moment she stood nude, her skin a bronze color in the orange-yellow light. Her body was stocky, like Pixtila's, and the fullness of her breasts were in contrast to Apsa's smallness, yet there was total sensuousness in the woman's movements. She took my hand in hers and brought me to her bed to unfasten my trouser lacings and pull off my shirt.

"We must take our time," she said, caressing my chest, then lay on her stomach half-under the fur covers. "Kelt, rub my body."

I began to stoke Frieda's skin, awkwardly at first, exploring the warmth of her curves and hollow places. My touch became more sensitive, lingering whenever I induced a moan, then moving my hand to another place that gave the girl pleasure. Swept up in experiencing her flesh, I also was aware of my own body. When she turned on her side and saw my erection, I tried to cover myself with a hand.

"I am your first woman?" Frieda seemed only slightly surprised at my nod, perhaps knowing that Celtic men sometimes lay with other men. She reassured me, "Among our people, he who remains a virgin the longest is held in honor."

She half rose and turned me on my back, then reached for a jar of scented oil.

"We are not all as barbaric as you believe." Frieda shushed my protest at the accusation, poured oil in her hand, and rubbed my chest in slow sweeps. Her nipples touched me and hardened. I trembled as her fingers caressed my groin. "So...I am your first? You had no Kelten filly?" She smiled as her hand reached my manhood.

When my breath came in gasps, the girl knew the sign and lay back to receive me. "Enter gently," she whispered, "not with the auroch thrusts of some men I know."

When I fumbled, her hand guided me into her wetness and she raised her hips to sheath me. The sensation of pleasure penetrated my groin as deeply as I was inside her.

"Follow my movements..." Frieda breathed in gasps as she thrust against me. As her rhythmic moves brought me to the edge of climax, she closed her eyes. Her breathing became one with the quickened motion. My sudden outcry as I released caught her a few seconds before her own rush of excitement welled from the depth of her being. She stiffened and exhaled a deep sigh of gratification.

Joined and silent, we lay soaked in love-wetness. I nuzzled her damp, scented hair while she traced gentle circles on my back.

"Ah, Kelt," she finally murmured, biting my ear, "It is not this way with the others. No man has moved me as much." I flushed and said I would like to rub oil on her body again She rolled onto her stomach. "Your hands on me are good. The others may as well stick a boar! They finish and are asleep."

I paused, upset at her remarks. Frieda constantly brought up different men and a feeling of jealousy was new to me. She sensed my unease and reached up to smooth my hair. "The others? No more than dreams in the night." She kissed my hand and whispered, "Rub me again, Kelt."

After I traced out the full curves of her body with oil, I entered her once more. This time she moved so that our release was together. Afterward, we lay on our sides, half covered with furs, watching flickering shadows cast on the wall by the oil lamp's flame.

I laughed at one. "That looks like Tergwath the sorcerer."

"Tergwath?"

"An old magician who destroyed one of our villages. That shadow reminded me of him."

"Kelt, my people have sorcerers, too."

We lay holding hands as she told me of Gudrun, the chieftain's daughter who was abducted and held in captivity because she refused to marry an alien king's son. Her perseverance was rewarded with freedom and revenge. The names were strange to me—Harmut, Herwig, Gerlinde, Hettel—I didn't understand everything she said, but it was enough for me to see Frieda's eyes shining as she lived a life of imagination through her stories.

In the telling, the brazier coals died and the room grew cold. Gray ashes lay in the iron grate when she told one last story of a warrior named Sigfrid, who lived in a village on the ancient Rhenus. Clasped in a woman's moist embrace, I felt a pleasure I had never before known, and fell asleep. When I abruptly awoke, the room was almost dark, the lamp barely alight.

I gently shook Frieda in our cocoon of scented warmth. "It's time I went before your father returns."

"He will be back tomorrow evening for the solstice. Remember your promise to take me away with you at the moonrise we agreed."

I kissed her, found my clothes, went back to my room and slept until dawn, aware of Frieda and the scent of her oil that lingered on me.

୭ഴ

Frieda was wrong. Her father returned in early afternoon, bringing a temper as dark as the overcast skies that threatened imminent snow. Word of his hiring Romani to train his warriors, and the poor showing of the men, had circulated among his lien vassals. Laughter had barely been concealed in the farmsteads he visited. Humiliation, and the realization that his ambitions were in tatters rankled the chieftain.

"CENTURIO!"

Ogerth's bellow was heard throughout the longhouse. Silanus came out of his compartment holding a leather belt he had been shortening.

"Bring your Shorthairs outside," he ordered, fingering his belt knife. "The Kelt, also. I have words for all of you."

A nervous Silanus sent Nonius to summon the men. I came with him to the open space outside the lodge. When we had assembled, Ogerth's guards formed a half circle around us. Each wore a sword. None of us was armed.

The chieftain scowled from astride his horse. "There was laughter at me yesterday. I was not pleased, yet do not reply to the cackling of hens." His look at Silanus held menace. "They say, *centurio*, that what you teach my warriors is like the training of dogs that run for sticks and amuse women. My seeresses tell me that Tiwaz wishes a taste of Romani blood."

At Ogerth's signal, two warriors seized Nonius, the messenger who summoned me on the night of my abduction. When the other legionaries instinctively reached for swords that were not there, the Suebii unsheathed theirs with an audible swish.

"Hold off, Ogerth, "Silanus protested. "Your men won't obey orders. They do what they please."

Ignoring him, Ogerth raised his voice, "I will offer this Romani honor in the sacrifice. Do you not behead your citizens?"

Silanus paled, but the chieftain answered his own question. At a guttural command, Nonius was forced to his knees an instant before the steel blade of Gurther's sword slashed through his neck. The legionary's body slumped forward. Gore from the stump seeped into the frozen ground. His severed head rolled into a hollow, where hounds sniffed at it and lapped the warm blood.

Ogerth's stiff grin held a threat. "Tiwaz is pleased. We train again after the solstice fires. Each quarter moon will bring either improvement or another sacrifice to the god."

I called out, "Allow us a funeral for Nonius."

The chieftain dismounted and frowned. "Kelt, bury him and do not waste wood on a funeral pyre."

Silanus's hands shook as he gripped the belt and went back inside the lodge. I helped the legionaries wrap their companion's head and torso in his cloak. While they dug a grave in the loose soil of the riverbank, I looked downstream in the direction of the hut where the skiff was hidden. I decided to make my escape shortly after sunset and not wait for Frieda to join me at moonrise. *She might not be able to get away from the ritual. The risk of being discovered is less at that time, since villagers will be at the scared grove. This is the longest night of the year, so I would gain additional darkness in traveling earlier down the river.*

As I trudged back to the longhouse, I decided to leave a message that Silanus would find and read to Frieda in the morning. I had realized that I could never bring her to Wermaros, even as a wife. The Suebi woman would be ostracized in the Sequani village, and there would be the presence of Apsa and her child. I had forgotten her in the sweetness of the past night.

❧❧

Near sunset, Belenos settled over the palisade on the last day of his journey to the south. The weather had cleared, as if my sky god, Teutates, wished to help me escape. There would be moonlight and enough snow on the ground to reflect its light and help me see my way to the hut. Villagers did not eat their usual evening meal. Feasting would come later.

With Ogerth and his family leading the procession, they filed out the gate to assemble in the oak grove. I told Silanus that I would watch from the ramparts. He waved me out, lost in his own plans. Before I left, I slipped my message to Frieda inside his helmet.

When dusk arrived, I eased through the unguarded gate and crouched low as I ran toward the river. My boots crunched in the snow more loudly that I wished, but watch dogs had gone with the villagers. None raised an alarm. Scrambling along the dark bank, my feet slipped into icy water several times before the stone hut came into view. I wrenched the door loose, pulled out my bow, and a deerskin bag of bread and dried venison that Frieda had hidden there. With effort, I wrestled the boat sideways through the door, laid it on the ground, and threw in my weapon and food. The flat skiff slid easily through dead marsh grass and scraped across a sand bank before slipping into the black water. I clambered aboard as the current caught the stern and glided the light craft downstream, toward its junction with the Rhenus.

Hunched low, I steered a clumsy course with unfamiliar cross-handled oars before I understood how they worked. As the boat slid silently past darkened farmsteads, I caught an occasional glimpse of orange bonfires speckling the countryside. The moon rose to mask the feeble lights, yet also to dangerously silhouette the skiff in a path of dancing brightness. I could be spotted more easily, yet at this time of year, I estimated that darkness extended for five watch periods.

By first light, I had drifted safely on the Lagona as far as its junction with the Rhenus. I guided the boat into the broad river until the current caught its stern and swept my small vessel north ward, amidst sunken trees pushing above its swollen surface.

Once again lured back by solstice bonfires, including our Celtic blazes, a pale smear of sun colored the eastern sky. The boat passed the now-dismantled remains of Caesar's bridge, where upright pilings stood like dark offerings to the mystical river. I wondered about the outcome of the raid into Germania; the silent palisade and vacant, snow-filled tent areas of the abandoned legion camps on shore were all that remained. Only ravens were left to quarrel over the bloated carcasses of fish that the river washed ashore during the night.

I was drifting away from legion camps and, moreover, Wermaros, toward the Sea of the Germani.

During the solstice rites, before the bonfires were lighted, Frieda slipped out of the darkened grove and walked her pony through the woods. When she felt it safe to mount, the woman trotted the animal to the river. The moon was at the height agreed upon with the Kelt for their escape and the night was clear. The luck of the youth matched the legendary fortune of his commander.

When Frieda approached the hut by moonlight, she clearly saw the black rectangle of open door. Alarmed that her lover might have been discovered, she jumped from her pony and looked inside. The skiff was gone. Anger slowly replaced her alarm as she saw the flattened grasses and slid down the sand bank to where the boat was dragged to the water.

Frieda lingered only a moment to ponder her betrayal, then returned in anger to the village.

Publius Silanus read the note, but burned the message instead of giving it to the chieftain's daughter. When she learned of Alberix's escape, the woman's fury would match her father's rage. His apprehension was justified. Ogerth decided to vent his frustration and anger by duplicating Roman gladiatorial combats of which he had learned. With a grim smile, the chieftain assigned three of his warriors pitted against each legionary, odds he considered fair in view of the vaunted fighting skills of the Shorthairs.

Encounters were predictably short. Desperate legionaries fell to the blades of furious warriors avenging the many humiliations they had endured during training sessions. Silanus was matched against a trio of Ogerth's bodyguards, the elite of his warriors. At the evening meal, the chieftain remarked that the *centurio* had fought with the fury of a wounded boar. His face brightened in admiration as he recalled how Silanus had killed one of his opponents and wounded the other two. Ogerth boasted that it was he who leapt through the circle of spectators and finally killed the Roman with a single knife thrust.

His men drank and listened in silence. No one dared remind their chieftain that they had been forced to pull him away from Silanus; he had continued to visciously stab him as he lay dead on the frozen earth.

That night Frieda slept in the bed of the warrior who had beheaded Nonius. The woman's lovemaking was so fierce that Gurther wondered at the cause of uncommon tears in her eyes. No one before had seen Frieda, daughter of Ogerth, weep.

Chapter XXXIII

As I fell into an uneasy sleep, the skiff wedged itself into a tangle of branches near the river's bank and abruptly awakened me. As I tried to free the boat by pushing at the brush with an oar, I was challenged by a group of Ubii fishermen, one of the few transrhenus tribes friendly to Romani. When they saw my legion clothing and asked why a Gallic auxiliary was on their side of the river, I decided to tell them the truth. The men sneered at a Suebi chieftain's ambition to become "Caesar of the Germani" and escorted me back to their village.

At Bonaz, I was surprised to find one of the Romani merchants Simonides had mentioned, wintering in the lodge of Galerth, his Ubii agent. Junius Balbus was concerned to hear of Publius Silanus's treachery and Ogerth's schemes of conquest. Gallic tribes, too, were learning Roman tactics in order to counter the legions' military advantages. When Balbus pointed out that Suebi renegades had raided Sequani villages before the defeat of Ariovistus, I realized that it was Ogerth that Pixtila and I had watched from the height above Wermaros. The mercahnt confirmed that Simonides, my Greek friend, had passed through Bonaz earlier that autumn.

Pleased to have my company for the rest of the cold season, Balbus failed to tell me that Legio XIV was in winter camp about one-hundred-fifty miles to the west. After Caesar's brief thrust across the Rhenus, his strategy was to quarter his legions in Gallia by building camps within a hundred miles of each other, or about a three-day forced march apart.

During the snowbound days that followed, the talkative merchant found me a good listener. He said that Caesar had ordered the bridge into Germania destroyed after staying in the countryside less than three weeks. Soon after, in late summer, he made the bold decision to send a legionary force onto the island of Albion. The tribune I knew from Octodurus, Gaius Volusenus, was send to gather information. Meanwhile, Caesar assembled a fleet of some eighty transports and warships and landed two legions, the Seventh and Tenth with their cavalry, on the island. After a series of inconclusive battles, poor weather hampered his effort. In late September, Caesar returned with his men for the winter.

I began to make another crossbow whenever Galerth was away—the Ubii fishermen had "lost" the one I escaped with. I, of course, thought of my night with Frieda, but without much guilt at leaving her behind. Like a wild creature, she would not have survived the captivity of living among tribes alien to her in language and customs. Apsa seemed more and more far away: I had no idea about how I could return to Wermaros from this remote place on the very rim-edge of my Wheel.

✌⤆

Despite rumors of Gallic unrest and conspiracies among barbarian tribes, Balbus remained convinced that Bonaz eventually would become an important transit station for Roman goods imported to the east. His commercial imagination was as wide as the dark forests that stretched toward the sunrise, but information that came to him from the direction of the sea to the north was of more immediate interest. Informants reported that Caesar was again assembling galleys at the legion winter camps for a spring expedition to Albion. Balbus realized that an invasion force needed supplies. Supplies were bought from merchants. *Ergo*, he decided to find the legions by sailing down the Rhenus and around into the channel that divides Gallia from Albion. He invited me to join him. In that way I could return to my unit of *auxilia*, perhaps even to Wermaros when the fighting ended.

✌⤆

We left with a guide, Herteg, on the calends of March, in a boat fitted with a small wicker cabin and sail. Riding the current, our voyage proceeded without incident. Balbus said the local tribes, who valued his trading goods, would recognize his bear totem painted on the sail. None would bother us.

In a swift current, on the first evening we reached a point where the river turned westward to form islands as it entered its delta. A tribe called the Batavi lived on one of them nearby. Balbus had brought gifts. Tribesmen rowed out in flat boats to receive them in exchange for fish and bird's eggs. Their chieftain invited us to spend the night in their village, but Balbus, no stranger to treachery, made excuses. We slept in the boat cabin with Herteg outside as watchman.

Next morning our guide steered us through a maze of channels. Around midday, I caught my first glimpse of the sea, its clean, sharp horizon straighter than any I had seen before. The sensation was unsettling, as if the distant flatness was a dangerous edge of the Now-world. The round earth that Simonides described was contrary to what I could see. When we entered the blue expanse, I admitted to Balbus that I was worried that we might fall off at some point. He laughed, said he was familiar with the Briton Sea, and no one ever had disappeared in quite that way. Herteg turned the boat south, steering close to a low, indented shoreline.

Balbus dozed in the cabin and the sun lay low in my line of vision, when I called our guide's attention to a dark shape silhouetted against the horizon.

Herteg stood up to squint in the direction I pointed. "War trireme, trainin' out of Gesoriacum," he said casually, and sat down at the tiller again.

He was not concerned. I didn't know the word he used to describe the shape, but to me it resembled a monstrous water creature with six sets of flailing legs. As it came closer, I saw that it was a large galley with a pointed bronze beak and enormous oars. They moved in rhythm to a hammer beat I could hear from below its deck.

Abruptly, a trumpet like the legion *cornua* signaled. The shrill sound carried across the water. Oars on the left side paused in mid-air, trailing salt water, then the right bank dipped into the water and turned the pointed prow toward our boat. The *cornua* sounded again, louder this time, and the opposite oars angled awkwardly into the sea.

Alarmed now, Herteg stood up. "What's that galley-master up to? They been known to ram barbarian craft as practice."

I saw that if galley's intent *was* to collide with us, their turn might be too sharp. At a new signal, the right bank of oars tried to compensate and the behemoth angled in our direction again. The splash of oars and curses of the pilot carried over to us clearly on the wind.

Balbus awoke and stood unsteadily at the cabin entrance. Seeing the danger, he came to a rail to wave his fur jacket and shout that he was a Roman citizen, "*Civis! Civis! Civis Romanus!*"

Fortunately, the wind was at our stern. Herteg steered us beyond the reach of the massive hull that foamed past, but the thrashing oars were barely five spear lengths away!

"*Excors*...idiots!" Balbus screamed as he steadied himself against the boat's mast, to counter rocking caused by the galley's passing. "I suppose they're novice sailors. Neptune's Balls, Herteg, can't you move closer to shore to avoid such fools?"

He said, "They thought we were Morini and would sport with us. We should be in Gesoriacum by morning. Look off to your right."

The featureless horizon was topped by a pale, bluish line that could have been low clouds.

"Albion." Balbus identified the place Dividiac had called "The Island of Blue Warriors."

I forgot the near collision with the galley, excited that the spokes of my wheel had extended this far.

At dusk, Herteg anchored as close to shore as he safely dared. Overhead, a clear night sky hosted the mid-March constellations. To the north, our guide pointed to what he called the Two Women, but to me the stars outlined Arctos the bear. I hadn't seen the entire body of Draco at Wermaros, but here was the dragon's body and square head threatening Hercules. The gentle bobbing of the boat eventually rocked me to sleep. I dreamed of Lucius and Psen-Ammon, because of the nearness of the legion camps.

❧

Herteg's navigation was as good as he predicted. By mid-morning, fishing boats appeared amid flat-hulled transport galleys, whose crews struggled to master oars and rigging. On shore I saw newly carpentered ships being completed or fitted out with naval stores that Balbus said had been brought in from Hispania. Above the beach, legionary tents blanketed the heights in tan leather. The air smelled of forge smoke and echoed with the pounding of mallets.

Angling around a cape that jutted from the coastline before it turned south, Herteg soon called out that Gesoriacum was in view. In the bay, transports, and war galleys similar to the one we encountered, crowded the harbor.

Astonished at the activity, Balbus marveled, "How does the man do it? Caesar is again planning to invade the Britoni! Herteg, put me ashore! Caesar's *quaestors* should meet my agent here."

Herteg guided his boat between the anchored galleys and beached it close to a new dock. Balbus hailed the first centurion he saw, pressed a coin into his hand, and demanded to know the location of the praetorian tent.

I went to see if the Tenth or Twelfth legions were among those assigned to build the invasion boats. At one site, I recognized the limp of Publius Baculus, the centurion who helped save Legio XII at Octodurus. He explained that Galba had gone back to Roma to campaign for a consulship. The legion was under a new commander. After Baculus mentioned that I was suspected of deserting the legion, he was surprised to learn of Silanus's conspiracy and Ogerth' plans to train his warriors in Roman tactics. I asked about Lucius. Most of Legio X was with Titus Labienus, keeping watch on the tribe of Treveri, but some engineers were further down the coast constructing boats. Baculus suggested I go there and report to a tribune on what I had seen in Germania during the previous months.

I procured a horse from the *auxilia* pens and rode along a road lined with workmen fashioning oars, wooden anchor shafts, rigging bits, and other galley supplies. Rows of legionaries sat on benches in the fields, struggling to master the unwieldy oars—to the curses of equally frustrated timekeepers. I reached a river named Cancos, and found a Legio X engineer's camp near an estuary of its delta. I walked among the tents without seeing anyone I knew, then spotted a familiar figure beneath the awning on a beached galley's deck.

"Psen-Ammon!" I called out.

He turned toward my voice. "Ah, White King. Are you well? Come up and speak with me." He touched my hand in greeting, then pointed to the galley's hold. Men were roughing in reed partitions and spreading straw in them. "Berths for the wounded. It seems our Caesar is not satisfied with his Gallic victories, but must threaten Britoni."

I ignored his criticism. "Have you heard from Lucius? How is he?"

"The arm is well, but his mind has sickened."

I wasn't sure what that meant. "Will he return here for the invasion?"

"Who can know the thoughts of Caesar, yet he undoubtedly will use his personal legion in fighting, as happened last autumn."

Psen-Ammon poured me a cup of wine. As I watched him sip from his silver cup, I gulped a drink and decided to confide in the surgeon. "Lucius is in love with my mother, but tribal law forced her to marry Cluvios, my father's brother."

"As I suspected. The Greek poetess, Sappho, describes love as one would an illness. One of their physicians used the passage to diagnose an illness in a young man that resulted from a love for his father's wife."

"Lucius made plans for her...for himself...to farm in the Narbonensis."

"White King, Time has much experience as a healer. Your friend will recover." Psen-Ammon sipped again from his cup. "Your two constructors are nearby. Have you seen them?"

"Marius and Cornelius? No, I just arrived from Germania."

He waved a hand toward activity along the riverbank. "They would be at the Cancos, where they repair galleys."

"*Grates*, Surgeon. I hope to sail with the legion when it leaves."

"Then may Tem protect you," he replied tersely and turned away.

The Egyptian did not seem pleased at my decision. I found Cornelius and Marius working with shipwrights brought in the year before from Hispania and the Narbonenis. After I told them of Ogerth and my abduction, I went with Cornelius to a tribune under the command of Gaius Fabius. The man knew Balbus and agreed to listen to testimony I had given him after I arrived at Bonaz.

When Marius heard the story, he offered me congratulations. "Your own people might have killed you, then belatedly wondered about what questions they should have asked. The information you gave that tribune won't hurt his career when he passes it on to headquarters."

"Are you becoming one of those cynics you talk about?"

Marius laughed at my question and didn't answer. "Alberix, we can use you here. No one believed that we could recondition so many galleys. I mean, sixty transports, as well as a number of triremes from last summer's foray onto the island. We still need ironwork and there's a forge up on that bluff where the wind is strong. Can you help us melt down what's left of the weapons we captured?"

"I can, Marius, but why is Caesar attacking the island again?"

"Politics, probably," he shrugged. "The Senate gave him a twenty-day public thanksgiving for being over there last year for a short period. This time we might winter in Albion. I expect the commander to arrive any day now."

"I saw Psen-Ammon. He's not pleased about the invasion."

"Look, Cornelius keeps reminding us we're soldiers not politicians. Alberix, let's get supper and you can tell me about all the ravishing girls you met in Germania. After that, I want to show you an idea of mine near the estuary."

I ate with Marius and some other engineers and listened to their crude talk about Gallic and Germanic women. I did not mention Frieda at the meal.

❧

When Marius took me to the mouth of the river, he was disturbed to find a company of slingers lining the banks of the waterway. Curly haired, stocky, wearing short-sleeve tunics cut square and embroidered along the hem, the men were natives of the Baliares islands. The mercenaries practiced for range and accuracy. Accompanied by the swish of the sling-strap, their stone or lead missiles plunked into the water or rattled off target barrels floating in the estuary.

"Pluto take them!" Marius complained. "I set up a *scorpione* on shore that can be operated by two men, even one if need be. I wanted to demonstrate it for you."

As we walked down to the beach, I watched the islanders. Several were drunk and slung the stones more in sport than training, yet I was surprised at the number of hits on the distant bobbing targets. At the small catapult, Marius was further annoyed to see several slingers poking at the instrument, trying to find out how it worked.

"Move back!" he shouted at them. "Get away from this machine!"

The slingers reacted with anger in a language neither of us understood. I was aware of Psen-Ammon watching us from the top of the embankment. *Why is he there? Has he followed me?*

Marius had finished explaining the cocking mechanism—the machine was a large, powerful crossbow set on a stand—when I heard the whistle of an approaching stone. Whether the missile was launched intentionally or from an erratic aim, I never found out: it struck the back of my head and pitched me forward into the wet sand. Stunned, I slowly lifted my head. Very slowly, it seemed, Psen-Ammon drifted down the embankment and toward me. His features were essentially those of the surgeon, yet before I lost consciousness I saw that the approaching figure had the head and lunar-disc crown of Khensu, the Egyptian god of healing.

Chapter XXXIV

Briga watched her as Apsa eased the walnut statue of Lug-Find, "The Fair-haired One," into the pool's still water. The offering to the god bubbled beneath the dark surface of the spring and disappeared. I waited until the votive was out of sight, then turned to embrace my mother and jest, "Much better than a funeral offering!"

Mother held me more tightly. I had reminded her of a husband with the same blue eyes and sandy hair, who had not been as fortunate.

When I went to embrace Apsa, she stared off into woods surrounding the shrine. She did not dare pull away—I had saved her from death yet the touch of a man brought back the terror of her months with Publius Silanus.

Although ill, Cluvios clasped my shoulder and tested my recovery from the head wound. "If we were at Sequana's shrine, and that carving of Lugos floated to the surface, where would it end up?"

"The Middle Sea, by way of the Arar and Rhodanus rivers."

"Nephew, you remember well..." He turned away to cough up bloody sputum.

When I had seen him that spring, Uncle's emaciated condition distressed me. Since offerings to the gods had not helped, how much longer could he live before his body succumbed to the evil inside?

Briga had brought a basket of food. Alone at this small shrine outside of Wermaros, where Dividiac occasionally had gone, we shared the meal in silence. Samain was over a moon away and druids were still at the High Assembly at Carnutum, in central Gallia. This year's conclave was especially important. Traders reported that archdruids had called together tribal chieftains opposed to Romani and planned an expanded war against the occupying legions.

That summer, Targetios, a Carnute chieftain friendly to Rome, had been restored to the Celtic title of *rix*—king—of his tribe. Shortly after, he was assassinated, prompting Julius Caesar to order a legion be stationed near Carnutum. Spies in the *auxiliae* reported that the names heard most frequently as potential rebel leaders were those of Ambiorix and Catuvolcos, chieftains of the Euberone tribe. All this was far from the warmth of an early October afternoon, as I repeated the circumstances of my injury.

"I recall Psen-Ammon, the legion surgeon, coming toward me. Marius helped carry me to the medical tent. My good fortune was in having the Egyptian there. He knew how to treat head wounds."

"All the same," Briga recalled, "you were not yet conscious when they brought you here."

Cluvios grudgingly admitted, "This Caesar must think well of you, to not leave you die in Gallia."

"Uncle, wounded *auxiliae* from Vesontio were being sent back, so I was put in a wagon with them. Caesar doesn't like to see training wasted. Besides, *quaestors* complain that deaths use up a legion's funeral fund."

I tried to make light of the incident. Cluvios spat aside before saying, "You and Apsa should spend a few days at a lake north of us. I need to repair tools there."

Briga protested, "Husband, you're too ill."

Angry at at being contradicted, he snapped, "Local crafters are helping the Helvetii rebuild and I must do the same! It will be good for Apsa to be away from the child awhile."

I looked at her for approval. Used to having decisions made for her, Apsa said nothing. The energetic woman I knew at Octodurus no longer existed.

Apsa's child had been born in the month after Beltaine. After my message about her arrival, Cluvios had gone to Vesontio to meet the young woman, yet had been unable to find more about her Raurici kin. Briga received her well, but Apsa half-kept to herself, silently helping with household tasks until she gave birth. A black-haired boy now seventeen months old, Ger, was docile and loving, as if the gods of retribution had offered an opposite to the brute that had sired the infant.

Under Romani custom, the father ritually accepted a male child and hung an amulet around the newborn's neck, to ward off evil. Since we had a similar custom, Cluvios adopted the child and gave him a pendant that depicted the sacred crane of Esus. Apsa had named her baby Ger; the word imitated the cries of the crane, as well as the lusty bawls of her newborn son.

While Cluvios visited local farmsteads and repaired tools, Briga worked a small hand loom in our wagon. I tried to relax Apsa in the tranquility of the lake. The beauty of the forested hills displayed patches of autumn color, yet the talkative girl with whom I had explored alpine meadows near the pass remained withdrawn and distant.

Unlike Silanus, Magha and her kin had not been cruel to their slave, yet expected Apsa to work with little concern for her own desires. Life was harsh in a remote valley, where gods were those of the hunt and storm or dark beings in legends, who fed on the blood of villagers caught in the forests after sunset. Healing was based on plant remedies and heavy doses of superstition and charms, such as shape-shift stones that resembled animal or human forms. Apsa's time with the brutal Roman was a walled void that made her tremble whenever her mind tried to understand. After six terrifying months in legion camps, Apsa had looked beyond the abyss that separated the Now- and Other-worlds and found them equally dark. In desperation, she had tried to consign herself to an unknown void, rather than continue in the known horror of Silanus's abuse.

On the second day, I borrowed a boat from a farmer and rowed with Apsa to the center of the narrow lake. She sat as far back as possible in the stern, clasping her knees in a protective stance. After a long period of silence, I almost regretted my decision to take her out in the boat. I tried reassuring her. "Apsa, you...you're free now." She nodded without looking up at me. "I may own you, but that's only tribal law. We...we could try to find your kinfolk. Where were you born?"

"My parents sold me as a child."

"I knew that much. So...so you don't remember."

"No."

Most of the Raurici joined the Helvetii migration, but how many returned? It's pointless to try and locate her relatives among remnants of the tribe. I'm trapped with a non-responsive woman. I tried to arouse her interest, "You haven't seen the country-side around Wermaros. In the spring we'll go to *Benn Samain*. From there you can see the White Mountains. Would you like that?" After Apsa's absent nod, I asked. "Do you remember Simonides? Magha cured his fever."

"I remember him."

In the moments that followed, the only sound was the lapping of lake water against the boat's hull, and distant calls from a flock of scavenging gulls on shore. I gave up trying to talk to Apsa and pulled on the oars to return. I understood how she had been hurt, but she was safe now. I thought should be more appreciative and responsive.

❧

Next day, we returned to Wermaros, where the descent of cattle from highland meadows, and the winter swine slaughter was underway.

Samain came, but Cluvios was not well enough for a pilgrimage to the mountain for the New Year fires. I had seen Fodla in the village, where Mother said he continued to exploit Liscos's vanity and ambition. On hearing of my wound, the one-armed chieftain's anger at me had softened, yet as the winter days lengthened, so did his drinking bouts.

At Imbolc, Liscos finally agreed to host a meal and celebrate my recovery. The chieftain drank too much and goaded me about again rejoining my auxiliary unit. He implied that the legions were in such danger that Caesar had feared to leave Gallia for the winter. In a drunken admission, Liscos revealed that Fodla and other druids were conspiring to incite local tribes toward rebellion. I reminded him that he had welcomed the Romani when they came, and he had profited though them.

Cluvios told a few stories of our people that were Liscos's favorites. One of them was intended to caution the chieftain from rash actions. It left him depressed, yet he invited us to return at the next market day if Cluvios brought happier stories.

Liscos drank less at that meal and here was no confrontation. Derona went to her room early. Soon after, Briga and Apsa returned to our lodge. The chieftain and I were left alone to refill our cups and listen to Cluvios's stories. He chuckled over the tale of a practical joker who ended up falling into his own manure pile, when a gate guard burst into the common room. The man was breathless from running the distance from the mountain gate to the lodge.

"Lucius," he gasped, "come...from Vesontio...with two others."

Liscos frowned and looked toward me. "Your *centurio* from the tower?"

I told the guard, "Bring them in here. They must be half-frozen."

When Liscos stood to walk with the man to the door, I noticed him whisper something to him.

Shortly afterward, Lucius came into the lodge, his face raw from a cold wind. The faces of his two companions were concealed by hooded cloaks. One pushed back his hood. "Simonides! What power brings you here in the dead of winter?"

"In the footsteps of Polybius and your commander."

When his companion revealed the lean features of Julius Caesar, I stammered, "*Im...Imperator!*"

He chuckled at a visit he knew was unexpected. "*Celeritas! Oppimere!* 'Swiftness. Surprise!' At Vesontio Simonides suggested this village would be a quiet place to work on my manuscript of the war."

Liscos recovered from astonishment and offered Caesar a chair. "Sit by the cook-fire. We are...my village...is honored by your visit." He called out for Arduinna to fill a flagon with mulled wine from a cauldron. Gentle swelling beneath her night tunic revealed that Liscos might soon have another heir.

When I introduced Caesar to Cluvios, the commander praised me. "*Fine auxilia* member, your Alberix. A natural leader on the mission I gave him to prepare the way at Octodurus for my legate, Sulpicius Galba." He indicated Lucius. "You know my First Centurion. I brought him as a guide since I want to explore a supply route up the Sequana River to Vesontio. In spring, I intend to build a road connecting with Bibrax in the land of the Remi."

Cluvios frowned but did not respond. After Arduinna set down the flagon, Liscos poured hot spiced wine into cups. He had overcome his surprise at Caesar's arrival and I thought he saw an opportunity to get information. His first question convinced me.

"The tribes in the north are quiet, Commander?"

Caesar sipped wine before answering. "Our legions have pacified much of the region. Thank Jupiter, things *are* going well." He glanced toward Arduinna. "That beautiful woman is your wife, chieftain?"

Liscos grinned. "My newest."

Caesar lifted his cup to him. "Then Fortuna smiled on you!"

Lucius exchanged looks with Simonides. Both knew of the commander's reputation as a seducer of females, and Simonides had confided that the Tenth referred to him as *calvus moechus*—"bald adulterer." On the eve of the campaign against Ariovistos, legionaries had jested that men at Vesontio should hide their wives and daughters. Later, as they tramped across the bridge into Germania, the bolder veterans chanted a warning to the Sugumbri.

Germani vigilante	Germani watch out
Feminae adhere	Hide your women
Romani venabent!	The Romans are coming!
Sugambri, cavite	Sugambri, beware
Uxoris concludere	Lock up your wives
Moechus venat!	The adulterer comes!

As Caesar warmed himself with the wine, he said to me, "Alberix, I must humor Simonides for a few days. He wishes me to write about the Britoni campaign while details are fresh. I'm told the Helvetii are rebuilding, but I would like to ride out with you to confirm that myself."

"Of, course, *Imperator*. Whenever ready." His quiet request was an order.

⸬

Snow had come to the Jurassos region in the full moon after Samain, blanketing the green and umber mountains in a thick mantle of white. On bright afternoons when the clouds resembled the sheep herds of Taranis, Mother encouraged me to take Apsa and Ger along the river road in a pony sledge. Nestled in furs, we shared bread, cheese, smoked pork and *cervisa* near the sparkling ice-rimmed Dubis.

On our third outing, Apsa smiled after I touched beer foam to Ger's lips and he puckered his face at the taste. With the passing days, dark circles around her eyes lightened. She had no longer tensed her body when I helped her onto the sledge.

Early one morning, Apsa left Ger with my mother and walked with me to the remains of the shelter, where I had helped Dividiac plot the location of sunrises. I checked the location of Belenos and compared his rising with the unfinished stonework of the distant menhir.

"It's getting close to the equinox," I estimated, "and then nights become shorter. Will you be glad to see spring?"

Apsa asked her own question, "You...you will go away for the war season?"

"I must, I'm in the *auxilia*." I realized that I also would be unhappy at the prospect of leaving.

"You are too kind to kill others," Apsa said, then groped for words. "It is like...like the lark flying with falcons."

"*Aulauda*, a lark?" I laughed and slowly eased an arm around her. She did not resist. "We do have another month together."

Apsa leaned into my arm. The closeness of her body aroused a stirring in my groin. Before I realized it, my hand fumbled under her tunic to fondle a breast. She pushed me away and bolted up, The look of terror had returned to her eyes.

I tried to ease her fright. "I...I'm sorry, Apsa. I had no right."

She leaned against a pine tree until her breathing calmed. "Magha protected me. She told village men that only a virgin could find plants that healed them."

"Why did you stay with her when Veragri left the village, then attacked us?"

"The old woman was all I had. Could I leave her alone?"

I recalled my own panic at Ogerth's anger and my broken promise to his daughter. Apsa's faithfulness in the face of certain death transcended any rationalization I had made to escape the Seubi. I felt ashamed. A slave girl was teaching the son of a clan chief about honor and trust.

Apsa came to pull me up and place my hand on the tunic over her breast. "Perhaps one day I will feel as when we were at Octodurus. Silanus—"

I gently put a finger on her lips. Apsa need not finish the sentence. Tears in her eyes spoke of the pain. Later, as we returned, she noticed a live hare in a hunter's snare cage. While I watched, she bent to set the creature free. After straightening up, tears glistened in each eye. I drew her to me, touched their saltiness with my tongue, and cushioned her head on my shoulder. I stood, gently rocking her for a time.

We held hands and half-walked, half-slid down the road to the river gate. I felt for the first time that Apsa would heal.

That night Apsa fell asleep alone to dream of the white hare scampering to the freedom of snow-filled woods—and of Alberix's warm touch.

Lucius remained at *Castor* with the few legionaries that made up the winter garrison. To keep his centurion active, Caesar ordered him to copy the sections of his manuscript that were complete. Simonides brought him the account of the capture and death of Dumnorix. The commander was concerned about the Aeduan chieftain's desire to be appointed king of his tribe. He had claimed that the Romani supported him in this. To keep watch on the *vergobret*, Caesar ordered that he accompany him on the second invasion of Albion. During the legions' embarkation, the Aeduan deserted to reach Bibracte. Pursued, he resisted returning, and was killed. Simonides added that Caesar decided to title his account *Commentarii de Bello Gallico*— Commentaries on the Gallic Wars.

Liscos recalled the previous celebration of the Roman Saturnalia in midwinter. Even though that time was past, he offered to host a banquet for Caesar, Cluvios, Briga and me. Apsa preferred to stay in our lodge and I did not object.

The commander was pleased. He planned to preside over a sacrifice and dinner of suckling pig for the tower legionaries, but asked Liscos to include Lucius at his dinner. It was also a command to the centurion, who avoided visiting Cluvios and Briga at their lodge. Simonides was not invited, but my friend came with Caesar anyway.

Snow fell lightly when Lucius arrived at the chieftain's home. He was as surprised as I was to find Ollam Fodla among the guests. Although Fodla said little during the meal, Liscos seemed nervous. I surmised the druid had insisted on being present to meet the commander. Caesar dominated the conversation with a charm and wit that came as easily as the ruthlessness he displayed in slaughtering tribes, or individuals, who opposed him.

Mother sat next to Cluvios, relieved that she needed to say little because of Caesar's flow of words. She glanced at Lucius when she dared. Once, when his glance caught hers, he quickly picked at his food. She ate little and helped clear dishes from the table afterward. After listening to the first of Caesar's stories, Mother excused herself to return to her lodge. Cluvios motioned that one of his brother-in-kin's slaves go with her.

After only drinking horns remained on the table, Fodla summoned Finan to entertain us with his hero songs of Inisfail. The melodies were sonorous, but the two Romani and Simonides did not understand all the words. Nor did I, but we applauded him. As gifts, Caesar selected gold or silver Gallic coins from a coffer Simonides brought with him.

Fodla fingered a silver coin with the letters R I M O stamped along the edge of the face. "The tribe of the Remi, I have been to Bibrax."

I thought it clever of Caesar to give out coins of a friendly tribe. He said, "Iccus and Andecombonios are friends. After the Belgae tried to take Bibrax—"

Fodla interrupted, "Your legions massacred women and young ones!"

Lisco's hand and wine cup stopped in mid-air. Lucius tensed at the accusation.

Caesar flushed, but held his temper. "Not so, priest." He took back the coin and put it in the center of the table. "Bibrax was here"—he nudged another coin against a knife—"and the legion camp thus. Iccus asked for help against an attack." The commander asked Simonides, "How many Belgae?"

"Well over two-hundred thousand, among them forty thousand Germani allies." He added with mock innocence, "Sir, the numbers were given us by Iccus himself."

To support his commander, Lucius noted, "You are well aware, druid, that it's common for tribes to hire mercenaries when attacking neighbors."

Fodla ignored his remark. "Caesar, that was the winter you stayed at Vesontio. Why be up there, when your province is far to the south?"

Liscos's taut expression suggested that he tried to walk a plank over a manure pile *without* falling off.

Caesar replied easily, "We need to protect the Sequani from Ariovistos. Even this village would have fallen to the Germani king."

Fodla countered, "Ariovistos was dead by winter. Murdered by your legions."

Liscos attempted to deflect the verbal swordplay. "Commander, what do you hear from Roma? Our small village is so far away."

Caesar stared into the dying coals of the fire pit. "My...my daughter, Julia, died in childbirth while I was on Albion. I only heard at Samarobriva."

Liscos murmured a condolance. Fodla smirked in silence.

The commander continued, as if speaking at the fire to unburden himself in this remote place. "Crassus should be in Syria by now. He wants me to send him a thousand Gallic cavalry and a like number from his son's legion. The man should have stayed a businessman instead of requesting another command!" Caesar swallowed a gulp of wine in frustration. "We have no consuls for the year. I backed Mammius and Messala, but Pompeius wants Scaurus as one of the men. The Senate postponed elections because of some reported bribery."

Lucius and I had noticed Fodla's eyebrows rise at mention of transfering two thousand horsemen from Gallia to Syria. We tried to signal caution, but Caesar had not looked away from the fire and continued speaking. "I don't trust Pompeius. He has seven legions in Hispania and recruits more in Italia. 'To cut grain,' he says! At Lucca, I never should have agreed to his governorship of Hispania...."

Already aware of the report, Simonides dozed. Lucius yawned in the pause. Liscos had fallen asleep at the table. Fodla remained impassive. Drowsy from the wine, I had missed some of the commander's words.

Lucius rubbed his eyes. "With your permission, *Imperator*, I should return to *Castor*."

"What...?" Caesar roused himself and passed a hand through thinning hair. "Oh...yes, it's late. Alberix, we'll ride out tomorrow and see the Helvetii resettlement. Have horses ready by the second hour."

I told him I would, then stood to go with Cluvios and Lucius. Fodla slipped out without speaking again. Liscos slept, his head resting on the table. When I looked back from the entrance ramp, Caesar again stared into the cook-fire embers, perhaps for a sign. Simonides forced himself awake to share the vigil.

❦

I rode out with the *Imperator*—as Lucius called him—through the river gate in the brilliant whiteness of a late February morning. Caesar wore the clothing of a hunter, with a hooded cape covering his head. Cluvios had lent him slitted-horn eyeshades against the glare, which further hid his features.

Instead of following the main road, I led the way through less traveled trails that Cabirios had shown me on the trek to *Benn Samain*. Shrill cries of jays warned of our passing. Fir branches slid an occasional fall of snow on our hoods and shoulders as our mounts struggled up narrow forest paths. On horseback, we made good time.

"Tell me of your Jurassos," Caesar asked, once the trail widened enough for him to ride abreast with me. "I had only seen an area of Gallia around Genava when we put up earthworks against the Helvetii."

"I helped build them."

"You, Alberix? How so?"

"I had just enlisted in the *auxilia*. I thought I worked hard at the forge with Cluvios, but digging those camp ditches was worse!"

Caesar laughed and commented, "Blisters are a small price for victory."

"As is *celeritas*."

"Exactly. Along with the smile of Fortuna, swiftness is the most important element in war. A goddess is less predictable, yet those tribes never expected my legions to be where they were. Certainly, not the Helvetii, or Ariovistos."

We fell silent until our mission brought Caesar back to the present. "I didn't realize you were at Genava. Because of Lucius Velcanius?"

"Yes. When I was at the tower, he would talk to me about your laws... Senatus... things I hadn't heard of."

"You saved his arm, perhaps his life. Psen-Ammon told me about that shrine of your goddess, Sequana, and her healing earth."

"And *your* goddess smiled on Lucius, Adherbal and you!."

"Fortuna again! She *has* been kind to me. When I was Pontifex at Rome...a kind of archdruid...I sacrificed at her temple each day."

I hesitated before asking, "Do you believe the gods give rewards for sacrifices?"

"Don't men behave the same way? Even your Celtic deities require a life for a life."

"Not always," I told him. "Druids teach truthfulness in the heart, strength in the weapon arm, and honesty in speech."

"As do our philosophers," Caesar noted, "yet to teach and to do are not always the same."

The path narrowed again, forcing us to ride single file. We turned our faces to sunshine that filtered through overhead branches and soaked up its pleasant warmth.

Around midday we reached the base of the mountain. I suggested we rest the horses before going on the trail to the summit. We dismounted, tethered our mounts, and sat on a fallen log.

Caesar resumed his questioning. "I asked about your region. Were you born near that village?"

"No, Arialbinnum, where the Renos bends to the north."

"Lucius said your father, Alrix, was killed by Germani, while building a new village. Where was that?"

"A short distance east of Arialbinnum. Father wanted to bridge the Renos there, and negotiate treaties with the Germani."

"A statesman of vision!" Caesar exclaimed. "My first teacher, Antonio Griffo, was Gallic. That's why I grant citizenship to *auxiliae*...even if the Senate disapproves."

"Who, again, is this Pompeius you mentioned last night?"

"Gnaeus Pompeius!" Caesar spat out the name with disdain. "He had Roma in his hands and threw it to the wind! He could have passed laws reining in the Patricians, but the fool disbanded his legions. Senators realized he had no real power without the army's backing., so why should they pass laws compromising their privileges? Pompeius didn't understand that, but when I become—" The commander caught himself and stood to untether his horse. "Shall we move on?"

At the summit of *Benn Samain*, we gazed over a panorama that stretched below and was patterned with afternoon cloud shadows. Blue smoke marked rebuilt Helvetii settlements. I pointed to a dark smudge at the right side of a small, middle lake. "Aventia, capital of the Helvetii."

"Ah, there..." Caesar pondered the location a moment. "I'll call the place Aventicum when this area is made our province."

He again unintentionally revealed his plan, but before I could question him, he started along the crest. The air was cold, so he pulled back his hood to absorb more warmth, or perhaps identify himself to whichever of our Celtic gods or goddesses were watching. On the ground around us, patches of darkened snow marked charred sites where the Samain New Year fires had been lighted.

Caesar noticed the shaft for ritual offerings and peered into the dark opening. "Your priests...druids...worship here?"

"They try to reach gods living in the Other-world with offerings thrown down the shaft."

Caesar straightened up. "Druids consider me a threat to their power and rightly so. I intend to replace their barbaric laws with those of our Republic. I need...Roma needs...loyal Galli to administer conquered tribal lands. Men like Diviciacus of the Aeduii and the Remi *vergobret*, Iccus."

I kept silent, but he came and put a hand on my shoulder. "You're Raurici, a Helvetii sub-tribe." When his gray eyes locked onto mine, it was impossible for me to look away. "Alberix, I see a place for you in a year or two as a magistrate working with a Roman governor to bring a *Pax Romana* to your people. Your father built a village, but you can help birth a Gallo-Roman country."

Seeming in a state of rapture as he envisioned the future, Caesar turned away to scan the ghostly line of Alps in the distance. Just as abruptly he pulled up his hood and went to stroke the muzzle of his horse. His mood of confidence and vision had passed with the swiftness of shadows on the plain below.

"*Imperator*," I said, "we can spend the night in a hunter's shelter we passed."

Caesar nodded agreement and remounted. *In this high place had he hoped for some sign from a god: an eagle grasping prey...unseasonable lightning to the north... or any omen that might predict success for his ambitions?*

As our mounts eased their way back down the trail, Caesar turned for a final look at the rich silent land that rolled away from us. I thought I heard him mutter, "The fool disbanded his legions, but I won't make the same mistake." Anything else he said was inaudible.

We found the hut stocked with kindling twigs, flat stones, a wooden bucket, cups, and straw bedding. After lighting a blaze in the firepit, I melted the cleanest snow I could find with heated rocks dropped in the bucket, then steeped rubus and mint leaves I had brought in the hot water.

Caesar seemed lost in his thoughts as he sipped the fragrant beverage. Finally, he commented, "A tranquil land. These mountains are gentle, not like the Apennines. The earth is fertile. How strange that Helvetii, an undistinguished barbarian tribe, now direct the course of my life."

And possibly the world, I thought, without protesting his term, "undistinguished barbarian," to describe my countrymen.

While I cut up dried venison, cheese, and bread into smaller pieces, Caesar took out a wax tablet and stylus from his saddlebag. He stared at the ceiling a moment, leaned forward to catch the firelight, and began to speak as he wrote.

> *"Oh, Jura, dark-forested Earth Mother,*
> *Your fruitful body lies in opulent pregnancy.*
> *What goddess this, disguised as common clay?*
> *Mimicking azure lakes and surging rivers free?*
> *Bursting forth to offer yellow grain.*
> *Teasing with dew-dropped fruits.*
> *Seducing Sons of Men, then with the spite*
> *Of fickle women, breathing out an icy breath,*
> *Then bringing snow to garment self in white.*
> *Yet no death-shroud this, for melting into spring,*
> *Her moisture enriches fields to blossoms fair.*
> *Jewels finer than daughters of mortal men can wear."*

Caesar paused, lost in imagery, trying to find correct words for ending his poem, before the moment passed.

> *"Ave, happy Jura! Like a maiden's secret,*
> *Your shadowed valleys hint of mysteries.*
> *Youth's embracing pleasures, laughing play.*
> *Innocent...Innocent as...."*

Caesar suppressed a yawn, laid down his stylus, and closed the tablet covers. After we finished our meagre supper, he said he was tired and would finish his poem in the morning.

After we wrapped ourselves in our cloaks and pushed into the straw, Caesar looked toward me. "Think about what I offered you, Alberix. I believe all Gallia will be peaceful at this time next year."

I doubted that, knowing the tendency of tribes for fighting each other, when not attacked by a common enemy. I tried to picture the role that Caesar offered me, but my regular breathing quickly joined with his. The quietnes of sleep overlaid the dark silence of the hut.

❧❧

Even before we reached Wermaros, the idyll ended the next day. Lucius had waited for us at the top of the road that looked back over the valley of Delsa. He reined in his horse next to Caesar and reported, "*Imperator*, poor news. This morning a messenger came from Samarobriva. Legio Fourteen was attacked and virtually destroyed. Both Legates, Cotta and Sabienus, were killed."

"How?" Caesar demanded. "Were they outside the camp?"

"Ambushed. Only a few survivors made it back to Labienus's position."

"The Fourteenth was in Euberone territory."

"Their chief, Ambiorix, led the attack. That's as much as we know."

As Caesar trotted his horse forward, he called, "Alberix, at dawn I return to Samarobriva to know which tribes are loyal. Take four men from *Castor* and ride with them to Lucius Roscius's legion near Cenabum. Ambiorix's success may encourage western Gauls to rebel, even the Belgae. Velcanius will write you an authorization."

❧❧

That evening, while Caesar made preparations to leave, Mother and Apsa packed food for me to take along. Cluvios sat hunched apart, polishing a bronze statuette of Taranis. I knew Uncle was disappointed that I was returning to serve Romani. I tried to explain to him that we could benefit from the kind of peace they imposed on their Narbonensis province. My father would have approved of that.

Briga agreed, "Alrix abandoned the sword to favor arbitration and treaties."

"We have no tribal council as powerful as the Senatus," I added.

Cluvios corrected me in anger, "You mean we have no Caesar!"

"Lucius told me their law is above any one man..." I paused, fearful of Uncle's reaction, but said, "Caesar offered to make me a magistrate, a kind of *vergobret*."

His reprimand was immediate. "Now you look to the Romani for future bread?" I knew his sickeness and anger had exhausted Uncle, yet he stood slowly to clasp my shoulder. "If you wish to follow your father's path, it should be with men who are Celts. Find a Caesar from among your own tribes!"

I didn't respond, although I felt that Father's vision had been larger than any one clan. I helped Apsa strap shut my saddlebags, then went to my sleeping area. There I tossed restlessly, pondering what the legion defeat might do to Caesar's plans. Apsa must have heard me, for she came with Ger to lie next to me. I cradled her head in an arm with the infant between us.

She asked me, "Do you believe what the Caesar told you?"

"Lucius trusts him, and he did send the Helvetii back to their lands. What Celtic chieftain would not have sold them off as slaves?"

"As I was by my parents."

"They had little choice at the time."

Apsa shrugged. "Magha was good to me. Cabirios brought me shape-shift stones from the mountains."

I stroked her hair when she laid her head on my chest. "Because of Silanus I feel differently about men than your village women do. Perhaps one day...." I touched her lips with my fingers, before she could complete a thought I anticipated. But she asked, "You will come back to me...to Ger?"

"The first thing I will do is make you a freedwoman!"

"I will try to be...to love like other women by then."

In the semi-darkness I tasted a salty trickle when I kissed her cheek. "Apsa, it's only important that your spirit is well again." I held her until Ger whimpered in hunger and she left to nurse him in her room.

Afterward, the report of the legion defeat, and Uncle's comment about finding a Celt that would lead our people, were raw concerns in my mind. Was the war beginning to go against Julius Caesar? Cluvios had reminded me of the old Tigurini chieftain's warning at the Arar, not to let the Romani weld chains onto my spirit. These were sentiments I could agree with, and yet *would* a leader ever arise from among our people?

FEBRUARY / 54 BCE — SEPTEMBER / 53 BCE

The wind shakes the twigs and weeps the leaves; the red rose drops its pedals.
Look! The blue-black ravens fly to the south

Chapter XXXV

The report of Amborix's victory over a Roman legion spread as rapidly as winter demons that caused raw throats, fever, chest disease and, often as not, death.

The news elated Ollam Fodla. He increased his pressure on Liscos to commit his dwindling group of warriors as a band around which rebelling clans could unite.

The druid's associate, Triccos, was at Vesontio, contacting Gallic nobles opposed to the Romani, when Fodla sent him a message. He was to bring the leaders he recruited to a meeting in a sacred cave near Lugdunacium. The druid knew he must use magic to impress the superstitious warriors. They would demand the help of supernatural deities to defeat Caesar, already rumored to be a reincarnation of Cú Chulainn, or another ancient Celtic hero-warrior.

Fodla timed the assembly for the beginning of Ogron, the month that ended winter, and a *Mat...lucky...*phase of the moon. The cavern was two days ride from Vesontio, yet the invited men should have no trouble in arriving on the appointed day.

❧

Apsa halted Derka a short distance from the entrance to a cave she visited whenever she felt a need to touch the Earth Mother. In the first days of his recovery from the head wound, Alberix had encouraged her to ride, as much to give the woman a diversion as to exercise his mare.

Briga's son had been gone from the village only five nights, but Apsa felt a yearning for him she had not thought possible. To fill her emptiness, the slave-woman rode Derka along river trails to collect dried berries and mistletoe. Apsa discovered the cavern after following a small steam that flowed from its entrance. The fantastic-shaped stone galleries were quiet places of transition between outer and inner worlds, shelters where the sources of the Mother's energy were tangible.

Apsa always used caution when approaching the entrance, checking for signs of other intruders. This time she was surprised to find several horses tethered nearby. Alarmed that their owners might be inside the cave, curiosity nevertheless overcame her fear. She left Derka hidden in the woods, circled back on foot through the trees to the cave, and slid into a hollow where a small opening led to a rubble-strewn ledge. Low and cramped, the stone shelf was just inside a gallery she had never entered. Crawling carefully to not dislodge stones, Apsa stretched out on the ledge and peered over its edge.

Orange light flickered off the cave's ceiling from a number of torches placed around an altar-like limestone formation. Incense burned in clay pots set to each side of a row of oval white objects lying on the stone. After a moment of uncertainty, she realized they were human skulls. Ollam Fodla stood in front, watching one of his blue-painted druidesses give a sip from a silver bowl to warriors entering from one side. As the men filed in, Fodla motioned for them to sit on the ground. Liscos was among them. After the last man entered, the druid stood in front of the skulls, facing the warriors. His black tunic made him almost invisible in the dim light—as if his waxen face were detached from his body, like the relics behind him.

"Men of Gallia," he intoned, "as in the days of our ancestors, only death awaits our enemies today."

Attracted by movements on the altar, Apsa bit into a jacket sleeve to keep from crying out: the jaws of the skulls had moved! Voices repeating Fodla's words seemed to come from between their yellow teeth: ...Death awaits our enemies today. ...Death awaits our enemies today.

On witnessing the horror, the warriors rose to a protective crouch. After one man unsheathed his belt knife to attack the phantoms, Boccus darted out of darkness beyond the torchlight and wrenched his weapon away.

Unaffected by the brief struggle, Fodla continued an invocation to Celtic gods.

"I call upon the spirit of the forests to help us."

A figure of fir branches and holly leaves emerged from the gloom and glided in a circle around the altar. Apsa recovered from her fright and imagined the impression the apparition made on warriors. She was sure their perception had been altered by a potion the twin druidesses gave them on entering, a practice familiar at Octodurus. She caught the gleam of an eye reflection when the forest-creature passed a torch,

Fodla continued his bizarre ritual. In succession, the triple Celtic gods of Earth, Sky, and Water entered, and then the great Lugos. Harp music sounded in rippling cords as the god-effigies swayed in a dance around the altar. Apsa was caught up in the melodies. As the music of the harp grew softer, the deity figures slipped back into the darkness. Fodla let the effect of the apparitions penetrate the warriors' minds, then stepped forward. He called on the men to support a sacred war against the Romani and bind each one by a sacred oath.

"Swear, Liscos of the Sequani, by the god of your clan to drive out the Romani."

Still reeling from the narcotic and mesmerizing dance, Liscos raised a sword with his good arm in assent.

"Swear, Critognatus of the Arverni." The sub-chief unsheathed his weapon. "I do swear."

"Swear, Commius of the Atrebates." The friend and former ally of Caesar signified his consent.

"Swear, Epedorix of the Aeduii."

"Swear, Virodomarus of the Aeduii."

Both warriors of a tribe allied to Rome voiced agreement.

After administering the oaths, Fodla raised his hands. "Let us assure the success of our cause through the sacrifice of a great warrior."

Boccus led in a gray-haired oldster and stood him before the assembly. At a nod from his druid master, the Mauritanian slashed the man's abdomen and stepped back. The old warrior fell to his knees without uttering a sound and toppled onto his side. Moira crouched nearby chanting a death ritual. In moments, the victim's twitching was still. Only his neck torc and a glisten of blood seemed to move as they reflected flickering torchlight.

Fodla examined the position of the body and patterns created by a flow of gore. "The omens are *Mat!*" he announced in a joyful shout. "Lugotrix predicts the defeat of our enemies!" He reached for the nearest torch, extinguished its burning end on the ground, and prophesied, "Thus will Romani die!"

With the ceremony over, the druidesses snuffed out the torches. Triccos ushered the unsteady warriors back to their mounts.

Apsa lay on the ledge until it was dark, when she felt it was safe to leave. At the lodge, she was unsure about what to do with the information she learned about a conspiracy to attack Romans. No details had been revealed. She thought to warn Cluvios, but word would get to Liscos and he might confront her. As a slave, her testimony would have no value, yet a vivid image of the old warrior's murder kept her awake that night, or brought on frightening nightmares in which Publius Silanus again violated her.

❧

Two days later, Apsa blurted out to Briga what she had seen. Alberix's mother decided that after supper the young woman should tell Cluvios. The dying crafter ate little. He had no appetite and food could not neutralize the metallic taste in his mouth. Coughs and headaches were constant. Vomiting was frequent.

Listening to Apsa, he shrugged a lack of sympathy. "If there is rebellion, the Shorthairs brought it on themselves."

Briga protested, "My son is with the legions!"

"And so is your Lucius."

"Husband, what does that mean?"

"Alberix should have stayed at the forge."

"To host evil in the metals as you do?" Briga asked.

Cluvios coughed blood, wiped his mouth, and rethought his opposition. "Perhaps your centurion should be told."

Briga touched his shoulder. "Cluvios, warning Lucius could avoid a slaughter that might kill Alberix."

"Then run to your Roman. He no doubt has a straighter spear than I."

Stung by the veiled sexual accusation, Briga retorted, "Husband, I have been faithful to my contract with you."

Cluvios stood and shuffled off to sleep without replying.

Briga motioned for Apsa to come to her compartment. The two women sat on furs covering the bed. "This evil makes my husband a different being, one that I don't know."

Apsa offered, "I could go to Vesontio and warn Lucius."

"You?"

"I know the camp." When Briga stared at the floor without replying, Apsa suggested, "I'll take Ersa with me. If you asked Anvalos, he would drive us."

Briga looked up. A slave woman that her son had sent to Wermaros was telling her, the widow of a clan chief, how to help save his life. "Alberix means that much to you?" When Apsa flushed and nodded, she said, "Take Anvalos, then. I trust him. Go with Ersa and I'll watch Ger in your absence."

Briga held Apsa tightly as tears welled in her eyes. "Go," she repeated softly. "Let us see if two women can exchange the gods of war for those of wisdom or peace."

Apsa found Lucius in the old legion camp south of the fortress. News of the conspiracy she had witnessed in the cave alarmed him. If rebellion festered among the Sequani, the legions in northern Gallia would be caught between them and the Belgae. He decided to see the cavern, confront the dark druid, and alert the tower garrisons, even though the few men would not be much of a deterrent in a sustained attack. He dressed in Celtic clothing to leave with her.

As Anvalos drove back to Wermaros, Lucius complimented Apsa. "Clever of you to realize I would be at Vesontio. Caesar ordered me to form as many cohorts of Sequani auxiliaries as I could." He glanced at the driver and lowered his voice, "I'm wondering how trustworthy they'll be." They rode in silence until Lucius asked, half in jest, "If I'm challenged, will I pass as one of your people in these trousers?"

Apsa laughed. "No, you smell much better."

"Ah, we Romani are forever bathing. How...how is Briga?"

"Worried about her son. And Cluvios is very ill."

Lucius did not pursue further questions. Since the cavern was a short distance west of Wermaros, he ordered the driver to follow Apsa's directions and go there.

Inside the cave, the Roman looked around by the light of a pine-pitch torch from Apsa's cache. The skulls were gone, but scattered remains of wilting evergreen branches and holly leaves testified to the figures Apsa reported seeing. Gnawed by ferrets, Lugotrix's desiccated cadaver still lay at the place where he had died as the instrument of a sham divination.

Outside, Lucius tried to anticipate the conspirators' next move. "Apsa, how long has it been since this assembly?"

"Six nights."

"And how many chieftains?"

"With Liscos, five."

"If each recruited twenty warriors, a hundred armed men could coerce farm-steaders into joining them. Did you find war preparations at Weramos?"

"Not many that I could see. A few warriors are in tents on the common pasture. Liscos is more boastful."

Lucius said, "They need a sober leader. Would to Minerva that I knew more about this Ambiorix."

"When Veragri threatened war at Octodurus, only a few warriors joined them."

"Galli have that reputation, Apsa, yet they might surprise Caesar this time."

When they had almost returned to the village, Lucius asked Anvalos to unhitch one of the horses so he could ride to *Castor*. As the driver undid the harnessing, Lucius told the woman to visit Ollam-Fodla. The druid was away, but his assistant, Triccos, was in the village. She agreed to try and learn about sedition preparations.

Lucius arrived at *Castor* to find Marcellus and the garrison waiting for an accurate report of events in the north. He reassured them, then, while a runner brought word of his return to *Pollux*, Lucius sent half the legionaries out to hunt and secure a reserve of salted meat.

In the early evening hours of the ides of Martius, unseasonal white flakes floated down past *Castor*'s high window. Marcellus called out to Lucius that it had begun to snow. The two men were alone in the barracks. Lucius sat behind the curtain of his room, warmed by a charcoal fire, and tried to block out Briga's nearness by looking over Simonides's latest map of the area. He heard Marcellus open the tower door and thought a hunting detail had returned. He saw the *optio*'s shadow outside the curtain.

"*Centurio*, there is a woman outside. She wants to see you."

"Apsa? Now? Let her in, she may have discovered something important."

In a moment the curtain parted. "*Salutatio*, Lucius..." Briga's Latin greeting was soft as the snowfall outside.

"Briga?" The map fell aside as Lucius stood up and caught at her hand.

Marcellus grinned and said he would go check men on signal watch at the tower's top level.

Lucius pulled Briga to him to kiss melting flakes on her cheeks. There was no restraint in his embrace, no hesitant touching. She pushed hard against him in response. He drew back her hood to nuzzle the warmth of her neck, then cursed softly when he fumbled in undoing the brooch at the shoulder of her tunic. She smiled at his impatience, but her own hand shook as she unfastened the bronze pin. The tunic fell around her feet.

After taking off his own garment, Lucius was hardly aware of the creak of the mattress's leather thongs, as he lowered Briga on his bed. The couple's breathing came in gasps at the release of months of frustration. He worried that his calloused hands were too rough on her body, but the caressing was hurried and short. Lucius kissed her breasts. Briga cried out softly as he entered her—she had not lain with a man since Alrix. As she pressed her face against his beard stubble, Lucius moved with her, trying to be gentle and give Briga pleasure. When his body spasmed in release, she pushed against him with a force that almost hurt, yet the pain was in their bodies, unlike the dull ache of separation that had drained each of them for months.

Sated, both lay back, damp with perspiration and smelling of mingled love-wetness. While Lucius's fingers traced the curves of her body, Briga lay on her side, staring at the glowing coals in a brazier that Cluvios had made. Despite the frustration that had prompted her visit to the tower, the iron grill was a reminder of her dying husband. She remarked, "How poorly the gods repay Cluvios for his work."

"Cluvios..." Lucius pulled back his hand. "Why always bring him up?"

Briga shifted around to face him. "Don't be angry. He...he's dying."

"Sorry, it's just that something or someone always kept us apart."

She touched the scar on his shoulder, then sat up. Before she put on her tunic, Lucius handed her a towel. "Come back with me to Vesontio,"

"To do what, Lucius? Gossip all day with camp followers while you're gone?"

"No, No... I told you that after this season I can apply for a discharge and receive a land allotment."

She shook her head. "I came because I no longer could bear the pain, yet am still contracted to Cluvios."

"Break it!" he insisted. "In the name of Pluto, break tradition! We can go to my family farm in Campania or live in the Narbonensis."

Briga let him kiss her again, then finished dressing and reached for the curtain to leave. "This memory of our time together will ease my pain." Lucius pulled her back. She slumped in his chair to ask, "What of this rebellion Apsa speaks of? I worry about Alberix."

He told her, "I sent word to Titus Labienus. He may get loyal Aedui to arrest this druid, Ollam Fodla." When Briga sobbed, Lucius knelt beside her to quietly urge, "Break this contract. What could Cluvios do?"

"Banish me from the clan or even order my death. Triccos...any druid... could authorize it. As punishment, I could be hung, drowned or burned inside a straw man."

"Cluvios would never let a druid do that."

She stood up to leave. "You wouldn't know him. Evil is destroying my... my husband and controls his actions."

Lucius squeezed her hand. "Strange, Briga, but for over twenty years I've solved most problems with a sword. I probably owe my life to an Egyptian surgeon and one of your goddesses. Now I just want to marry you and go manage a farm."

"When will you return to Vesontio?"

"Before the end of this month. Your Ogron, isn't it?" After Briga nodded, he quipped, "See, I *am* learning more Celtic."

She half-smiled, then slipped on her cape. After she descended the ladder and brushed snow from Derka's back, Lucius called down, "Remember, I share Caesar's luck." He returned to lie down on a mattress that held Briga's scent and curse the fate that kept her apart from him.

The centurion returned to Vesontio the next week without seeing Briga or hearing from Apsa again. She had decided not to speak with Triccos too soon, fearing he might suspect that she knew about the conspiracy. But now, with the new moon of Cutios in its first quarter, she felt courageous enough to visit the druid's lodge.

A gray sky masked an afternoon sun, and a brisk northwest wind sent crystals of latent ice spinning from thatched roofs. Apsa hurried past the row of storehouses along the west palisade. She had put on a circlet of artemisia leaves as protection against evil spells Triccos might attempt, yet wondered exactly what she would ask him.

The druid answered Apsa's knock, concealing his surprise as he admitted her into the lodge's smoky interior. She recognized the smell of kannabis. Two other people were in the room.

Wary, Triccos said, "A pleasure, your visit. Do you know Sabia and Epanactos? He is the head of Liscos's guards."

Sabia, lying under the furs of a sleeping ledge, did not speak.

Epanactos grinned. "Ah, the slave of Alberix. What are you here to sell us?"

She ignored him. "Triccos, I hoped to see Ollam Fodla."

"The archdruid is not here now."

"Alberix's mother and I are worried about him and reports of rebellion. I...I hoped Fodla could help us."

Epanactos chuckled. "Of course you would. Your lover-of-Romani is with Caesar."

"Rebellion?" Triccos repeated. He wondered if the woman was clever enough to seek information, and replied in calculated innocence, "The interests of warriors are not those of Men of the Oak. Our concern is to placate the gods."

Epanactos muttered, "Like Caturix." Apsa caught his reference to the Celtic war deity.

Sabia moaned, and Apsa glanced toward the woman.

"She is with child," Triccos explained. "Her bleeding did not come in the moon after Samain."

"I can help her," Apsa offered. "I have herbs to ease the condition."

"Ah, no," he declined. "She is a druidess and the conception is of the gods. No human may interfere."

Epanactos stood up and circled Apsa, plucking at the fur of her jacket. "Woman, I see you riding along the river. Where do you go?"

"To gather plants like mistletoe."

"Mistletoe? You are not a druidess."

"At Octodurus we—"

Epanactos cut her short. "This is not Octodurus and your Alberix won't be returning. I'll pay Liscos your ransom price, but first need to know if you're worth it."

He moved to pull Apsa to him, but Triccos stopped the warrior. "Fool! She is kin to Cluvios."

Epanactos cursed and shoved Triccos aside. In that distracting moment, Apsa ran up the ramp and out the lodge door. She angled across gardens behind the house and looked back. Epanactos had not followed her.

Once inside her lodge, Apsa crouched in a corner, breathing hard and fingering the artemisia circlet that had protected her.

Briga came and sat next to her until she caught her breath. "I went to Triccos, as Lucius wanted," she explained. "Epanactos was there. He tried to… to—" Briga cradled the young woman's head, recalling the time the warrior had challenged Lucius and been humiliated. After a moment, Apsa said, "Triccos pretended to know nothing. Can we help Alberix?"

Briga shrugged and looked over at Cluvios and Ger playing with the infant's cloth dolls. Apsa followed her gaze. "Is there nothing to counter evil in his body?"

"My husband won't give up the forge! You would think the gods could take better care of their own."

A bout of coughing seized Cluvios. When Briga went to help him, Apsa took Ger to her room. She laid her artemisia circlet on a brooch Alberix had given her with a silent petition. *Arduinna, goddess of the forest, help him. Help me.*

Chapter XXXVI

The next day Epanactos disappeared from the village. Triccos came to Cluvios and blandly told him he knew of no sedition against the Romans.

In the greening valley, the possibility of imminent fighting did not cause alarm among the farmsteads. As Beltaine approached, the main topic of conversation at Wermaros was the sun god's slow journey toward his festival day and the return of cattle to their summer pastures.

≈≈

Rumors of the Gallic war in the north reached Massilia and Nikomaxos, Simonides' father, by way of Rhodanus bargemen. A fragment of his son's letter, recovered after a courier's packet fell overboard when the barge carrying it capsized, did not reassure his father...

> *who were attacking the camp, left the area and went back into the Arduinnian forest to hide out.*
>
> *I wrote you earlier that if the Galli did not produce a leader who might unite them, then Caesar could well conquer the entire country, tribe by tribe, with the few legions he commands. Gallia will become another Roman province like the Narbonensis. Will Ambiorix be that leader? He displayed a rare shrewdness in luring Sabienus out of camp and escaping the Romans in their relief effort.*
>
> *Indutiomarus of the Treveri is also a capable chieftain. He survived exile during Caesar's support of Cingetorix, then rallied enough of a force to threaten Labienus. If either or both chieftains controlled tribal infighting, they could well be the ones who can unite the Galli in a common effort to drive out the legions. I stop now, but will send a separate account of what I think was an unwarranted and bloody campaign against the Eburones.*
>
> *To my mother and sisters, whom I would very much like to see, and to friends in Massilia, greetings. Simonides*

In the letter, the historian did not mention his recent break with Caesar. After an angry confrontation over the commander's brutal tactics against the Eburones, and exaggerated reports of success to the Senate, Caesar dismissed Simonides as secretary. He ordered him returned to Massilia under guard, but south of Durocortorum the Greek youth slipped his escort and rode to Carnutum, where the high assembly of Gallic druids recently ended. He mingled with a few priests assigned there, but was recognized by Ollam-Fodla and barely escaped after being mauled by Boccus.

In pain, riding south for half a day and exhausting his horse, Simonides reached Cenabum on the Liger River, where a colony of Roman merchants resided. One of them, Gaius Fufius Cita, was from Massilia and a friend of his father.

❧

"You actually went to Carnutum?" Cita's question reflected disbelief as he watched Antiochus, his house slave, examine the youth's ribs for a possible fracture.

"I never reached the main nemeton, itself," Simonides admitted. "A druid from Wermaros recognized me, and his African brute threw me around a bit..." He winced, "Aaaah...easy, man!"

Antiochus apologized and told Cita that nothing seemed broken, only sprained.

"Bandage him," the merchant ordered. "Young man, what in Tartarus persuaded you to go to Carnutum?"

Simonides knew of the merchant's friendship with Caesar. "The commander and I had...a...well, a slight disagreement. He sent me home, but I wasn't ready to return just yet. I'm writing a history of the war."

Cita shook his head. "I recall once...you were twelve or thirteen...and became lost around Glanum. 'Exploring' you said when we found you. It seems you still crave adventure."

He nodded as Antiochus wrapped his chest with a linen band. "I have a friend, Alberix, who's now with Roscius's legion. Their camp is north of here, isn't it?"

Unsure of what Simonides had done to displease Caesar, Cita avoided the question. "Alberix? That isn't a Roman name."

"No, he's a Kelt. We were with Caesar at Wermaros, when we heard about the ambush of the Fourteenth Legion and rumors of a possible uprising. The commander ordered Alberix to go there. I would like to know that he's all right and what is happening."

Cita admitted, "I've only heard rumors myself. Caesar put me in charge of the supply commissary here at Cenabum, so I should very much like to know if rebellion is in the air."

When Antiochus finished his bandaging, Simonides tested his chest. "*Efharisto*, the tightness feels good!"

After the slave bowed and left the room, Cita smiled. "You'll mend, but I'm concerned about a lack of accurate reports. Did you see any confirmation of these rumors at Carnutum? Caesar is adamantly opposed to these druid priests."

"The assembly had ended, but a few tribal chieftains were there. Ollam Fodla, the druid I mentioned, took particular interest in a man named Vercingetorix."

"Arvernian, and his father was killed at Gergovia for trying to make himself king. What did you think of the man?"

"I was impressed with Vercingetorix..." Simonides accepted a cup of wine Antiochus brought. "I wouldn't trust Fodla with a lead sestercius, but the chieftain acted like enough of a leader to attract sub-chiefs as clients."

Cita pondered his assessment a moment. "I would like to speak with your Gallic friend, if he's still there."

"Alberix? Antiochus could ask dock slaves about him. Bargemen know everything that's going on."

"Hear that, Antiochus?" After Cita called out, his slave appeared from the behind an atrium curtian. "Take a few denarii with you. If Alberix is at the camp of Lucius Roscius, bring him here."

After he left, Cita observed, "A good man and an eavesdropper like all slaves, but I suppose I owe him his freedom by now." The merchant filled both their wine goblets again, then sat across from the youth. "Tell me about your trouble with the commander. Perhaps I can repair any damage to Caesar's pride."

∾

Alberix had written briefly at Beltaine that the western Galli were quiet. Later, a letter from Marius to Cornelius, who had been given leave to return home and bury his father, summarized the trouble Caesar had encountered that summer with several tribes.

Marius suo salutem, Cornelius:

I trust your mother and sister are well after the unfortunate death of your father. I am blessed that both my parents live, yet I share your loss; may he be welcomed in Avernus. I find myself on the Rhenus again, two seasons after the construction of our bridge into Sugambri territory. We put this new one a bit above the old site, to Suebi lands. They are suspected of sending cavalry and foot warriors to aid Gallic seditionists. Before I relate that, and your grief notwithstanding, I hope you again are able to enjoy some of the refinements of our Roman civilization. What I would give for half-a-watch in the caldarium of the smallest public bath!

Since you left, our campaign against the Treveri has been as swift as a race between the greens and whites in the Circus. Even I, cynic that I become, was impressed with the speed that the legions—two new ones actually—were sent to us at Samarobriva. One is a replacement for the Fourteenth. May Mars and

Fortuna grant it greater success than that of Sabinus!

A Fifteenth, again recruits from the Cisalpina, and a borrowed unit of Pompeius—his Legio I, which Caesar renumbered VI. The Imperator has let his hair and beard grow long in token of mourning after the loss of some five thousand legionaries and auxiliae of the old XIV. The replacements arrived before winter ended, bringing our strength now up to ten legions.

The Gallic council we convened this spring went badly. You had just left when tribal vergobrets assembled. Since the Senones, Carnutes and, of course, the Treveri sent no representatives, Caesar thought the worse. He ordered the council transferred to Lutetia, an oppidum of the Parisii. Immediately after, Caesar moved against the Senones, who live to the south. Acco, their leader in sedition, tried to crowd his tribe into oppida at Metlosedum and Velaunodunum, but our legions arrived before he could complete the transfer. Through the intercession of the Aedui, Caesar accepted peace envoys from Acco. We took a hundred hostages to assure his cooperation. The usual sword-shakers among our younger tribunes—who have sausage meat where their brains should be—wanted to massacre the lot, but Caesar was relieved to keep the legions out of battle and intact, should further trouble break out. Of course, it did.

You recall that the most troublesome tribe after the Nervii is the Menapii, who never sent peace envoys. Their lands are on the northern flank of the Nervii and Eburones, in Hades-like terrain. In our autumn campaign against them and the Morini, three seasons ago, rains almost washed away our camps. This time, Caesar divided five legions into three commands under himself, Fabius, and Crassus. Instead of facing us, the Menapii thought they could hide in their forests and marshes. It was not autumn this time and the weather was good. We crossed rivers so rapidly that we captured cattle and herdsmen right in their fields. Warriors still were around campfires! It took their vergobrets only a short time to ask for peace. Caesar accepted, but warned them not to give Ambiorix any refuge or aid.

After that, I had hoped for leave time in Samarobriva, but the Treveri were on the move again, trying to force Labienus from his camp. Fortunately, Caesar established a base camp there before going after the Menapii, and had sent Labienus two legions and our heavy equipment. Gallic deserters told the Legate that Treveri were encamped about XV miles away, waiting for Germani mercenaries to join them in an attack. Titus Labienus, as you know, is not one to sit on his shield in camp unless he has no choice. He took XXV cohorts and a large cavalry troop to go after the Treveri, hoping to lure them into attacking on his terms before Germani arrived. Provoke them he did! I believe many of our men would do well as actors in the new theater of Pompeius at Roma. Labienus had then mimic panic and passed word around that we would attempt a retreat out of fear of the Germani. He felt confident that the Treveri would not let the loot they planned on slip away. The Legate was correct. As our men marched off, displaying signs of fear and haste, the Treveri crossed the river to chase them like hounds after a crippled stag. Our rear guard kept drawing the warriors toward higher ground.

When we reached a favorable position, Labienus ordered his centurions to turn their men around and form an acies triplex. He urged them to display the same courage as if Caesar himself were watching. The first javelin throw of hastati confused the lead warriors, who thought we were running away. The princeps and triarii followed up so rapidly that the enemy broke for the woods where our cavalry waited. Miratio! I had set up the line of scorpiones we designed on the flanks of the supply train. Labienus gave permission to shoot their bolts at the same time the centurions turned their men. Our range was good and quite a few of the missiles found flesh among the massed warriors. Our maneuver surprised the enemy and add to confusion. The weapon as now built is for long-range siege operations, and Legates are reluctant to adopt new tactics. Blame our Senate for this. They give us conservative leaders in warfare and senators seem to think that the reforms of our ancestors were intended to be set in pozzuoli. Look at Crassus' defeat. Parthian horse-archers destroyed his legions, yet we still use our cavalry as auxilary units – and half of them dismount to fight on foot. Can you envision several troops of horsemen armed with the Greek bow design of Alberix, shooting from the flanks? Or hastati discharging bronze bolts from thirty or forty paces, before throwing javelins?

All that I write explains why I am on the Rhenus again. Once Germani heard of the Treveri defeat, they never came to help. Leaders of the sedition, relatives of Indutiomarus fled eastward across the river. Cingetorix is restored as Treveri chieftain. Caesar's reason for building another bridge is to allow our legionaries to more easily cross to Germania and assure that Ambiorix will not find refuge there. The other is to pursue the Suebi, yet we have been here a moon phase with no sight of them. We finished a four-story tower to protect the Gallic end of the bridge, but orders for tomorrow are to destroy the half of the roadway that touches Germania. Some men complain about the possibility of being assigned to the guard detachment and rumors persist that ten cohorts of veterans will stay the winter.

But enough of battles. I must tell you the sequel to the wounding of our friend Alberix the Celt. One of the engineers from Cohort V, Lucus Granius, stopped by one evening after you left. He had been nearby when Alberix was struck and ran to help. While Psen-Ammon bound the wound, I picked up the sling-stone and handed it to Granius. He thought I wanted to keep it and stuffed it into his pack. While fitting out to pursue Ambiorix, Granius found it and brought it to me with a story of his own. Seems he had been wounded in the Hispania campaign by a Cretan arrow. After recovering, he dedicated the arrowhead to

Apollo Curatio and had it made into a pendant for his wife. She wears it as an amulet for his safe return. The sling-stone is too heavy to be worn by that girl Alberix saved from suicide, but she may want it as an offering to one of her gods. We can give it to Alberix when we see him again. Even if the stone has no value as a charm, it should be good for conversation over a horn or two of his kin's wine. Since I'm reminded of Wermaros, have you heard anything of Tullius Tilius since you returned? He must have oozed his way into the Senate by now.

This summer I attained Grade III of Miles—in our Mithraic brotherhood. As you know, his planetary sign is Mars. I find it fitting that my initiation as Soldier took place under Caesar's command.

Crops ripen in the fields. This time of year makes me miss the peaceful Campania even more. In a few days, we shall try to find this Ambiorix to the south, in the Arduinnian forest. More roads to survey!

Again, bonus amicus, condolences on your loss! Vale.

≈≈

Ambiorix was caught by Roman cavalry, yet Fortuna deserted Julius Caesar's men for the moment. After abandoning his followers, the Eburone chieftain escaped north.

≈≈

Ollam-Fodla was still at Carnutum when the report of Ambiorix's defeat reached central Gallia. The news was a setback to the nascent rebellion, but Fodla determined to salvage the situation by haranguing warriors and druids who had not yet left Carnutum after the assembly.

Fodla stood near an altar to Taranis as he shouted rebukes to those listening.

"Ambiorix was a fool, hungry for his own glory, and glory has been the death shroud of our people. We need a leader willing to turn aside his pride and bring other sub-chieftains to fight in unison with him. They must humble themselves beneath his sword until the Romani are destroyed."

Vercingetorix, standing nearby with his friend, Lucterios, listened to the druid.

"The priest speaks silver words," Lucterios said quietly. "Too often our tribes put clan interests first."

Vercingetorix pointed out, "My father united many of our clans. He made the Arverni feared, and yet what was his fate?"

Lucterios touched his arm. "Our people were not ready for a king again."

Fodla's voice ranted on. "Caesar's legions are not sent out like chaff on the wind. They unite under one command. This is why they occupy half our lands in Gallia."

A warrior called out, "What are druids doing to stop the Romani?"

Fodla controlled his voice at the taunt, "We have agents among the tribes and your own Gutater has sworn to join us. Commius the Atrebate, even Epidorix and Viridomarus of the Aeduii are with us."

"The dark druid is a fanatic," Lucterios whispered, "yet even such a man can move people like the chaff he mentions. We should ask him more about the *vergobrets* he names as allies."

Vercingetorix asked, "Where would your Cadurcans stand?"

"Most would follow me. The Narbonensis borders our lands. Rich treasure waits in provincial towns."

Doubtful, the Arvernian insisted, "I would want a sign from our gods that such a war would succeed." Vercingetorix took Lucterios by the arm and turned away. "I leave for Gergovia at dawn. Bring the druid to my tent after the watchfires are lighted."

That evening Ollam Fodla told Vercingetorix about the meeting of chieftains and his ritual sacrifice in the cavern. In a month, one of his druidesses would give birth to a miraculous equinox child. The infant would be dedicated to Belenos and Caturix and would assure the success of his plan in driving out the Romani. The Arvernian chief agreed to be at a dolmen near Saumis for the child's birth.

જ⁀ç

After the ambush of Legio XIV, Caesar had me to go to the camp of Lucius Roscius. A promising, but inexperienced commander of *quaestor* rank, Roscius had situated Legio XIII in the territory of the Esubii, a Channel seaboard tribe subdued by Publius Crassus three years earlier. Despite Ambiorix's success, the area remained peaceful, except for a few warriors of the neighboring Armoricans, who had harassed Roscius's camp.

The *Quaestor* was pleased with me as an interpreter, yet had not quite known what to do beyond Caesar's brief authorization that I gather information on the mood and intentions of local tribes Esubii, Lexovii, Aurlerci, and the trouble-making Armoricans.

A tribune wrote down my reports and included them in his summary of activities by Legio XIII.

Time passed quickly for me. Thoughts of Apsa filled my nights, and I intended to return to Wermaros when the campaigns ended for the winter.

Roscius's camp was located near Dunfrontum, where I went to look at forge work. Only one old crafter lived in the village, but I made friends with Trebios, his son. At first both of us had trouble understanding each other's different dialects. We laughed about it, yet soon after came a potential conflict between us.

One day, after I watched a tin pouring, Trebios asked, "Why are you in Romani service? These Shorthairs are another conqueror imposing themselves on us."

Taken by surprise, I replied, "Celtic chieftains war with rival tribes and even clans. A victorious tribe inflicts their will on the loser."

"We are Celts!" Trebios replied in anger. "The Shorthairs are not."

I told him, "The Romani could unite our warring tribes and institute peace, as they have in their Narbonensis province."

Trebios countered, "How many of our people were killed in the raping of that land? I went to Carnutum for the High Assembly. Many *vergobrets* and sub-chiefs listened to druids preaching rebellion against your masters." I resented his implication and thought Trebios had ended his criticsm, but he admitted, "I almost joined warriors my age, who had vowed to burn out Romani merchants at Cenabum."

"Cenabum?"

"South of here, the oppidum of the Carnutes, and Carnutum is the most sacred nematon in our lands. Druids call it "The Navel of Gallia'."

Trebios calmed a bit and offered me supper, yet I wanted to get back to my tent and sort out his words. The ideas confused me. How many others felt as he did?

That night, before sleeping, I compared the idealism of Lucius's brotherhood of men with the reality of injustices happening around me each day. *Were* Romani ways superior to Celtic ones? Tribunes constantly reminded legionaries that Gallic chieftains had invited Romani to help them against their enemies, yet Trebios had made clear that the opposite was true and forged the unrest. In questioning local tribes, I had heard the name of Vercingertorix, an Arverni chieftain. His father, Celtillos, had become the most powerful man in the region, then, in what Simonides would have called a supreme act of *hubris*, the man rejected our election process and declared himself king. Angry warriors killed him. I told Roscius about Vercingetorix, but he was scornful. Caesar would deal with the Arvernian as he had with Ambiorix.

Roscius copied my report and ordered me to take it to Durocortorum. I don't know if he changed anything, but I felt he was glad to see the last of me—poor news is never welcome to those who must deal with it. Next day I left with an escort of cavalry on the road to the Remi capital.

When we stopped by a stream at midday to rest the horses, I lay apart from the men. As I half-dozed an image of the Wheel appeared in my mind.

Eight spokes radiated from the hub, each representing a crucial event in my life. One began with the Harude raid, seven years earlier, where Father was killed. Our stay at Wermaros was another. People—Mother, Cluvios, Dividiac, Liscos, and Ollam Fodla were a third. The fourth spoke was Pixtila, Frieda, and especially Apsa, the Raurici girl I thought about so often. Lucius and Julius Caesar were another spoke—certainly the two Romani had made the most change in my life.

I saw that three spokes were empty. Then, inexplicably, the name of Vercingetorix came to my mind. It meant "King of Great Warriors" in our language.

Before I could grasp a meaning from the dream, I awakened at a cavalryman's call to continue the journey.

On the road, the name of the Arverni chieftain remained in my mind, seeming to keep cadence with the fall of my mount's hoof beats. Eventually, this repetition of Vercingetorix transformed itself into the phrase Cluvios had spoken to me as a plea on the night I left Wermaros:

"Find yourself a Caesar among our own people."

I abruptly determined to find out of the Arverian would fit that mould.

High in a grove of oak trees still green with summer foliage, ravens glutted on harvest grain, watched our line of horsemen move along the road below. Croaking protests at this intrusion into their territory, the black birds flapped up and flew alongside. I watched those Birds of Death, the incarnation of the dreaded Babd, until the dark specks turned away over ochre grain fields.

The ravens winged south in an erratic wave, straight toward where I turned off and headed to meet with Vercingetorix in the heartland of Gallia!

About the Author

An artist and writer, Albert Noyer was born in Switzerland but raised in Detroit, Michigan. After Army service, he pursued degrees in art, art education, and teaching humanities, at Wayne State University. He subsequently worked as a commercial artist, taught art in a Detroit Public Schools technical/vocational program, and art history at a private college. Noyer retired to New Mexico with his wife, Jennifer, where he exhibits watercolor paintings and woodcut prints in galleries and regional exhibits. His artwork has been featured New Mexico Magazine and the Mature Life in New Mexico supplement of Albuquerque's Sunday Journal. He is a member of the New Mexico Watercolor Society, SouthWest Writers, Sisters in Crime, Croak & Dagger, and New Mexico Veteran's Art.

Noyer first published A.D. fifth century novels, the *Getorius* and *Arcadia* mysteries, set in an era now seen as critical in creating the political, religious, and cultural institutions that survive into modern times. Published by Plain View Press, his contemporary Fr. Jake Mysteries, *The Ghosts of Glorieta* and *One for the Money, Two for the Sluice*, are set in Michigan and New Mexico. *Alberix the Celt* is the retelling in two volumes of Julius Caesar's conquest of Gaul, but from the viewpoint of a Celtic youth caught up in the Romanization of the country now called France.

www.ingramcontent.com/pod-product-compliance
Lightning Source LLC
Chambersburg PA
CBHW070759120726
47910CB00001B/236